EVERYTHING'S BETTER WITH BACON, AND YOU CAN NEVER HAVE ENOUGH BUTTER

(but karma's a bitch...)

Book One

THE FIRST CHILD

S. F. Goldsholl

D1738706

ISBN: 9798877183698
Independently published

Acknowledgments

I could not have written–or finished–this book without the constant support of my husband, Paul Goldsholl, or my son, Tom Brindisi. My late brother Stan ("Sandy") Fila was my chief cheerleader. I always hit your Chinese gong, Sandy–which is hanging at the bottom of the steps outside–whenever I pass by it, and your gigantic wind chimes are hanging from a pine tree. I'm sorry you didn't get to read the completed novel, but you did get to read a lot of it.

Special thanks to my soul-sister, Marian Clatterbaugh Owens, for her editing work.

And thank you to Bob & Judy Fila, who are always there for those they love, to Catherine Weber, Deborah Albrecht, and Jim Blucher, for their encouragement, and to cousin Debra Sharp, for her editing assistance.

In memory of brother Sandy, my mother, Catherine Fila, and my father, Stanley Fila, on whom the character of Stanley Ostrowski is based.

There are universes where the dominant species live by the Golden Rule, treating other conscious beings as they, themselves, would want to be treated.

Our own universe is not one of them.

Table of Contents

Part I

Chapter 1

Extermination Camp Redux

Kate is having one of her many nightmares. She is sitting in a chair in front of a large-screen television and watching a reality show competition.

The stage set consists of a concrete gas chamber and a single adjoining room. The second chamber contains four waist-high, metal gurneys. The gurneys are slanted, top to bottom. There are raised edges and channels on the sides of each gurney.

Large crates sit under the gurneys. The crates are filled to the brim with saws, butcher's knives, chef's knives, scissors, razors, and other dismemberment tools. A pair of elbow-length rubber gloves, goggles, a mask, a lab coat, and a chef's apron are neatly arranged at the top of each of the gurneys.

Four Waffen-SS storm troopers march a group of fifteen naked, emaciated, terrified people into the gas chamber. All of the prisoners—except for one young woman, who somehow slipped by the guards without experiencing that mortification—have had their heads shaved.

A voiceover says, "Don't worry, folks! None of that hair is going to be wasted. We've distributed it to our factory bosses. They will, in turn, use it to stuff pillows and to produce bomb ignition mechanisms, and a bunch of other cool stuff."

The SS storm troopers exit the gas chamber and close a steel door behind them. The door has a small viewing window in it. The captives stand in the center of the room, confused, not knowing what to expect next. Overhead shower heads above them begin to make a fizzling sound. The people look up and brace themselves for a deluge of cold shower water.

Zyklon B gas is released, and not cold water. The men and women scream. They grab at their throats and make choking and gurgling sounds.

The scene fades to black, but the sounds continue. Kate hears someone in the chamber pounding on a wall.

Red letters appear on the screen: "Fifteen Minutes Later." The gas chamber reappears.

All of the people are dead. Some of the bodies are in half-squatting positions. There are red spots on their skin and foam around their mouths. Blood has streaked from their ears.

An old woman is hunched against the wall. The front of her forehead is crumpled inward. The pounding sound had, apparently, come from the woman beating her head against the concrete wall and crushing her own skull, to stop the agony.

Kate wants to cry and scream and tear her eyes away from the television screen. She cannot. She has sleep paralysis. She cannot even close her dream eyelids.

The SS troopers re-enter the room. They are led by an officer with the rank of lieutenant-colonel. The officer turns to the camera. He steps around the bodies of a few of the deceased—knocking one of them to the side in the process—grins, and throws open his arms.

"Hello, everyone—welcome, once again, to the Gas Chamber! I am your host, Rottenführer Friedrich Becker."

An unseen audience claps wildly.

"Tonight, we have the semifinal for Auschwitz's next Top Mass Murderer! The last man standing will go into next week's finale. He will be joined by the other three men from the prior weeks' semifinals.

"Before we get started, let's take another look at our contestants. Our first competitor is Storm Trooper Max Möller."

The camera pans to a youth with a rectangular, blocky head. Möller has short, thick, wavy blonde hair. Another of the men has greased-back, blonde hair. The remaining two men sport bald heads. The lack of hair on one of them reveals that he has two large, round knobs on the back of his head. The other has a low, sloping forehead and huge brow ridges, as if he were the child of Neanderthals.

A cloud of dry ice fog pours around the four men. They immediately strike menacing, gangster poses. They fold their arms over their chests, compress their lips together in ugly pouts, thrust out their jaws, and tilt their heads back at an angle. The poses—rehearsed for many hours beforehand in front of the mirror—give the general impression that they are ignorant, brutish thugs.

The scene switches to a previously-filmed video of Trooper Möller. He is wearing civilian clothes. He is on a farm. Two other men, who resemble him closely and are likely his siblings, hold down a baby lamb. They are pressing the animal's head and legs against the ground.

Möller kneels and sticks his tongue out of the side of his mouth. He begins to saw at the lamb's throat with a long knife.

The lamb looks, disbelievingly, at the trusted men she had thought of as the leaders of her flock. Blood spurts from her neck and mouth. The lamb's mother, standing in a nearby stall with her head pressed against the slats, emits a heartbreaking wail.

The video ends. The camera pans back to Möller. "My parents own tens of thousands of cattle, sheep, chickens, and pigs. They are quite wealthy. I, however, am a self-made man. I've actually developed dozens of other farms all by myself. My father never gave me a nickel."

Becker snorts. That's a lie, the rottenführer thinks. He has no problem with that particular alternative fact, though. He is actually impressed, and believes Möller will go far as a politician. The Nazi propaganda machine welcomed any man who could blithely let falsehoods roll off the tongue, especially if they did it with faked indignation.[1]

The storm trooper pretends he does not hear the sound of Becker snorting. "You can see that I've been doing this sort of work my entire life. I've <u>trained for this moment.</u>"

---

[1] One of Becker's descendants would, decades later, emulate the Nazi tactic of repeating lies enough times that those lies would become adopted as the truth by—not only the descendant, himself—but also a large percentage of his gullible and receptive followers.

Becker moves on. "And here are our other contestants." He sweeps his arm toward the men.

The camera zooms to the second trooper for a moment. Another video follows. It shows the trooper stabbing a crying calf, repeatedly, in the head, neck, and chest.

The third youth is introduced by a video of the trooper hacking flesh from a live, squealing pig, and the fourth by a video in which the trooper is chasing chickens around a yard and lopping off their heads.

The camera pans back to Rottenführer Becker. The host feigns humility. What he actually wants is nonstop attention and praise. He is, after all, the man in control of the show. He has the final word on the contestants, the judges, and the scenarios.

The troopers pretend to hang on the puffed-up narcissist's every word.

"All right. Now that you've met our contestants, it's time for our first butchery challenge. Men, you will select a cadaver and come up with the most useful product from it. Your stations and tools are in the adjoining room. You have thirty minutes. Your time starts... *now!*"

"Heard!" one shouts. Another whoops, "Let's *go!*"

The troopers tear off.

Each of the four chooses a corpse from the floor, throws it over his shoulder, runs with it into the adjoining room, and tosses it on a gurney. The men don elbow-length rubber gloves, goggles, masks, and lab coats. They each pull a chef's apron over the lab coat, and get to work.

"Don't forget," Becker calls after them. "Arbeiten sie zielgerichtet! Work with purpose!"

Becker stands next to the doorway that adjoins the two rooms and watches the men work.

An old man rushes into the gas chamber, which is behind Becker. The man is wearing a torn and sullied uniform. He stops in front of Becker, bows, and hands him a paper-wrapped, fast-food hamburger. Becker tears off the paper, flings it to the concrete floor, and begins cramming the hamburger into his mouth. Ketchup drips from his mouth and down his chin.

The old man bends and picks up the trash. He exits the room backward, bowing to Becker the entire time.

Becker turns to the camera and holds up the remnants of the greasy burger. "I could live on these." He grins and bites down on the last pieces of animal flesh and adds, as an afterthought, "I think their thirty minutes are almost up."

It seems to Kate as though only a moment has gone by since the troopers began their obscene labors.

Becker rejoins the troopers and shouts, "Thirty seconds—*come on* guys—you *got* this—bring it *home!* Sign the painting!"

The men work furiously at their stations. Sweat pours from their foreheads, directly onto the human remains in front of them.

"Time's *up*."

The men jump back from their respective tables. Their arms shoot straight up into the air.

"Let's meet our judges." Becker's voice drips with simulated respect.

The far side of the room is in darkness. A light goes on. It illuminates three attentive, uniformed men, and one woman. They are seated at a long table. The table is on a raised platform, so that the judges are gazing down on the proceedings. The judges have donned stoic, grim looks for the occasion. They look like they are about to sentence condemned rapists.

"Our first judge is Hermann Göring. You all know Reichsmarschall Göring. He's the man who brought us the answer to the Jewish Question."

The unseen audience claps loudly and enthusiastically. Göring looks at Becker with feigned worship in his eyes.

"Our second judge is Josef Goebbels. Josef's propaganda machine has, with his complicit followers, rolled over and *crushed* the free press in Germany. We recognize that the free press is the enemy of the people, and we thank you, Reichsleiter Goebbels, for abolishing it.

"That is, with the exception of the indoctrination programming our party controls, such as "Fixed News" and "Newsquax." And we cannot forget our own "OAF" which, as we all know, is short for the "Only Alternative Facts" network."

Goebbels preens at the audience's crazed applause, and chuckles. "You're *welcome*, Nazi Germany. But, sir, may I ask that you don't overlook the commentary program I, myself, started?"

"Ah, yes," Becker responded. "Please, everyone, put on your tin hats, later tonight, and listen to our "Mightyfart" program. If its brainwashing screeds don't turn you into a Hitler-loving Nazi, nothing will. Anyway, let's get on with our introductions. We cannot forget Camp Guard Wanda Klaff." Becker nods at the middle-aged, homely woman.

Wanda Klaff—unlike the other judges, who are duded up in stiff uniforms and weighed down by dozens of big, fantastical medals—wears civilian clothing.

Klaff sneers at the show's host.

"Do you think you'll have that same sneer on your face during the Allied Command's war crime tribunals in Poland, a few years from now?" Becker asks.

He points at the woman's plain dress. "Maybe you'll wear that to your hanging, after the Allies convict you of the war crimes you'll have committed on Nazi Germany's behalf."

Everyone on the panel looks at each other. They are mystified and confused. Klaff's sneer deepens and becomes a snarl.

"Oops—*spoilers!*" Becker has a faraway look on his face. He shakes his head to clear it, and gets back to business.

"Last—but certainly not least—Josef Mengele. Hauptsturmführer Mengele could have been the father of this very competition. You know him for—among many other wonders—the procedure in which he switched the eyeballs of one Jewish teen with those of her twin. Not to mention the one where he pumped water into tubes shoved down the throats of Jews, just to find out how much they could hold before their stomachs exploded!"

The audience screams its approval. Mengele looks adoringly at Becker. His adoration, unlike the others, is not feigned.

"Ok, let's go to our first contestant." Becker moves to the table closest to him and peers down at it. "What do you have for us, Trooper Möller?"

The young man stands proudly by the table and his work product.

"In front of you we have teeth, which I've extracted." He nods at the emaciated dead man on the table. "This once vital young man had excellent teeth. I was disappointed when I discovered he had no gold fillings. But, we all know how expensive good ivory is. His teeth are of such quality that they are ivory-*adjacent*."

He glances at Becker, seeking approval.

"I'm here for it," someone yells from the audience.

"*Smart*," someone else shouts.

"Hmmm." Becker frowns. He evidently disagrees with the audience members. "And that took you all of thirty minutes?"

The trooper tries to defend himself. "It's not easy to pull healthy teeth from healthy bone, sir."

Becker turns toward the judges. "Thoughts?'

Mengale closes his eyes, considering. He opens them and leans forward.

"First of all, I commend you, Storm Trooper, for trying to make sure that no part of the body goes to waste. But, I just wish you had done more in the allotted time. I think you could have done something like, maybe, harvested the organs, as well."

"Thank you," the trooper responds. He gives the judges a slight, begrudging bow.

Becker moves to the next table. "It seems our second contestant had a different focus."

The trooper—the one with the slicked-back hair—nods.

"Today, for you, we have a beautiful hide. You will notice that we were able to keep it in one piece. We kind of skinned the abdomen, and then we kind of skinned the back, and then we kind of skinned the buttocks of this old lady. Her skin can be tanned and made into a small coat and a pair of shoes or a couple of lampshades."

He raises his chin, puffs out his cheeks, and holds up a stretched-out length of the woman's skin.

The camera pans to the excoriated female for just a second and then moves back to Becker.

"I see." Becker is noncommittal. "Judges?"

Klaff tugs at the collar of her plain dress. "I think what you have done here is impressive. This is definitely a fine substitute for leather. My only criticism is that there are small tears in the hide."

"Thank you, chef. I mean, *ma'am*." The trooper, imitating the first contestant, bows.

The host turns to the third trooper, the man with the bald, lumpy head. "What have we here?"

"For you, today, we have a woman who was

in the prime of life. This person's head was not shaved, as were the others. So, I decided to scalp her."

The man holds up a length of beautiful, thick, long black hair, still attached to a cap of skin.

"Oh... kay," Becker does not try to hide his evident disappointment. He glances at the judges. They shake their heads.

"And our last contestant. I hope you did something better than that, which any simple guard can do in five minutes."

"I *did* do better than that." The next contestant is the Neanderthal-looking man. He has symbols tattooed all over his head.

Kate would not have been able to identify the symbols while awake but can do so in her dream. An Othala rune, SS lightning bolts, a Nazi eagle, crossed grenades, a sun wheel, a life rune, and a wolfsangel. She recalls seeing those same symbols tattooed on people in modern-day United States of America.

The trooper points to a pile of glob, next to the body of an elderly gentleman. The man's chest has been pried open and his abdomen slit all the way to the groin. "Organs, sir. I did just a *little* bit of cutting." (The man's voice has gotten playfully high and squeaky, pronouncing the word "little" as "lée-tul.") "And then I pulled out the guy's organs."

"Why?" Becker seems amused.

"We all know that Karl Maria Wiligut is Reichsführer Heinrich Himmler's personal occultist. I believe Herr Wiligut can use these entrails in his divination rituals."

Becker speaks for all of the judges. "Das ist *Licht aus*. That is *lights out*."

The trooper blushes. He smiles shyly and looks at his feet, reigning in his inflated ego and, for a moment, humbling himself.

"You came to *play*," Becker turns to the panel. "The judges will now confer. And remember, the winner is not only playing to be in the finale, but also for bragging rights."

The judges hold their hands in front of their faces to hide their lips, and murmur among themselves. They reach an agreement. They nod at Mengele.

Mengele looks at Trooper Möller. "We think you could have done a lot more in thirty minutes." His voice is stern. "I'm sorry to say that I have to ask you to remove your apron, and leave."

Möller nods. The camera follows him as he removes his apron and neatly folds it. He places it on the gurney next to the carcass, as the camera pans in.

"Thank you for allowing me to participate in this wonderful competition. It has been a pleasure," Möller says. His face is red. He backs away from the now-toothless, human carcass on the gurney. He leaves the room.

A producer stops the storm trooper as he exits through the gas chamber. He holds a microphone up to the trooper's face. "You are the first to be eliminated. What do you think went wrong?"

Möller's anger is obvious. He looks like he wants to kill someone. The camera closes in on Möller's purpling face. "I don't believe I should have been eliminated. I think my dish... I mean, my creation, was far superior to the others."

He lifts his head and juts out his chin. This is an apparent, but unsuccessful, attempt to prove that he is a testosterone-packed, manly man, and not a simple, sadistic, entitled, and pompous douchebag.

Mengele next turns his attention to the would-be barber. "I just wish you hadn't taken off the woman's scalp along with her hair. It makes it much more difficult to utilize the product efficiently, later on. The hair requires more processing."

Becker wears a solemn expression, as if he were a physician breaking the news to a patient that that the diagnosis is not only cancer, it's terminal. "Please pack your blades and go."

The scalper hangs his own head. "Thank you, Rottenführer, thank you judges." He departs.

"And the winner is... " Mengele pauses for a full thirty seconds, looking at the two remaining contestants, and drawing out the suspense. The camera zooms back and forth between the two men. It stops for a close-up of the face of the skin-flayer, moves to the tattooed-head eviscerator, and then back to the flayer.

Mengele finally utters the judges' decision. "The *disemboweler* is the winner of this challenge!"

The audience claps and shouts. The tattooed, bald trooper throws up his arms. Grinning, he stomps around the gurneys on which the ravaged bodies lay.

The other, remaining trooper congratulates the winner. Becker turns to the loser. "I guess it goes without saying, but you're *fired*." The loser quietly withdraws.

"Congratulations, Trooper," Becker exclaims. "First, Let's get one thing very clear. You knocked it out of the park. Now, let's get down to business.

13

You've all been playing for charity. What is your charity, should you win the finale next week?"

The trooper rubs the Nazi eagle tattoo on his forehead. "There's an animal rescue I like, in Berlin. They take in homeless cats and dogs and place them with good families."

Becker nods. "A suitable charity."

The people turn their attention to the gurneys. The figures on the gurneys begin to wiggle, and to shift and change. The eviscerated man's form shrinks, alters, and grows a coat of soft wool. His nose elongates. His body shrinks into that of a baby lamb.

The ruined form next to him transforms into that of a skinned, open-eyed calf. The next table holds a now-tailless racoon. A piglet, her toothless mouth hanging open, lies on the last table.

Becker reluctantly tears his gaze away from the mutilated bodies. "Join us next week for the finale, where the finalists will be making some dynamite, banging dishes. And, they'll be using the corpses that were butchered today.

"The corpse each contestant will use shall be decided by lottery. The winner of the finale will receive 250,000 Reichsmarks for their favorite charity. That man will become Auschwitz's next Top Mass Murderer!

"Plus, I have a *treat* for all of you. My daughter just turned eighteen. She will be joining the judging panel next week."

The judges ooohh and aaahh. Kate, somehow, understands that they are buttering up the dispenser of their paychecks and the promoter of their fame, and that their happiness at Becker's nepotistic move is a pretense. The judges do seem to acknowledge that this is supposed to be a family-oriented show, which means that viewers *like* it when children of the lead cast members become part of the ensemble. The move also allows the next generation of charismatic predators to do their thing.

"But, there's going to be a twist." Becker looks at the camera.

"Oh, boy. Here we go," Göring says.

The other judges shake their heads and grin. That Becker, always with something up his sleeve. What a card.

"The troopers will be required to use five unusual ingredients in their dishes. In addition, there will be certain staples that they will *not* be allowed to use. They'll find out what next week. And, they'll only have four minutes to shop from our well-stocked pantry. They'll have to fit everything they get into a small leather duffel case. That means they'll have to shop smartly.

"I'll give you one other piece of information." He pauses, letting everyone appreciate the coy look on his face. "The contestants will be required to use the eyes and gonads of their victim in their preparation. They have a week to think about a recipe that highlights balls!"

"This will be an eye-deal, ball-busting competition." Göring winks.

"I see what you did there," Becker chuckles. He loves a good pun. He turns to the audience. "I advise the competitors that they must always remember: Mit Speck ist alles besser! Everything's better with bacon!"

The judges waggle their heads up and down so furiously that Kate thinks their necks are going to snap.

Becker glances at the bodies on the gurneys. The bodies are continuing to alter. They are morphing back and forth between those of tortured animals, and those of tortured men and women.

"Hmmm. It's true that *people* taste like pork, correct?" He turns to the judges. "What would you do, then? Make a breakfast dish?"

"Whatever they make, I hope that they don't forget to season, season, season," Mengele comments, "and to have a pop of acid on their dishes. Salt and acid are always nice on my tongue, on my palate."

Goebbels leans forward. "I *do* love a nice offal stew, but it would be a shame to waste those bones." He looks at a body on one of the gurneys which is, momentarily, that of a young man. "I'd definitely do something with the marrow. Maybe a nice bone marrow and offal soup-type-situation? I *do* like to see nose to tail cooking. Nothing wasted, that way."

Camp Guard Wanda Klaff touches her hair. "I'm on "team texture." There should be some sort of crunch factor. I would throw pieces of that woman's skin into a deep fryer, make cracklings, and sprinkle that on top of the dish."

Goebbels nods. "Same. Dare I say, that would also taste a lot like bacon."

Göring straightens in his chair. "I hope one of the contestants does a good barbecue. Or a smoked brisket. There has to be a good "bark" on the skin—at least to the level of third-degree burns—if they expect to win. Because *brown food tastes good.*"

"I love the brown bits," Becker agrees. "Now, to make the finale even more interesting, I am going to work alongside them and prepare a dish under the same constraints. Just for fun."

The judges immediately start with the ooohhing and aaahhing. "We can't wait to taste *your* dish," Göring simpers.

The other judges start nodding again, so frenetically that Kate, this time, expects their heads to pop right off of their necks and go flying.

∞

Kate is traumatized. Her dream throat is dry, and her dream body paralyzed. Only her eyes are able to move. She looks past Becker and notices another man in the room. He is standing in a dark corner. It is difficult to see him.

Kate suddenly knows that this man is not part of the dream. He is another sleeper. He is *sharing* the dream with her. The man has poufy white hair that crests into a pompadour. His head resembles that of a bat. He is wearing a chalk-striped dark suit. He looks pompous and scornful. He seems to be riveted by the scene in front of him.

He glances past Becker and the tables. His gaze falls on Kate, *right though the television screen.*

He stares for a moment, lunges forward, and shouts, "*YOU!*"

The man's head and body alter as he charges out of the dark corner. His eyes lighten in color, and the muscles in his arm begin to swell, as if

17

someone has inserted an air pump into them. His suit melts into black clothing. The shirt has an emblem on it. The insignia is a golden "P," laid on top of SS lightning bolts.

The man's face becomes ovoid and his jowls fill out with fat or, possibly, excess fluid. His hair begins to recede, even as it turns a weird, dyed, reddish-blonde color. A meager, new-growth beard crawls around his jowls, as if in compensation for the lack of hair on his head.

A jolt of terror shoots through Kate's body.

~

Kate opens her eyes. She is awake. She has witnessed horrific events that seem to be roughly based in history but which are still happening all over the world, every day, to other conscious beings. She wants to cry.

Her sorrow turns to anger.

And then she thinks about that other person in the dream, the one who had been a watcher, like her. He had seen her. He had been coming toward her. No. He had been coming *for* her. She believed that, if she had not awoken, he would have come right out of the television.

Her anger grows. Screw him, she thinks. He, whoever he is, has no idea what she is capable of.

Kate, herself, has no idea what she is capable of.

~

Everywhere on Planet Earth

The world economy is built upon animal suffering, grief, trauma, and death. Most people suspect the truth but would rather not know anything about it. Humans prefer to pretend that the agribusiness industry, which feeds and clothes the population, is nurturing, pragmatically kind, and paternal.

There are no "sunshine" laws enabling us to see the dark secrets that lie behind our plates of food, our shiny leather shoes, and our agreeably scented bath products.

There are, conversely, criminal laws which protect the agribusiness industry's horrendous secrets. "Ag-gag" laws have been introduced in more than half of the states in the U.S. It is a crime, in the states in which those laws have been passed, to film, record, possess, or distribute video, photographs, or audio, of the colossal misery that is happening, twenty-four hours a day, seven days a week, behind the high walls of industrial factory farms, slaughterhouses, and even small, family-owned farms.

Hitler likely would have enacted the same types of laws with respect to his extermination camps, had it been even remotely necessary.

Many of the enterprise's stakeholders, ironically, *do* make donations to organizations that benefit cats, dogs, elephants, and tigers, it being the puzzling human consensus that those are the only non-human animals who have pain receptors, intelligence, and emotions.

The public welcomes the manipulative tactics used in the industry's many-armed, Lovecraftian marketing.

Non-stop commercials flaunt the beauty of skins torn from animals and used to make shoes, handbags, sofas, and car seats. Pervasive ads pay tribute to the delectability of animal babies and animal fragments, secretions, and reproductive cells. The sound tracks to the ads permanently plant the subject matter in the viewers' brains.

Human vanity causes people seeking fewer wrinkles to use "serums" that are primarily composed of collagen drawn from animal bodies. If these same people weighed the pros and cons of using animal substances to stave off the normal wear and tear of aging, it would go like this: "Animal cruelty and sacrifice... fewer wrinkles... The win goes to... *fewer wrinkles.*"

∞

The industry supports the holiday traditions that focus on preparations of specific animals, like turkeys, baby sheep, or pigs. Industry sales skyrocket during those happy holiday times.

The public rallies around the notion of farm-to-table animal "husbandry," while ignoring the obvious, underlying horror in this setup. The farmers in the business raise animals as if they were their own pets. They then betray their charges in the most terrifying and horrendous way, by either sending their wards off to dreadful and agonizing slaughter, or committing the horrendous acts, themselves.

Charismatic chefs, some as legendary as superstars, are filmed rending apart the carcasses of animals and serving them up in amusing and trendy dishes. The industry continually seeks out cooks who have that certain, indefinable quality known as "gravitas."

Some of the shows build up the excitement by presenting the cooks as omniscient, god-like beings. The performers enter the stage in slo-mo, their heads slightly bowed, lost in thought so lofty and deep that it is, apparently, unfathomable to "everyday people." The performers stop and strike well-practiced, ominous, intimidating stances, as a fog machine works overtime to envelop them in a low-lying bank of clouds. The doting audience frantically claps.

The shows often start with highly-charged music. The music ranges from ultra-virile rap, to Wagneresque orchestration, to hip jazz, to bouncy country, to current and self-congratulatory pop songs, to elegant classical. The music is switched to the underscoring mode when the cadaver slashing starts. This makes whatever is happening feel momentous to the viewers, who are not consciously aware of the musical manipulation.

Food competitions—centered around the cooking and dressing up of animal parts and animal secretions, and often featuring celebrity cooks in one capacity or another—are a raging success. No one minds that the dishes are seasoned with the sweat that pours from the cooks' brows, as the contestants feverishly work, directly over their preparations.

Semi-retired singers and once-famous actors have gotten in on the action with their own cooking programs. A number of television and movie personalities engage in self-promotion by guest-starring on cooking shows, in an attempt to hang on to their fame and to remain relevant.

That this is done at the expense of animals says a lot about all of these people. Many of the performers project kindness and compassion. Those supposed feelings are reserved for others of their own kind and for some of their pampered pets, with none at all for the other conscious creatures who share this planet with them. They have no issue brutalizing the latter in service of their own appetites, fame, wealth, and smooth rubbery faces.

The cooks call each other "chef," the word weighty in the mouth, as if the designation indicates the cooks are as exceptional and important as surgeons and scientists. Each cook, moreover, uses the royal "we" when pontificating about a dish created from the remains of once vibrant beings.

They talk, non-stop, about the need for "seasoning." The cooks prefer an excess of high blood pressure-inducing salt on decaying flesh. This is likely because salt covers up the ongoing process of rot, which starts the moment an animal's throat is slit from ear to ear.

These entertainers are representative of our culture. Many are as fit and beautiful as models. Others are plump, with a down-home, grandparental vibe. Others could be the typical boy or girl next door. They assign each other kitschy, precious street handles. Many of them sport goofy, whimsical, and considerably fortified hairstyles.

The industry is an equal opportunity death dealer. The spectrum of ethnic groups is represented. All are welcome in the animal exploitation arena.

A number of the cooks have sleeve tattoos, presenting themselves as "gangsta," as opposed to pampered celebrities in the pocket of their industry handlers. Some of the group enjoy receiving compliments for their physiques and their workout regimes. They preen at the praise, even as they barbeque the once-fit and beautiful bodies of animals.

The cooks sometimes mention their various, worthy charities. These, paradoxically, are often "animal" rescues, but the definition of "animals" is limited to dogs, cats, elephants, and tigers. The viewers are left believing that these entertainers not only can whip up a mean plate of corpse, but are also very fine people.

The performers, to this end, incorporate dad jokes and puns into their banter. "I see what you did there," a cook will respond to the punster with a wink, flipping the horror of what is happening on the stage into light comedy.

The entertainers will watch a cook, who is up at bat, prepare a dish. They punctuate the segment—as they look at the mutilated parts of a prettily plated cadaver, and stuff small forkfuls of a dead animal and other animal secretions into their mouths—with, "My mouth is watering," or "This is *craveable*, or "This is *off the hook*," or, "*Look... at... that*," or, "This is so *intentional*," or, "This is *sexy*," or "I love the *mouth feel*," or "You can never have too much *butter*, you know what I'm sayin'?"

A fellow cook, with freakily pumped-up lips and her hair done up in two cat-ear buns—rocking the *"Please, viewers let's all pretend I'm a sweet, innocent girly-girl child, even though everyone knows I'm a jaded adult and outgrew this hairstyle decades ago, but my boyfriend really likes it when I do this to my hair and, on top of it, when I wear a high school cheerleader outfit"* look–will say, "You claim that you're just a home cook, but this *eats* like a high-end dish.[2] This totally has that extra somethin' – somethin'." And then she will groan–her mouth stuffed full of animal carcass–"Ummmm! UMMMMMM!"

Another will playfully brush her lovely, black hair extensions away from her cheeks (which have recently been subjected to buccal fat removal), and look down at the steak on a plate in front of her. "Yes, this does *read* like upscale cuisine," gaslighting the viewers into equating now-lifeless animals on a plate to literature. She will then grab a bottle of ketchup and pour the red liquid on the meat, while the other actors laugh at her antics.

"I can't help it," the performer exclaims. "I love ketchup on my steak!"

The camera will zoom in on a forkful of the flesh and switch to slow motion. The meat will tremble slightly. Secretions and ketchup will drip from it, giving a nod to the blood that had poured out of the animal during its terrible slaughter.

"This has such smoky, warming notes," still another will add. She will genteelly cover her mouth so that she doesn't spray pieces of deceased animal fragments across the table. "I'm definitely getting barbeque vibes."

The industry's use of the foregoing, ritualistic protocol beguiles the public into trusting that what the cooks do is delightful and fun and has nothing to do with pain, horror, and death. How could this industry have a thousand-mile-high mass of anguish and grief behind it, when these

---

[2] Industry cooks have made the verb "to eat" intransitive, in trade-approved vernacular.

people seem so happy, authentic, lovable, authoritative, fun, kick-ass and sometimes, even, silly?

Widely advertised food festivals feature celebrities. The festivals make a *party* out of animal carnage.

The marketing arm of agribusiness is masterful at reinvention. Years of subtle references by the submissive celebrity chefs to "protein" has largely erased the reality that the served-up "protein" is actually the flesh of a dead animal, who has suffered a horrible, terribly painful and lonely life, and death.

The industry doesn't overlook minors. It lures the younger generation into its fold by promoting competitions between child cooks or bakers.

All of the foregoing is done with calculation.

An industry cook may occasionally go rogue and demonstrate a vegetarian or even a plant-based recipe. This is the industry's attempt to pull in non-carnivore viewers. The co-hosts always indulge the rogue cook and pretend to observe the process carefully.

The usual format for this segment is: The other hosts take a small taste of the dish. They agree, with a wink or a smirk, "I can't believe how yummy this is—I don't even *miss* the meat." Another—the self-deprecating, comic relief host— will wrap it up with, "But bacon would make this so much better, wouldn't it? I mean, *everything's* better with bacon!"

The crew, the audience, and the culprit who has prepared the bacon-less cuisine, laugh heartily.

The industry is relentless. An incessant, ceaseless barrage of promotion is fired at us, from cradle to grave.

In light of all of the above, don't be surprised if any aliens, who might have visited this planet, are of the opinion that the human race sucks.

But, like the concept of "hope" at the bottom of Pandora's Box, not all famed chefs, actors, entertainers, influencers, writers, educators, and thinkers are owned by the industry. There are those like Elisa Aaltola, Chad Ackerman, Bryan Adams, Carol J. Adams, Nadia and Omowale Adewale, Casey Affleck, Afia Amoako, Kip Anderson, Pamela Anderson, Sébastien Arsac, James Aspey, Michael Aufhauser, Sadia Badiei, Yvette Baker, Matt Ball, Leslie Barcus, Brigette Bardot, Travis Barker, David Barritt, Luke Barritt, Gene Baur, Steve Bellamy, Rynn Berry, Ryan Bethencourt (the CEO of the groundbreaking vegan pet food company, Wild Earth), Tom Beauchamp, Ed Begley Jr., Marc Bekoff, Steven Best, Mayim Bialik, Choice Bison, Linda Blair, Shari Black Velvet, Michelle Blackwood, Will Bonsall, Cory Booker, Kirsten Ussery-Boyd and Erika Boyd, Shemirah Brachah, Sean Brennan, Beau Bridges, Bonnie Brown, Patrick O'Reilly Brown, Tabitha Brown, Mel Broughton, Carlota Bruna, Joseph Buddenberg, Gisele Bündchen, Genesis Butler, Ned Buyukmihci, James and Suzy Amis Cameron, Lydia Canaan, David Cantor, Michelle Carrera, Joey Carbstrong, Michelle Cehn, Alka Chadna, Jenné Claibone, Stephen R. L. Clark, Katie Cleary, Sue Coe, Pinky Cole, Chris Comer, Jake Conroy, Allison Corbett, Rod Coronado, Chloe Coscarelli, Simon Cowell, Sarah-Jane Crawford, Joe Creaco, James Cromwell, Alan Cumming, K.

Ward Cummings, Luke Cummo, Mac Danzig, Brian and Gloria Davies, Amy Jean Davis, Angela Davis, Babette and Ron Davis, Steph Davis, Camille DeAngelis, Jan Deckers, Lisa DeCresente, Thomas Dekker, Chris Delforce, Nimai Delgado, Emily Deschanel, Peter Dinklage, Ivan Di Simoni, Anita Dongre, Michael C. Dorf, Amy Dumas, Jermaine Dupri, Joan Dunayer, Ava DuVernay, Akisha Townsend Eaton, Diana Edelman, Peter Egan, Billie Eilish, Kimberly Elise, Heather Rae El Moussa, Christopher "Soul" Eubanks, Edie Falco, Anthony Fantano, Kendrick Farris, Pamela Ferdin, Craig Ferguson, Lawrence Finsen, Jerome Flynn, Jonathan Safran Foer, Michelle Forbes, Gary L. Francione, Joe Fredericks, Sharrod Fredricks, Shenarri Freeman, Bruce Friedrich, Tony Frier, Daisy Fuentes, Rodrigo y Gabriela, Maneka Gandhi, Sharon Gannon, Leah Garcés, Juliet Gellatley, Christen Gerhart, Ricky Gervais, Sara Gilbert, Tal Gilboa, Antoine Goetschel, Jane Goodall, Brigitte Gothière, Kat Graham, Ariana Grande, Michael Greger, Grey, Gregory Gude, Jane Halevy, Lewis Hamilton, Daryl Hannah, Amy Breeze Harper, Woody Harrelson, Mark Hawthorne, Elaine Hendrix, Alex Hershaft, Richa Hingle, Ally Hinton, Oscar Horta, Sarah Howlett, Wayne Hsiung, Kyrie Irving, Nina Jackel (the founder of "Lady Freethinker"), Holly Jade, Elgin James, Melanie Joy, Tyra June, Avery Yale Kamila, Tony Kanal, Tonya Kay, Shannon Keith, James Keen, Asa Keisar, Lisa Kemmerer, Jamie Kilstein, Dexter Scott King, Aph Ko, Niko Koffeman, Anita Krajnc, Lenny Kravitz, Keegan Kuhn, k.d. Lang, Carla Lane, Addison K. Lantz, Charlotte Laws, Preacher Lawson, Jessican Mei Lee, Ronnie Lee, Tobias Leenaert, Carl Lewis, Leona Lewis, Valerie

Libutti, Angela Liddon, Chris Liebing, Bob
Linden, Eric C. Lindstrom, Ludvig Lindström,
Cody Linley, Andre Linzey, Howard Lyman,
Evanna Lynch, Dan Lyons, Toby Maguire, Tomi
Makanjuola, Keith Mann, Kate Mara, Rooney
Mara, Katherine Maraveyas, Liz Marshall,
Richard Marx, Jim Mason, Dan Matthews, Gauri
Maulekhi, Bryan May, Peter Max, Jo-Anne
McArthur, Jenny McCarthy, Mary McCartney,
Paul and Stella McCartney, Melanie McDonald,
JaVale McGee, Colin McGinn, Angela Means,
Tracee McQuirter, Erica Meier, Sara Millman,
Heather Mills, Chetana Mirle, Stewart Mitchell,
Moby, Shaun Monson, Richa Moorjani, Victoria
Moran, Joseph Morgan, Morrissey, Mýa, Petra
Němcová, Ingrid Newkirk, David A, Nibert, Jack
Norris, Jade Novah, Martha Nussbaum, Gaz
Oakley, John Oberg, Natasja Oerlemans, Michael
and Masa Ofei, David Olivier, Esther Ouwehand,
Wayne Pacelle, Alex Pacheco, Sara Pascoe,
Colleen Patrick-Goudreau, Charles Patterson,
Chris Paul, Michelle Pfeiffer, Joaquin Phoenix,
David Pearce, Joseph Poore, Natalie Portman,
Gregston Van Pukeston, Ian Purdy, **Maggie Q,
Debby Querido, Christopher Dillon Quinn, Bella
Ramsey, Romesh Ranganathan, Dawn Richard,
William Riva-Rivas, John Robbins, Ruby Rose,
Bernard E. Rollin, Craig Rosebraugh, Kirsten
Rosenberg, Zoe Rosenberg, Mark Rowlands,
Nathan Runkle, Richard D. Ryder, RZA, John
Salley, Becky Sanstedt, Pria Sawhney, Sadaa
Sayed, Miyoko Schinner, Matthew Scully, Jérôme
Segal, Ryan Shapiro, Sia, Alicia Silverstone, Isaac
Bashevis Singer, Peter Singer, Sadie Sink, Kevin
Smith, Snoop Dog (who's trying!), Amy Soranno,
Caitlin Stasey, Gary Steiner, William O. Stephens,
Jon and Tracey Stewart, Styles P, Kurt Sutter,

David Sztybel, Nora Taylor, Sunaura Taylor, Marianne Thieme, Haile Thomas, Dominick Thompson, Darren Thurston, Bob and Jenna Torres, Lauren Toyota, Chrissy Tracey, Will Travers, Eloisa Trinidad, Sam Turnbull, Michaela Vais, Jerry Vlasak, Nisha Vora, Louise Wallis, Tony Wardle, Robin Webb, Paul Wesley, Stephanie Redcross West, the beloved Betty White, Persia White, Will.i.am, Ed Winters, DeWanda Wise, Steven M. Wise, Philip Wollen, Stevie Wonder, Roger Yates, Gary Yourofsky, Joy Zakarian, and Duna Zulfikar—to name just a few— who do not appear to accept the popular notion that any non-human creature is fair game.

These rare individuals are likely able to peer into the eyes of other animals, and not just cats and dogs, or elephants and tigers, and see that they, too, have personalities and—to the extent that humans do—souls.

Chapter 2

Toads and Other Animals

Maya Jackson pulled her foot back in mid-step and stared at the tiny toad sitting in the middle of the garden path. The toad ignored her.

"What's up, friend?"

The toad did not respond.

"Huh." Maya stepped over the small being and continued on the path toward the open sunroom door. She'd finished inspecting her flower and vegetable gardens and the condition of the cherry laurels that grew next to the fencing around her peaceful, quiet enclosure, located smack dab in the middle of an old Los Angeles suburb.

The young woman raised her hand to her head and rubbed her short curls. The mood in her sanctuary was peculiar today. She normally felt safe and protected here. Today, she was so tense that she'd had to resort to a breathing exercise. Inhaling and exhaling air, however, had done nothing to ease her anxiety.

Maya inhaled deeply again, through her nose, to give the diaphragmatic breathing another try. She caught the smell of sautéing mushrooms as she breathed in. Shoot. She hoped the mushrooms weren't burned. She hurried into the sunroom and through to the kitchen.

Maya heard footsteps coming from the front of the house. Had she locked the door? She was always forgetting to lock the door. It couldn't be Dad, she thought. He's not due home for at least another half hour. Her shoulders tightened.

She heard a man's voice. "I'm home, Maya."

Her shoulders relaxed. She quickly walked to the stove and began to move the sliced mushrooms around with a spatula, pretending to be preoccupied with cooking.

"How're you doing, sweetheart?" Eli Jackson walked through the archway from the dining room and into the large kitchen.

"Fine, I guess. I'm making dinner."

"I can see that. What do you mean by "fine?" Is everything ok?"

"Yeah... Just a little off, today."

Eli moved to her side and rubbed her shoulder with one hand. "What's for dinner?"

"Tortillas." Maya pulled the pan of mushrooms away from the gas burner. "Why are you home so early, Dad?"

"We finished insulating the house. I let the crew go early. We'll start drywalling tomorrow."

Eli had been working as a project manager for Colombera Homes for the past twenty years. He was respected by the owners, to the extent that they gave him control over his jobs without input or interference.

"Congrats. You're making good time on that one." Maya began spooning the mushrooms into a small bowl. "I can work for you on Saturday, if you need me."

"Thanks, but no thanks. We're ahead of schedule. I'm shutting it down for the weekend. And shouldn't you be working on your dissertation?"

"My paper is almost done. It's not due for another two months. My advisor says it's pretty tight. So, I'm taking a break this weekend."

"The Uncertainty Principle and Wave-Particle Duality." Eli recited the title of his daughter's paper. He had repeated the title many times and to many people. He was proud of Maya. (He was almost as proud that he could remember the name of her paper.) "I would need the rest of my life to write about something like that. I guess I'd have to take a few math and science courses first."

"I'm pretty sure I got my IQ from Mom."

Eli ignored the comment. "I'll help with dinner. What do you want me to do?"

"Wash your hands—"

"Duh... " Eli cut her off and walked to the sink.

"—Rinse off some cilantro and romaine lettuce and give them a quick chop, please," Maya finished.

"What else do we have?"

"Chopped, toasted walnuts. Avocado, lime juice, cherry tomatoes, red onion, pico de gallo, black beans, chick peas. I think that's it. Oh—and cashew cream. It's all ready to go." She nodded at the kitchen island. "The tortillas are already warmed and in the oven."

Eli's movements were precise and fast. The skills he'd learned over the years in the construction business seemed to transfer to the kitchen arena, as well. "This is going to be good."

Maya looked at the bowl of mushrooms. "Should I add some roasted tofu?"

"No, thank you. I had a tofu scramble for breakfast." Eli looked at his twenty-three-year-old daughter with a critical eye. She may have inherited her brains from his wife, but she'd gotten her build and appearance from him. Tall, trim, and muscular, rich dark hair, and mahogany skin with bronze undertones.

He did not, however, like the way she was screwing up her gorgeous face right now. He stopped working.

"What's going on, Maya?"

She looked up at him, and squinted. She did not answer.

Eli pushed. "Are you thinking about those job offers?"

Maya was, hopefully, soon to receive a Ph.D. in physics, with a concentration in quantum mechanics. Several federal agencies and a number of tech firms were already seeking out his brilliant daughter.

"No... " Maya forced her face to relax. "It's not that. Something's... off."

Eli dropped the fork he'd been using to mash avocadoes. "Sorry?"

Maya turned her head and stared toward the garden out back. "Our little friends—the toads in the garden—are... fidgety. I swear they're trying to tell me something."

Eli smiled, relieved that's all it was. "You've always been intuitive and perceptive, tuned in to our sisters and brothers. Some people in our family would have called you a "sensitive." If you say something is off, I believe you." He nodded once, to stress the point.

33

Maya shook her head, walked to a cabinet, and pulled out two plates and two glasses. "Water ok, or do you want something else?"

"Water is fine."

She filled the glasses from the reverse osmosis tap, took the plates to the island, and began assembling the tortillas.

"So, what do we do about it?" Eli asked.

"I don't know. I have no idea what's wrong. It's just a feeling."

"A strong feeling, I take it."

She nodded. "Let me think about it. Something is up. I wish I could communicate with them." She finished wrapping the tortillas. "I could throw these on the grill for a minute, if you want."

"I'm too hungry. They're perfect as they are."

Eli grabbed the plates from the island and took them to the rectangular kitchen table. Maya followed with the glasses of water and a pile of napkins. They'd be eating with their hands. It could get messy.

"I wish Ben would come over for the weekend," Maya said. "It's been too long since he's been home."

Eli frowned. "I sure do miss that boy."

"He's not a boy anymore, Dad."

"I raised him since he was three, after your aunt and uncle were killed by that drunk driver. Both of you will always be youngsters to me."

"Ok, Dad, whatever. Just don't call him that to his face. He's moved out and is on his own now. He's an adult."

"I don't think of twenty-one as an adult," Eli groused.

~

Professor Michel Arnaud placed his hands on the lectern. He bent his long body forward and peered at the students who were seated in the tiered rows of desks.

One of the scholars was sound asleep. Michel shook his head. This caused his wild shock of white hair to whip back and forth for a moment. Most of the students reacted by straightening their backs and trying to look more attentive.

The majority were keeping their eyes on him and entering notes into their laptops. A few were whispering to each other. One guy was ignoring the professor and hitting on the girl in the next seat.

The student who had caught the professor's attention was resting his head on his desk. At least Mr. Benjamin Jackson wasn't snoring. The professor knew the student well. Ben dropped by his office at least once a week.

The young man planned to become a naturalist. The two men—one in his early seventies and the other just starting out—had a comfortable connection. The college was short-staffed, and Professor Arnaud's schedule was packed. His time was valuable. He rarely wasted it on non-mandated student meetings.

He always had time for Ben, though. He had mixed feelings about the fact that Ben was–as soon as he took a couple courses this coming summer–about to wrap up his four-year degree program. He was happy that Ben would be moving on to post-graduate work, but would miss their conversations.

Michel found the young man to be charismatic and compelling. Michel guessed this was due to Ben's intensity and drive, his combination of strength and vulnerability, his openness, insight, determination, kindness, frankness, and curiosity. Ben had a brilliant and genuine smile which–as the professor had witnessed first-hand–would often cause its recipient to stop speaking for a moment.

Ben's self-composure was profound and contagious. The professor felt serene just standing next to the young man (who was almost as tall as Michel). Ben's physical features, which were irrelevant to Michel, were of the same quality as his mind and spirit. He had lean muscles—the result of actual work—and a face that attracted young people of both sexes. Ben stood out among the thousands of students whom the professor had taught.

Now, as he stared at the close-cropped black hair on the top of Ben's head, Michel said in a loud voice, "Mr. Benjamin Jackson. What do *you* think?"

Ben jerked upright in his seat. He shook his head and straightened his neck and back. He flushed.

"Sorry, sir," Ben answered. "Could you repeat the question?"

Some of the other students snorted. Every one of them had fallen asleep in at least one class, at some point. College was grueling.

"Yes, Mr. Jackson, I will repeat it. What are the two fundamental processes in evolution?"

Ben sat up straighter. He ignored the laughter and rubbed his head for a moment.

"The two fundamental processes in evolution are change within a lineage and formation of new lineages."

"Please provide examples of each."

"The pint-sized dawn horse Hyracotherium evolved into today's Equus through directional succession, which is an example of change within a lineage. The chimpanzee line and the Homo sapiens line resulted from a split in an ancestral primate lineage, which is an example of formation of new lineages."

"Correct." The professor relented, and moved on to another student. "Miss Lucia Sanchez. Is natural selection a factor in the former process, the latter process, or both?"

Michel listened to Miss Sanchez's answer, but glanced back at Ben. The boy worked too hard and for too many hours. He wished there was something he could do to make Ben's life easier. He saw that his protégé was bending his elbows on the desktop, cupping his chin in his hands and drifting back to sleep. Michel decided to leave him alone and let him take his needed nap, in peace.

∞

Ben was exhausted. He'd only had two hours of sleep the night before. He tried to fight his fatigue after answering Professor Arnaud's question about evolutionary processes, but he was too tired to fend off the darkness into which he was falling. He finally gave in.

He allowed his eyelids to close, and reached for the vivid dream the professor had interrupted.

Lucia Sanchez was answering the professor's next question. Ben began to hear Lucia's voice, and the quiet background whispering drone of other students in the classroom, as a low-level, white noise. The grayness, filtering through his eyelids from the room's fluorescent lighting, turned black.

∞

Ben opens his eyes. He is outside in a forest. It is nighttime. He is freezing. He is not in Los Angeles. He looks around at snow-covered trees, and then down, at the top of a small boy's head. The boy has soft, wavy, dark hair.

The child tilts his head upward. His eyes are the exact shape and dark color as Ben's. His golden-brown skin glows in the dark.

Ben *remembers*. He knows this is a dream. He's been dreaming of this boy his entire life, even when he, himself, was a child. He thinks hard for a moment, and remembers past dreams of the boy, which he can never seem to recall when he is awake.

The boy's eyes are banked embers. The child lifts his hand and takes Ben's strong, smooth brown hand in his own. The child gestures around them with his free hand.

Ben looks up. They are standing at the center of a snow-filled clearing, bordered by trees. A bright, shimmering light of some sort, on the ground behind them, allows Ben to see that they are surrounded by a circle of animals.

His dreams of the boy, until now, have been of just the two of them, holding hands and sitting under a tree at the top of a mountain and looking down at a springtime valley, or standing on a

38

cloud and gazing at ocean swells far below, or body-surfing waves together by a long, white beach.

Being with the child in those settings has filled Ben with a peace which has, unconsciously, carried him through the difficult times in his life. The age of the boy has varied in the dreams.

It is different now. It is no longer just the two of them. Something is happening. Perhaps he will be able to remember the boy, this time.

The animals are sitting in, or perched on, the snow. Ben squints. He tries to focus his eyes in the dark. He can make out several crows. And... wait... A cat, a fox, and... is that a hedgehog? His eyes adjust, and he turns.

An incongruous assortment of animals surrounds Ben and the boy. A calf, a wolf, an owl, a coiled eastern diamondback rattlesnake, an eagle, a shrew, a chickadee, a possum, a raccoon, a cottontail, a chipmunk, a Canada goose, a hippopotamus, a chicken, a black bear, a pig with a monarch butterfly resting on its rump, and a salmon, who is sitting straight up on her caudal fin. A salmon?

The light from behind them is strong and gleaming, but Ben notices that neither he nor the child are casting shadows. His eyes adjust to the illuminated night. He watches a dragonfly land on the salmon's head. A firefly, next to the salmon, shimmers on and off.

The group is a random, impossible assortment. Ben stares at its members, considering. He suddenly understands who they are.

"You're... representatives," he says, out loud. "Representatives... of the Animal Kingdom."

The light source behind him: what is it? Ben spins around. What appears to be a two-foot tall, radiant, squirrel-shaped candle, a brilliant torch with wings pressed against its sides, is in the center of the circle. It is so bright that it causes an afterimage.

Ben leans over and reaches down to touch the squirrel-shaped torch.

A few things happen at once. The light goes out and is replaced by a much smaller, flesh-and-blood squirrel. The squirrel leaps backward.

Startled, Ben loses his balance. His fingertips scrape the snow in the place where the animal had been and he pitches, face-forward, into the snow.

He rolls over onto his back and watches the child drop to his knees next to him, in the icy snow. The boy leans forward, until his forehead brushes Ben's. Ben digs his right hand into the snow and freezes in that position, his fingers wrapped in snow and his head touching the child's.

A startling blend of scents pours from the child's skin. Ben pulls in a deep breath through his nose, as if he is inhaling during a stethoscope examination of his lungs. The boy's natural scent... the mixture is exactly right. Ben closes his eyes and whispers to himself, "Lotuses, oranges, peppermint, fir needles, vanilla, cinnamon, and rain."

He opens his eyes. The child is back on his feet.

The child stares at Ben. The banked embers in the child's eyes are not quite ready to ignite.

The boy speaks. It is the first time he has done so, over Ben's long years of dreaming about the boy. His young voice is authoritative.

"You know what to do. You have the information you need."

"Wha...," Ben starts to say.

"*Find me,*" the child commands.

It is now daybreak. The rising sun highlights a tall mountain next to the clearing. Ben looks toward the mountain, drawn by a sudden movement. A man is sliding down some kind of chute etched into the mountain. He is halfway down and picking up speed. He will be at the bottom in a few moments.

The man is tall and thin, with a long, skinny neck, a small, round, bald head, and eyes that appear to be pure-white, ceramic balls. Ben blinks. The man changes, and is replaced by a short and stocky man who has weirdly colored, reddish-blonde hair.

The men are dangerous, no matter what they look like. And they are coming for the boy. Ben has to find him, before they do.

∞

The world in front of Ben's eyes became murky. The boy's world grew faint, and then was gone. Ben was looking at the back of his own eyelids, lit once again by the fluorescent overheads of the classroom. The fingers of his right hand were freezing but were working with the fingers of his left hand and entering words into his laptop.

He looked down and saw that he had typed: "lotuses, oranges, peppermint, fir needles, vanilla, cinnamon, and rain." The words tickled his nose.

"I'll find you," he whispered, and then said aloud, "What does that mean? Find *who*?"

The red-haired girl sitting at the desk next to him turned her head. She raised an eyebrow.

"Were you speaking to me?" The girl made her voice soft and musical.

The young woman, whose name was Madison Gagnon, had told her circle of friends about Ben, the arresting guy in her class. She had entertained them with the story of her futile attempts to get him to notice her. She could tell the story without embarrassment because she was sought after, her family was rich, and she was her father's princess. No boy had previously rejected her.

The circumstance Ben presented was a novelty, a one-off. Talking about him served to underscore the fact that it was rare, if not impossible, for a male not to succumb to her.

Madison had made it a point over the past few weeks to get to class early enough so that she could scope out where Ben was sitting in the room, and to take the seat next to him before anyone else could. Ben, so far, was oblivious. He kept to himself and tried to sit away from others. He had never acknowledged Madison's presence.

Her friends were surprised by her failure to capture Ben's attention. This was a first for her. It was baffling. She had studied the art of flirtation. Men of all ages were drawn to her like she was a lobbyist handing out bribes, or like her pet cat had turned her into a sexual magnet by infecting her with the parasite Toxoplasma gondii. Her associates were making bets on how long it would take Ben to cave.

And, now, it seemed that he had. He'd spoken to her. He was making his first move. Madison prepared herself for Ben to turn those dark brown eyes her way, those eyes that seemed to absorb whatever they fell on. She was ready to be soaked up. It was past time for Ben to be added to her roster of conquests.

She had decided, in fact, that Ben might be her final victory. His continual lack of interest, his apparent and single-minded determination to achieve whatever goal it was he had in mind, his looks, the indefinable way he smelled, and some other quality she couldn't put her finger on, had elevated him to the top of her list.

She had been fantasizing, for the past month, about how they might look standing at an altar together. Ben in a black tux and Madison in a white gown. His long, slender brown fingers entwined in her own alabaster white ones. They would be a dazzling couple. They would take the social world by storm. Madison and Ben. People would refer to them as... as what? Benjamad? No, that sounded too... foreign. Badison? Badison. That was it. They would be a badass L.A. power couple, with a handle to match.

Madison had a moment of self-doubt. Ben did not interact with the other students. She had, by stalking him, found out that this class was his last of the day. He always popped up from his chair when class was dismissed and headed out of the building, like he had places to go and things to do. Maybe he didn't even know her name. No.

That was ridiculous. Men made a point of finding out her name.

"Sorry, no," Ben said, without turning those eyes to her. "I was just talking to myself."

He was embarrassed. He had fallen asleep in class again. He tried to pick up the thread of the lecture, but his thoughts were dominated by random images of a cup of coffee with a cinnamon stick in it, a grated orange peel, and fir trees that dripped rain from their needles.

He really had to get some sleep tonight. He thought how nice it would be if his bed were to be covered, not with his parents' old blanket, but with a blanket of tiny peppermint leaves and enormous pink flowers that smelled like bubblegum. He shook his head to clear it.

Something clunked down onto the floor by his foot, and then a warm arm brushed his own. He glanced to his right. The young woman seated next to him was reaching downward. She had moved her arm into just the right position to touch his.

Ben had done his best to ignore this girl. He was aware she'd been chasing him all semester. He was not interested. Apparently, she was upping her game.

He sighed. He had zero interest in dating her or anyone else. No girl or boy had ever appealed to him. He had no idea whether he was heterosexual, gay, or asexual. It did not concern him. He would figure it out in time, or he wouldn't. What *did* bother him was that people of both sexes were attracted to him and routinely tried to invade his space. This is why he tried to sit away from other students.

Madison straightened in her chair and held up her handbag. "Sorry," she breathed. "Dropped it."

Ben saw that the girl's bag was made of leather. Madison held the handbag higher, to draw his eyes from it to her face. She knew how lovely she was. She and her parents had put plenty of time and money into her appearance. All Ben had to do, for once, was get a good look at her.

"Do you like it?" Madison asked, her voice quiet. "It was a birthday present. Refined calfskin. From Tuscany."

The image of a baby calf with its skin flayed off popped into Ben's head.

This time Ben *did* turn his eyes to Madison. He was not judgmental. Maybe this young woman had not thought about the fact that calfskin came from an actual *calf*. He looked past the young woman's heart-shaped face, tiny flared nose, conditioned and exfoliated pale skin, long wavy red hair, and right into her big eyes, the doorways to her soul (which doorways were accentuated by blue contacts, dark brown eyeliner, and extremely long false eyelashes, which he guessed were made of fur scalped from a mink). He frowned.

Madison dropped the bag on the desk. She gasped. This was unbelievable. Ben was looking at her as if she were... as if she were... ugly. Ugly! Her.

"You've mistaken me for someone else." Ben's voice was as quiet as the young woman's. "I'm not a fan of refined calfskin handbags, wherever they come from." He grabbed the backpack hanging from his chair, unzipped it, shoved the laptop inside, stood, and walked to the door of the room.

Professor Arnaud glanced his way. Ben nodded, in apology. The professor turned his attention back to the classroom. There were still fifteen minutes left in the class, but the day's lecture was over for Ben.

∞

Madison walked out of Professor Arnaud's classroom after the class was dismissed. She went straight to the Registration Department to withdraw from that Genetics and Evolution class. It was past the drop/add deadline. She wouldn't be getting back the tuition for the class. She did not care. She didn't know why Ben had rejected her so forcefully and, worse, with such apparent disgust.

It couldn't be because he did not like her handbag. He couldn't be that petty. She was humiliated. Madison had never experienced humiliation. She intended to avoid Benjamin Jackson from there on out. And, she would not be telling her friends this story. She would instead tell them (if they asked) that it turned out Ben was not up to her standards.

Madison's handbag swung against her leg as she left Registration. She glanced down at the thing banging into her thigh. Its soft feel and luxurious gleam no longer appealed to her.

She looked past the handbag and down at her expensive leather athletic shoes. She had the sudden urge to pull them off and to walk barefoot. She thought of the short, black mink coat hanging in her closet. Her parents had given

46

it to her last Christmas. I'll donate it, she thought. To a women's shelter. Or, better yet, maybe I'll donate it to a women's shelter, and then volunteer there in my spare time.

What was happening to her? Maybe she should schedule an appointment with her father's therapist.

∞

Ben walked across the campus toward the bus stop. He pushed the incident with the pale, red-haired girl from his mind. His thoughts drifted back to evergreen forests and cinnamon sticks. What was the deal? Something to do with that short list of words he'd been entering into his laptop when he awoke from his nap in class. He couldn't remember what he'd typed. He would pull it up when he got home, later that night.

Ben wished he could spend the coming weekend with Uncle Eli and cousin Maya. He needed them, but he had too much schoolwork to finish, and he had to work at his grocery store job on Saturday. He hoped he wasn't cracking up. Maybe the trauma of the sudden deaths of his parents, back when he was a little kid, was manifesting itself again, and he was losing his grip.

A man slipped over the lawn behind him. The man stopped at the base of a fern pine and stood alongside the tree. He was tall and thin and wore gray clothing that blended into the tree's shadow. Anyone walking by would have mistaken him for part of the tree trunk.

He had a little round head in the shape of a perfect globe, stuck on top of a long stick of a neck. His eyes appeared to be carved from milky quartz into two smooth globes.

The man's head swiveled, tracking Ben. His nostrils flared. He was blind, but could strongly sense things of which other people could only get, at most, a hint. The man inhaled the robust scents of cinnamon, vanilla, lotuses, and peppermint, all coming from the direction of Benjamin Jackson. In addition, he detected the faint, fading traces of oranges, fir needles, and rain.

The man, who had called himself "Mr. Anthill" for so many years that he couldn't remember his first name, smiled.

Chapter 3

Carpentry

Katherine Birdsong heard the sound of her foster mother's long cotton robe rustling against the hallway walls. The woman was walking the short distance from the main bedroom to the kitchen. A man coughed, and the bathroom door banged shut.

Kate was only partially awake. One foot was stuck in dreamland. Her dreams were usually borderline (or not so borderline) nightmares. What was it this time? She struggled to remember the dream before it faded away and was lost in the morning sunshine.

The setting had been that of a gigantic, limitless park somewhere in the center of the country. A monstrous granite *face* had been chasing her. Well, it wasn't exactly her it had been chasing. She had been someone else, another young woman. Her body had felt different and smaller, and with shorter legs. Dark brown hair, instead of her own light ash brown hair, had whipped across her face.

The thing had been on the verge of catching her—or her borrowed body—right in the middle of a sunny, poppy-covered meadow. She'd known that if it was able to catch her, the rock monster was going to enfold her in its stony structure and absorb her, down to her last molecule. She'd worked as hard as she could to run. It had been like moving through heavy clay.

The bones of hands had suddenly sprung up among the bright flowers, grabbed her by the ankles, and pulled her down through the earth and into a silent, cold, dark, tight underground cave. The earth had closed above her as she had fallen to the floor of the cave. There had been hard round lumps and other pointy things under her body. She'd reached down to feel what they were.

Ribcages, skulls, and other bones. A warm glow had radiated from the bones. The glow had lit the cave, enough for Kate to see the body of a young man lying next to her. A tiny toad had been sitting on his chest. It had gazed at her.

Oddly, she'd felt warm and safe. The ending of this dream had been much more tolerable than the earlier one she'd had about a televised concentration camp competition, which had, thankfully, mostly faded from her memory.

Kate opened her eyes and saw the bright sunlight streaming in through the one window in her room. She let her eyes go out of focus and tried to remember the nightmares. No luck. That was just as well. She did not know why she felt compelled to recall them but, somehow, it seemed important.

She let her thoughts wander to her current obsession. It was less than one month until her eighteenth birthday. Freedom, she thought. Goodbye, foster care.

She pushed off the covers with her feet, threw her legs over the side of the bed, stood, and stretched her five-foot, six-inch body. She made the bed, grabbed clothes from a small dresser, and put them in a neat pile on top of it. She sat on the edge of the bed and listened for her foster father to get out of the bathroom.

She could barely wait until she got her own place and did not have to share a bathroom.

Kate looked down. A small black spider was marching across the wooden floor toward her bare feet. She leaned over and placed her hand on the floor next to the spider. It climbed onto the back of her ring finger.

"This way," she said, and stood.

She walked to the window over her bed and opened it. She flattened the hand–on which the spider was catching a ride–against the exterior brick wall of the apartment building. The spider raced off her finger and onto the wall.

"Go, little one. The garden is three floors down. Watch out for birds."

Kate liked to pretend that animals could understand her. She knew they could not, of course, but she never tired of trying to communicate with them.

She heard the bathroom door open. "It's all yours, Katie," a man called.

"Thanks, Oscar," she called back, and closed the window. She picked up her clothes from the bed and headed for the bathroom.

The spider raced down the brick wall toward the garden. The little guy, as instructed, watched out for birds as he descended.

Kate showered and dressed in ten minutes. Her routine was short and to the point. She didn't wear make-up and she didn't fool around with styling her long hair. Her hair was as straight as a rail and would dry on the way to school. She looked in the mirror and considered, as she did every morning, grabbing a pair of scissors and cutting it off at her shoulders. She would probably make a mess of it. Better to leave it alone.

Kate made her way to the kitchen. It did not take long. The apartment was small: two little bedrooms (one slightly bigger than the other), a bathroom, a kitchen, and a tiny living room.

Matilda Wright, in a floral, patterned robe, was leaning over an old white electric stove in a corner of the room. Matilda had short, frizzy, dyed brown hair. She was small in stature and about a hundred pounds overweight.

Matilda referred to herself, with a smile, as "fluffy." She was preparing a large omelet. Oscar, her husband, was seated at a round, blue-painted aluminum table in the center of the kitchen. He was reading the *L.A. Times*. He, too, was short. He had a protruding belly and a bald pate fringed with neatly trimmed, gray hair.

"Morning," Kate said.

Oscar looked up from his paper. "Good morning. How'd you sleep?"

"Well, thank you. You?"

"Like a rock." Oscar went back to reading his paper.

"What do you want for breakfast, honey? Would you like some of this?" Matilda gestured at the frying pan. "I know you don't eat eggs or cheese, but this omelet does have spinach in it. Maybe this once?"

Kate tugged her wet hair away from her face, and pulled it through a band into a ponytail.

"No, thanks. I'll make myself a sandwich, if you don't mind."

"What's on your schedule today?" Oscar asked, without looking up from the paper.

"Getting ready for finals."

"I can't believe you're almost done with school," her foster father said, "and that all of your classes are electives."

Kate had been in an accelerated academic program. She'd been able to maintain her grades even when shoved from pillar to post, from home to home, from school district to school district. She had taken a number of high-level courses. Biology, advanced biology, botany, marine science, zoology, plant and soil science, animal behavior, oceanography, geology, environmental science, and ecology. These were all subjects related to, or having an impact on, plants and animals.

Kate found it difficult to be open with people, but not so with animals. She had lived in a number of foster homes where there had been dogs, cats, rabbits, hamsters, birds, and/or tropical fish. Kate connected with animals on a level far beyond the claims of dog whisperers or horse whisperers or cat whisperers. She tried to downplay it when someone noticed, but the intensity of the connection was there. Even aquarium fish tracked her movements when she passed by their tank.

This unusual magnetism had presented a problem with some of the foster families. Those adults believed Kate had, somehow, underhandedly commandeered their pets' affections.

The hardest part about leaving those particular homes had been saying goodbye to the animals. She remembered every single one of them. Each had a unique and remarkable personality.

It was obvious to anyone who paid attention, or gave a damn, that every single animal on the face of the earth experienced joy, happiness, gladness, playfulness, attachment, anxiety, sadness, pain, and fear, just like people did. The difference—when it came to a domesticated animal or a farm animal—was that the animal's state of mind was largely dependent upon the actions of its human caregivers, which actions could range from responsible and caring, to neglectful, to brutal, to sadistic, to actual slaughter and dismemberment.

Kate spread peanut butter over a piece of bread and sliced a banana on top of it.

"Coming straight home after school, are you, or do you have plans?" Oscar asked.

Kate sliced the sandwich in half. She did not look up. "I have a job interview."

"A *job* interview? What? Why didn't you tell us?" Matilda turned from the stove. Oscar dropped his newspaper on the tabletop.

"No big deal. I've been looking for a job online. They're hiring carpentry apprentices at Colombera Homes. I thought I'd give it a shot."

Matilda pressed a hand against her cheek. "Honey, we thought you were going to go to college. Why would you want to be a *construction* worker?"

"A summer job." Oscar turned his head to Matilda. "Just for the summer. That's great! I did the same thing myself. Construction. No reason, in this day and age, a girl can't do the same. Kate

54

will save money for the fall and then go on to college and become a marine biologist or the head of an animal rights organization, or whatever else it is she wants to be."

Oscar knew that there wasn't a snowball's chance in hell Kate could get a job with a contractor, unless it was as an office worker. The personnel director would take one look at this scrawny kid and send her on her way.

"Sure. A summer job," Kate said. "If I can get it."

"But why a carpentry job?" Matilda asked again.

Kate took a small plate from a cupboard and placed her sandwich on it.

"You know that woodworking class I took in school, when I needed a fill-in elective?"

"Of course! You made my beautiful jewelry box, and the wall cabinet that I keep my collection of salt and pepper shakers in." Matilda pointed at the cabinet on the wall. "And you made Oscar that wonderful chessboard and those chess pieces, which gave him the incentive to learn to play and to join the community chess club."

"Yes. Well, I really liked it. I think I might be good at carpentry. I'd rather get a job at the nearby wildlife rehab center, but there aren't any openings for a trainee. Or at a botanical garden, but they're all too far away. Too long a commute."

"Are you going to get your college applications in on time?" Oscar asked.

Kate moved away from the counter and carried her plate to the table. She sat down across from Oscar and looked at him. "I don't know, Oscar. I don't think I'm ready. I first have to get my life in order."

Matilda steadied herself against the counter. Oscar's face fell.

Kate turned toward the older woman. "Don't worry, Matilda. Carpentry would just be a short-term job. Not a career."

Kate did not add that the woodworking course she had taken had been one of the rare bright spots in her life. There had been a purpose to measuring, sawing, routing, using a planer, and drilling wood. She'd had a sense of accomplishment when she'd held a final product created by her own hands.

She wanted a career, one day, that was centered on animals or plants, but she knew that would require years of education. She could save money, in the meantime, working at what she thought might be her second calling.

Matilda took a breath. She looked at Kate's elfin form. The girl was too skinny. "Well, if you get that construction job, maybe you'll build up some muscle, put on a little weight. That, at least, would be good."

Oscar exhaled. "Listen, Katie. We talked about it, and we want you to stay here with us, even after you turn eighteen. We want this to be a real family. No more foster system. We get it. You'll be out of it at eighteen, no matter what you decide. But we want to *adopt* you. Make you our legal daughter, and us your legal parents. You wouldn't have to work while you went to college. But you could, if you wanted to. It would be completely up to you."

56

Adoption? Kate thought of her biological parents. Her real parents. Wouldn't adoption be a betrayal of them? One of the few details she knew about them was that "Birdsong" was a Navajo surname which meant "magical power." She assumed, therefore, that her father had some degree of Navajo ancestry. Her mother's maiden name—which was on Kate's birth certificate—was "Èbren," the Hungarian word for "awake."

One of Kate's caseworkers had taken an interest in the girl and had done a little research on Kate's parents. She had discovered that the couple had been in their early 40's when Kate had been born. Their immediate relatives had predeceased them. In sum, after her parents died, Kate had had no one but herself and the people who were part of the system.

Her parents were executed in a mass shooting at a grocery store. Kate had just turned two. She had a searing memory of a woman—who must have been her babysitter—picking her up from her crib and placing her in the arms of a strange man who was dressed in dark blue clothing. She remembered looking up at his big, olive-skinned, man-face and staring into his sad eyes. He had taken her away from her crib and to another place. She didn't remember where. She now knew that he'd been a police officer and that he'd taken her to his station.

That was the point at which her foster care journey had begun. She was left with nothing to remember her parents by, other than a tiny gold heart on a fragile gold necklace. It had been her mother's. The necklace had, somehow, come with her from home to home, even when she had been too young to wear it. It had never been stolen or lost which, in itself, was a miracle. Now, she never took it off.

Her memories, after that, were of a series of foster families: promising beginnings followed by an equal number of sudden displacements. Children were naturally open and vulnerable. Her vulnerability had long since been layered over with years of trauma, fear, disruption, and loss. There had been no one upon whom she could rely. Only her friendship with animals had relieved the loneliness and isolation.

Kate felt like people viewed her as an immaterial, valueless shadow. A family would decide that it was inconvenient to continue to foster her and, voilà: a social worker would appear out of nowhere and order her to pack up her belongings. Bam. Get out. Gone in a moment to another scary, unknown place full of strangers.

She had lived, at times, with families who had what Kate viewed as *real* children. Real biological or adopted children, permanent family members, who were loved. Kate never felt truly real. She saw herself as a shadow intruder whom a family was obliged, by their contractual requirements with Los Angeles County, to clothe, feed, house, and monitor.

She had decided, at the age of nine, to leave the foster system and its trappings behind as soon as she turned eighteen. She would move on from the trauma of her past, go out on her own, and stop being a wraith.

Kate understood that a child's well-being and psychological development were tied to consistent love, support, and affection. How much had she had, prior to her time with the Wrights? About a "two," on a scale of one to ten.

She had continually lived with the legitimate fear that, when she got off the school bus, a social worker would be waiting, in whatever home she was then living in, to rip her away to another place. Kate had never known security until the past couple years with the Wrights. By then, unfortunately, she was no longer able to accept what they wanted to give her.

She knew that she had a form of post-traumatic stress disorder. She did not know whether she could heal. She was aware that one of her primary PTSD symptoms was her inability to feel a connection to other people. She feared that she might have a schizoid personality disorder. And, to top it off, she had night terrors.

She had lost the foster care lottery. Until the Wrights, that is.

Kate sat still and stared at Oscar. How could she respond to Oscar's offer without hurting him and Matilda? She had made her decision. If she were to overcome her condition and become a whole individual, she first had to put her sad, painful, distressing youth behind her. That meant severing all ties with the foster care system and with everyone associated with it, including the Wrights.

Oscar looked back at the girl. "Like I said, you could work if you really wanted to, while you went to school. And then you could just put that money into your own bank account." Kate didn't answer, so he added, "You would be moving forward with your life."

He continued to look at her. He wondered why no one, other than he and Matilda, could see that the girl was beautiful. He did not know that Kate thought of herself as invisible and that, as a result, she had almost become so to other people. The Wrights *saw* her, though, in spite of her best efforts to erase herself from the awareness of others.

Matilda and Oscar had a large extended family of sisters, brothers, nieces, nephews, aunts, and uncles. They had not been able to have children of their own. In vitro fertilization had been beyond their means. Kate was kind, smart, and hard-working. She was a girl they would be honored to claim as their own. And, maybe, one day, she would marry and they'd have the addition of a son-in-law to their immediate family. And then there might even be grandchildren.

"We'll help you apply for college grants," Matilda added. "If you wanted to get a student loan, we'd help you pay it back. But you have to do this fast, Katie. It's already pretty late to get accepted for the fall semester."

Kate looked down at the floor. She had lived with the Wrights for two years. She was grateful to the couple. She was vaguely fond of them and knew that a *real* person would feel more than that. The last thing she wanted to do was cause them pain. They were good people and had been very good to her. But she did not have it in her to give them what they wanted. She was too damaged.

"I don't know. I appreciate your offer. I'll think about it."

She was lying. She would not think about it. She would take her finals. She would turn eighteen. She would graduate. She would start work as a carpenter's apprentice. She would find a place to live that had no connection to the foster care system. She would put her past where it belonged, in the past. There would only be the present and future, which she, herself, would control.

She did feel regret. She would find a way to let them down gently. She knew that her plan was a betrayal of their hopes. But, it was her life. Thus far, the losses she had sustained, beginning with her parents' deaths and continuing throughout her childhood with the ongoing rejections–that had been, in her case–an integral part of the foster care system, had allowed her little happiness.

There was something special waiting for her out there. She had to leave and go out on her own, if she were ever to find it. Put, for once and for all, the concept of temporary housing and the foster care system in her rearview mirror. It was unfortunate that Matilda and Oscar had entered her life right at the end of her foster care journey. Maybe she would have been a different person, a *real* person, if they had become her foster parents when she was younger.

The girl looked up. Matilda and Oscar were watching her. Her eyes met Matilda's and then moved to Oscar's. Both of the Wrights straightened their shoulders. Kate normally avoided eye contact with anyone. Kate's direct gaze had different effects on different people. The girl might seem to be introverted and introspective, but her eyes told a different story.

Sadly for the Wrights, the only message Kate's eyes were showing them at the moment was *flight*. She was not going to stay.

"Oh." Oscar looked down at the table

Matilda walked to Kate and put her arms around her. "We have faith in you." Matilda's eyes filled with tears. "You're going to be an amazing woman and have an amazing life."

Matilda looked at the window over the sink. An Allen's hummingbird hung outside. The bird was looking back at her and the girl.

"Oh!" Matilda said. She wiped her eyes, put her hands on Kate's shoulders, and turned the teen around so that she could see the bird. "Look!"

Kate glanced toward the window but, by the time she did, the bird was gone.

~

"Enter," a voice called from inside the room. There was a small sign on the door that read, "Mr. Poggi, Personnel Manager." Kate opened the door and walked inside.

"Sit down, please," the man said.

He gestured to a hard wooden chair in front of his metal desk. Kate sat, as instructed. Mr. Poggi was engaged in answering emails on his desktop computer and had not yet looked up at the girl. Kate sat in her chair, as still as a statue. He waved one hand in her direction, and asked, "Name?"

"Katherine Birdsong."

The man began scrolling through the files on his computer and clicked on one of them. He read for a moment. "Not much of a resume, eh? I see you're about to graduate from high school. So, tell me why you think you're qualified to be a carpenter's apprentice."

"I, well... ," Kate began.

On the bus ride over, she had pulled her hair into a knot at the back of her neck. She was making a conscious effort to keep her hands in her lap, instead of tearing away at the knot. Why *did* she think she was qualified for this job?

All she could come up with, on the spot, was, "I loved woodworking in school."

She always prepared well for everything she did. She was totally unprepared for this interview, however. Why hadn't she thought about what she was going to say? Had she just assumed she could get the job by sheer force of will?

Kate looked at the man. She wished he would stop fooling with his computer and pay attention to her. Kate wanted this job. She *needed* this job. She believed that it would, somehow, change her life.

This was the first step toward her real future. She could not recall ever wanting anything so badly, other than to have her parents back. She touched the little gold heart hanging from her necklace and thought, "I have to get this job."

"Woodworking?" Ridiculous. Mr. Poggi stopped fooling with his computer. He looked up. His eyes met Kate's.

He pushed back into his chair, dumbfounded. The girl's eyes were like twin furnaces. They radiated some sort of massive potential. As if—had she not been a frail-looking, white girl—she might have been a daughter of Genghis Khan.

Mr. Poggi's lips moved and he started talking, the words erupting from his mouth on their own. "How much weight can you lift?"

"Fifty or sixty pounds," Kate exaggerated.

She wondered what was wrong with the man. He was taking deeps breaths and sucking in his cheeks and then puffing them out. She decided to ignore his odd behavior and push forward. She hoped he wasn't having a heart attack.

"We have a weight room at school. I've been using it two or three times a week. I'm sure I could build up to lifting even more weight, on the job."

The manager's eyes were glued to Kate's. His face tightened, and lines creased his forehead. Words were coming out unbidden. "We've sometimes employed apprentices with no experience, but those have always been big *guys*."

"Please give me a chance," Kate whispered. She leaned forward, trying to figure out what was up with the man. Her hazel eyes peered into his tired brown ones, pressing her case.

Mr. Poggi felt like he was being tumbled by a wave. His eyes widened. He looked, for the first time that day, like he was fully awake.

"Ok," he said, back in control of his speech. "You're hired. You can start the Monday after your high school graduation. You'll be working directly under the supervision of Eli Jackson, our senior project manager." He added, as additional enticement (as if *he* had to convince *her* to take the job), "He's also our senior master carpenter."

Mr. Poggi looked down at his computer and began pecking at the keyboard.

"There." He looked back up at the girl. "Done. Everyone's been notified. I've emailed you links to the forms you'll need to complete and then email back to me."

Kate stood. "Thank you, sir." She extended her hand. Mr. Poggi took it and gave it a squeeze.

Kate left the office and closed the door behind her. Mr. Poggi rubbed his neck. The memory of the power of the girl and her gaze did not fade with her departure. His eyes lowered. Tiredness seeped back into them.

He wondered how he was going to explain why he had hired her, and why he had assigned her to Eli, of all people. Any carpenter's apprentice at Colombera Homes would have given part of their pay to be on Eli's team and to work under his guidance. Only those with the most potential were assigned to him, and all who were so assigned made it to full carpenter status, on a fast track.

It was true that Mr. Poggi had often, in the past, employed people with no experience. Those hires had been sturdy young men. Each of those muscular lads had worn the title of "apprentice," but had actually started out with the company as a simple laborer. The young lady did not fit into that category. She was not strong enough.

He had already assigned her to Eli. She would, therefore, truly be working in the capacity of an apprentice. A random thought popped into the man's head.

"Hmmm," he said aloud. "This will improve our female gender participation rate. It's good for the annual stockholder report, isn't it?"

This was a solid rationalization, an acceptable justification. Mr. Poggi pushed the matter of Kate out of his mind, leaned forward, and began answering emails again.

~

Benjamin Jackson took a bus from the college to his job at an auto repair shop.

He worked for four hours, until the shop closed at 8:00 p.m. Ben cleaned his tools and put them away, washed the oil and grease from his face and hands, took a change of clothes from his assigned locker, rolled up the dirty clothes, put them into a tote bag, and stuffed the tote bag into his backpack. He said goodnight to his coworkers and left the garage.

He had a second job at a grocery store, working the after-hours, part-time, night shift. He ran the five blocks to his bus stop so that he could reach it before the bus did. Missing the bus would mean he'd have to wait twenty minutes for the next one. This had often happened. The grocery store owners were kind, understanding people and did not require him to show up at a specific time.

Tonight, he was fortunate and made it just as the bus pulled up. Ben relaxed for the fifteen-minute ride. He got off a few blocks from the small corner market.

Mr. and Mrs. Patel owned the business and the building in which it was located. The couple liked Ben. His work ethic, moral compass, and intelligence reminded them of their only child, Krish. The young man had been a Special Forces officer in the U.S. Army. Krish had died while protecting his team in Afghanistan. It had been his third tour of duty in Middle East hot zones.

Both of the Patels, now without a living son of their own, had a strong urge to help Ben. They knew he wouldn't take handouts so, instead, leased him a clean, snug, fully furnished studio apartment upstairs from the grocery store. They charged him a ridiculously low rent. Ben was happy with the space and grateful for the arrangement.

Ben arrived as Mr. Patel was leaving. "Need anything special done tonight, sir?" Ben asked.

"No, thank you, Ben. Just the usual. In fact, while Mrs. Patel was doing the accounting, I swept and washed the floors and dusted the shelves. Not much left for you to do. Just fill in the shelves. Try to get out of here early so you can get some rest tonight. Mrs. Patel is waiting for me in the car. Very impatiently, I'm sure. I didn't want to leave until you got here. I'll go out the side door. Good night."

"Good night, Mr. Patel. Say, "hi" to Mrs. Patel for me."

The older man went to the back of the store and into the storeroom. A side door in the storeroom led to the alley, where the car was parked.

Ben flipped the "Closed" sign, so that it faced outward on the door window, and locked the front door. He went about his routine of stocking shelves. He was fastidious about rotating the stock, with the newest items behind the older products.

At 9:30, Ben heard a noise outside. He stopped working. It came from the back of the building. He went into the storeroom. He usually had just one overhead light on in that room, to conserve energy. Now, he turned on all the lights and looked around. He checked the side door. No one was in the store with him.

He shook his head. He was tired and starting to hear things. Ben normally did not secure the front exterior of the store until he was getting ready to leave. He decided to do it early, this night. He unlocked the front door, went outside, relocked the door, and reached to the right to grab the exterior steel gate which protected the entire storefront. He pulled it across, fastened it on the other side, and deadbolted it.

He went around the building, to the left, and entered the alley. He took out his keys, unlocked the side door, went inside, and locked it behind him. He leaned against the metal door and looked around the storeroom, searching for... searching for what? He was so jumpy. What was wrong with him?

Ben went back to work. He moved canned tomatoes from the storeroom to a partially empty display shelf. He was still uneasy. He stopped and listened. Nothing. Not even a passing car. His uneasiness grew.

He did not take Mr. Patel's thoughtful advice to leave work early. His shift was over at midnight and there was always enough work to keep him busy until then. He needed the money and was paid hourly. Never mind that the Patels probably would have paid him for a full shift, whether or not he finished it. He would not take unearned money from his own uncle, and certainly wouldn't take it from anyone else.

The Patels had received a shipment of flour, rice, and canned goods earlier that day. The unopened cases were stacked in the storeroom. Ben cut open the cases, checked off the received items on the packing list, noted any shortages or damaged goods, and shelved the products in the storeroom in their proper places. He gradually relaxed, dismissing his earlier apprehension as the result of simple exhaustion.

A little metallic noise interrupted his work. This sound did not make him edgy. He knew what it was. He looked under the shelves and spotted the three, no-kill, "Havahart" traps he'd set up in the room. One had been triggered. He leaned over, pulled the trap out, stood up, and held the trap in front of his face.

He looked at the tiny rodent staring back at him. "Ok, little guy, you're going out into the big, wide world tonight. I hope you stay safe. Avoid rat poison and cats."

He unbolted the side door, went into the alley, and released the mouse. The mouse did not run away. He stayed where he was and continued to stare at Ben.

"I hear the next alley over has a lot of trash in it. Head there. You'll be fine." Ben yawned and put a hand over his mouth. "Goodnight, mouse." Ben went back inside.

The mouse looked toward the end of the alley, at the dark brick wall. The fur on his back rose. He turned and ran off in the opposite direction.

Midnight arrived. Ben washed his hands, grabbed his backpack, and went out the storeroom door. He double-bolted it behind him. A metal staircase, fastened to the brick wall near the front of the alley, rose to the upper levels of the building. Ben's apartment was accessible only through this stairway.

Ben was too tired to be alert, too tired to observe much of anything. He failed to notice the peculiar man who was wearing dark clothing which bled into the darkness. The man was standing, motionless, against the back wall of the alley. Ben climbed the metal stairs to the second level. He walked a few feet along a metal balcony and reached the door to his flat. He unlocked it, went inside, and pushed the door shut behind him.

An insect crawled up the back of his neck. Ben's hand jerked and gently touched the spot. No bug. Ben turned and looked at the solid metal door to his studio apartment. The disquiet had returned. He reached to test the door handle, to make sure it had automatically locked, and shot the deadbolt for good measure.

Ben tossed his backpack on a coffee table—the only table in the small flat—and walked the few steps to the bathroom. He stripped and put his dirty clothes in a small combination washer/dryer in the corner of the bathroom.

He took a long, hot shower. He finished by wiping down the glass door and the tiled wall of the shower, to prevent the formation of mold. He stepped out of the shower stall, removed the dirty clothing from the backpack, added the clothes to the washing machine–along with his wet towel and washcloth–and started the load.

Ben went into the tiny kitchenette. There was a half empty pot of coffee left over from breakfast. He poured himself a cup and microwaved it for a couple minutes. Ben inhaled the fragrance of cinnamon-infused coffee. His Uncle Eli had instructed him to always put a piece of cinnamon stick in with the coffee grinds when brewing coffee. Uncle Eli had read that the sticks—but not ground cinnamon—were good for diabetes prevention. Ben just liked the taste.

He took a container of homemade white bean puree from the refrigerator, spread it on two slices of twelve grain bread, and added sliced avocado and tomato. He squeezed a fresh-cut lime on top, sprinkled on a little salt and pepper, and slapped the two slices together. Dinner was ready.

He set the cup of coffee and the sandwich on the coffee table and plopped down on the sofa next to it. The sofa did double duty as Ben's bed. He pulled the backpack forward, opened it, and drew out a textbook. This was his study time. He hoped he could get in two or three hours before he fell asleep.

His thoughts drifted to the advanced geology paper on which he'd been working. He had chosen a project involving geological maps of Ohio. He'd noticed major discrepancies among the maps. He'd given a draft to Professor Arnaud for his input, but hadn't yet heard back from the man.

Ben had been able to trace the inconsistencies to one specific location, the City Park in Cutter City, Ohio. His attempts to research the area had ended in frustration and disappointment. Little had been written about the Park, and none of the data added up.

Ben hadn't been able to help himself. His paper went off in an unexpected direction. It had become all about that damned and, so far, unmeasurable, parkland. Oh well, Ben thought. My paper had probably sounded, to Professor Arnaud, like the rantings of a loon.

"Whuh?" Benjamin's body jerked, startling him awake. He was lying at an uncomfortable angle on the couch. He rubbed his eyes and sat up. The floor lamp was still lit. He looked at the coffee table. His sandwich was half-eaten. The coffee was untouched. The textbook was on the floor. He glanced at the clock. Three a.m.

"I was dreaming," he said aloud. "What was I dreaming?"

The answer to that question seemed more important to him than the fact that he had slept through his limited study time.

He rubbed his face with the back of his arm. The strong, combined scent of lotuses, oranges, peppermint, fir needles, vanilla, cinnamon, and rain permeated the room. Ben inhaled deeply. The scent filled the flat, and Ben remembered a fragment of his dream. The dream had revolved around a familiar boy. He needed to write down the small bits he could recall, before it slipped away. He reached for his backpack, pulled out the laptop, and opened it.

He began to type: "The boy told me his name is "Samuel." He's looking up at me, and smiling. There is this incredible smell-"

He struggled to remember more, but the rest of the dream slipped away. Ben stopped and pressed "Save."

He had to see Uncle Eli. His head filled with fog. There was no way he could attempt to read a textbook right now. He laid back down, and fell asleep.

The man with the small round head and stick neck and eggshell eyes stood by the back wall of the alley. He twitched. He had been standing motionless for hours. He was right!

He was one of the few living people who could *taste* Ben's soul. It was like cinnamon, vanilla, lotuses, and peppermint. That taste, that soul, had lured the man all the way from LAX, the Los Angeles airport, where Mr. Anthill had had a layover on a business trip to Hawaii. He had not gone on to Hawaii. He had, instead, left the airport in L.A., fixated on finding the person with the elusive smell. It had drawn him right to Ben, the way people and flies are drawn to a bakery by its fragrance.

Now, Mr. Anthill smelled and tasted the rest of the Scent, as he had earlier that day at the college. It was so strong that it spilled out of Ben's dream and into Ben's studio apartment. It contained all of the young man's scent, plus the three missing pieces: rain, fir needles, and oranges.

There was no longer any doubt. One of the Children was on the way. The man's mouth split open into the suggestion of a smile. His teeth were little and white, like tiny Chiclets.

He'd have to think about his next move.

Chapter 4

Working for the Man

Eli took one look at the silent, skinny, fair-skinned girl who stood before him in the partially constructed mansion. He immediately made a bet with himself that this girl would not last a week on the job. He wondered why Lorenzo Poggi had hired her. Maybe Poggi was friends with her parents or owed someone a favor. He was definitely going to speak with the man about it. He'd have to make time to visit the main office.

"You finish high school?" Eli asked.

"I graduated this past Saturday, Mr. Jackson," Kate replied.

"Name's Eli. No "misters" on the job. Put this on." He handed her a blue hard hat. "Do you know how to fit it?"

"No, sir."

Eli retrieved the hat from the girl and spent a few minutes adjusting the suspension mechanisms to fit her head. "Rule number one: Always wear your hard hat on-site. Ok. Let me show you around a little bit, and then we'll meet up with my crew. We're in the process of framing out the rooms."

And so, Kate's training began. Eli's instructions were curt and to the point. He was reserved and did not often smile. That suited the non-chatty Kate. Eli showed her what to do and she did it, copying him and her coworkers to the best of her ability. Kate had known that there would be a lot of lifting involved. The actual work was surprisingly comparable to a laborious, synchronized dance. It certainly required skill and coordination.

The workday started at 7:00 a.m. and ended at 3:30 p.m. The house was "dried in," meaning that the roof, exterior walls, windows, and doors had already been installed. Kate was weary, but also happy that she'd survived her first day.

Eli said to the girl, as she was leaving the site, "You did a good job today. I must admit, I was a little concerned when I first got a look at you. You have surprised me. I don't surprise easily." He handed her a key to the temporary lock on the front door. "Go ahead and let yourself in, if you ever get here before the rest of the crew."

Kate walked with a crowd of other construction workers to the bus stop, a few streets away. She was pleased to be carrying a hard hat. It was a symbol that she belonged to an exclusive club.

Her bus pulled up within twenty minutes. She had to take three buses, which involved two unreliable transfers, to get to the Wrights' apartment. She got home after 5:00. She was tired and didn't have much to say to Matilda and Oscar, other than she liked the job. Matilda had prepared beans and rice for her.

Kate scarfed down a bowl of it and put the bowl in the dishwasher.

"I'm pretty beat. I think I'll go to bed early."

It wasn't even 7:00 p.m., yet. Oscar and Matilda looked at each other. They both wondered whether Kate would last longer than a few days in the job.

"Sure," Oscar said. "Get your rest." He glanced at the blue hard hat, sitting on the kitchen countertop.

∞

Kate wanted to get to the site, the next morning, before anyone else. She wanted to show Eli that she was handling the job well, no matter how hard it was.

She arrived at 6:30 a.m. Eli's black Chevy Silverado pickup was sitting in the as-yet unpaved driveway. The front door was already unlocked. Kate put on her hard hat and went inside.

Eli was standing in the center of the room next to a tall, young woman. The woman had a blue hard hat tucked under her arm. Eli held a tablet in front of him. The young woman touched a finger to the tablet.

"So, the little powder room goes there." Her voice echoed throughout the large, empty room. She stopped and waved her hand toward a spot near the front of the big home.

"That's right," Eli said. His eyes followed the woman's gesture, and landed on Kate. "Kate. You're early."

The stranger looked at Kate. "You work for my dad?" she asked. She lifted one eyebrow.

"If Eli is your dad, then yes," Kate replied. Kate looked from Eli to the woman, and saw the resemblance.

"Wow," the woman said.

"Hmph," Eli muttered. "You're supposed to be a feminist."

"But she's... ," Maya replied softly.

76

"Skinny? Looks weak? Don't judge a book by its cover." Louder, he said to Kate, "Come on over and meet my daughter. This is Maya. Maya, Kate."

The two young women walked toward each other, stopped, and shook hands. Maya gave Kate the once-over. "Well," she said. She chewed on her lip. "So, Kate, why do you want be a carpenter?" She looked at her father as if to say, "You're kidding, right?"

Kate looked back at Maya. Eli's daughter had lanky arms and legs and a long, swan-like neck. Her face was angular and bare of makeup. She wore large glasses and had a short haircut. Her slender fingers ended in clipped, unpolished fingernails. She watched Kate studying her, and grinned. Maya's teeth were even and white. She had a big, brilliant smile. She was stunning.

"Holy," Kate said. She couldn't stop herself. "Are you a model?"

"Hardly," Maya snorted.

"You could have been," Eli said. "It's not like you didn't have offers."

"There're a lot of things I want to do. Modeling isn't one of them. What about you, Miss Kate? Why are *you* here?"

Maya's voice was warm and melodic. The sound went as straight and sure as an acupuncture needle to a spot in Kate's brain, causing the release of endorphins. It calmed her. She wanted to hear Maya's voice again. "I like working with wood," she replied and thought, what a dumb thing to say.

"I guess that's a good enough answer. I do, too. Anyway, since you're early, do you want to go over the plans with us?"

"Yes, please."

Maya took Eli's device from his hand. She scrolled for a second, then handed Kate the tablet. "These are the house plans."

Kate—with Maya's instructions—ran the program's tutorial for the next ten minutes, and then Maya went over the house plans with her. Kate absorbed the knowledge that was delivered on waves of Maya's musical voice.

The other workers arrived at 7:00.

"I think I'll team up with Kate," Maya decided. "That ok with you, Dad?" This young girl who wanted to be a carpenter, and who was hanging on Maya's every word, intrigued her.

Eli felt dizzy for a moment. He closed his eyes and took a breath. He smelled orange, fir needles, and... and... rain. Like a rainstorm-kind of smell. Eli had never had a seizure. He wondered if he was about to have one now, and if this was some kind of pre-seizure aura. The smell dissipated. He opened his eyes. "Sure," he said.

Maya looked at him closely. "You ok?"

"Yeah, I'm fine." He looked at Kate. "Are you wearing some kind of perfume? It's probably not a good idea on a job site."

"Really, Dad? Why not?" Maya asked, confused. "I mean, I wouldn't wear a scent because so many people are allergic to them—plus, most perfumes and colognes are loaded with carcinogens, neurotoxins, and phthalates—

but why is it a bad idea, specifically, on a job site?"

"I'm not wearing perfume," Kate interjected. "Not a fan."

"Don't mind me," Eli said. "Forget I asked. Go ahead and get to work now."

"You mind partnering with me?" Maya asked Kate.

"Sounds good," Kate replied, and beamed.

Maya put on her hard hat. "We're framing in the office today. Come on."

Working with Maya turned out to be even better than working with the men. The two women fell into a rhythm that was more like a ballet than a simple dance. Maya recognized in Kate the same eagerness and capacity to learn that Eli had seen in the girl the previous day.

~

The interior framing was completed by mid-July. They were to begin the finishing work on the portions of the house that had been drywalled. Kate was keen at the prospect. She was going to help give this home its own personality.

Maya no longer thought it odd that Mr. Poggi had hired the young girl. Kate was quick to learn and contributed as much as anyone who had ever held that position.

Kate, on the other hand, was beginning to question her belief that she couldn't connect to people. She certainly connected with Maya.

Maya liked talking with individuals and getting to know them. And people, in turn, liked hanging out with Maya. Kate surreptitiously observed Maya greet their coworkers. She noticed that the men's faces lit up whenever Maya directed her intelligent, curiosity-filled eyes their way.

Maya had, in turn, been watching Kate. She felt compassion for her. Kate reminded her a bit of a wounded bird.

Maya decided that it would be worth the effort to get the reserved girl to open up. She figured the best way to do this would be to talk the other girl's head off. This was a skill at which Maya excelled.

She began her campaign. Maya avoided personal subjects but, during their labors, informed Kate about her opinions on a broad range of subjects including, among other things, politics, the environment, the racial divide, animals, the road infrastructure in L.A., her relief the university's acceptance of her dissertation defense, her decision-making with respect to the job offers she was currently evaluating, flowers, dating, living in the city, why both sexes should know how to use a sewing machine and how to change an automobile air filter, the beauty of antique clocks that played "Westminster Quarters," veganism, the best places to shop for vegan ingredients, Ferris wheels, socks, the misogynistic cultural pressures that caused women to think they had to wear high heels and dye their hair and smear their faces with questionable cosmetics and use toxic chemicals on their nails, why food coloring sucked, how wrinkles made a person look interesting as opposed to being stamped out of a rubber mold, the importance of pulling your shoulders back so that—among other things—you could breathe properly, and the pros and cons of soup.

Kate did not care what Maya talked about. She loved listening to her. The sound of Maya's voice alone, no matter the subject, was soothing to the girl. It was starting to heal the jagged places inside her.

Maya and Kate were assigned to the installation of the kitchen's upper cabinets. Maya thought it was possible that she might now be able to have an actual two-way conversation with the other woman.

"I won't be working here past mid-August," Maya said.

She was holding up the corner cabinet while Kate, standing on a stepladder, drilled in screws through the back of the cabinet.

"What?" Kate asked. She stopped drilling. A screw fell from her hand to the floor.

Maya's left hand was still supporting the cabinet. Kate noticed a tiny tattoo on the interior of the other girl's wrist.

"This is just a summer job for me. You know I'm done with school. I have to choose, in the next few weeks, where I'll be working. It might even be on the East Coast. I haven't decided yet."

"Oh." Kate picked up another screw and restarted the drill. She looked lost.

"It's a ways off yet. It's only the middle of July. Almost a whole month to go."

Kate nodded. She continued working, in silence.

"What about you, Kate? Don't you want to go to college? I mean, you do have an aptitude for carpentry, but it doesn't hurt to have a degree."

Kate didn't answer. She concentrated on making sure the screw was going straight into the wall beam behind the cabinet.

"I'd think that any person who has your potential and drive would at least want to give it a shot."

Kate stopped drilling again. She looked down from the short ladder on which she was standing. "I *do* want to go to college. I need to save money first, so that I can go out on my own."

"Where do you live now?"

"With my foster parents."

"Oh." Maya didn't know what to say. She had previously avoided questioning Kate about her life, and Kate hadn't offered up anything. This was the first important thing she'd learned about the girl.

"They're kind people," Kate continued, "but I can't wait to get out of the system." There. She'd said it aloud.

"How far away is it?"

"Our apartment? I mean, my foster parents' apartment? It's a little more than an hour away, depending on the buses."

"You take buses?"

"Yes, three of them."

Maya thought how nice it was that she herself came to work in style, chauffeured by her father in his Chevy Silverado truck. "Do you mind if I ask what happened to your parents?"

Kate didn't answer for a few minutes. She finished drilling in the last three screws. She stepped down from the ladder and turned to Maya. "They were killed in a mass shooting. When I was two."

God, Maya thought. We're going from zero to sixty in a matter of seconds. She really needed to do a breathing exercise to calm down. She didn't, because Kate was watching her. "I'm so sorry. Do you have any other family?"

Kate shook her head. "My parents were older when they had me. I'd supposedly had a couple of uncles, but they and my grandparents were all dead by then. So, I was put into foster care."

She stepped from the ladder and leaned against a wall. She began to let it all out, for the first time in her life. She told Maya about the policeman who had taken away her from her home, never to see the place or her parents again. She talked about the foster parents with whom she'd never been able to connect, and how she'd always been an outsider. She blurted out the summary of her sad story within twenty minutes.

"Aww, I'm so sorry," Maya said, when Kate had finished. She walked the few feet to Kate and put her arms around her. Kate began to sob.

Eli, in the great room adjoining the kitchen, was going over the project schedule with the master plumber and the master electrician. He looked up at the two girls, perplexed. He'd noticed when they'd stopped working in order to talk, but had not interrupted. It looked like the quiet young apprentice was opening up, and he was glad. Maya caught her father's eye and shook her head.

"Come on Kate, let's go for a walk. Dad, we're taking our lunch break now," she called. He nodded and went back to the discussion about the upcoming schedule.

"There's a vegan café down the street," Maya said to Kate. "My treat."

Kate pulled off her hard hat. Her long hair spilled past her shoulders. She wiped her eyes and nose on her sleeve. "I'm not a crier," she mumbled. "I can't remember the last time I did that."

"Wow. I cry at anything and everything. I'd say you're making progress," Maya smiled.

They walked on the sidewalk to the café, without speaking. The place was packed. "Maybe takeout?" Maya suggested. She looked at the line of people waiting for tables.

"Yes, please," Kate replied. She was exhausted from what appeared to be the major psychological catharsis she'd just experienced. She felt much calmer, though. She was tapped out, at ease, and feeling better about herself. The big hole she'd felt in her chest, since the day her parents had died, felt like it had shrunk significantly.

Maya ordered two teas and two portobello mushroom burgers. Kate carried the teas and Maya carried the bag of burgers to a bench in the nearby park. They sat and ate in silence, warming themselves in the summer heat.

∞

Eli finished his conversation with the other two men, who went back to their crews. He walked into the kitchen and looked at the sole cabinet hanging on the wall. He reached over and tried to move it. It was solidly in place. He looked behind it to see if there was a gap. There was none. The two girls had done well.

"Hmph," he muttered under his breath. That Maya, he thought, and shook his head, her and her strays. He thought about Kate. There was something more to her, beyond that scrawny exterior.

He'd been meaning to pay Lorenzo Poggi a visit but had been putting it off for weeks. Now, as he watched Maya and Kate leave the job site to go to lunch, he decided, on the spot, to go downtown to the personnel director's office. He needed to find out why Lorenzo Poggi had hired Katherine Birdsong, although his reasons for the upcoming interrogation had changed. Eli got in his truck and made the thirty-minute trip to the main office.

~

"Good afternoon, Lorenzo." Eli pushed open the personnel director's door without knocking.

Mr. Poggi looked up, startled. He saw Eli, sat back, and sighed. Eli closed the door.

"You've come about the girl," Mr. Poggi said. He had been expecting this visit.

"Right."

"Well... how is she doing? Is everything all right?" Mr. Poggi asked. He was stalling. He needed time to collect himself, and to think. How could he justify the hire to Eli? The front office was one thing. Those staff members had bought the "improvement in gender numbers" thing. Eli, however, was not quite so gullible.

"She's fine," Eli replied. "Now, tell me."

"Tell you... ?"

"Tell me why you hired her."

"Well, I... uh... , you see, she's a female and... "

"Stop," Eli said. "No bullshit, Lorenzo. I'm asking you again: Tell me why you hired her."

Mr. Poggi looked up. "I can't tell you, Eli. I don't know why."

"Try to figure it out." Eli's voice was gentle. He plopped down in the chair facing the desk.

The personnel manager broke. "Ok." He couldn't handle the intense scrutiny of Eli's dark brown eyes. He let his own gaze overshoot and travel to the wall behind the other man. "It can't leave this room," he whispered, looking toward the door. "They'd think I was losing it. I could be fired." The man looked helpless and scared.

"Go on," Eli replied. "I'm not going to say anything. The last thing I want to do is get you in trouble. I just want to know what it is about Kate that caused you to hire her."

Mr. Poggi grabbed onto Eli's words, and looked directly at him. "That's it! There's something about her. Something astonishing. I saw it when I looked into her eyes."

"You saw something astonishing in her eyes?"

"Yes," the man replied. He was engaged now, thinking how best to explain what had happened with the girl. "She's like a force of nature. I can't describe it. I just knew that she could handle the job."

Mr. Poggi wondered if he'd said too much. Maybe Eli would think he was nuts and notify the bosses upstairs, after all.

"Hmph," Eli said, He sat back in his chair. "Ok." He didn't speak for a few moments. Then he stood. "Thanks." He put out his hand. Mr. Poggi also stood, took Eli's hand, and shook it.

"That's it? You don't have any other questions?"

"Nope. That's all I needed."

"You're not going to say anything?"

"You have my word." Eli strode to the door. He opened it. He started to walk out, stopped, turned, and said, "You... you didn't notice anything different about the way she *smelled*, did you?"

"Smelled? What do you mean?" Mr. Poggi asked.

"Uh... " Eli was now as reluctant to continue as Mr. Poggi had been. Eli stopped, thinking of sitting in front of a kitchen window and watching rain drip from fir trees while peeling an orange. "Nothing, never mind." He added, "Don't worry about it. I'm not mad at you for hiring Kate. She's working out fine. I've got to get back to work now. See you, Lorenzo." He turned and left the office.

"Goodbye, Eli. Take care," Mr. Poggi called after him. He felt an enormous sense of relief. He, too, went back to work.

~

Maya crumpled up the paper in which the burgers had been wrapped. She tossed them into a trash can a few feet from the bench. She sat

87

back, took a gulp of tea, and looked up at the tree limbs that hung above them.

"You remind me a lot of myself."

Kate jerked her head in surprise. "Me? What?" She snorted. "You're smart and together and... I mean, look at you."

Maya raised an eyebrow. "Look at me? What do you mean?"

Kate stared down at her feet. "You're... well, people really *like* you. I don't think I'm very likeable except, maybe, to my foster parents."

Maya lifted her hand, put it under the other girl's chin, and gently pulled Kate's face up so that she could meet her eyes. She dropped her hand. "There's more to you than you think, Kate. I'm not going to list the attributes I think you have. Right now, you would find that to be a bunch of babbling. I'll just leave it at this: *I* like you."

Kate gave Maya a little smile. "Thanks."

"Let's finish our tea and get out of here."

A cedar waxwing began to sing in the tree above them. Two lazuli buntings, a bushtit, a horned lark, and a blue grosbeak joined in. It was an unlikely assortment of songbirds, forming a surprising chorus. Maya and Kate looked at each other and then up at the colorful birds.

Neither woman was startled. Both of them, throughout their short lives, had had extraordinary interactions with animals.

Maya inhaled and smelled something wonderful, orange peels and fir needles and a rainstorm. She closed her eyes and inhaled again. Kate also closed her eyes and took a deep breath through her nose. She caught the faint whiff of vanilla and peppermint. They both drifted for a time, enjoying the birds' music, the uncanny but welcome smells, and each other's company.

The intertwined songs of the birds faded, along with the scents. The girls heard the small flapping of wings as the birds left the tree. Maya and Kate shook their heads, to clear them, and stood.

"Back to work, I guess," Maya said.

The pair walked out of the little park. Maya asked, as they walked, "What are you doing for dinner tonight? Want to come over? I've got a mean, plant-based stew heating in a crockpot."

Kate touched, through the fabric of her work shirt, the heart hanging on its little chain against her chest.

"I'd love that." She'd never been to a friend's house for dinner before. But then, she'd never really had a friend.

They reached the construction site and went into the front foyer of the house. The place was coming along. A man was applying drywall mud to the living room ceiling.

"Hey, Hugo! Where's my dad?"

"Dunno. He left in his truck a while ago."

"Huh." She and Kate went back to work on the cabinets.

Eli walked in, a few minutes later. "Hugo says you're looking for me?"

"Just wanted to let you know that Kate's coming over for dinner tonight," Maya replied.

Eli nodded. "That's fine."

"Do you need to call your foster parents and let them know you'll be home late?" Maya asked.

Kate had not thought about checking in with them. She always came home on time, and hadn't had to consider whether they'd worry if she failed to show up at the appointed hour. "Yeah, I should call them." She looked around the job site. "Is there a phone somewhere I can use?"

Maya and her father glanced at each other. "You can use mine," Maya said. She pulled a phone out of her pocket and handed it to Kate. Kate looked at the face of the device. She had never used a smartphone before. The Wrights only had a landline. She had no idea what to do with the phone.

"Here," Maya said. She took the phone back. "What's the number?"

Kate made the call, with Maya's help, and informed the Wrights she was going to a coworker's for dinner.

∞

"She's making friends," Matilda said to Oscar. "That's a good thing. Maybe she's coming out of her shell."

"Fingers crossed," Oscar said.

∞

Eli drove them to the Jackson home in his pickup. Kate sat in the back seat. Maya turned in the front seat to look at her. "We live alone in an old house. It's pretty big, for just the two of us."

Eli didn't know what to make of the sudden friendship between his daughter and this quiet kid. He liked Kate, though. There was something about her that reminded him of Maya. This made no sense. Maya was a grounded, powerful, charismatic young woman, whereas Kate was a timid slip of a girl who seemed to want to fade into the background. There was something about her, though, as if she was hiding something from the world. And from herself.

Kate *had* taken on more substance since she'd started to develop a friendship with Maya. Eli, himself, did not allow too many people in but was, however, warming to the girl. His daughter always had a natural, fresh-washed smell. Kate, too, had a natural, fresh-washed smell, but it was different than Maya's. I'm losing it, he thought. Why am I tuned in to how these girls *smell?* What's the deal with that?

Eli parked in the driveway of a well-maintained, Craftsman home. The two-story house had an attic, green siding, and a white-trimmed front porch that ran the width of the house. Eli unlocked the front door and pushed it open. Maya entered after him and waved to Kate to follow.

The front door opened onto a large, airy, family room. The smell of baking bread permeated the house. "I set the oven timer, so we'll be having fresh bread with dinner," Maya said.

Kate inhaled. Her face lit up, and she smiled. She took in the big windows, the built-in cabinets and shelves full of books, and the warm, inviting, overstuffed furniture.

Kate had never before doled out compliments or criticisms. Why would anyone care what she thought? "Wow—this is *awesome.*" This was a home.

"Wait 'til you see the rest," Eli said. Maya glanced at him and smiled. Her father loved their home. It felt... safe, and welcoming.

The first floor of the house was only one room wide, but thirty feet across. A set of steps on the left side of the living room led to the second level. An archway at the back of the room opened onto a wide dining room. They passed through it and into a massive country kitchen at the back of the house. The fragrant smells coming from the crockpot on the counter made Kate's stomach growl. French doors at the rear of the kitchen opened onto a large sunroom.

"Come on out here," Maya said. She looked over her shoulder at Kate, and opened the French doors.

Kate walked onto the porch and gazed at the garden outside. A ten-foot-high, red cedar privacy fence surrounded the small outdoor area behind the house. It was enchanting. Kate did not wait for an invitation. She pushed open the exterior door and went out, past a large fir that grew next to the sunroom. Maya followed behind her.

A cobblestone pathway cut through flowering bushes and led to a screened gazebo that contained cushioned, sectional seating and a table. Blooming bougainvillea covered the top of the structure and twined down the sides. The path split to the left and right, in front of the gazebo. A thriving, mature vegetable garden was on the left side, and a riotous flower garden on the right. Kate heard birds singing and watched a chipmunk race under a shrub.

Kate stared. "It's amazing."

"It is peaceful out here," Maya said. She thought about how unnerved she'd been, just a few months ago, by the little toad. He had seemed to be trying to tell her something, something important. She shook it off, and continued. "My cousin Ben used to live with us. He slept out here in the gazebo as often as he slept in the house. It's a beautiful place to spend the night. Like camping, but cozier."

Kate thought of what it would be like to camp out in the gazebo and felt a rush of envy toward the unknown Ben. She wondered what had happened to *his* parents.

The three had dinner at the large, oak kitchen table. Kate was quiet, thinking of the gazebo and about how Maya's cousin used to sleep out there. It made her curious. She wasn't used to conversing with people other than the Wrights, or being interested in other people's lives, and she had not developed the best social skills.

"So, what happened to your cousin's parents?" She broke off a piece of bread from the round, homemade loaf, and dunked it into the stew.

"His parents were killed by a drunk driver," Eli said.

"Oh." Kate's face reddened and she dropped the piece of bread into the bowl. "I'm sorry." For his parents being killed, and for having asked such an inappropriate question.

"It was a long time ago," Eli said. "Ben has become like my own son."

The cozy kitchen, the warm bread, and the company had an effect on Eli. The normally taciturn man suddenly felt comfortable with getting personal. "My wife, Jennie, died of cancer a few years after Ben's parents died. The three of us—Maya, Ben, and I—are all we have left." He glanced at Maya. "Until I met Jennie, I hadn't really had time for dating, or any of that nonsense. I ran into her in a grocery store. Literally. I wasn't looking where I was going and smashed

my cart right into hers. We were married six months later."

Kate thought of her own lost parents. "I'm really glad you and Maya have each other. And Ben." She played with the drowned piece of bread, swirling it around in her stew while it dissolved. "So why doesn't he live with you anymore?" She bit her lip as soon as she asked the question, hoping she hadn't opened the door to some other tragic story.

"Ben moved out when he started college," Maya said.

"He had to prove that he could take care of himself," Eli grumbled.

"I can relate to that," Kate responded. "Does he still visit, and sleep out on the gazebo?"

"Hmph," Eli replied. "That boy just works, goes to school, works some more, and goes home and studies. He doesn't have any time for us."

"Please stop referring to him as a boy," Maya said. "But, yeah. It gets kind of lonely around here without him, sometimes. I miss him. He's like my little brother."

Kate kept picturing a teenaged boy, the way they were describing Ben. She imagined he might be around her own age.

The three fell into a relaxed silence and concentrated on their dinner. "This is the best stew I've ever had," Kate said, finishing her second serving of stew and bread. Maya grinned, pleased. Eli pushed his empty bowl away from him. "You made dinner. I'll clean up the kitchen."

"No thanks, Dad. We got this." Maya smiled at Kate, who immediately stood and began clearing the dishes from the table. Eli got up and wandered off into the family room to read the newspaper. Maya winked at Kate. "One day, my dad will join us in this century and read the news online."

Kate finished drying the last dish. "Do you want to see the rest of the house?" Maya asked.

"Yes, please, but then I should get home. Do you have a bus schedule? And where's the closest bus stop?"

"Oh, don't be ridiculous. It's early. And I'll drive you home. Come on, let me show you around the house."

There was a second stairway on the side of the kitchen. This steep, narrow staircase, unlike the larger one in the family room, went all the way up to the attic. Eli had converted the attic into a bedroom suite for Ben when the child had been newly orphaned, so Ben could have something to call his own. Maya had moved into the attic, after Ben had vacated it.

A wide hallway ran the length of the second story. Eli's bedroom suite was on the eastern side and overlooked the garden at the back of the house. A library/study was next to his bedroom. Two guest bedrooms, connected by a bathroom, were on the other side of the hall.

The two girls went up to Maya's attic suite. "This is awesome." Kate said. "Look at the view from your windows," as if Maya had never noticed the view before. "And this bedroom!"

"Check out my bathroom," Maya returned.

"I hope you don't mind if I use it, while I'm checking it out."

"Mi casa es su casa."

The bathroom was clean and bright, with a clawfoot tub and a shower. The best thing about the bathroom, though, was the big window that provided a view of the back garden and the gazebo. Kate imagined a young Ben sleeping in there at night.

She looked into the bathroom mirror and splashed water on her face. She noticed how white her skin was. She thought about how much healthier she would look if she had a little more color in her skin. Would the Jacksons like her better if she weren't so pale or her hair so straight and... and... flimsy? (Evidently, some of her mother's Hungarian genes had overruled some of her father's Navajo ones.) She wished she had been part of a family like this one. No, not *like* this one. *Just* like this one. She dried her face and hands on a clean towel and left the bathroom.

Maya was sitting in a large armchair, the only chair in the room, and looking out of a window. She gestured toward the bed. "Sit."

Kate gingerly sat down on the bed.

"Make yourself comfortable," Maya laughed. "Stretch out. Relax. It's not late. You have time before you go home."

Kate smiled back at Maya, and relaxed on the bed. It was a very comfortable bed. It had been an emotional day, and she had also worked very hard. Plus, her stomach was full. She felt quite sleepy.

"Let's talk," Maya said. "Nothing heavy. Just tell me what you want to do with your life." She grinned.

"I'd like to do something with animals," Kate volunteered.

"That's awesome."

"There's so much more to them than people see." Kate felt like she'd been drugged. It must have been all that crying earlier in the day. She had to let her eyelids close for a second.

"My cousin wants to become a naturalist," Maya said. "He's passionate about animals, too. Ben's already taken courses like ecology, biology, zoology, botany, chemistry, math, geography, and environmental science. Right now, he's taking his second course in evolution and genetics. He has to take summer courses to finish his degree requirements because he works two jobs and can't take a full course load during regular sessions. I think he works until midnight. And *then* has to study. Can you imagine?"

"That's a lot," Kate mumbled.

"I saw you looking at my tattoo today, when I was holding up the cabinet we were installing. It's teensy-weensy. You almost need a magnifying glass to read it." Maya peered at the inside of her left wrist, and at the script inside of a small black circle. "It says "Jennie." My mother's nickname. I never thought I'd get a tattoo, but I had to do it in her memory. Dad was *pissed*. He doesn't like tats.

He said that if he'd gotten tattoos of the names of every person he'd lost over his lifetime, his entire body would be covered in ink, and he might even have to grow some more skin." She chuckled. "It's not funny," she added. "It's sad. I don't know why I'm laughing." She tried to look serious. "I guess it's the thought of my dad covered in tattoos."

There was no answer. Maya pulled her gaze away from the tattoo on her wrist, and glanced at the bed. Kate was sound asleep.

"Ok," Maya whispered to herself. "I guess you'll be spending the night."

She quietly walked to the bed, leaned over, and pulled off Kate's shoes. A light coverlet was folded at the bottom of the bed. She picked it up and draped it over the sleeping girl.

"Sweet dreams," Maya whispered, and left the room, closing the door behind her.

∞

Maya's phone rang as she was walking down the stairs from the attic bedroom. She dug the phone out of her pocket and looked at the number. It was Ben.

"Hey!"

"Hi, Maya. Can you and Uncle Eli use some company this weekend?"

"You know it! And thank you for fitting us into your schedule."

"Come on, cuz. I've been trying to get over there for weeks. Something always comes up."

"I know, I know. A paper deadline, overtime at one of your jobs, your active social life."

"Humph," Ben snorted. "Guilty of the first two, though. Nothing I can do about the last."

"When're you coming?"

"Tomorrow morning. I expect breakfast."

"Good to know. See you then. Love you, Ben."

"Love you more."

Maya joined her father in the family room. He was sitting on the sofa and reading a book by the light of a single floor lamp.

"Ben's coming over tomorrow morning. He's going to spend the weekend."

"You just capped off my day," her father said. "That'll be fine. Looking forward to seeing him."

"Tea?" Maya asked.

"Sure. Where's Kate?"

"She fell asleep. While I was in the middle of a conversation with her. I guess it was a long day for her. She called her foster parents from my phone, so I have their number. I'll call them and let them know she's staying over. I'll sleep in my old room."

"You've been bringing home wounded animals your entire life. Birds with injured wings, baby mice with no mother. That coyote someone had trapped. You paid the veterinarian a lot of money to fix the coyote's leg. That was one very surprised vet."

"What're you saying?" Maya narrowed her eyes.

"Nothing. I'll take that tea now, if you don't mind."

Maya got up and went into the kitchen. She returned ten minutes later with two steaming mugs of chamomile tea. She handed one to her father and sat down on the other end of the sofa.

"Thanks," he said. He went back to reading his book.

"I was wondering, Dad. Did you notice anything about Kate's... smell? I don't mean perfume. She made it quite clear she doesn't wear any. I'm talking about her natural smell. Have you noticed it?"

"You talking about that orange smell?"

"Orange? It's more like fir needles. You know how they're kind of grapefruity when you touch them?" Maya asked.

"Yeah. I don't know. She also sometimes makes me think of the smell the air gets during a rainstorm," Eli replied.

"A mystery," Maya said. "She doesn't wear a fragrance. Maybe she's some kind of witch."

"Let's hope not a bad one," her father smiled.

Maya smiled back at him. "That quiet little thing? I doubt it."

"You have to watch out for the quiet ones." Eli grinned. "They're trouble."

"Can you get any more clichéd?"

They continued to sip their tea. Eli put his book on a side table. The two of them sat and listened to the small sounds the house made as it continued the years' long process of settling itself.

~

Ben awoke in his little flat over the store early the next morning. He'd been dreaming again. His dreams of the boy had started to stick, a little bit. He had a vague memory of the child.

He brushed his hair and teeth, washed his face, dressed, shoved his laptop into his backpack, and left the apartment. He only had to wait for five minutes at the bus stop before his bus pulled up. Ben had no idea that a blind man followed the bus in a black, self-driving car.

Chapter 5

Smells

Kate had an internal alarm clock. Her habit, since she'd started working for Eli, was to awaken at 5:00 a.m. She opened her eyes and looked at the ceiling. It was the color of a forest. A green ceiling? Where was she?

She sat up and looked around. It came back to her. She was in Maya's room. She'd been too tired last night to notice that the walls of the room were painted white and the baseboards, window trim, and ceiling were painted green. She glanced at the clock on the side table. It was 9:00! She threw her legs over the side of the bed. A coverlet fell to the floor.

Kate could not face Maya and Eli without first taking a shower. Maya was obviously in agreement with the plan, as a terrycloth bathrobe and a large towel had been placed on a little chair next to the bed. Kate hurried to Maya's bathroom to shower.

She was finished in fifteen minutes. She made her way halfway down the back stairs to the kitchen. She was barefooted and dressed in shorts and a short-sleeved shirt. She heard Eli's and Maya's voices. A stranger's voice answered them. Kate smelled coffee and something baking in the oven that smelled of oranges.

She stopped for a moment, overcome by shyness, and embarrassment at being who she was. She felt like an intruder. She didn't think she deserved to be here. She took a deep breath, and stepped down into the kitchen.

∞

The man with the small round head and stick neck and eggshell eyes sat in a black car, down the block from the house. He had followed Ben to the uncle's house early this morning, tracking Ben's scent like a bloodhound on the trail. The man twisted the fingers of both hands together, untwisted them, and twisted them again. Patience, he thought. Patience.

And then he began to think randomly of toads, of all things. He became drowsy. He rarely slept, because his body no longer required sleep.

His eyes shut. He began to snore.

∞

A young man was sitting at the table with Eli and Maya. He glanced up at Kate.

Their eyes met. They both froze.

The coffee pot on the stove began to shake. Its cinnamon-infused contents boiled over onto the stove and floor.

Thunder cracked overhead. Cumulus clouds, thousands of feet above the house, instantly darkened to black. Rain launched itself from the clouds and knocked needles from the fir tree onto the roof of the sunroom. The oven rattled and the fragrance of Maya's eggless orange olive cake escaped from it. The door to the freezer flew open and a carton of home-made, frozen peppermint cashew cream fell to the floor, spilling its contents. A glass jar of vanilla, that had been sitting on a shelf, toppled over and shattered. Roses in a vase on the kitchen table filled the room with a floral scent, which was not that of a rose.

Maya stood in the middle of the maelstrom. An odd thought flashed through her mind: "A rose by any other name is not a rose, but a pond flower."

Kate knew her flowers. "Lotuses," she murmured. "Why do your roses smell like lotuses?" And then she and Ben toppled over onto the floor, unconscious.

∞

Maya was bending over Kate, with her head against Kate's chest. This was the third time in the last five minutes she had checked Kate's heartbeat and respiration.

The coffee pot had stopped shaking. The rainstorm had ended, as suddenly as it had begun. The fir needles had blown off the sunroom's roof. The roses smelled like roses again. The oven was behaving like an ordinary oven.

Ben sat on the floor a few feet away. He slowly scooted over to the prone Kate.

"Move away." He gently pushed his cousin to the side.

"Katherine Birdsong," Ben breathed. He touched Kate's wrist with his fingers. "Kate, Kate, Katie, wake up. Come on."

Maya jerked her head. "Do you *know* her? Have you met before, Ben?"

It seemed so unlikely. The two did not travel in the same circles. Kate had just graduated from high school and had no social life. Neither did Ben. They didn't live near each other. How would they have met?

Ben ignored his cousin. He watched Kate open her eyes. He became very still.

"I remember your smell," Kate said. "I remember *you*." She smiled.

Ben leaned forward and inched his right arm around her shoulders. "That is good news." He grinned, then seemed to collect himself, and blushed. "Let me help you up. Easy." He pulled her to a sitting position.

"It's still there, but faint," she said. "Your smell."

Cinnamon, vanilla, lotuses, and peppermint. She took in a deep breath and lifted her hand to his face.

Ben inhaled Kate, in return. She was a rainstorm, she was a forest of fir trees, she was an orange grove. He didn't know if the fragrance was in his mind, or if it was coming from her. He lifted Kate's hand and kissed it.

Eli and Maya stood over the couple and looked at each other.

"What is going *on*?" Maya whispered urgently to her father. In a louder voice, she said, "I think she's ok. You're both ok? No need to call 911?"

"Can you stand?" Eli asked the couple on the floor.

"I think so," Kate replied. She and Ben helped each other to their feet.

The pair stood, facing each other. Maya didn't think she could have slipped a piece of paper between their bodies. Kate looked up at Ben.

"Who are you?" she asked.

"Benjamin Jackson," he smiled.

"I know that. I mean, who *are* you?"

"I really have no idea," he replied. "I'm more interested in finding out who you are."

Kate wrapped her arms around Ben and laid her head against his chest. "I'm pretty sure you and I know everything there is to know about each other. Except who we *are*." She closed her eyes. "I'm so tired." Ben pulled her in tighter, leaned his chin on her head, and closed his eyes, too.

Eli turned to Maya. "I have no friggin' idea what's going on. This is totally beyond me. They're strangers, but these two act like they're newlyweds on a honeymoon. And what are they talking about, who they *are*."

He looked around the kitchen. Eli was a practical man. He turned his head to Maya, accusingly. "This has something to do with your toads, doesn't it?"

Maya shrugged, at a loss.

Eli continued. "I don't want to think about it, or talk about it, right now. I'll clean up the vanilla and coffee messes. You can clean up that melted pool of cashew cream, Maya."

Ben and Kate untangled from each other and sat down at the kitchen table. Ben pulled his chair next to Kate's, so that his knee touched hers. She put a hand on his thigh. Both of them were as exhausted as if they'd run a marathon. They watched the cleanup but did not offer to help.

Eli and Maya were soon finished. Maya asked, quietly, "Is anyone still hungry?"

"Look outside." Eli's voice was strained.

It was pitch-black outside the windows.

"What?" Maya asked. "We were eating breakfast a few minutes ago. It was morning. What's going on? Is there an eclipse?"

Eli pulled out his phone and looked at it. "It's 11:30 p.m."

He dropped into the chair across from Ben. Maya also sat down. Everyone looked at each other.

"So... where did the day go?" Eli asked Ben and Kate, as if they knew something he and Maya didn't.

Kate spoke. "So much... has happened."

"Ok," Maya said. "So, what exactly *has* happened?"

Kate looked at Ben. He nodded, encouraging her.

"I saw Ben, sitting at the kitchen table. And then the room was filled with an unbelievable smell, like what Christmas morning would smell like in the best of all possible worlds. I can't describe it. The scent filled my head. And then he and I were alone in a huge clearing in a forest. We were surrounded."

She stopped, and looked up at Benjamin. "We were surrounded by these moving shapes. By... beings... beings made of light." She closed her eyes. "They had *wings*."

"Animals," Ben said. "*Animals*, with wings, made of light. Birds, cows, sheep, moose, bears, pigs, chickens, groundhogs, possums, geese, rabbits, dragonflies, horses, bats, elephants, wolves, lions... " He closed his eyes.

Kate twined her hands in Ben's. "But they weren't making sounds that animals would normally make. They were speaking in English. I could understand what they were saying. At first, there were only a few, and then there were dozens, and then there were hundreds of them. It went on and on and on, for a long time."

She glanced at Eli and then at Maya. "They said they were called "Apalacheela" and that they were on our side. Whatever that means."

Eli saw a flicker in Kate's eyes, as if they were backlit by fire. It was disconcerting. Her sudden, peculiar intimacy with Ben was even more perturbing.

"More and more came, until there were thousands of animals," Benjamin said. "And then they began chanting. It was so loud I could barely stand. It felt like the words and the volume were driving me to my knees."

His eyes, too, seemed to spark and flare.

"And then... ," Kate murmured. She caressed the back of Ben's hand with her fingers.

"And then?" Maya pressed. Kate and Ben looked at each other and smiled. Neither answered.

Eli and Maya stared at Kate and Ben and at their curious, compelling eyes. Eli recalled what Lorenzo Poggi had said about Kate being a force of nature. He now saw, clearly, that she was. And so was Ben. Something had happened to the two during the span of the storm that had caused the innate force in them to grow, exponentially.

And it had connected them.

Maya wondered where shy Kate had gone, and who this person, sitting next to Ben, was.

Maybe this Kate still liked tea. "I could use a cup of tea," Maya said. "I think we all could."

Tea was Maya's cure-all. It had helped her through the death of Ben's parents and that of her own mother. Tea represented security, comfort, fond memories, and relief from pain.

The other three sat at the solid table and looked out at the darkness beyond the windows. Maya carried the pot to the table and then brought in four mugs.

"Chamomile. If it's really nighttime, no point in having caffeine."

It was soothing to sit, without speaking, and to drink hot tea.

Maya broke the silence and asked, "So... what did the animals say, or chant, or whatever? Were they all saying the same thing, or was it like being in a noisy crowd of people? I mean, with everyone talking at once, over top of each other?"

Kate refilled her mug. "No, it wasn't like that," she replied, slowly. "They were all saying the same thing. It was rather... urgent."

She glanced at Ben, and back at her mug.

Ben said, "Let's talk about this tomorrow. I think we're all pretty tired. I feel like I've been working for twenty-four hours straight, with no sleep. He leaned toward Kate. "Do you need something to eat? The three of us had breakfast before all this happened. You must be starving."

"I feel fine. Not hungry at all. I'm just sleepy."

Eli stood. "We'll talk about it tomorrow. Why don't we all go to bed, now? I don't know whether we've been up for a few hours or for an entire day, but I'm done. Goodnight, all."

He walked over to Maya, leaned over and kissed her on the forehead, and patted Kate and Ben on their heads. "I'm going to lock up the front," he said, and left through the dining room.

Maya stood. "Goodnight, you guys." She rubbed Ben's shoulder. "It was great seeing you, cousin. Even if you did bring chaos with you." She smiled.

"You too, Maya. I've missed you." He put his hand over hers, which was still on his shoulder. "You know what? I think I'll sleep in the gazebo tonight."

"Your safe place," Maya said. She dropped her hand from Ben's shoulder and turned to Kate. "You coming, Kate? You can have my room again. I'll take the guest room I slept in last night."

Kate looked at Ben. "Thanks. I think I'll stay down here."

"Oh... kay." Maya shook her head, and went upstairs.

Ben got to his feet. "Stay here, Kate. Please. I'll be right back."

He went into the dining room, opened the door of a built-in cabinet, and pulled out the blankets and pillows he kept stashed there. He carried the pile back into the kitchen.

"Come on," he said. "Maybe we can stay awake long enough to talk about what happened to us. If we don't, you'll love sleeping out in the gazebo, anyway."

"As long as *you're* there," Kate said. "I'm happy to sleep on concrete."

"It's a little better than concrete."

He took her hand and pulled her to her feet. She wrapped an arm around his waist.

Kate was beginning to feel substantial, *real*, for the first time since she'd lost her parents.

~

Mrs. Moretti lived next door to the Jacksons. She and her husband had emigrated from Italy forty years ago. They were childless, but she'd thought they had a happy marriage. And then, fifteen years later, Mr. Moretti had presented her with divorce papers. He'd immediately married a much younger woman, who had presented *him* with a baby girl a year later.

Mrs. Moretti had been disgraced and humiliated and, thereafter, never again showed her face in public during the day.

Her practice was to sleep from 7:00 a.m. until 6:00 p.m. She would then get up, bathe, dress, prepare a dinner of spinach and steak (cooked rare), run errands as necessary (as soon as it was dark), do household chores, and spend the rest of the night wandering the house. She would go from window to window, upstairs and downstairs, pulling back the curtains and peering out of the windows.

This evening, she'd noticed a strange, dark car parked on the street toward the end of the block. All of the homes in this neighborhood had driveways. People who lived there generally did not have to park on the street. Mrs. Moretti also knew that the house the car was parked in front of was vacant, the owners having gone to visit relatives in Mexico for a month.

The car was still there at midnight. Mrs. Moretti decided it was time to investigate. She walked out of her front door, down her front steps, onto the sidewalk, and to the car.

She looked in the car window. She could see, by streetlight, a man slumped over the wheel. She wondered if she should call 911. She didn't want to make a fuss if the person was just resting. But what was he doing here, in the first place? He could have had a heart attack or a stroke. She had a responsibility to do something.

Mrs. Moretti tapped on the front passenger-side window. The man behind the steering wheel started. He sat straight up and turned to her. His head was tiny, bald, and perfectly round. It sat on a long skinny neck that seemed too thin to contain both a larynx and an esophagus. He opened his eyelids and Mrs. Moretti saw the pure white marbles that passed for his eyes.

The woman threw up her arms and shrieked. She turned and tore back along the sidewalk, up the steps to her house, and through the doorway. She slammed the door and shot the deadbolt. Trembling, she looked down at her feet. One of her shoes had fallen off somewhere on the sidewalk.

Mr. Anthill was glad the woman had intruded on his space. There was something he was supposed to be doing. Something to do with toads.

It so happened that a dozen tiny toads were, at that moment, sitting under the car in the dark. They began a chorus of croaking. Mr. Anthill's eyes closed, and his head again dropped against the steering wheel.

~

"Strange things live in our garden," Ben said. "I hope you don't scare easily." He pulled her by the hand out of the house, into the darkness beyond.

"Not at all. I should fit right in."

"We went through a lot today," Ben said.

"That we did."

They had made love in the clearing. They knew that the act had been in their heads and had not been an actual physical event, but that was the point. Their minds had been so linked, during the act, that they had each lost the sense of self, and had not known who was who.

The consequence of their union was that Ben now knew everything there was to know about Kate and Kate now knew everything there was to know about Ben, including their smallest foibles and their greatest aspirations.

Ben laughed. He was happy and giddy. The sound that came from him made Kate think of the one time, when she was a small child, a case worker had taken her to the ocean for the day. She'd sat in the shallows and splashed in the little ripples for hours. It was the closest she'd come to experiencing joy. This was much, much better.

Kate's train of thought was interrupted by the sound of a faint shriek coming from somewhere in the neighborhood. She cocked her head and listened.

"What was that? Did you hear a scream?"

Ben listened for a moment. "Probably teenagers." The sound was actually coming from

Mrs. Moretti, who had just gotten a good look at Mr. Anthill through the window of his car.

"Do you think we should check it out?"

Small sounds came from several little toads, who were in hiding next to the garden path. Their sounds replaced the shriek. Ben leaned over and listened to the miniature symphony. He squeezed Kate's hand. "If we hear it again, we will."

It was a moonless night. The couple felt their way along the path. Ben led the way to the gazebo. The blankets were draped over his left arm. His free hand found the screen door handle, turned it, and pushed the door open. Kate followed and tumbled up the steps in the dark.

Kate's bare toe nudged a squishy, fat little object on the top step. She leaned over and peered through the black night, her eyes adjusting. It was one of the tiny toads. She dropped the pillows she carried to the ground, and ran her fingertips over the animal's soft skin. The toad leaned into her touch, the way a dog or a cat would. A mockingbird, sitting on top of the gazebo, began to sing.

Ben pulled cushions from the furniture and placed them on the floor. Kate picked up the pillows, straightened her back, and made her way inside. Ben covered the cushions with a blanket, while Kate placed the pillows at one end. She sat down on the bedding and pulled another blanket up over her knees. Ben dropped down beside her.

"I just petted a toad," Kate said.

"I used to be friends with a toad, when I was a boy," Ben remarked. "He lived under a rock by the path. He wasn't afraid of me. He would even let me pick him up. Maybe the one you met is one of his descendants." He smiled, in the dark. "Or maybe it's even him, welcoming you."

It wasn't necessary for him to tell Kate about this. She had explored his memories in the clearing, as he had hers, and she already knew the story. It was still nice to hear Ben voice the story aloud.

"The way the...animals, or whatever they were, welcomed us today." Kate felt for Ben's hand.

"Find the boy," Ben said. "Find the boy. Over and over. That's what they were chanting." He thought for a moment. "But, before that—when they introduced themselves to us as Apalacheela—did you hear that one opossum say something to the effect that we shouldn't be afraid, because they weren't Killapaka?"

"I did hear that." Kate shuddered. "The Apalacheela were awesome. I got the idea that meeting the Killapaka would not be so awesome." She stroked Ben's arm. "But, as far as a boy goes, what did we do? We didn't find any boy."

"No, we didn't." Ben closed his eyes and thought about what they'd done in the forest clearing. They'd given themselves to each other, opening themselves up completely while a horde of animals chanted at them about finding the boy.

Kate remembered the voices that had wrapped around them. The chorus had pounded at her eardrums. It had hypnotized her, made her senses come alive. The clearing had filled with an incredible scent.

It had been coming from Kate and Ben, themselves.

"I'd like to do that again, here and now, in real life," Kate said. She remembered the urgency in the animals' voices, and the exhilaration she'd felt with Ben. "Somehow, I think it's important." She wanted him, whether or not it was important.

"We can leave out the head games. That was pretty intense. I don't think I could do that again, at least not tonight," Ben said.

Kate rolled next to him and ran her hand along his hip. "I guess we're both, in reality, still virgins," she murmured. "Although I don't feel like one any longer."

The smells of lotuses, oranges, peppermint, fir needles, vanilla, cinnamon, and rain rose up around them in the gazebo. Ben and Kate did not notice. A hawk dove from the sky and landed on the top of the gazebo, and then another, and another.

∞

Ben stirred shortly after 3:00 a.m. and turned over to face the side of the gazebo. He opened his eyes. It was still dark. A bit of light, from the headlights of a car going by the front of the house, reached the back garden. It was enough to light up dozens of pairs of eyes in the darkness around the gazebo. Some were low to the ground, others at Ben's level or above, still others high in the air. Some were like blazing spotlights, some like sparkling lanterns, some like glowing flashlights, and others like flickering torches.

"Hello, my friends," Ben whispered. "I've missed you. I'm glad you're back."

He stared upward and smiled in the darkness. So, as a boy, those glowing eyes hadn't

116

just been part of a dream. He sat up on his elbows. Kate had to see this for herself.

"Katie," he whispered. He touched her shoulder.

"Ben!" Kate sat up, startled. "Ben, we have to go. Right now." Her right hand moved to her lower abdomen and lightly rubbed it.

"What? Go where?"

He wanted to tell Kate about the glowing eyes. He looked around. There was no longer anything to see. All of the lights had winked out.

"I'm pregnant." She pushed her hand against her stomach. She cocked her head and listened, as if she were communicating with someone through her palm. "And we've all got to leave. Right now."

"Pregnant?!"

Kate took his hand and pressed it against her abdomen and then Ben felt what Kate felt, and knew what she knew. His mouth dropped open.

He instantly remembered all of the dreams about the boy. About Sam.

"It's *Samuel!* We found him!"

"Samuel?" Kate's mind reached for that of the fetus in her belly, and then grabbed Ben's hand. "You're right. Our baby is the boy you've been dreaming about all your life."

Ben laid his hand on her stomach again. "And *you're* also right. He *does* want us to leave. He's telling us we're in danger."

Ben jumped to his feet and leaned over to take Kate's hand, to pull her up beside him. "We have to get Uncle Eli and Maya."

117

"Uncle Eli—wake up!" Ben was leaning over Eli and shaking the man's shoulder.

Eli opened his eyes. "What is it?" he asked, sitting up. "What's the matter?" He glanced at the illuminated clock on his nightstand. It was 3:13 a.m.

"We have to go. Now," Ben said.

"Wha... ? Why? What's happening?"

Eli got out of bed, even as he questioned Ben. He opened his dresser, took out clothing, and started to put on a shirt. "Does this have something to do with what happened yesterday?"

"Trust me, for now. We don't have time to talk. Kate's getting Maya."

Eli pulled on his pants. "You're carrying your backpack. Should I grab a suitcase?"

"No time. Just your keys and wallet. And some cash. Do you any have cash in the house?"

"Three or four hundred. Where are we going?"

"I'll explain, once we're on the road."

They heard footsteps on the stairs, coming down from the attic room. Ben went to his uncle's bedroom door and looked down the hallway to the staircase.

"They're ready," he said. "Let's go."

They were on Route 10, heading west out of Los Angeles.

"Which way?" Eli asked. He was driving. Maya sat next to him on the front passenger's seat. Eli had brought his phone with him, ignoring Ben's instruction to take only his keys and wallet. Maya always had her phone in a pocket. She had pulled it out and was currently looking at a map.

Kate was curled up in a ball on the back seat of Eli's Silverado truck. She raised her head. "Take 10 to Route 15, and 15 to Route 40," she said. "Drive until you can't anymore. Then let Maya or Ben take over." Her head dropped back to Ben's lap. She was asleep within seconds.

Oddly, it didn't seem extraordinary to Eli and Maya that they were taking orders from an eighteen-year-old slip of a girl, Eli's entry-level carpentry apprentice. They both felt as if they were half asleep and dreaming. Maybe it was because they'd been shocked out of deep slumber. Neither asked any questions, until they were leaving the city limits. It was 4:15 a.m., and there was little traffic. Eli relaxed behind the wheel.

"Talk to me, Benjamin. What's going on? What kind of trouble are you in? Are we running from somebody?"

"And where are we going?" Maya asked.

"Let's get you caught up," Ben said. "Kate's pregnant."

Eli and Maya watched the empty road in front of them. Neither spoke for a few moments.

Eli finally broke the silence. "What? Who's the father?" *Ben* couldn't be. They'd just met.

And then Eli became aware of what he'd been smelling, ever since Kate got into the car and they'd closed the windows to turn on the air conditioner. It was an amazing scent, a mixture that was just right, complete. It made Eli feel like

119

a kid who'd been given a puppy on his birthday. He glanced at Maya. Maya's head was back against the headrest. Her eyes were closed. She was smiling.

"*I'm* the father. We didn't think to use protection. It just happened." Ben cupped one hand on top of Kate's head and the other on her flat stomach. "And the baby is... the baby is communicating with us."

Eli and Maya relaxed into the Scent, as it flowed into their own skin. Of course. It all made sense, everything that had happened. The Scent was creeping into their noses, down their throats, into their lungs, and into their bloodstreams. It made them even more open and receptive than they already were. It made them trust Ben and Kate, completely.

"The baby is talking to you?" Maya asked. She craned her neck around to look at Kate's stomach.

"*You* try." Ben nodded at his cousin, and patted Kate's tummy.

"Ok." Maya undid her seatbelt and half climbed over the seat so that she could reach into the back. Ben took her hand and placed it on Kate's stomach. Maya closed her eyes.

"Ohhh... ," she said. She stayed in that position until the truck hit a pothole and she nearly fell into the back on top of Kate. Maya pulled herself back into her seat and refastened the seatbelt.

"It's no joke, Dad. Sam... the boy's name is Samuel, right Ben? He *is* communicating with us. He says there are some dangerous people... people? Did he say people?"

Ben picked up where Maya had left off. "All we have been able to understand, so far, is that we're going to be completely screwed if we stay in L.A. Some bad stuff is coming this way." He stroked Kate's head. "And it's all because of *him*, because of Sam. Our only job, from here on out, is to protect him."

Eli believed them. His senses were awake. Long dormant neurons were firing across synapses in his brain. Connections were being made. He was beginning to grasp things about the world that he had partially comprehended as a child. He believed, but he also needed more information. He wanted to fully grasp their situation.

"Why?" he asked. "Who—other than us—cares about this one baby? Especially a baby who's just an hours-old fetus?"

Ben shrugged. Eli's eyes were on the road. He did not see Ben shrug, but he knew Ben had.

"I've been dreaming about Sam all my life." Ben said.

He noticed his backpack, which he had tossed on the floor in front of him when he got into the truck. He reached for it, pulled it open, drew out his laptop, and opened it. He pulled up the notes he'd taken in Professor Arnaud's class, and handed the laptop over the front seat to Maya. "Look at this," he said.

Maya read aloud. "'Lotuses, oranges, peppermint, fir needles, vanilla, cinnamon, and rain.' So... you're saying you wrote about this awesome smell, which now seems to be coming from Kate, before you even knew she existed."

"It's not coming from Kate," Ben corrected. "It's coming from Sam. I had a big part of it. I guess it's genetic. I think you have a few parts, too, Maya. Kate had the missing pieces. It was like fitting an extremely difficult jigsaw puzzle together. She and I did it. And then we found Sam."

"You mean you *created* Sam." Maya replied.

"No," Kate mumbled. "He was already out there, waiting for us to find him and bring him here. We're... I'm just giving him a lift." She was too drowsy to stay awake. She could feel the baby commanding her. "Rest, Kate. We need rest." She was safe and warm, and with the three caring, grounded, magnificent people she had already come to love during the past twenty-four hours, not to mention the child growing in her uterus. She slept.

"Do you know where we're going?" Eli asked. "Or are we just going to wing it?"

~

Mr. Anthill had fallen asleep in the back seat of his car, which was still parked at the end of the block from the Jackson home. He had neither sight nor a driver's license, but his otherwise heightened senses gave him the ability to zip in and out of traffic and to avoid the police, even when he wasn't using a self-driving vehicle.

His sleep was long and deep that night. He was not aware of the vibrant, incredible smells that rocketed from the Jackson home, nor was he aware of the family's hasty exodus.

He felt drugged and hungover when he awoke in the morning. At least he supposed this was what the abuse of alcohol and drugs felt like. He stepped outside of the car, raised his nose, and inhaled.

He didn't just pull aroma compounds into his nose, as a normal person would do. The sensory neurons in the back of his nose had been reconfigured many years ago, and the neurons could now detect any motes of energy that were saturated with the essence of lotuses, oranges, peppermint, fir needles, vanilla, cinnamon, and/or rain. Motes of energy generally weren't saturated with those things, so sensing any one of them was a major find.

Now, there was *nothing*. He didn't have to inspect the inside of the Jackson house. His nose told him all that he needed to know. They were gone. He was at first furious, at himself and at the Jacksons. And then, he became fearful.

He decided that honesty would be the best policy, under the circumstances, and considering for whom he worked. He got back into the car, picked up his phone, hit the speaker, and said, "Boss."

There was one ring. A deep voice, which sounded like it was rising from the bottom of the ocean, asked, "What have you found, Mr. Anthill?"

"I followed the subject," Mr. Anthill replied. "He has certain pieces of the Scent. The Scent became complete for the first time, during his Stage 4 REM sleep, the night before last. He was evidently in a dream state when it happened. And then something significant happened here yesterday. I don't know what. I feel like I've been drugged. I'm fairly certain there were Cheela here, and that they knocked me out, somehow, for the entire day and night."

"And, he's gone, of course," the voice at the end of the line said.

"He and his entire family are gone. A girl was also there. She's gone, too."

"A girl. How old is this girl?"

"Late teens, I guess." Mr. Anthill stopped. "You don't think... "

"I don't think. I *know*. I can smell it from here. A Child."

"Wait. You think one of the *Children* was conceived last night?"

"Yes. You would have known, and would have been able to take control of the parents–and thus, the Child–if you'd been able to stay awake."

"What do you want me to do?"

"Get back here. I'm sending Kills after them. They should not be hard to find. The Child's Scent is like a fireworks' display to us."

The line went dead.

Mr. Anthill felt like he'd been slapped. He had failed. He prided himself on his ability to detect the Scent and every one of its elements. He was among the handful of humans who could. But he certainly couldn't pick up the Scent from twenty-five hundred miles away, like Saklas, the being for whom he worked, could. His own range was, at most, one hundred miles. And Saklas, clearly, was correct. The parents and the unborn Child had been right under his nose.

He switched on the car, and told it to take him back to the LAX airport. He would be returning to Cutter City, Ohio. His failure was bitter. He'd have to come up with a backup plan on the flight. He was good at making backup plans.

Part II

Chapter 1

Meanwhile, on the Other Side of the Country

Beau Wald was sitting in a sturdy rocking chair on the front deck of the Wald home. His wife, Annie, was seated in a rocker next to him. Pink lotuses bloomed in the large pond, down the slope in front of the house. The couple sipped their morning coffee and watched the sunrise.

Beau was in his mid-sixties. He wore shorts and a gray t-shirt with "Venice Beach" printed on it. He was lean, and had sharp features and light gray hair. Annie, the same age as her husband, wore jeans and a black t-shirt with a silkscreened pink lotus on it. She had chin-length, blondish-white hair.

A red-tailed hawk soared across the sky from the west. The bird plummeted toward the couple. She spread her wings and landed on the railing in front of the man and woman.

"Falke—you're back!" Beau exclaimed. Both he and Annie stood.

The bird exploded into a huge, shimmering, hawk-shaped light form, hung in the air in front of the deck, and spoke.

She said, in word-shaped, fluting sounds, "We found the parents of one of the Children."

The man and woman gaped.

"Is this possible?" Annie asked, turning to her husband. "They found parents? Which means... "

"That one of the Children may be born during our lifetimes," Beau finished.

"You are correct," Falke replied. "The woman is pregnant."

"Pregnant! With a Child," Annie repeated. She dropped back into her chair, stunned.

"Yes. I was there when he was conceived." There was pride in Falke's fluted words.

"Holy crap," Beau said.

"Where *are* they?" Annie asked.

"And will the Apalacheela Deor bring them here? As they've been planning, for like, forever?" Beau asked. He sounded like an excited teen.

"The parents live near the Pacific Ocean, on the other side of the country. They're starting their journey here, now."

"How are they coming? Are they flying? Are we picking them up at an airport?" Annie asked.

"No. They are coming in a vehicle. It is too dangerous for them to be in one of your airplanes. They could be found by the other side and trapped."

"How could the Killapaka Deor find them?" Beau's face hardened at the thought.

"The Child is brand-new. He is a miniscule grouping of cells. He is too immature and too inexperienced to hide his Scent. Anyone who has the ability to detect it will be able to do so, from anywhere on this planet. I, myself, can smell him, right now, and determine his exact location."

"But that means they're in real jeopardy," Beau said.

"Of course, they are. We *have* been protecting the home from which they left, a short while ago. A man named Eli Jackson has lived there for years. He had a small part of the Scent, but it was very weak. We've always known that he was somehow related to one of the future Children. His daughter, Maya, also had a small part of the Scent. That, too, was very weak.

Benjamin Jackson—had four, extremely strong, components of the Scent. We have been watching him closely.

"Ben is the Child's father. We have guarded Ben and his family, as we do with anyone we have found who has even a *trace* of the Scent. A knot of toads—ones who are Apalacheela Deor—took up residence in the home's garden, years ago. They've been watching over these people, ever since."

"A knot of toads?" Annie asked.

"That means a group of toads," her husband explained.

"The toads had been sensing that a momentous event was about to occur. It all came together, yesterday. We discovered, years ago, that a female, by the name of Katherine Birdsong, bore the final three components of the Scent. Those components were very strong in her. So strong that we are amazed humans—with the exception of people like you—could not sense her uniqueness."

"How did it all come together yesterday?" Annie asked.

"The girl visited the Jackson home, where she encountered Ben Jackson. Their connection was instantaneous. The two had no choice in the matter. The Living World used its operative, the Scent, to bring the two together. The Scent wanted to be complete. The couple make it complete.

"They immediately mated. Kate–that is the abbreviated version of her name– is now carrying the fetus-Child, Samuel, in her womb."

Beau shook his head. "They had no choice in the matter? That seems like a Killapaka move."

The bird spread his huge, glowing wings. "They have been made for each other. Their very genes would draw them to each other even in the absence of the Scent. There is no one else, for either of them."

"I guess that's ok, then, right, Beau?" Annie asked.

"I... guess. It sounds like they'll be happy together."

"Yes. Considering their genes and all," his wife replied.

Falke continued. "A strange man was watching their house last night. The man has, at a point in the past, been touched and changed by the leader of the Killapaka Deor. He's become something other than human. It is disturbing to sense Deor power in a human, where it does not belong. And he certainly had no business stalking our humans. We think the other side sent him. The toads put the man to sleep to stop him from spying, or from doing even worse."

"Yikes. It seems as though the other side, too, has been able to recruit humans," Annie said. "That is bad news."

"Is Meska going to provide safe passage for the mother and her group?" Beau asked. He pictured Meska, the gigantic bear, in his mind. He couldn't imagine anyone going up against her.

"Yes. Meska—our leader—is already traveling with them. She has plenty of support. They will get the Child here."

"I haven't seen Seta today." Beau looked around for the large brown dog who had been his companion, in one dog form or another, since Beau, himself, was a child.

"Seta is also with the Cheela who are shielding the boy. Everyone from the Motherland is, with the exception of Tembo the elephant. Did you not notice that none of us were around today?"

"We just got up a little while ago," Annie replied. "We hadn't yet gone up to the forest for our morning walk."

"Only Tembo and I have stayed behind," Falke said. "She, as you know well, has never fully recovered her power, after her selfless act in the Cutter City Park, the heart of enemy territory. The rest of us are with the boy. I wanted to be with him as well, but Meska told me to come back and let you know the situation, especially because you have to be ready to receive the Child and his family."

"It feels weird, not having Cheela around," Annie said. "I feel... naked. Vulnerable. You've been with me since I was a kid."

"I am here now," Falke said. "I will be up in the forest. If you need me, call. Or ring the little bell in your kitchen."

There was a blur of light too confusing for human eyes to follow, and Falke was gone.

"I guess Meska wants us to batten down the hatches," Beau said.

"Let's go over our lists. Good thing we've been working on this for over thirty years," Annie said.

~

Interlude
The City Park

The City Park, located in Cutter City, Ohio—and simply referred to by the Cutter City residents as "the City Park," or just "the Park"—was peculiar. It had been the subject of Ben's paper for his advanced geography class. Ben had gone off on a tangent. His analysis of specific geographical features was replaced by the study of an enigma.

No one had ever been able to map the City Park. People who entered it disappeared. Search and rescue parties got lost for weeks at a time, or disappeared themselves. Planes and drones that flew over it vanished. Satellite images of it were always blank. No cell or internet service was available anywhere within the Park, even though there were nearby cell towers.

The City Park was bordered by an ancient, twenty-foot-high wall. It was composed of hand-placed stones. Archeologists hired by the city were not able to determine how old the wall was. They posited that it had been constructed by cave-dwelling Paleoindians, no later than 10,000 BCE. The wall, which by all rights should have been reduced to rubble by wind and rain, was in remarkably good shape.

The size of the City Park was indeterminate. It could be thousands of acres, or it could be thousands of square miles. One city road ran next to a small section of the Park. It had taken years for a series of contractors to accomplish that feat. It turned out to be impossible to construct a road bordering any other portion of the Park's perimeter. The road crews would forget what they were doing, and would eventually find themselves constructing a thoroughfare anywhere but alongside the Park.

Articles about random, weird events, which regularly occurred in connection with the City Park, vanished from newspapers, leaving behind columns of empty spaces, or just a series of random letters and numbers. Television correspondents who attempted to report on Park happenings suddenly got laryngitis, or could not recall what they had been talking about; that is, if the station signal hadn't died first.

The City Park returned no telemetry. No instrument could detect any information about the Park. This should have set off alarm bells. It did not. All data about the size and layout of the State of Ohio—and even of the United States, as a result—was incorrect, as it was impossible for the City Park in Cutter City to be taken into account.

No one seemed to care much about this fact. Most people—except for the rare ones like Benjamin Jackson—could not remember the issue for more than a couple of seconds.

People who lived inside Cutter City avoided the Park, or even thinking about it. People who lived *outside* of Cutter City avoided Cutter City, or even thinking about it, or about Cutter City's strange, depressing aura.

The City Park, from a data standpoint, was a great big section of nothingness in the center of the country. That which lived inside it, though, was far from nothing.

∞

Fifty million people died in the 1918 influenza pandemic, six hundred and seventy-five-thousand of them in the United States alone. A number of freed slaves had settled in Cutter City during that time. The flu killed about two hundred of those good people.

So, there the Cutter City Planning Commissioners were, with a couple hundred bodies on their hands. The Commission consisted of twelve old men and one (seemingly) youngish woman. They had rather unusual character flaws. Fear of the "other" was not one of them. They viewed everyone and everything as resources, regardless of ethnicity. They decided that the best course of action was to order that the bodies of the freed slaves be buried in the city cemeteries.

A large segment of the citizenry was horrified and incensed by the decree, and immediately took action. They wrote letters, carried placards outside of the government building, threw rotten eggs and tomatoes at the homes of the City Planners, and stood on top of soap boxes on street corners, shouting through bullhorns. Their message: The city churchyards were for the remains of *white* people, and no one else. Period.

The efforts of these loud, repugnant people had the same effect on the City Planners as extreme right-wing media radio and television personalities have on gutless, blustery leaders in the present day. The City Planners did not like being railed against by even a tiny fraction of the people they governed.

It was clear that the most obnoxious members of their community were vehemently opposed to people of African descent being interred in white people's cemeteries. The Planners bowed to the screaming bigots, and reversed course. They decided, instead, to send the deceased off to be buried in the City Park.

The Good Ol' Boys and their women gave that proposal their full-throated approval.

∞

The Planners were able to find a contractor who was willing, for an eye-popping sum of money, to expose his hired hands to the vague and sinister dangers that, for generations, had been associated with the City Park. The contractor's employees just happened to be Black, themselves freed slaves.

The contractor had thirty employees. He called all of them to the little building that served as his main office. He explained the job, and added, "I'll pay double time to those who volunteer for this mission. I won't pretend it's not dangerous. You'll have to go at least five miles into the Park." The contractor did not want white people to stumble upon the burial ground. He would definitely hear about it from the City Planning Commission, if that were ever to occur.

All thirty employees stepped forward. They did not volunteer for the money. They would have taken on this task for free, creepy Park or no creepy Park. The decedents were *their* people. It was important that their sisters and brothers be interred with honor. If any of the men sustained injury or death in the course of their performance, so be it.

The men[3] loaded the bodies onto mule-drawn wagons. The contractor stood by the open park gate, and said–as if the men had not already thought of this themselves–"You might want to mark the place in some fashion, in accordance with your tradition."

The workers were, like anyone with a grain of sense, afraid to go into the City Park. They were more afraid to travel the long, five miles into it. No one who had gone that far had ever made it out.

The men went in, anyway, and without pausing. They walked alongside the mules and spoke softly to them, urging them through the gate and into the City Park.

The contractor closed the gate behind them. He thought for a moment, and then decided to hedge his bets by going straight to the local newspaper and placing a "Help Wanted" advertisement. Just in case.

The men trudged alongside the laden wagons up steep, tree-covered hills, down into valleys, across streams, and through a wide river. They walked in a northwesterly direction. It was mid-summer. There had been little rain in weeks and the water levels were low. It was easy to ford the deep streams and the river, with the assistance of

---

[3] In those days, women in Cutter City were not eligible for paid labor jobs, apart from the usual women-folk type work, such as cleaning, washing, nannying, prostitution, and cooking.

rope. Surprisingly, no injuries occurred, not even a sprained ankle.

The account that was handed down about the burial ground contained only tidbits regarding the route the men took and a description of the gravesite. The more important parts of the story were unknown to the local human population. Even the workers who had gone into the City Park were unaware of critical events that occurred in connection with, and as a result of, their entry into the Park.

For example, they did not know that a creature–an "Apalacheela Deor"–went into the City Park with them.

Tembo, an elephant Cheela (which is short for "Apalacheela"), had noticed the group entering the hazardous Park. She soared above the men, unseen, and spread her wings. She imagined a bubble of her energy surrounding the men who walked alongside or led the mule-drawn wagons through the Park.

The bubble formed as soon as Tembo thought it into existence. It pushed away the other, opposite force that filled the Park.

The men could have buried the bodies anywhere. No one would ever have known if they had failed to comply with the charge to go in at least five miles. They had a calling of their own, however, which was unrelated to the instructions of their employer. They intended to ensure that their brothers and sisters were treated with reverence, and placed in the most beautiful location the men could find.

The band of men eventually came to a large prairie that was covered in wild poppies and bordered by soft hills. It happened to be exactly five miles inside the Park, unbeknownst to the men, who had no instruments by which to gauge the distance they had traveled. It was the wildflowers that did it. The men looked at each other and nodded. They had the mules pull the wagons to the center of the prairie.

The men dug the graves, interred the bodies, and completed their task.

These people or their parents had come from various African countries and tribes. There was no single death tradition among them, as their employer had ignorantly assumed. They sat in their camp at the edge of the prairie, as evening fell. Beans bubbled in cast iron pots that were placed above campfires. The men discussed the best way to commemorate the site. The place was important and sacred. It was the first location in the Midwest where honorable people of African descent were buried in their own marked cemetery. Their descendants and other people of color might, one day, visit it.

They ate the beans out of wooden bowls while they talked. It did not take long for them to reach a consensus. The shortest man among them stood.

"We are agreed," he said. "Stone death mask."

The others nodded, one by one. Eleven other men put their bowls on the ground, and also stood.

The short man led the other eleven men up the nearest hill. They brought along two mules, hitched to a single wagon. It was getting dark. That did not matter to them. The men had decided on a grave marker. That marker was out there, calling to them. They agreed that the first appropriately-sized stone they found would be the one. The leader walked seven hundred feet up the steep hill and there it was, a three-and-a-half-foot-tall granite rock, lying on its side on the ground.

"This is it," he said.

It took all of them to lift it onto the wagon. Other men might have thought the wagon would splinter to bits with the weight of the thing, but these men knew that it would not. The stone was ordained to be the graveyard marker and would reach its appointed position. The wagon was too heavy for the mules to pull, so three of the men positioned themselves at the back and pushed. Their route was downhill, but it still took six hours, pushing and heaving the wagon in the dark, to reach the camp.

The men who had stayed behind at the camp took over. They maneuvered the wagon to the head of the burial ground, released the mules to graze with the other mules, and heaved the rock onto its resting place.

One of the men searched through the tools he always carried with him. He pulled out several hammers and chisels. Three of the men took the tools and went to work on the stone.

The men sculpted the stone in shifts. It took two weeks to finish the marker. The final product was a smooth, androgynous face with high cheek bones, closed eyes, a distinctive nose, and full lips.

The men packed up the wagons with their supplies and hitched up the mules. They stood by the wagons before they left, bowed to their brothers and sisters in the ground, and then began their trek out of the Park. They stopped at the edge of the prairie to look back at the three-and-a-half-foot-tall sculpture of a face, now standing at the top of the burial ground.

Bigots have built countless monuments throughout the United States to glorify the institution of slavery. These dedicated workers, by contrast, had created a single small monument to venerate the African men and women who had been imprisoned and tortured by comrades of those other monument builders.

∞

Tembo watched the men leave. She hovered over the burial ground. She wondered who the bodies in the ground had been in life. She touched the soil over them, and learned that they had been men and women of great spirit, nobility, and goodwill. The City Park was especially treacherous to living people who had those qualities. These departed were now beyond the reach of the Park, but they might just be able to help others like themselves.

The elephant Cheela leaned forward. She allowed almost all of her essence to seep into the bodies under the earth.

"Protect any who come to this place who *deserve* your protection," she whispered.

Tembo swooped into the air to follow the retreating men. She saw them safely out of the Park, and then flew east.

The elephant had been stationed, clandestinely, in the area of the City Park for years. She had intervened, time and again over the millennia, in the destinies of those humans she had deemed worthy of her help. Each such intervention had depleted her. This last one had left her with only enough strength to go home. It was dangerous for her to remain in the Midwest any longer. She was too weak. It was time to go back to the Motherland.

Every one of the workers, to a man, walked out of the Park, leading their mules and empty wagons. The contractor and the City Planners had not expected to see the workers again. People who went into the Park, for a period longer than a few hours, generally did not come back.

The contractor was impressed. He not only paid each of them the promised double time pay but also gave them bonuses. He put them on his best jobs, from that day forward, and gave the white men he had just hired the more grueling work.

∞

Saklas, also a Deor, like Tembo—but of a different camp, the "Killapaka Deor" (also known as the "Kills")—dwelled in Cutter City. He had once lived in the City Park, but had moved his center of operations to Cutter City itself, decades ago. He did visit the Park at least once a week. Feeling the lifeblood of the Park gave him focus and reinvigorated him. The Park was his refuge and his sanctuary.

Saklas had the particular form of a winged goat.

The being also had an extremely bad temper. He was hostile to humanity, which he considered his personal enemy. He was pacified by the fact that the City Park was the stomping grounds of

140

the Killapaka and, as such, was also hostile to humans.

He made a trip to the Park a few days after Tembo's intrusion. Saklas realized that something was wrong, as he soon as he flew past the stone walls surrounding the Park. Humans had made their way far into the Park and out again, and had survived without injury. Worse, they had done something that felt *off*. He turned to fly toward the source of the problem and, in less than a minute, found it.

It was an *atrocity*. There, right in the middle of a flower-covered savannah, lay a defilement, created by the other side. He could feel the elements of Tembo within the dead human bodies that were interred in that Park's ground. He had to get rid of them, to purge the place of Cheela essence. He would snatch the dead from his Park, and tear them to atoms.

The being reached down to rip out the intangible substance his enemy had planted there.

Saklas immediately shrieked and whipped backward. In agony, he saw that his claws had been pierced through and through, and were dripping his elemental light, like blood from a deep wound.

Furious, Saklas stared down at the offending ground. The creature spotted the carved stone object that sat like a sentinel in the middle of the field. He saw that the object had not been defiled by the energy his enemy had fed into the bodies below the ground.

Saklas knew what to do, how to counterbalance the effect of the filthy energy the other side had somehow introduced into his Park. He opened his wings, pulled part of his essence into his damaged claws, and slammed it down into the stone figure.

People in Cutter City looked up and saw, far off in the City Park, a massive bolt of lightning crack down from the otherwise clear, blue sky.

The monument began to make creaking noises, and to grow. The stone figure stopped growing when it reached a height of ten feet. It opened its eyes.

Saklas looked at the smooth hills surrounding the prairie. This place had been made unholy by his adversaries. He wanted it, in the future, to be as unapproachable as possible. He sent another massive bolt of energy into those smooth hills, and reversed gravity. He held out his arms like a conductor, curled his claws, and *pulled* at the slopes. The hills lurched upward from the ground like drunks, rocking back and forth.

Satisfied, Saklas released his grip on the hills, which were now massive, majestic, snow-topped mountains.

His work was done. He flew off, exhausted and in pain, to return to his home and his disciples, and to heal. He decided, from that moment on, that Cutter City was *his*. He would never again permit an Apalacheela to invade his home.

The Stone Face watched Saklas, who had given it life, leave. It turned to look at its surroundings. Another being, who was greater than Saklas—and who was actually the father of all the Deor, Cheela and Kills alike—had spent time in the Park, millennia ago. The Deor Father's essence saturated the place.

Some of that energy now entered the Stone Face, along with a very small part of Tembo's competing energy that was being emitted from the freed slaves buried under the earth.

The Stone Face became more than Saklas had intended. It knew everything its creators knew.

It was, by its nature, a wild card. It moved slowly across the graveyard, out of the field, and up a mountain. It was off to explore its domicile, the City Park.

The word-of-mouth tale (which did not include anything about the winged beings or the Stone Face), told by Cutter City denizens, ended in a mystery. The mountains were high enough that they could be seen at a far distance. People swore that, before the men buried the freed slaves in the Park, no mountains had ever been in that part of Ohio. Certainly not in the City Park.

This part of the tale was hard for modern-day residents to swallow. There were no photographs of the City Park from an earlier time, so there was no way to prove the story, one way or the other.

~

By 9:30 p.m., the Jacksons and Kate were nearing Denver, Colorado. They had driven for eighteen hours straight. All of them, except Kate, had taken turns at the wheel. Kate had wanted to drive, after she had awoken from a six-hour nap, but the other three had vetoed this idea. Sam had not weighed in.

"I feel good. Great, even. I'm not tired at all anymore," she said.

143

"No need, little mama." Eli said. "We don't know what's going on with you and the baby. It makes sense that the more rest you get, the better both of you will be. And we all feel fine. *Better* than fine. Awesome."

The others *should* have been exhausted. The wonderful Scent, however, filled the car and energized them. They spoke little during the journey.

Ben was recalling in vivid detail all of the heretofore forgotten dreams about Sam that he'd had.

Eli and Maya were recalling the most wonderful events in their lives.

Eli was reliving the rare moments he'd had as a little boy with his hardworking father, before the man had died at a young age. Those events had happened so long ago. Years of subsequent life had pushed the memories far down in the brain cells that stored them.

He remembered them vividly, now. Holding his father's hand and walking into a repair shop that smelled like grease, where his papa purchased a new exhaust pipe for their old car. Sitting on their small, rundown porch, and watching his father push a mechanical reel mower over the tiny patch of front lawn. Lying in bed, while his father read him a bedtime story.

Maya was thinking about her mom, and how it had been before her mother had become ill. The disease that had wracked her mother's body had been terrible and had caused Maya to forget how good life had been, prior to its coming.

She remembered, now. It was like a movie being played in her head. Her mother had had a beautiful voice. The woman had always been singing, whether cooking, cleaning, gardening, sewing, or playing with Maya. Her dad had whistled along when he was home. Their house had been a noisy, happy place.

They'd been driving for the past eighteen hours, though, no matter how good they felt. They had taken Route 70 across the Mojave Desert, through Utah, and into the Rockies. They had almost reached Denver. They'd only stopped three times for fuel, bathroom breaks, bottles of water, and stale peanut butter crackers and corn chips from vending machines. The foursome, who were little traveled, would have been stunned and delighted by the mindboggling scenery and the staggering topography, had this been a simple road trip rather than an escape of some sort. As it was, during the daylight hours, they still took turns grunting in surprise or saying, "Whoo!" or "Holy!" or "Do you see that?" or "Awesome!"

Kate had had enough rest but knew that the others had not. She was becoming concerned. She leaned her head against the window and spotted a sign for a place called Lakewood. They were now a couple of hours from Denver. "Take Route 6 to Lakewood, please," she said to Maya, who was currently driving. "We need to find a place to stop and get some sleep."

Maya was intently focused on the road in front of her and, at the same time, daydreaming about her mother, pre-cancer. "Will do."

It seemed as though the extraordinary, lush smell that filled the car was being refreshed, moment-to-moment, by a fan blowing it through the interior of the vehicle. It was not, however, being blown in by a fan. It was coming from every pore in Kate's body.

"I'm not sleepy. Not even hungry," Maya said. "I feel like I could drive forever."

"I know. I do, too. But we *do* need to rest, when you think about it," her father said.

Maya glanced at her father, then at the road, and then at the rearview mirror, in which she caught a glimpse of Kate. Kate had become the *de facto* leader of the group, by virtue of the bossy little person she was carrying in her belly.

Ben had been quiet for the past hour. He had been trying to think through the logistics of their journey, even though he had no idea what their destination was.

"We need to get rid of our phones," he said. "I'm afraid we can be tracked through them, even though they're turned off. We'll smash them, and leave them in an outdoor trash can."

"I hate doing that," Maya said.

"I'm not crazy about it either," Ben answered.

The three Jacksons felt naked and vulnerable, thinking about going through life without their phones. Kate, of course, had never owned a smartphone and was the most unaffected by what the others viewed as a momentous event. But it was not like they would be calling anyone, anytime soon.

"I'm also going to have to disable the tracking device in this truck," Ben added.

"Do you know how to do that?" his uncle asked.

"I think so. I learned a lot at the repair shop about the different trackers."

146

"There's a motel up ahead." Maya said.

"I wonder if they have a restaurant?" Kate asked.

The place was an old, blocky, road motel next to a strip mall, but it did have a little eatery. Meatless chili, amazingly, was on the menu. They rented two rooms. (Eli paid in cash.) They decided they would eat first and then go to their respective rooms, Kate and Maya in one, Eli and Ben in the other.

Ben, after darkness fell, would drive the truck to a dark location and disable the tracking. They just hoped that no one had already tracked them to the hotel. The three Jacksons, reluctantly, smashed their phones on the parking lot pavement, and pushed them down into a trash bin.

~

Annie and Beau were sitting at the little dining room table. Annie's laptop was on the surface in front of her. She was scrolling through their inventory list.

"Read what we have," Beau said. "Let's see if there's anything important missing."

"Ok. In the basement: Bottles of vegetable seeds in one of the basement refrigerators, and flower seeds, just because. Large glass containers of almonds, walnuts, cashews, pistachios, chia seeds, flax seeds, pumpkin seeds, sesame seeds, poppy seeds, pine nuts, sunflower seeds, tofu, vegan cheese, yeast in bulk, and Beyond Meat and Impossible Food products, along with vegan puff pastry, in the upright freezer. Also, a lot of mung bean egg substitute. I've found it freezes quite well. I stockpiled it when the manufacturer began having fiscal problems. Our milks—oat, hemp, flax, rice, almond, cashew, and soy—fill three of the chest freezers. Peanut butter, almond butter, vegetable shortening, ginger root, chopped herbs, frozen vegetables, frozen fruits, frozen berries, dried fruits, miso paste, and other miscellaneous food items that hold up well when frozen, in the fourth chest freezer. Coffee beans and flours—including whole wheat, all purpose, almond, barley, rice, and arrowroot, along with corn meal and corn starch—in the fifth chest freezer.

"On the basement shelves: first aid supplies, reading glasses in various strengths, dried herbs, baking soda, baking powder, vanilla, vanilla beans, cinnamon sticks, olive oil, coconut oil, peanut oil, grape seed oil, maple syrup, coconut milk and cream, hot sauces, coffee, teas, sugars, kala namak black salt, sea salt, peppers, vitamin B-12, vegan vitamin d-3, prenatal vitamins, condiments, nutritional yeast, and bottles, tins, and boxes of spices.

"In the stacked-up storage containers: dried legumes, textured vegetable protein, farro and other grains, moong dal, lentils, lentil pastas, regular dried pastas, oatmeal, freeze-dried coconut and fruits, vinegars—including large bottles of white vinegar for cleaning—organic unsweetened juices, apple cider, jellies, anti-viral elderberry extract, canned goods, jars of olives, capers, peppers, and other pickled items, whole grain crackers, rice, jars of vegetable bouillon, toiletries, batteries, towels and wash cloths, linens, toilet paper, women's sanitary supplies, canning supplies, and natural detergents, all properly labelled. The items to make vegan meats

148

and cheeses are in separate containers: vital wheat gluten, pea protein flour, chickpea flour, tapioca starch, agar—"

"Hold up," Beau interrupted. "What's agar?"

"If you ever helped me make panna cotta, or mousse, or vegan cheese, you'd know that agar is derived from seaweed. It takes the place of animal products like gelatin and rennet."

"Do you have everything you need to make vegan butter? I hope you didn't store the junk from the store."

"I do, and I didn't."

"You know that stuff they sell is mostly palm oil, and cutting down all those palms is causing deforestation of the most biodiverse forests in the world?"

"Why do you always find it necessary to preach to the choir? Of *course*, I have everything I need to make butter. Coconut oil, canola oil, almond flour, nutritional yeast, coconut cream, apple cider vinegar, salt, and turmeric. And why are we even talking about this, right now?"

"Sorry. I get carried away. Continue."

"We have cases of dehydrated versions of oat milk, coconut milk, almond milk, and soy milk. And then we have vegetable bouillon, tahini, fava flour, liquid aminos, wasabi, mirin, and dried mushrooms. Tons of dried beans. Vegetables that you so helpfully assisted me to can. Cases of vegan wine, beer, and other spirits."

She smiled and took a breath. "Then, there are the water system supplies: the bags of salt, boxes of reverse osmosis filters and inline filters, and bottles of seven percent peroxide. We've got them in our basement and in the cottage basements. I've made sure to repackage everything possible into glass canning jars of various sizes. Nothing is in plastic. We will be reusing the jars to can vegetables.

"The basements in the two cottages are also filled with extra cases of paper goods, canned goods, and some other food items. We'll figure out ways to upcycle the used tin cans. And under the overhang next to the garage, sitting off the ground on pallets and covered by tarps, two hundred and fifty bags of high-quality hard pellets for the two stoves in our house. Not to mention all of your stuff in the basement and the garage. Then there're the potatoes, carrots, onions, apples, sweet potatoes, cabbages, parsnips, and turnips in the root cellar."

"Sounds tight," Beau said. "And I can say, without being smug, that we've done a damned good job."

Annie closed the laptop and stood. "And I keep tabs to make sure everything has long dates. Why don't we take a walk up to the cottages and make sure the lodgings are still in good shape?"

"Our guests might just want to stay with us in our house," Beau replied. "The two bedrooms upstairs should be enough space."

"I don't know. We went to all the trouble to have the cottages built, for this very purpose. Why not use them?"

"Those little homes are pretty far back, up there in the woods. The newcomers might feel like they're too remote and isolated. They can decide for themselves when they get here," Beau said. "We'll get one of the cottages ready, in the meantime."

"It *would* be nice to have them stay in our house for a little while, at least," Annie agreed. "Get to know them. Get to know a Child's parents! And, they're probably going to be traumatized and exhausted from everything that's happened to them. I can't imagine that their trip from the west coast is anything but wild. It might help them recover if we treat them as our honored guests–which, of course they are– and take care of them. Wait on them."

"We'll see," Beau said. "Whatever they want."

∞

The couple walked up an incline toward the forest behind their home and entered the woods. The air was cool and clean under the tree canopy. They continued upward for about five minutes, until they reached an impenetrable, solid stand of pine trees. Impenetrable, that is, except for a narrow opening between two of the pines. Beau went through it. Annie followed behind.

They emerged into a small glade. A little, slate-roofed, stone cottage was in the center of the clearing. A solid oak door was set in the middle of the home's front wall, with a window on each side of it. Heavy oak shutters framed the windows.

"We kept saying we were going to come up here and spend a few days and nights," Annie said. "We never did. Wonder if we'll ever get the chance, now?" She unlocked the front door of the cottage and went into a small, bright kitchen.

"I'm sure we will. One day." Beau looked around. "Everything looks spotless."

"I guess the Cheela have been seeing to it," Annie said. "We need to put sheets, pillows, and blankets on the beds. I doubt the Cheela would realize that was something that needed to be done."

"Our Cheela are getting pretty hip to the human condition, and to our needs."

"Doesn't it seem like just yesterday that the groundhogs and moles were digging the foundations for the cottages?" Annie asked. "And Meska and a few other bears were carrying the stones and building the structures?"

"No, it doesn't seem like yesterday to me. It took forever, getting contractors up here to put in the electrical, the plumbing, the wells, and to hook up to our septic field, which—fortunately—is downhill from both cottages. And then installing solar panels on the roof of our house and another array in the side field, so that we could provide off-grid power to all the structures on the property. On top of that, getting the solar battery bank set up in a new shed, and then getting all the buildings connected to each other, communications-wise."

"I guess it seems like it was yesterday, and also like a hundred years ago. It *was* a massive undertaking," Annie said.

"I'll help you do the beds." Beau headed to the short hallway, which adjoined the kitchen on the left.

Annie opened a pantry door on the side of the room. The pantry was packed full of the food and kitchen supplies she and Beau had carried up to the cottage, with the help of the Cheela. She closed the pantry door and walked into the room behind the kitchen. It was a small, cozy den, with a wood-burning stove that was connected to the ducts in the house, a sofa, two comfortable armchairs, and footstools. She glanced around. Nothing for her to do in here, either. She thought that weary travelers would find the room inviting. She went back through the kitchen to the bedrooms, to help Beau.

Beau and Annie finished making the bed in the tiny main bedroom, and walked across the hall to the even smaller, second bedroom. It was crammed with furniture and baby things. There was a single bed, a crib, a bassinet, and a changing table. They had prepared for the eventuality, over the past two decades, that they or their successors would be providing shelter to a child whose unknown age could range from newborn to seventeen years. A baby required a lot more provisions and gear than did an older child, but the Walds were ready. They had stocked the currently unoccupied cottage in the woods as if it were going to be a prepper's maternity ward.

A door on the side of the main bedroom opened onto a storage closet that was larger than the bedroom. Shelves lining the left wall of the closet were stacked with gender-neutral clothing, sized for a newborn, on up. Various sized shoes were on the bottom shelf. Bins labelled, "baby food/baby dishes/spoons," "cloth diapers/bibs," "wipes/changing pads," "bottles/bottle brushes," "bedding," "misc. baby supplies," "stuffed animals," and "misc. maternity supplies" were stacked at the back of the storeroom. Baby equipment, including a baby carrier, stroller, high chair, and baby bathtub, lined the wall on the right.

The couple put sheets, some pillows, and a blanket on the single bed, and sheets, only, on the crib.

Annie opened the window in the room. "Let's open *all* of the windows. Get some fresh air in here."

Beau walked back into the hallway. A small laundry room was on the right, past the second bedroom. The bathroom was at the end of the hall. The floor in front of the bathroom was covered with a small braided rug.

Beau leaned over and slipped his hand under the rug. He stretched forward and felt around under the rug. His fingers found the handle that was inset into the wooden floor. He lifted the handle. The rug was tacked to an oak trapdoor. Beau pulled it open. The underside of the trapdoor was lined with thick sheet metal.

"Shall we check out the basement?" he asked.

"I don't want to climb down there. We know what's in the basement: a water heater, solar batteries, a bed, a refrigerator, a toilet, a sink, some other equipment, and more supplies. I've got the entire inventory on our computer." The notion of unnecessarily climbing down extremely steep steps into the windowless cellar did not appeal to Annie.

Beau lowered the trapdoor and stood. "Ok. I'll open the rest of the windows, and then we'll go. We'll come back up, before dark, and close them."

The couple finished readying the cottage, and then went back outside.

Do you think we missed anything?" Beau asked. He was standing next to the closed door of

154

the cottage. "Do I need to make a run into Vestal?" (Vestal, which had a number of big box stores, was twenty miles east of Owego.)

"We should probably get some maternity clothes. But I have no idea what size the mother is, so no point in even thinking about that right now. I have lots of fabric and can always whip up whatever she needs. Except underwear and bras." Annie sighed. "I can sew, but I'm not exactly a seamstress."

"We can always have things delivered," Beau said.

"I guess. I don't know. I think we're going to have to do one more shopping run after they arrive, when we can figure out what we need and don't currently have."

"That will depend on whether the Cheela tell us it's safe or not. Meska believes that a Child's Scent will be so all-encompassing that even our clothes will be saturated with it. How will we be able to leave? It would be a red flag to the other side. And then they'll be able to find us. Home delivery might be our only option."

"Well, maybe I'll go into town today, then. I'll buy different-sized maternity clothes. I'll lean toward larger sizes. I can always take them in, but it's much more involved to make them bigger. And I'll get assorted bras and underwear. I'll pull up a home-birth checklist online before I go, to double-check that we've covered everything."

"I'll come with you. We'll take the truck. If we can't leave here for who knows how long, I want to make sure our stock of organic fertilizer and vegetable seeds will get us through." Beau locked the door of the cottage behind them. "Kind of dumb, isn't it? Considering that all the windows in the house are open."

"It's not like anyone is going to break in," Annie said. "We're in the forest. And Tembo is still here, on guard. Should we go up to the other cottage, and open that one up too?"

"I don't think it's necessary. We'll do it if we find that these travelers want or need more space."

They walked out of the forest and down the slope toward their house, passing their large composter on the way. "I know we're missing something," Annie remarked, "besides what we already discussed."

"There's always going to be something else we could have gotten. We've done our best. That's all we can do. And the vegetable garden's going strong. We've got enough to feed and care for an army. I'll go inspect what I've got in the garage. See if I can think of anything else. You go ahead and do your research about home births. We'll leave for Vestal in say... an hour?"

"Sounds good, honey."

Chapter 2

Boner's America First, Last, and In-Between Militia, (aka The Unidentified and Incognito P Company, LLC, aka The Pee Company)

Rex Boner did not know what to do with himself after high school graduation. He'd had big plans in school. His goal was to set the world straight by making it, once again, the domain of white men. The problem was that he didn't have a clue how to go about doing it.

He sulked for days, in his bedroom in his mother's crappy apartment. Rex could not stand the woman. He viewed her as a bloody idiot and, therefore, communicated with her as little as possible, simply growling or yelling orders at her. Get me dinner. Clean my room. Wash my clothes. Go to the store and buy me this, or that. He'd treated her in this manner since he was a little boy. She had tolerated it, as though she had deserved it.

Bertha Boner had raised Rex by herself. Rex had no clue who or where his father was, or even the man's name. Boner was his mother's surname.

Bertha supported them by cleaning homes for other people. All of her friends' kids had worked part-time jobs and summer jobs while in high school. Not Rex. He'd spent all of his free time conducting what he called his "research" or his "project." He did not share any information about it with his mother. She wouldn't consider trying to open the locked file cabinets in Rex's bedroom. She feared what she would find there.

Bertha had dropped out of high school, at age sixteen, to work; otherwise, she would not have had a roof over her head or food to eat. She certainly was not a bloody idiot, as Rex thought. Her behavior was motivated by her understanding that Rex was always on the verge of violence. She'd been afraid of her son since he had been three years old. She'd had no information or resources with which to deal with the situation. The thought of him obsessing over some "research project" terrified her, especially in light of the crude, racist, xenophobic, misogynistic, homophobic things he continually muttered under his breath.

She blamed herself, with reason, for Rex's apparently psychotic, sociopathic personality. She had been a heavy drinker throughout her pregnancy. Unbeknownst to anyone, Rex would have had some remarkable genes–similar to that of Samuel Jackson and Katherine Birdsong–had his mother abstained from drinking. The alcohol had, unfortunately, modified and twisted what should have been a rare and spectacular genetic structure.

Rex's mother was obsequious, almost groveling, in her attempts to placate and calm the boy. He had never attacked her, but he frightened her. She was more afraid that he would leave her, though, than she was of his potential violence. Her greatest fear was being alone. She had the self-esteem of the stereotypical domestic violence victim.

Rex had thought of joining the military. The thought lasted about a minute. Why would he voluntarily subject himself to authority? And a lot of the people above him would surely be minorities. No doubt some of them would be Black or Latino or gay. Some of them might even be women, a double whammy. The existing authority structure sucked. He needed to shake it up.

He started to formulate a plan.

Rex sat in his bedroom for several weeks. He came out only to eat, to use the bathroom, or to order his mother to wash his dirty laundry or to pick him up something at the store. He went through all of the materials in his file cabinets during the day. He lay in bed staring at the ceiling and thinking for hours at night, until he fell asleep.

His scheme finally took shape.

He took his mother's shredder from her living room desk (where she paid their bills every month), and set to work shredding all but the materials that were most important to him. These primarily consisted of neo-Nazi, white nationalist disinformation and propaganda. He also retained maps of sites that were significant to the white race, in one way or another.

A novelette he'd read as a child, *The World Tilters*, was in his file. The book, if you could call it that—as it was only about twenty pages long—had been out of print for years. Why had he bothered to hang on to it? He recalled that it was a fictional story about two children who were supposed to change the world. The animals in it were big creatures made of light and energy. They called themselves the "Deor." What a load of crap.

Rex would show the world some magic, all right. Rex Boner's kind of magic. Presto, everybody back in their correct places. White men at the top, attended to by their white women. Rex had read his history. He was fully aware how remarkable a place the world had once been. He would dedicate his life to making it so again.

He was about to start tearing pages from the book to run through the shredder, solely for the fun of destroying it, but stopped. He touched the cover of the book. There was a funny, almost imperceptible sensation in his fingertips. The sensation went up his arm and into his head. It was like the book had cast a little hook into his brain. The part of his brain that had been hooked was telling him there was a clue in the book about his mission.

He reread it that night, and again the following night. Animals and children. What did they have to do with his plans? They did, though. He knew it. Rex had, throughout his life, used his gut feelings as his North Star. He had a strong feeling about this.

Ok, so in the book, animals in their true, light and energy forms were called Deor. Those who wanted to eventually live alongside mankind were "Apalacheela," or "Cheela." There were also those Deor who wanted to exterminate people. They called themselves "Killapaka," or "Kills."

And then there was the "Scent" by which the two "Children" would be known. The two Children would somehow change the balance of the world, and *right* it. They would have some kind of power. A godlike entity, called the "Living World," had created all life on Earth. It had planted the seeds which would, one day, give rise to these two kids. The brats would fix what was wrong with the planet.

Rex snorted. Power. Not if he had anything to do with it. He resolved that, if these kids were born during his lifetime, he would find them before they knew what they were doing. He would force them to use their power to his own ends.

He had bought the story about the Children, hook, line, and sinker.

The story did not have a conclusion, which Rex found to be quite unsatisfactory. It focused on describing the Deor and the Deor factions, the Living World, the Children, and the Scent. It was written more like a factual treatise than a piece of fiction.

He sniffed at the air in his room. He didn't smell anything, other than his socks and underwear. He wouldn't be able to smell the Scent anyway, according to the rules of the world described in the book. You had to be a Deor or have the right genes, or something. Oh, well, he'd figure something out.

∞

Rex finished his sorting and shredding operation by mid-August. A small stack of papers was on his nightstand. A neatly folded stack of clothing was on a chair, along with a few other personal items. A beat-up black suitcase was on the bed. Rex picked up the stack of papers and put them in the zippered compartment of the suitcase, packed the clothes and personal items, and closed and zippered the suitcase. He glanced at the clock next to his bed. 6:00 a.m. He'd been up all night, getting ready.

Rex opened the door of his bedroom. He was fully dressed and he was carrying the suitcase in his right hand. His mother was cooking her breakfast in the kitchen. She heard her son's movement and came out into the small living room. She was surprised he was up so early. Rex, heading to the front door, pushed past her.

"I'm out of here," he said, as he opened the door.

"Where are you going?" Bertha asked.

He did not bother to answer her. He strode through the door and left. He also did not bother to close the door behind him.

He headed to the bus stop in front of the apartment complex. His friends, Ethan Miller and Arnold Mudak, had, after graduation, gotten jobs at a big box store. They made just enough money that they were able to move out of their parents' shoddy flats and get their own dumpy apartment together. Rex had decided–without telling the other two boys–that he was going to move in with them.

Rex showed up at his friends' new place, unannounced. Ethan answered the door.

"Hey, Rex," Ethan said. "Come on in." He looked down at Rex's suitcase. "What's up?"

"You've got a new roommate," Rex replied. He picked up the suitcase and went inside. "Where's Arnie?"

"In the bathroom, getting ready for work."

"Is your bedroom the biggest one?"

"Yup."

"Does it have its own bathroom?"

"Sure does. We worked it out so I pay a little more rent, based on the *pro rata* square footage of the two bedrooms." He raised his chin.

"That's pretty cool, that you figured out that formula. Very adult of you."

"Yeah. And then we don't have arguments over who's got what and who pays how much."

"Well, speaking of who's got what, I'm taking your room," Rex said.

"My—"

"You can sleep with Arnold or you can sleep on the sofa. Or you can tell Arnie to sleep on the sofa. Your call. Maybe you can figure out a rent formula for that one. Lead the way. Show me to my quarters."

Ethan bit his lower lip and flushed. He turned and led Rex to the master bedroom. Bertha Boner was not the only person who feared the potential violence that animated Rex Boner, leaked out of his every pore, and manifested itself in the look in his eyes and the expression on his face.

Rex settled in, while Ethan moved all of his own belongings into Arnold's room.

"I guess we can both sleep in here." Arnold's voice was sheepish. "It *is* a double bed."

Ethan looked doubtful. "We'll have to start splitting the rent fifty-fifty."

"Rex will have to pay his share," Arnold said, in a low voice.

"Yeah? You going to be the one to tell him that?" Ethan snorted, and then he sneered. He emulated Rex whenever possible, without realizing he was doing it.

∞

Rex, Ethan, and Arnold gathered in the living room.

"Get the guys over here tonight," Rex said. "I have a proposition for them."

"A proposition?" Arnold asked.

"That's what I said. Listen up. We had fun with our little 'Boner's Militia' when we were kids in school. We're out of school now. We're adults. It's time we did it for real. Created a real militia. We'll call it, "Boner's America First, Last, and In-Between Militia." How's that?"

"First, Last, and In-Between?" Ethan asked, puzzled.

"Think about it. We have to distinguish ourselves from those slackers who believe that being *first* is enough. We'll cover all the bases."

"Huh," Ethan said. "So, we take *all* the seats on the bus, not just the ones in the front."

"You're getting it," Rex smiled. "And we'll go with the ranks we gave ourselves as kids. That means, you're a lieutenant, Ethan.[4] And you're an inspector, Arnold."

Arnold looked up. He slowly smiled. Arnold was enamored with the British, including the idea of Scotland Yard inspectors. He sometimes faked a British accent (as long as Rex wasn't around, that is).

Boner continued. "And the others can go by the titles they had before, too. I know how much thought everyone put into their own

---

[4] Ethan Miller would later rise to the rank of "colonel."

designations, going all the way back to elementary school. I respect that."

"Are we going to do the things we talked about when we were kids?" Ethan asked.

"That's the plan. We're going to take over this loser country, do a reset, and put people back in their places. And then move on to other countries."

"And then get rid of all the—"

Rex cut him off. "Minorities. Get rid of all the *minorities*. Use the correct phraseology, boys. Right-thinking people will know what we're talking about, but we don't want to stir up the ones in the other camp. We don't want to draw attention, until it's too late for them to do anything about it. Then we can be loud and proud."

"Ok," Ethan said, "you mean how "European" is, actually, white people. "Thugs," "animals," and "dogs" are... "

Arnold cut him off. "The same thing as "urban" and "inner city." So, basically, *Black* people." He thought for a moment. "And anyone else who doesn't have white skin."

"These are private messages to our people," Rex said. "And when we're talking about "illegals," it only refers to Latinos."

"Women who are professionals are "uppity,'" Ethan added. He was enjoying this game.

"But if we're talking about a *minority* professional woman, the bitch is "low intellect" or "low IQ." At the same time, if she talks good, and some of her kind actually *like* hearing her speeches, she's "articulate" or she "performs

165

well." Rex sneered. "Like it's a surprise she could pull it off. You know the routine." He changed the subject. "You two will be my right-hand men, along with Edwin Perdet."

"How're we going to get started?" Ethan asked.

"We're going to find a place for our headquarters, big enough so that we can all move in together, like a barracks. We'll need money to do that," Rex said.

"We need money to do anything," Ethan said.

"Yeah. I've been giving that a lot of thought over the past few weeks. I think I know how to do it. I need you to do some research on what it takes to become certified as a home health care provider in California."

"A home health care provider? How are we going to get the capital we need doing *that*?"

"Just get me the information. I'll explain later, when all the boys are here. Saves me from having to go through the whole thing twice. Arnie, your cousin's a lawyer, right?"

"You mean Oliver Schlau?"

"Yeah. Is he any good at doing wills?"

"Sure," Arnold replied.

"Get him on the phone for me. I need to talk to him."

"Ok." Arnold was getting excited. His life was being given meaning. He had no idea what Rex's scheme to make money was. It did not matter. Arnold was a follower, and Rex Boner was his leader. He also no longer cared whether Rex chipped in toward the rent.

"Uh, General Boner?" he asked, tentatively. He hadn't called Rex "general" since they'd left school and, in school, it had been a fantasy. Now it was *real*. He thought it might be funny or weird to use the designation. It was not. It felt good. Arnold's voice got stronger. "What about uniforms, sir?"

Rex's back straightened. Arnold had called him "general," and then, "sir." He felt like a man who had just been knighted. He was grateful to Arnold.

"I'm thinking black clothing, Inspector Mudak." Rex's voice was abnormally kind. "We'll worry about that at a later date, though. Give the boys something to look forward to."

∞

Fifteen other young men crowded into the apartment that night, including Maynard Arshloch and Edwin Perdet. They sat on the soiled, threadbare sofa, on kitchen table chairs brought into the living room, or on the carpeted floor. Rex paced back and forth through the room. He was rubbing his hands together.

He'd presented his proposition to the group and was awaiting feedback.

"We all want the same things we wanted back in high school, right?" he asked.

The group mumbled its agreement.

"Ok. So do we agree that we'll form Boner's America First, Last, and In-Between Militia?"

He heard, in response, "Yeah." "For *sure*." "Absolutely." "Damn straight!"

"Any objections?"

All of the boys shook their heads.

"So, we need some serious funding. Here's how we're going to do it. We target old people who don't need their money anymore. Well, actually, old *dead* people who don't need their money anymore." Rex gestured at Ethan Miller. "My lieutenant, here, has looked into what you need to do to get certified as a home health care provider."

The response was, "What the ... ? You've got to be kidding."

Rex shook his head and smiled. "Calm down, boys. We're not going to be a bunch of nurses. Well, not any longer than we have to be. Do you know how many rich old pricks there are, who can barely remember their own names?"

He smiled again, and looked at the faces around him. They looked back at him, not grasping his point. They were anything but a group of rocket scientists.

Rex nodded toward Arnold Mudak. "Inspector Mudak has a cousin who's a lawyer. Guy by the name of Schlau. He mostly does criminal law, but Arnold says the guy can write up a mean will. I explained what we need and Schlau's on-board."

The boys' faces relaxed. An actual lawyer thought that what they were going to do made sense. This could work.

One of the crew, a smooth-faced young man named Erik Huber, stood. "I get it. We glamour those old farts. Do whatever it takes. Make them think you're their long-lost son, or the only person in the world who gives a shit about them, or that you want to get in their pants, or whatever."

168

Erik thought of himself as a ladies' man. He had, unsuccessfully, used the latter two methods trying to get women to go out with him.

"Exactly," Boner said. "Lieutenant, could you hand out the information sheets I printed out? Each of you'll go through some little state program to become certified. It only takes about twenty-four hours total to complete it. Stay focused, and you'll be able to whip through it in three days. Keep your eye on the prize. There are a number of small agencies throughout L.A. Each one of you will go to work for a different agency.

"You'll steal a copy of the agency's client listing, as soon as you're in a position to do so. I don't have to tell you boys how to handle that end of it. We've all done our share of breaking into school computers to download tests or to change our grades. This should be a breeze for you.

"Inspector Mudak will take the client listings to his cousin, Schlau, to find out which of the clients have nice bank accounts and no families. Mr. Schlau has different ways of getting that info. He'll tell each of you which one of your agency's clients is your mark. Then, you'll do what you have to do to get assigned to that client. Your aim is to suck up to the target and get in their good graces. You decide how to do it, based on the particular case.

"I'll oversee the operation. The lieutenant and the inspector will coordinate who works where and–most importantly–how to proceed with getting the client to make you a beneficiary under their will. Actually, *you* won't be the beneficiary. That will be the company we're about to form, "The Unidentified and Incognito P Company, LLC.""

~

The Significance of the Letter P

Rex liked the letter P. It was the sixteenth letter in the alphabet, and sixteen was a fortuitous number.

The M16 rifle, for example, was one of Boner's favorite weapons. Tarot Card No. XVI was the Tower. The depiction on that Tarot card was of a tower being struck by lightning and, as a consequence of the lightning strike, two men being thrown to the ground. Boner believed that he, himself, was that lightning.

Plus, the number sixteen, in numerology, was associated with the search—through both modern and ancient wisdom—for profound and consequential answers. Rex had been searching for just such answers most of his life.

The numerology profile of the letter P stood for shrewdness, influence, and knowledge. The downside was that it also suggested self-preoccupation. Rex would take that. He didn't consider his own egocentricity to be a bad thing. He would find it so in others, but not in himself. He believed he was so special that it would be weird for him to be anything other than self-obsessed.

Rex had considered the letter "Q." He had quickly steered clear of it. He despised the words with which it was associated. Queer, queen, quivering, queasiness, querulous, quick-tempered, quixotic, quisling, quack, quagmire, quarrelsome, quicksand, quashable, questionable.

Forget the letter Q. The letter P would help propel him to greatness.

~

"The something-something Pee Company? What?" Captain Edwin Perdet asked.

"Unidentified and Incognito, which we will be. Until we come into our own, that is. And I talked about the letter P and how it's the sixteenth letter, with some of you, back in school. The letter and the number are both auspicious and powerful. The name will bring us luck.

"But, back to the plan. The old people won't know what they're signing. We'll make sure that we have guys—meaning some of *you* guys—to sign as witnesses to the wills. The lawyer cousin or someone on his staff, to switch it up, can notarize each client's signature. The witnesses can attest that the client was of sound mind at the time the will was signed, if a will is later attacked. Questions?"

"I've got a question," Sergeant Maynard Arshloch said, raising his hand. He was diffident and self-effacing. He preferred not to have a rank higher than that of sergeant.

Rex stared at the raised arm, and lifted an eyebrow. Maynard reddened and dropped his hand.

"Don't the people have to die before we can inherit anything from them through their wills?"

"Well, Sargeant," Boner replied. "That's the easy part. Don't worry about it. All your clients will be in crappy health, senile, doped up out of what's left of their minds, and in hospice, or almost. I'll handle that end of it."

There were no other questions. The young men thought about their orders. The scope of the venture to which they had agreed was beginning to sink in.

Rex broke out the beer and potato chips. Ethan had forgotten the dip, so they had to do without.

~

The plan took several years. It worked, sometimes too well. Several of the heads of the targeted agencies became suspicious when their richest clients suddenly died, with the decedents' entire estates left to a secretive company called The Unidentified and Incognito P Company, LLC.

Oliver Schlau had done an amazing job, however. His wills were bulletproof. He was incentivized by the amount of money Rex paid him. Mr. Schlau had made sure that none of the targeted clients had any living relatives, and that no other people had reasonable claims to the estates. The few who did try to contest the wills were paid a visit by a few of Boner's boys. These people quickly withdrew their objections.

The Unidentified and Incognito P Company, LLC eventually had the wealth required to fund Rex Boner's plans.

The militia members started calling their limited liability company the "Pee Company," for short.

∞

Rex Boner was the head of a small empire, within three years. He'd always believed that success was his preordained destiny, but he was also convinced that his superstitious use of the sixteenth letter–incorporated into the name of his umbrella company–had sealed the deal.

His organization had grown so large that he'd made Colonel Miller his Chief of Staff (after having promoted him from lieutenant), Inspector Mudak his Minister of Defense, and Captain Perdet his Secretary of Covert Ops. Anyone who wanted to meet with him had to go through one of those three men.

He kept the little book, *The World Tilters*, in the top drawer of his desk and often pulled it out to reread the parts about the Children and how they would be found. He became obsessed with it. The book was out of print, so he made copies of it and distributed them to his inner circle. He ordered his men to familiarize themselves with it. They had no idea why they didn't get the same odd sensation that Rex did when he touched the book.

They did as they were told, however. It was not theirs to ask why.

Captain Perdet was a tech nerd. He believed that information was power. He convinced General Boner that they needed an Information Technology section, which they could use to spy on people (among other things). Rex approved the request.

Perdet performed an extensive search for talented IT people. The applicants were immediately rejected if they were not xenophobic, misogynistic, homophobic, white males. This actually did not narrow the field that much, and Perdet was quickly able to put together a proper IT team.

He discussed with the general the idea of bringing in some well-paid minorities as front men. The colonel argued that this was the standard in the industry for "white-oriented" organizations. Boner, however, despised the idea and immediately nixed it.

The swearing of loyalty to General Boner was a condition of induction into Boner's America First, Last, and In-Between Militia. The new member had to stand in front of Boner and bow his head.

Boner would ask, "Do I have your loyalty?" The recruit had better–very quickly–answer, "Yes." Anyone who hesitated, soon disappeared. People who got close enough to General Boner to be asked that fealty question already had way too much information, just to be cut loose.

The Pee Company was temporarily leasing office space in an office building in Los Angeles. Its ranks were rapidly swelling. They needed more room. Rex wanted to find a home for the Pee Company in a place that was located anywhere but the "Left Coast."

Chapter 3

Witnessing

Kate awoke with a start. She sat up, held her stomach, and rocked.

"What is it," Maya mumbled into her pillow.

"Time to leave." Kate pushed on Maya's shoulder. "Get up, Maya. I'm going to wake Ben and Eli."

Maya rolled over and looked at the clock. It read 2:30 a.m.

"That is one domineering little kid you've got growing in there," she grumbled.

The Scent filling the room hit Maya as soon as she lifted her head. It was invigorating and soothing. She got up and dressed, pulled on her shoes, walked across the room to the door, and went outside.

She knocked on the next door. "Ben, Eli — it's time to go!"

All four had slept in the clothes they had worn the previous day, in case they had to rush out of the place. This now appeared to have been a good plan. They splashed water on their faces, brushed their teeth, used the bathroom, and were on the road fifteen minutes later. Benjamin was driving. Kate sat in the front passenger seat.

"Do we get back on Route 70?" Ben asked.

"No," Kate replied. "We'll go down to Route 470 and southeast, around the city. We'll pick up Route 70 again when we're on the other side of Denver."

Eli had procured road maps that were in a display case by the front desk. He was lucky that the proprietors of the little motel were elderly and still thought it appropriate to provide such an antiquated amenity to their guests.

This is what we're reduced to without smartphones, Maya thought grimly. Maps made of paper.

Eli had a map open and was peering at it. "We could take Route 80, instead."

"No," Kate said. "It's a toll road. We're taking evasive maneuvers. The less interaction we have with anyone, the better. In fact, Sam is telling me that we have to go all the way to our destination on this next bit. No more stops to sleep. He says that someone is on our tail and getting close."

"*Who's* on our tail? *Who's* getting close?" Maya demanded, from a back seat.

"He hasn't told me," Kate replied. She touched her stomach. "I think he doesn't want to scare us. We have to move quickly, and we have to be smart."

"Has he told you where we're going?" Ben asked.

"Yes. Some place called Owego, in the southern tier of New York."

"New York!" Eli said. "That *far*? Isn't there some other place we can go, that's a little closer? How can we possibly travel that distance, in one hitch?"

"We're going to the only place we'll be safe," Kate replied. "There is no other choice."

"If that's the case, I suggest the two of you try to get some more sleep. Kate can navigate and keep me company. I'll drive for eight hours, and then we can switch," Ben said.

"Is anyone hungry or thirsty?" Maya asked. "We've got bottled water and some crappy snacks."

No one felt like they needed any water or crappy snacks, at the moment, so Maya curled up in a corner and fell asleep. Eli stretched out his legs and put an arm behind his head. He was snoring a few minutes later.

∞

Hundreds of Apalacheela flew above, and alongside, the truck. They formed a barrier between the vehicle's occupants and the Killapaka, who flew higher above.

∞

Kate had intended to keep Ben company, but could not keep her eyes open. The wonderful smell in the vehicle was evaporating. The air in the truck began to feel hot and oppressive. The others felt it, too.

"Hey, Ben. Is the AC working?" Eli asked.

Ben touched the controls, and then felt the air vents. "It's working, but it doesn't seem as strong, though."

Ben felt sluggish. It was difficult to keep his eyes focused on the road.

Kate's head lolled against the window. She drifted off.

∞

Several Killapaka soared far overhead. The Apalacheela spread the elements of which they were made across the sky. They became thin and stretched, and made themselves invisible to the Kills flying above them. At the same time, their stretched-out components created a blanket that hid the truck and the Scent from their opponents.

Sam, a tiny cluster of cells in Kate's belly, was more powerful than he had been just twenty-four hours ago. He did his best to pull the Scent into himself. He was able to do it for a short time, as miniscule as he was. The Kills glided in a circle for a few moments, then turned to the north and sped off.

∞

Kate is in some kind of blocky, windowless building. She has been trying all of the doors along the hallway. The recessed lighting overhead is so redundant that she does not cast a shadow.

There is only one door left, a solid one with no window It is at the end of the corridor. Kate is searching for something, but has forgotten what it is. Maybe it will be behind this last door.

She pushes on it with her hand. The door opens a crack. She uses both hands and it swings open. She walks into the room.

There are multiple rows of animals in cages. Dogs, cats, rabbits, white rats, birds, frogs, pigs, hamsters, fish, monkeys. The cages are so small that the animals can barely change their positions.

Kate moves forward down the first aisle of cages, like someone is ramming a cattle prod into her back. She sees:

A cat with the top of its skull missing, and a pronged metal crown with wires running from the top part of the cat's exposed brain. The pitiable cat sits, without moving, and stares at

Kate. Words are printed on a small placard in front of the cage. Kate leans forward and reads, "BENZENE TEST NO. 57-3426344D."

A pig with his eyes half eaten away, and tubes running from his chest. A sign on the cage reads, "SHAMPOO TEST NO. 72513687-4-B32."

A yellow Labrador Retriever, with the lower half of her legs removed from an earlier test, turning her head to look at Kate. The dog's face and body are covered in bone-deep ulcers. A sign on the dog's tight-fitting cage reads, "WINDOW CLEANER TEST NO. 4052849."

A monkey lying on its back, with its stomach opened and the skin pulled away and pinned down on each side, its intestines exposed. He, too, turns his head to stare at Kate. A sign on the cage reads, "ACID BLOCKER TEST NO. 360-1D-G204."

And others, hundreds of them, mutilated, with tubes and wires cruelly stuck in open wounds. They all suffer in silence, and they all turn their heads to stare at Kate.

Kate walks down every aisle, to see every last one of them. To *witness*.

Her path finally leads her back to the door. She walks into the hallway, closes the door behind her, and leans against it. She feels her baby move in her stomach and begins to hear the animals again, as she had in the kitchen of the Jackson home the morning she met Ben.

But this time, rather than voices, she hears animal *sounds*:

Chirping, crying, warbling, bleating, barking, roaring, mewing, growling, quacking, neighing, mooing, trumpeting, baaing, trilling, screaming, gobbling, oinking, hooting, chattering, howling, clucking, squeaking, bellowing, hissing, screeching, whining, whistling, singing, groaning, honking, chittering, clacking, grunting, croaking.

Kate collapses to her knees. She begins to cry. There poor, tortured, helpless babies. There had been another sign—a tiny gold one—on the cat's cage. The cat's name, "Petunia," was printed on it. And one on the dog's cage, "Bailey." And on the monkey's cage, "Dexter." And on the pig's, "Lady."

She clutches her stomach and curls up on the floor in fetal position. Sudden, uninvited images flood her mind. A dog in China being skinned alive. Kate can smell the dog's raw and bloody flesh and hear its screams.

A baby calf, also alive, aware, and screaming, in a Massachusetts slaughterhouse, followed by an image of a runway model strutting her shiny red leather high heels, and then one of a teenaged girl buying a faux fur coat. The coat was not so faux, after all, despite the claim on its tag, having been made in China of dog hair.

"You feel them," her son whispers to her. His wonderful smell fills the air around Kate and soothes her. "The Deor overhead. They are the Apalacheela and the Killapaka. And this is our story."

∞

Kate opened her eyes. Her left hand groped for Ben's right hand on the steering wheel. "I love you, Ben," she murmured, and fell back to sleep. This time, it was dreamless.

The invigorating smell was back in the vehicle. It cooled everyone off. Ben became fully alert again.

~

Annie came up the basement steps. She had just finished organizing the last of the items they had purchased a few hours ago, in Vestal's big box stores.

"There," she said. "Done. Birthing supplies, maternity stuff, etc., all stashed away. We'll just have to wing it if we need anything else. I'm operating under the assumption that Meska won't want us to leave here again, once our guests arrive. Would you like a cup of tea?"

"Sure. Let's have it on the sunporch."

Annie brewed the tea and brought the cups to the all-season porch on the side of the house.

"It will be all right if they stay in our house, rather than one of the guest cottages," Beau said. "It might even be fun. We have three big sofas inside the house. People could crash on those and, if necessary, we could always pull out an air mattress. And don't forget this porch. It's heated and air-conditioned, with its own pellet stove for atmosphere. Out here we have two arm chairs, a big sofa, and that queen-sized sofa bed. All of them are pretty comfortable."

Beau took a drink of his tea, put it down on a side table, and stretched out on a sofa. He closed his eyes. "I think I'll take a nap."

"I wonder how our soon-to-be guests are doing," Annie said to herself. "I hope Meska is able to protect them." She pulled a slender chain from around her neck and fingered the locket that hung from it. Falke, the hawk, was out and about, and not secreted away in Annie's locket. It made her feel better, anyway, just to touch the little charm.

People would be so freaked out if they knew what an awesome being usually hung out in my locket, she thought. And then she thought of the locket Beau always carried in his pocket. Beau's locket was also unoccupied. Seta, the dog, was with Meska the bear, about seventeen hundred miles to the west.

~

Route 81, a north-south passage from Tennessee to the Canadian border, lies in the everyday world. The dimensions *bend* where Route 86, an east-west road, intersects Route 81 to the west of Binghamton, New York. The anomaly was created, millennia ago, by the Mother of the Deor.

Owego is a small village on the Susquehanna River. Route 86 passes by it, on the opposite side of the Susquehanna. Owego lies in the Allegheny Plateau, the northernmost part of Appalachia. The evergreen-covered hills surrounding the village of Owego are steep and loom like gigantic, green tsunamis. A bridge runs over the Susquehanna to the village, at Exit 65.

A singularity begins at the high point of the bridge over the middle of the Susquehanna River, and stretches to the northernmost points of the Finger Lakes. Underground aqueducts spill the essence of the singularity into the Finger Lakes and throughout the southern tier of New York.

Owego is at the heart of the peculiarity. The Iroquois tribes in the region knew this, as did the Nanticokes, who ruled the Owego area until the English and French came. The Onondagas, who under Nanticoke rule occupied what was then called "Ahwage"–until they were driven out by Europeans in the early 1800s–were especially conscious of it.

Countless peoples have moved in the currents of the singularity. It has, among many other things, inspired individuals to become vegans and to create farm sanctuaries, such as the Watkins Glen Farm Sanctuary, the Broome Animal Sanctuary, the Coming Home Sanctuary, the Hullabaloo Farm Sanctuary, the Finger Lakes Farm Sanctuary, and the Happy Compromise Farm, to name a few.

Passengers, in cars moving by on Route 86, can view Owego from across the river. Lights sparkle at night along the little riverwalk, at the edge of the Susquehanna, and on Owego's brick buildings above the river. The bridge ends at the village square, with its bell-towered courthouse and Revolutionary War monuments. A painted, open-front gazebo, not visible from Route 86, is on the other side of the courthouse. Musicians perform in the gazebo, the center of local festivals, throughout warm summer evenings. Well-kept Victorian, colonial, Greek revival, and federal homes–that look like big dollhouses, no two alike–are along Front Street, on the Susquehanna.

A person who sees or enters the village, even with its familiar and ubiquitous donut shop, will feel the enchantment. The individual will not be able to recall the feeling later unless they live in

Owego. Owego residents know about the magic but don't talk about it. Few move away for good. Those who do move never forget the place, but can't remember it exactly as it was.

~

"Here we go again," Eli said. It was his turn at the wheel.

Light-filled fog was rolling into the tree-lined road in front of him. The trees vanished. The truck was moving through a channel that had walls of swirling light. The road was the only visible feature, apart from the tunnel of light that surrounded them. He felt Maya's hand on his arm.

"I don't know what this is, but it makes me feel safe," she said. Her voice was drowsy and calm. She felt like a child being rocked to sleep by her mother.

No humans before them had ever been so protected by Deor. There were so many Deor that their individual forms were almost indistinguishable. The occupants of the sheltered truck, apart from tiny Sam, were unaware of the beings who flew above and around them. They saw only the otherworldly, brilliant, dancing light, and the black asphalt in front of the truck.

More and more Apalacheela joined their entourage. The Cheela came by the hundreds, to ensure nothing prevented the group from getting to Owego. They blanketed the vehicle as it moved east through Kansas, Illinois, Indiana, Ohio, Pennsylvania, and, finally, New York.

The truck arrived in the southern tier of New York with no flat tires and no engine trouble. It was not slowed down by bad weather or major accidents. The Cheela saw to that.

Eli, Ben, and Maya might be oblivious of their fellow travelers and guardians, but the baby growing inside Kate was very aware of them. Kate quickly began to sense what her miniscule son did. She did not sleep for a long time after her terrible dream about the horrific animal testing lab, but instead kept her eyes on the sky and searched for something she could not see.

Seta the dog, who had spread himself directly over the truck, fired his thoughts at Meska the bear. "This is easier than I imagined it would be."

The bear had taken point in front of the vehicle. "The Child is adding his power to our own. His parents also have their own genetic abilities, and are, unconsciously, helping to hold off the Killapaka. They have no idea they are doing it. Even the other two, Eli Jackson and his daughter, are assisting. They are making us stronger."

The Cheela masked the Scent and the occupants of the truck, so well that the Killapaka lost the Scent somewhere in Indiana. Befuddled, they returned home, to Cutter City, to report their failure to their ruler.

"It does not matter. I know where they are going," Saklas informed his frightened disciples.

The motion of the vehicle, and the effort she was unknowingly making to buttress the power of the Cheela, eventually made Kate drowsy. She tried to fight it, but couldn't. She dozed off. No dreams interrupted her slumber.

∞

185

They changed drivers several more times. Eli was again driving, on the morning of the third day since they had left Los Angeles.

As he drove the truck across the bridge into the village of Owego, he asked, "Where to now, Katie?"

Kate rubbed her face. "It's a little fuzzy. I think the baby—"

"Sam," Ben gently corrected. "His name is Sam."

"Sam. I think Sam is trying to tell us that the place we're going is about nine miles out of town. West," Kate said. "He'll let me know if we're going in the right direction, and then I'll let you know."

They came to a small country road on the right.

"This is it," Kate said. She leaned back in her seat.

Kate had, until she'd met the Jacksons, been obsessed with the idea of being independent. That goal, which had driven her all of her life, suddenly seemed irrelevant. She was part of a team now. She needed them and they needed her. She felt a steadiness and strength that had, apparently, always been there. It had just been suppressed, waiting for the right circumstances to emerge.

Green, leafy trees branches met overhead on either side of the road, as they drove up a steep hill. The sun shone through patches in the branches. They felt like they were entering a cathedral. They drove past a few sharp bends in the road, down into a valley, and up another hill.

"Here," Kate said. A narrow driveway on the left wound off into a large grove of pine trees. "Turn into this driveway."

Eli pulled into the drive. He stopped, but let the engine idle.

"I don't see a house from here. What do you think?"

"Keep going. Don't stop," Kate said.

"Ok."

Eli drove the truck slowly up the driveway. A stream went under the pavement through a large pipe. They drove over the stream, around a bend, and spotted the house. It had the appearance of a chalet.

Eli parked in front of the garage, over which the house was built, and turned off the ignition. A series of steps led to decking on the right side of the house. They sat in the car, unsure what to do. A door opened, and a man and a woman emerged from the house onto the top deck.

"Hello," the man called down. "Welcome! Anyone want coffee?"

"Coffee?" the woman asked. "I think we can do a little better than that. Come on in, everyone. I can have breakfast ready in no time."

Annie did not let them talk or even introduce themselves, when the group came up onto the deck and into the house. She eyed the laptop Ben was clutching.

"We've come from Los Angeles," Eli started to explain. "We... we had to leave in a hurry because... because... "

"It's all right," Annie said. "Don't worry about anything, right now. Come on in. Freshen up in the bathrooms, and then have some breakfast. We can talk afterward. We already know a bit about you. And, lucky for us, we're one of the few people in the world who have a true sense of smell, thanks to the facilitation of the De–"

Beau cut her off, whispering, "I don't think they know about the Scent or the Deor, yet."

"Right." Annie turned back to the group. Annie looked directly at Kate. "Anyway, I believe that one of you has what we, in this place, call the "Scent." And we're grateful that we're part of this."

"It's *you*," Beau said, looking at Kate. "*You're* the one." He walked toward her and took a deep breath.

"Leave her alone, honey. Let's feed them."

Eli, Maya, Ben, and Kate suddenly realized that they were thirsty and hungry. Beau waved them over to the table at the side of the room.

"I think caffeine-free tea for you, is that right?" Annie asked Kate.

"That's true," Kate replied. "I'll be laying off caffeine for a while."

"Go on now," Annie said. "One bathroom upstairs and two in the back of the house. Plenty of washcloths and towels. You can all take showers after you eat. Just wash up for now."

The Jacksons and Kate felt like children being ordered around by their grandmother. They were content to feel that way, and did as Annie told them to do.

A pot of hot coffee and a kettle of boiling water for tea were on the stove. Beau grabbed both of those, took them to the table, put them down on trivets, and then brought over mugs, plates, utensils, napkins, and creamers of soy milk, almond milk, and oat milk.

Annie scraped sautéed sliced mushrooms, red onions, garlic, crumbled pressed tofu, and spices from a hot pan on the stove into a large bowl. She ladled vegan refried beans, from another pot, onto a dish. A plate loaded with vegan egg omelets was already on the table, along with a basket of homemade rolls, a small dish with vegan butter, and a bowl of spinach with lemon and garlic. Beau helped Annie carry all of the plates, dishes, and bowls to the table.

Falke had, earlier that morning, returned to the house and instructed the couple to prepare for the four people, and told them when those people would arrive.

"It's a good thing Falke came back this morning and brought us up to speed," Annie said quietly to her husband. "I'm happy to have all this ready for them." Beau nodded, and continued carrying dishes to the table.

The four travelers (who all imagined they should be traumatized by the events of the past four days, but weren't), sat down around the dining room table and let Beau and Annie wait on them. They filled their plates and glanced through French doors on the side of the combination dining room/den space. The doors opened onto an all-season porch, on the side of the home.

They could see, through the large windows in the porch, a strip of pine woods about thirty feet from the side of the house. The little strip was dotted with mountain laurel bushes, azaleas, rhododendron, and a variety of perennial flowers.

Vegetable gardens took up the top half of a large field, past the strip of woods. An array of solar panels filled the lower half. A row of raspberry and blueberry bushes was at the far side of the field, and dense trees beyond them.

The windows at the front of the dining room table provided a view of the half-acre pond that was downslope, several hundred feet below the house.

"Thank you for this," Maya said. "It's awesome."

"Yes. Thank you." Kate said. Ben and Eli both nodded, their mouths full.

Ben swallowed and looked up. "By the way, I'm Benjamin Jackson." He gestured at Kate. "This is Katherine Birdsong, and my uncle, Eli Jackson, and his daughter, Maya."

"Beau and Annie Wald," Beau said. "We know who you are, and we're pleased to meet you."

"How do you... " Ben started to ask, but gave it up, to concentrate on breakfast.

The older couple stood in the kitchen and watched the others eat for a few minutes. Kate crammed a loaded mung bean omelet into her mouth, spilling some of its contents down her shirt.

Beau and Annie glanced at each other. They had already eaten. Each grabbed a cup of coffee and went into the family room, to give the others some privacy for a few minutes.

The Walds were feeling elated. They both wanted to savor their happiness in silence. One of the Children, although unborn, was here and present, under their own roof. And the others! They were undoubtedly special. They had to be. They were related to the Child.

It would be interesting if a scientist could map their genetic structures, Beau thought.

They heard dishes clatter in the sink, fifteen minutes later. They got up to rejoin the group. Eli and Ben were carrying the dishware from the table to the kitchen.

"Nope," Annie said. "Sit down. We'll take care of it. You guys left the West Coast... when?"

"How do you know where we came from?" Ben asked.

"Ok. Let's get this straight," Beau replied. "We know more about your current situation than you do. We just don't know much about *you*, yourselves. Apart from the fact that Kate is pregnant."

"We left three days ago," Maya said. She was still sitting at the table. She yawned.

"Right," Beau said. "Do you have any luggage?"

"Uh... no, no luggage," Eli said. "We left in a hurry." He glanced at Ben. "I mean, Ben does have his laptop. That's about it."

Beau and Annie glanced at each other. "Phones? Other devices? Did you bring any of those?"

"We trashed them. I also disabled the GPS in the truck." Ben answered.

"That was smart, Ben," Annie said. "But do me a favor, and don't turn on your laptop."

Beau started to load the dishwasher, saying, "Ok. You'll probably feel better after you've showered. You'll find assorted bathrobes, pajamas, and slippers in the upstairs guest rooms. One of you can use the shower or the jetted tub in our main bath down here, someone else can use the shower upstairs. There's also a bathtub in the hallway bathroom downstairs. But I suggest you just take quick showers and then go to bed."

"That sounds perfect," Kate said.

Kate and Maya went first, Maya downstairs and Kate upstairs. Maya walked down the hallway next to the kitchen, which dead-ended in a door that opened onto the screened-in back porch. To the left was the hallway bathroom, to the right the primary bedroom and adjoining bath. She noticed the jetted bath in the main bathroom and wondered, if they were going to be staying for a little while, whether she would have the nerve to ask the Walds if she might use it, even though they'd already given all of them general permission.

Ben and Eli showered next, Ben upstairs and Eli down.

The travelers, feeling clean at last, gathered in the large family room. They sat on the three sofas. The sofas were arranged in a U-shape configuration. The four guests were dressed in night clothes and slippers, even though it was 10 o'clock in the morning. They had, per Annie's instructions, deposited their dirty clothes by the clothes washer and dryer next to the master bathroom, downstairs.

"So, can you please tell us what's going on?" Eli asked.

"Sure," Beau replied. "But not now. After you've slept. Suffice it to say that it looks like you're going to be living here for a pretty long time."

"*How* long?" Maya asked.

Kate was sitting on a sofa. She was leaning into Ben. Her eyes were closed.

"We don't know. We do know that you—well, all of us, that is—are safe here. This is the safest place you can be, for now," Annie said. "Look, we do have a lot to tell you. And I'm sure you have a lot to tell us. But you need to sleep first."

She nodded toward Kate. The girl appeared to be asleep already.

"There will be plenty of time to talk, later. Let's get you settled and rested. There are two bedrooms upstairs. Plus, you have these three large sofas in this family room. Decide who is going to sleep where. We'll get sheets and pillows for the sofas. There are other places to sleep in the house, but we'll figure that out later."

Beau added, "Whoever sleeps on a sofa can use the bathroom in the hallway next to the kitchen. We'll keep this door closed, in the meantime, so you won't be disturbed." He pointed to a pocket door which, when shut, separated the family room from the kitchen. "Figure out what you're doing, and we'll get the bedding for the sofa."

The Walds walked out of the room. Annie called back over her shoulder, "We also have two little guest cottages you can check out tomorrow or the next day, after you've recuperated from your trip. But this will do for now. We'll be right back with sheets and pillows."

Two guest houses, Maya thought. She looked forward to seeing them. Where were the other buildings hidden, and what other surprises were in store for them? She turned to the other three. "Ben and Kate will, of course, have one of the bedrooms upstairs. You take the other, Dad. I'll sleep down here."

"No, I will." Eli glanced at the front door. There were actually two entrances to the house off the front deck, one to the kitchen and one to the family room.

"Yeah, that's right Dad. You can protect us from whatever's out there that's coming to get us. I'm sure it'll be coming right through that door." Maya raised her index finger toward a three-foot tall, painted wood, pink flamingo that stood guard in a corner of the room. "Maybe use that as a weapon." She grinned.

The Walds came back into the room. Their arms were loaded with piles of pillows, sheets, and blankets. They dropped the piles onto one of the sofas. Annie walked around the room to close the shades and pull the curtains over the large windows, to block out the morning sunlight.

Beau grabbed a remote control from the large, oak entertainment center that faced the sofas. He tossed it to Eli. "This controls the mini-split." He nodded at the HVAC unit at the top of one wall of the family room. "Use the AC if it gets too warm in here."

"We can't thank you enough... ," Eli began. Beau cut him off. "Stop. We're just as grateful that you're here. We've been waiting *years* for this day."

Annie pulled Beau from the room. "Pretend it's nighttime," she called back, over her shoulder. "Sleep well." She drew the pocket door closed behind her.

Maya went upstairs, to the bedroom on the back side of the house. It had a view of the field on the side, and of the dark forest behind the house. Ben and Kate took the front upstairs bedroom, with its view of the field on one side, and the big pond in the front.

There were fans in both rooms and the windows were open. They immediately turned on the fans, and then hit the beds.

Eli took Ben's suggestion and turned on the AC. He tucked a sheet into the cushions on a sofa, moved a pillow to one end, collapsed on top of the sofa, pulled a light blanket over his head, and crashed.

∞

The Jacksons and Kate slept around the clock. They awoke at 10 a.m. the following morning, roused by the smells of cooking food. Ben and Kate stayed in bed for a few minutes. Their bodies were tightly pressed together.

"You know we can't make love again until after he... Sam is born," Kate said. "He's fully aware. It would be too weird."

"Yes. That would be bizarre," Ben agreed. He pressed his lips against the back of her neck and got a mouthful of hair. It was beyond his comprehension that he could be so completely mesmerized by another person and, apparently, she by him. He'd known Kate for less than a week, but could not imagine life without her. They could wait until after Sam was born to start a healthy, active sexual relationship. He was happy just to have this strange and unique girl in his arms.

The Jacksons and Kate again took turns showering. It felt, after their long journey, like a luxury. Dressed, they made their way to the enclosed sunroom. They sat in their freshly washed clothes (courtesy of Annie) in cushioned chairs or on a sofa. They placed their mugs and platefuls of food on the coffee table and end tables. The four newcomers were content to sit on the porch, eat at their leisure, and take in the views.

Annie brought Kate a second cup of non-caffeinated ginger mint tea with oat milk and a dash of almond milk.

"Umm," Kate said, taking a sip. "This is delicious. Thank you."

Beau followed behind Annie, carrying a cup of coffee. "Ok. I guess it's time to have a talk. Should we go first, or do you want to tell us your story?" he asked.

"I'd like to hear *their* story first." Annie said. She was sitting back in a chair. Her feet were propped on an ottoman. The Scent filled the room and, in fact, the entire house. She savored it. "Beau and I have been in suspense, the entire time you were sleeping, as to how it is you've brought a Child and the Scent into our home."

"Wait," Ben said. "That's what you're calling the wonderful smell, the smell that apparently started to come out of Kate's pores, the moment we conceived the child she's carrying. The scent?"

"The Scent with a capital S," Beau replied. "It's a specific term with a specific definition.

Long story. It's actually at the heart of a very old prophecy. Normally, I would say that you weren't going to believe it. I'm guessing you'll be open to what we have to say, under the circumstances, and after what you've probably seen or experienced for yourselves, by now."

"It's also Child with a capital C," Annie added, "which, too, is part of the prophecy. Anyway, tell us about yourselves first. Then, we promise, we'll tell you everything we know."

"Yes," Beau agreed. "You have to go first because, when we tell you our side of it, you might be too flabbergasted to tell us your story. For a while, anyway."

Ben shook his head. "Ok," he said. "Here goes. But I think Uncle Eli and Maya should start. Tell everyone how they met Katie and why she was at our house, in the first place." He looked at his uncle and cousin. "Even *I* don't know that part of it."

Eli began. He told them about the unusual placement of the girl on his carpentry team. The smell he was getting from her that reminded him, somewhat, of Maya's. Mr. Poggi's confession about why the man had hired her.

Maya picked up the story at that point. She described her immediate connection with Kate. She stopped, and looked at Kate.

Kate nodded, and said, "I told Maya about my background and some of my experiences in the foster care system. I was pretty emotional. Maya was kind enough to ask me to come to her and her dad's house for dinner. We ate, and then I fell asleep in her bedroom. I woke up the next morning and came down to the kitchen. And there was Ben."

Ben smiled. "Yes. There *I* was, about to come face-to-face with the person I now know was my missing half. The instant we laid eyes on each other... "

"You and Ben passed right out and collapsed on the floor!" Maya exclaimed.

"The kitchen went crazy," Eli added. "The oven door flew open. Things were falling over and breaking and spilling their contents. And some kind of major windstorm happened outside. And the smells... the "Scent" thing... was *everywhere*."

"It stopped after what seemed, to us, like just a few seconds," Maya said. "Everything went back to normal as soon as Ben and Kate recovered. And then we realized it was dark outside. We checked the time and it was almost midnight."

"And what was going on with you two during that time?" Annie asked. She looked at Ben and Kate. It was clear to her that a major event had occurred while they were, apparently, unconscious.

"Well, we were... we were somewhere else," Kate replied. "Like in a meadow, in a forest. But there were these... these big *light* things, all around us."

"They were *animals*, but they were made of light particles. The motes moved so fast that you couldn't follow them with your eyes," Ben said. "They were speaking to us, in a chorus."

"And then we made love," Kate said. Her voice was light, and matter-of-fact.

Eli and Maya looked at her. Maya's mouth gaped. "You *what*?"

"Come on, cuz. Are you saying the fact that Kate and I made love in a dream-place is weirder than anything that's happened to us since?" Ben asked.

Maya looked down, shaking her head.

Kate continued, pretending to ignore the interaction between the cousins. "In short, Ben and I came out of whatever it was. Eli and Maya cleaned up the kitchen and went to bed. Ben and I went out onto the gazebo in the back garden, made love–for *real*, this time–and then I woke up around 3:00 a.m., pregnant, and with the fetus speaking to me."

Maya and Eli looked up. "You made love for real," Maya said. "You only knew each other for a few hours. I don't get it. Knowing you Ben, and sort of knowing you, Kate, that's about as strange as anything else that has happened."

Ben smiled at Maya. "I know, right? But, to continue, I put my hand on Kate's stomach, when she woke me up with her story about being pregnant and the baby talking to her. You probably won't be surprised to learn that Sam talked to me, too. He made it clear that all of us had to vacate the premises, immediately."

"Sam?" Annie asked.

"Yes, Sam. That's his name. I've been dreaming about him all my life."

Annie took a good look at Ben and Kate. Their eyes were glowing, and almost seemed to be on fire. The two were in continual contact, one with a hand on the other's knee, or stroking the other's hair, or twining their fingers together.

They spoke in quiet, measured tones, but their words impacted Annie as though they were shouting into a bullhorn placed next to her ear.

Yes, these two were definitely the parents of the first Child, the boy. Kate and Ben seemed to have a bit of the Deor in them. That was impossible, though. They were human. Human, but infused with Living World magic. Annie had always thought that she and Beau were a perfect couple, but these two...

"About those dreams you've had of Sam," Beau said. "Can you give us an idea of what they were about?"

Ben nodded. "It started when I, myself, was a young boy." He could now remember the dreams in detail. He gave them an abridged version, finishing with, "And my laptop. I brought it because I'd typed words that made no sense to me, right when I was waking up. Now, I'm starting to get it."

"Those were some amazing dreams," Beau said. He turned to Annie. "Imagine spending an entire night dreaming of floating on a cloud above the Earth, accompanied by a magical little boy."

"You're right," Ben agreed. "It's wonderful that I can recall them now. But there's something else that may be tied into all of this. I used to sleep out on the gazebo at Uncle Eli's, fairly often." He turned his head to his uncle. "I never mentioned this to you—because I didn't think anyone would believe me—but I would get visitors out there. Toads. Little ones, medium-sized ones, big ones. There was always this one little guy who stayed right next to me while I was out there.

Maya looked at her father with a, "See? I-told-you-so expression on her face."

"And, the night Kate and I slept on the gazebo... " He stopped, lifted Kate's hand, and kissed it. She smiled. "They were *back*," Ben continued. "I saw their eyes, all around the gazebo, in the middle of the night."

Kate and Annie spoke at the same time.

"I think I met him!" Kate said. "When I was going into the gazebo."

"Deor," Annie said to Beau.

"What? Dee-who?" Eli asked.

"Yup," Beau said to Annie. "Falke said that the Jackson home was protected. By a knot of toads, no less."

Annie laughed.

"What are you talking about? What is a Deor? What is a knot of toads? Who is Falke?" Eli asked.

"Hold off and finish your story, please. We'll get to all that," Beau replied.

"There isn't that much left to tell," Eli said. "The kids woke us up and said we had to get out of there. We listened to them, for some reason. We drove for almost a full day. We stopped near Denver to rest. Kate woke us up after a few hours." He nodded at her. "She said we had to get back on the road and couldn't stop to rest until we reached our destination, because something was after us."

Maya jumped in. "Don't forget that amazing smell in the car, Dad." She looked at Beau. "That Scent of yours. None of us needed to eat or drink or sleep. We felt like we could drive forever."

"And there's another thing," Kate looked down at her feet. "When we were leaving Denver, the Scent, as you call it, went away. And with it, the astonishing feeling we'd had." She turned to the others. "Remember? It got hot and muggy? And then you know how your head gets heavy and drowsy, when it's too hot, and you feel like you can't breathe? I felt like my lungs were being crushed. I fell asleep, but it wasn't a good sleep. And, I had a dream."

The words were rushing out of her now.

"I was in an animal testing lab. I saw what corporations do to animals. When they're testing hair products and cosmetics and lotions and dyes and detergents and pharmaceuticals. This is not the first time I've had this type of nightmare, and I've seen other things, cruel and terrible things. The most horrible nightmares you could imagine.

"There's been this... man, I guess you could call him, in some of them. A terrible person. He made it clear that he was coming for me." She considered, for a moment. "But now, I think, he's actually coming for Sam."

Beau wrinkled his forehead. Annie looked perplexed.

Kate's throat was dry, and she coughed. Ben picked up her cup of tea from the coffee table and handed it to her. She took a sip. Ben put the cup back on the table and put his arm around her.

Kate found her voice again. "Sam spoke to me, when I was waking up from the first dream. I remember his words exactly. I've played them over and over in my head since."

"Why didn't you tell me?" Ben asked.

"I... I didn't know what he was talking about, and I didn't know how to explain it. I still don't." She turned to Beau and Annie. "But I have a feeling that *you* do."

"What did Sam say to you?" Annie's voice was gentle.

"He said, 'You feel them. The Deor overhead. They are the Apalacheela and the Killapaka. And this is our story.'"

"Oh. Wow." Beau stared at the four travelers. "You have no idea how lucky you are that you made it here."

Annie said, "The Kills were *right there*." She had directed those comments at Beau, but now turned to the others. "It was fortunate the Cheela got there in time to hide you."

"Oh, boy," Eli interjected. "Kills. Cheela. I believe it's your turn now."

"Wait," Ben said. "I've got a question, off-topic, but it's bugging me. You've got a small pond by the driveway, and another big one—I guess we are in the Finger Lakes region—and all these trees, yet I don't see a single bird or squirrel, or any other animal." Ben was always aware of animals. "Where are they?"

"Oh, believe me, they're around." Beau gave Ben a small, enigmatic smile.

Annie pulled her shoulders back. "Well, it's our turn. Beau's going to start off by telling you the little we know about something called the "Living World." Before he does that, could you guys write down your clothes sizes? We've tried to stockpile some clothes in different sizes, but I don't know if they'll fit. We're not supposed to leave this property anymore, and we're supposed to limit deliveries here. You'll understand why, in a bit. I do think it's worth chancing one more big, online order. I'll get paper and pens, so you can write down your info. Shoe sizes as well."

"Use this to pay for whatever you get," Eli said. He pulled out his wallet and started to select a credit card. "I can also have the funds in my checking and savings accounts transferred here."

Annie looked at him. "Right. Use one of *your* credit cards and have your funds transferred here. Not the best idea." She walked into the kitchen, opened a drawer, and grabbed a pad of paper and some pens.

"Oh, yeah, I guess you're right. If anybody is searching for us, our credit cards and our bank accounts would be the first things they'd monitor. Well, I do have a little cash on me."

"Don't worry about it, Eli," Beau said. "From here on out, you're going to have to start thinking of us as family. We're in this together. What's ours is yours, except our bedroom. We're not giving that up." He glanced at Annie, who was returning from the kitchen, and smiled. "Anyway, we've put away a bit of money over the years, with a lot of help from others."

"Others?" Ben asked.

"Why don't you stop being so mysterious and just tell them, already?" Annie asked.

She was tearing off paper from the pad and passing that and the pens around.

"Can you start with why we have to stay here?" Eli asked. "And, more importantly, who or what is after us?

"The *Scent*," Annie replied. "We have to stay here because of the Scent. It's all over this house now. I imagine it permeates my clothing. Regular people aren't able to perceive it, but there are others who can. It's not an issue, as long as we stay put. We're right at the edge of the Motherland, and we're especially safe here. All of Owego is fairly safe. We just don't want to take any unnecessary chances."

"In case of spies," Beau added.

"Right at the edge of the *Motherland*," Maya repeated. "What does that even *mean*? I think I'm going to have a stroke, if you don't tell us what's going on."

Annie touched Beau's shoulder. "You're up, sweetheart."

Kate put her lips against Ben's ear and whispered, "Awww. That's so sweet. I hope we're like that when *we're* old."

Beau stood, walked over to the back of the sunroom, and looked up at the forest. "I'll begin by explaining who the Deor are."

Part III

Chapter 1

The Legend of the Deor

Earth was one of the fortunate planets which was infused with a consciousness. It called itself the Living World. There was no life on the planet, other than that of the Living World.

The omnipotent entity's natural state was a dream-filled sleep. It dreamt of the past, the present, and the future. The entity knew there was loneliness in its future, unless it did something about it. So, it decided to do something.

It awoke from its long dream. It stretched, and oceans and rivers were born. It yawned, and flora sprang from the earth. All of that pleased the Living World, but it was not enough.

It realized it needed to make a big effort. It pulled heat, magma, and light to itself and, from that, created two powerful entities, the Father and the Mother.

The Father and the Mother perceived each other's strong presence. They instantly came together like opposite magnetic poles and joined, once. In that moment, the entire Animal Kingdom—which the Living World christened the "Deor"—was made.

The Deor were born in hydrothermal vents, as glittering, light-filled microorganisms. They communicated with each other by manipulating motes of light. Light was their sustenance, be it sunlight, starlight, moonlight, phosphorescence, or firelight.

The Deor gradually evolved, and began to select their individual forms.

The Living World was not pinned to Time. It understood the entirety, from beginning to end, of what would or could happen on Earth. It counseled the Deor that, as they moved on to more and more complex shapes, it would be good for them to leave behind physical manifestations of the prior forms they were discarding.

The Deor followed the Living World's instructions. They effortlessly fashioned from matter—as they allowed their shapes to evolve and to become more complex—those remains which would later become known to humans as "fossils."

The Living World created early humans—beginning with an ape, which was the only non-Deor animal ever to be created, and which evolved into Homo habilis—millennia after the Deor were well established.

The Father and the Mother did not understand what humans could add to this world. They did understand, however, that only the Living World was privy to the big picture.

The Living World planted, in a few, random humans, the genetic seeds that would one day evolve into two very special Children. Satisfied, the Living World settled back into its long slumber.

Humankind evolved. And then it began to take notice of the Deor.

Deor, in their natural forms, appeared as huge, winged beings of moving light to the human eye. They were difficult and terrifying to observe. Many humans went into mankind's default mode when faced with the unknown which, of course, meant that they began to worship the Deor.

The Mother was appalled at the notion of any creature idolizing another one. She did not know how to address the issue. She could not see anything good coming from it. She decided to seek counsel from the Living World.

This required that she fall asleep and enter the Living World's long dream. The Mother did so. She slept for centuries–which she had not intended–during which time she communed with her maker.

The Father did not wait for the Mother to return to him from her dream. He was disinterested in the Living World's verdict. He traveled, while she slept, to the places where his children were treated as idols by the local populations of early humans.

He spent time in each of the continents. He witnessed, in each of them, (except Antarctica) humans sacrificing to the Deor their enemies, their slaves, their virgin women, and their own young. He liked what he saw.

The Deor who lived with the Mother in her home, in the northeastern part of what would eventually be the United States, waited by her side as the endless years went by, and as the Living World showed the Mother what it believed would come to pass.

The Mother finally awoke. The Deor who had stayed by her side welcomed her back with delight.

She had seen the probable future, hers and theirs. Sadness was a condition formerly foreign to her. It bled from her now.

Meska the bear had become the effective leader of the Deor while their Mother slept. The Mother now asked the bear to gather representatives of the Deor from all over the world. Meska did as she asked. The Deor came.

The Mother told them, in a grave tone, that endless war would result from humankind's worship of the Deor. Enough damage had already been done that it was impossible for it not to occur. It was, however, possible to limit the coming destruction. Humans could not live with Deor until humans evolved.

The Mother requested that the Deor conceal themselves from humans in flesh and blood, animal bodies. She further asked that they submit, in these flesh and blood bodies to humans, until such time that the Living World determined men and women were ready to meet the Deor in their true forms.

The Deor were *desolate*. Give up their forms of light, and become matter? Submit to humans? The Deor were beings of joy, love, and peace. They understood that taking on physical forms, and allowing humans to dominate them, would cause the Deor immeasurable grief, loss, and pain. She told them that this was the only way their interactions with humans would not result in idol worship and war—war that would inevitably result in the final deaths of all of the Deor—as shown to her by the Living World.

But the Mother did offer them hope. She told them that the Living World had implanted a specific genetic code within a few individuals in the human race. The coding would, one day far in the future, cause two special, human Children to be born. The coming of the Children would be the Living World's pronouncement that men and women were evolved enough to meet the true Deor.

She explained that, as humans were the cause of the original problem, humans would have to be the corrective catalyst.

The two Children would have a gift. Their abilities would make it possible for Deor, unmasked, to live on this planet *alongside* humans. The Deor would know the Children by the Scent the Children manifested. The Mother listed the components of the Scent: lotuses, oranges, peppermint, fir needles, vanilla, cinnamon, and rain.

She also told them that some of the Deor, including Meska, should retain–for the majority of the time–their true forms. Those Deor would be responsible for connecting with and protecting the Children, and for bringing back the other Deor from their physical forms, when it was time.

The Mother dismissed them. She was listless and forlorn. She retreated, to be alone.

The Deor complied with her requests. The translation, into human speech, of that which they called their flesh and blood animal forms was "Camaflur."[5]

---

[5] The word might actually have been the origin of another word, spelled "camoufleur," which referred to someone skilled in the art of camouflage, and might also have been the origin of the French word "camouflet," which could translate to "a whiff of smoke blown in the face."

And so, the Deor became Camaflur, simple flesh and blood animals, condemning themselves to endless, painful cycles of birth and death. A Deor who died in a Camaflur animal body was immediately reborn, to start the cycle over. No Deor could be permanently destroyed, unless it was killed while in its true Deor form. This was quite difficult to do, except when the assassin was another Deor.

Residing for thousands of years in flesh and blood bodies, and dying in them, and being reborn, and dying again, and being reborn, was an insidious process.

Most of those who lived in their Camaflur bodies eventually lost themselves, lost their identities. They forgot their origins. They forgot that they were Deor. They were conscious and aware, and could feel pain, happiness, family bonding, and loss. Their little Camaflur animal brains, however, could not retain the knowledge and memory of who they really were (just as humans with their little animal brains could not remember who *they* really were).

The Camaflur animals, who so forgot, began to prey on each other.

The Father saw the transition, saw what had happened to his offspring. He was incensed that his children had assumed weak animal bodies, enraged that they were beginning to eat each other, and furious with the Mother for creating such a situation. The Deor had voluntarily diminished themselves, and made themselves subservient to a cruel and opportunistic race.

He believed the Mother's prediction about the future of the world, if the Deor did not do as she asked. He believed it was truly what the

211

Living World had foreseen and had revealed to her. He also believed that two human Children, who were destined to reconcile the Deor with humanity, would one day be born.

It did not matter. This was not *his* plan. *His* plan was for the human race—which was reveling in, and rationalizing, the enslavement and torture of his children—to become vassals themselves and, ultimately, to be wiped off the face of the Earth, altogether.

∞

The Father returned home. He was in a rage.

"Leave!" he roared at the Deor.

"Leave," the Mother whispered to them.

She knew what was going to happen. The Living World had shown her. She did not want any of her children to be injured or killed, in a fruitless attempt to protect her.

The Father attacked her as soon as the Deor had fled. She fought back, but was quickly overwhelmed.

The Father murdered his former partner. He ripped apart the light from which she was made. He threw it to the four corners of the Earth. There were no witnesses.

The Father knew that his act would rouse the Living World. The Living World knew everything. He began to feel it stir.

He had, in his travels, found Deor, here and there, who wanted the same things *he* wanted. He called to them and they came. He told them of his crime.

Together, they fled to the Midwest and hid in the land that would later be known as the Cutter City Park.

The Father had often observed the Mother, while he had lived with her, allowing some of her magic and power to seep into the ground, air, and water of their home. This made their habitat more suited to them and to their children, and caused their very surroundings to protect them.

He now imparted some of his own power and magic to his followers. He gave even more to one particular follower, a goat, whose name was Saklas. The Father put Saklas at his right hand.

Saklas determined that the Deor who followed the Father were something altogether new. They were no longer just Deor—they were *more* than that. They agreed to call themselves the Killapaka, which translated to "The True People Who Are the Eaters of Men."

"Kills," for short.

The Father also allowed some of his capacity to seep into the ground, air, and water around him in the Cutter City Park, as the Mother had done at their home.

He did this for two reasons. He concentrated the power and caused it to act as a magnet for the forbears of at least one of the two promised Children. He hoped, through that measure, to be able to find the Child when it was born, before anyone else could. He would capture the Child, control it, and use whatever power it had to reshape the world in accordance with his own vision.

He also compelled his surroundings to disguise and protect him and the Killapaka from the Living World.

This attempt did not work. His act of destroying the Mother had caused the Living World to come to full consciousness. It went after him.

He ran. He left his followers behind.

∞

Most of the Deor were stricken at the loss of their Mother. They did not know what had happened to her. She was simply *gone*. They began a frantic, worldwide search. No one could detect a trace of her.

They mourned, but did not stop following her instructions. They continued to submit to humankind. They believed that, if they were good and obedient children, she would come back to them.

They were spread throughout the world. Those in the Midwest who witnessed the rise of the Killapaka in that area took on their Deor forms and flew home.

"It is safe for us to be in our Deor forms here, in our Mother's home," Meska said. "We have to remain so, and we must remember who we are. We must do more than just *wait* for the Children, though. We cannot allow the Killapaka Deor to find them and take control of their power. It is certain that the Killapaka will want to use the Childrens' power–whatever that power is–to subjugate, or even exterminate, humans. That is not the result that the Living World or our Mother intended. We have to actively work toward her goal, which is humans and Deor reconciled and living side-by-side."

This faction of Deor decided to call themselves the Apalacheela ("Students of the Path"), or Cheela for short, to distinguish themselves from the Killapaka.

The Cheela did not know that their Father had murdered their Mother. They waited for her to come home. They went about their business, in the meantime.

∞

The Killapaka were bereft, at first, when their Father fled. The Living World hunted only the Father. It left the Killapaka alone and to their own devices. The Kills hoped to rejoin their Father, so they, too, hunted him. They were able to trace his flight to the eastern seaboard.

There, the salty ocean water ate his trail.

Time passed. Most of the Deor were patient, even those who were not part of the Apalacheela core group in the Motherland. They believed the suffering and agony that they had endured and continued to endure, over their countless life cycles, was the price for the future foreseen by the Living World, and by their Mother.

The Deor created a "Creed," over millennia. It was a plural first-person narrative, with an intended audience of future humans. The Creed set forth the Mother's story, and also affirmed the resolve of the Deor.

Some of the Deor, however, became angry and resentful. They began to hate humans for their selfish, callous, and violent exploitation of animals. These Deor were drawn to the views of the Killapaka. They joined the Killapaka, by ones

215

and by twos, and then by dozens, and then by the hundreds, and then by the thousands.

The Kills intended to take charge of their own destiny. They rejected the Mother's request. Forget the so-called flesh-and-blood Camaflur bodies. They were *Deor*.

They hid. They watched for thousands of years and debated what they should do. They finally determined, by the second decade of the 1800s, what their ultimate goal was and how to achieve it. The first step was to acquire wealth and property, and to become integrated into the human culture. They would use the human's own systems against them.

~

Beau talked, and talked, and talked. He allowed no interruptions or questions. "When I've finished," he said, when a stunned Eli tried, for the third time, to get clarification of a specific point or two.

They stopped for a lunch and bathroom break, and then Beau went on with the narrative. He related the story of the Living World, the history of the Deor,[6] and the Children.

Annie took over, at that point, and described the Apalacheela and their opponents, the Killapaka. "The Killapaka want to dominate people. They want to switch places with humans and become sovereign."

---

[6] The Apalacheela and, thus, the Walds, did not know that the Father had murdered the Mother; so, this part of the story was missing.

"Which we never should have been in the first place," Beau grumbled.

Annie continued. She explained how flesh-and-blood animals were in what they called "Camaflur" forms.

"It's important for you to know that some of the Deor attach themselves to specific individuals, for reasons that are related to their prophecy. Such a lucky person is allowed to carry a Deor in a further disguised "Masque" shape, which appears as a tiny, gold, animal-shaped charm."

"A charm? These gigantic Deor can live in a small talisman?" Ben rubbed his head. He should be thinking the old couple were senile, and that his family should be getting out of there. Instead, he was a rapt audience member. "You've obviously seen some of the Deor. Can you describe what they look like?"

"It's hard to describe what the Deor look like, in their true forms," Beau said. "You're just going to have to see for yourselves."

Kate rubbed her stomach. She felt more comfortable and at home than she had anywhere else, including the Jacksons'.

"So, our baby is one of these Children. And he's supposed to change the world."

"Yes," Beau said. "Not only one of the Children, but the first. The boy who is "awake" from the moment of conception, and able to use some of his powers. Whatever they may be."

"That's why he's been able to communicate with us," Ben said. He, too, felt amazingly snug, secure, and relaxed.

217

"How does he communicate with you?" Annie asked.

She was sitting next to her husband at a round table on the sunporch. Ben and Kate were leaning against each other on a sofa on the far side of the room. Maya and Eli were sprawled in lounge chairs.

"The knowledge of what he's conveying is just, suddenly, there in my head," Kate replied.

"Same thing with me," Ben added. "I put my hand on Kate's abdomen, and then I know what he wants me to know. I don't hear actual words."

"Happened to me, too," Maya said.

Everyone else in the room looked at Kate's flat belly. No one had the nerve to ask her if they could touch it, in light of what Ben had said. They wanted to do it even more than they had before, though. They'd ask later. Maybe.

"And what do you think about everything we've told you?" Annie asked.

"We have every reason to believe you, based on what we, ourselves, have experienced in the past few days," Eli replied. "It's pretty scary to think that those things–those Kills–were after us. *Are* after us. As for them... " He waved at Ben and Kate. "Your story explains a lot. I have one more reason to accept the account. I'll go into that after you've finished. You were talking about the Deor Creed, Beau. Do you know what it says? It would help to complete your narrative, in my mind."

Beau turned toward his wife. "Annie?"

"Sure, I'll be right back."

Annie stood and walked into the house. She retrieved her laptop from her bedroom and brought it back to the porch. She sat down next to Beau again, flipped open the laptop, and pulled up a document.

"I typed it up, at the Deor's request. They gave me the wording for some additional elements, to bring it into today's world. I don't recall if Beau explained to you *why* the Deor composed the Creed, in the first place."

Eli shook his head.

"There are several reasons. They wanted to memorialize the story their Mother told them, and the history of their current plight. Some of them thought that, when the Children arrived and the Deor were finally able to show themselves to people, the Creed would serve as an *introduction*. A first contact, if you will, to lay the groundwork for what would come afterward."

"Plus, their Creed gives them a focus. It gives the Deor the strength to carry out their Mother's wishes," Beau added, "despite how horrific it's been. I mean, think about being born into the body of a pig or a steer or a chicken. You know that, every time you die, you're going to be reborn as a flesh and blood animal, and you're going to die another terrifying, agonizing death in some ghastly slaughterhouse, or by some other, equally horrible means. And that, if you wanted to, you could just say "screw it," and go back to your natural form. But if you did that, you'd be disloyal to the Mother and...."

"Here you go." Annie stood, interrupting Beau's chain of thought. She handed the laptop to Eli. "Years ago, I asked Falke... " She paused. "I guess I should tell you, right now, that Beau and I both carry Deor with us... "

"Say what?" Kate asked.

"They're usually in Masque form. Falke is a hawk, who often stays in a locket hanging from my necklace. Seta is a dog, who often stays with Beau as a trinket in his pocket."

Eli did not seem surprised. He just nodded. Annie didn't know if Eli was nodding like a shell-shocked person, or to indicate his understanding.

"Anyway, I asked Falke to repeat it to me, slowly enough so that I could type it out. I've also saved it on a couple of flash drives. Read the document I've pulled up on the laptop," she said.

Eli glanced at the other three in his party, and then began to read aloud from the document:

The Deor Creed

We were here before you. The Living World gave birth to our Mother and our Father in violent volcanic eruptions, at the beginning of this world.

Our parents, as one, created us.

And then the Living World thought it good to fashion your distant ancestors.

Your slope-skulled forebears stretched upright, to pull the curves from their spines, and began to walk on two legs. Their attention—like that of their early quadrupedal relatives—was focused on avoiding foes and on finding food, water, partners, good spots to defecate, and safe and warm or cool sleeping places.

They were blind to us, at first, but soon they were able to open their eyes wide enough to see us. We were in the trees, in the clouds, in the rays of light, in the shadows, in the rivers, in the streams, in the mountaintops, and in the holes in the ground. They were able to see us and our glowing wings and eyes and bodies.

The brains of those early people worked the way yours do. They studied the problem of what it was they had seen. They came to a conclusion which seemed right to them, but which was a fallacy. They determined that we were divinities. And so, they fell to the ground, prostrated themselves to us, and slavered like dunces.

Most of us slipped away into the mist to flee the uncomprehending, demanding devotion in your distant relatives' eyes.

A few of us did not. These prideful Deor became the prototypes for your gods, your angels, and your demons. They are the one who laid the foundation for the mythologies of your ancient and current religions.

Our Mother reflected on the newly surfaced concept of worship. She feared that your useless adulation would taint and consume you, and would result in a world of turmoil and madness. She conferred with the Living World, in a dream.

When she finally left the dream, she told us that the only outcome of your devotion was utter devastation, to humans and to us. She intervened, in an attempt to mitigate the coming destruction.

Her intervention consisted of the following: She told us to change ourselves, to change our forms and substances, to the extent that you would no longer fall down on your faces when we were near. She advised us how to make the transformation.

She told us to hide right before your eyes in bodies which you, in your conceit, would believe were inferior to your own. She said that we were to live alongside you and under the same rules of survival that govern you.

We were to permit you to subjugate us, if you were so inclined. We were to do these things for the millennia it would take you to develop and evolve. Some of you would, eventually, begin to awaken and shake off the sleep that fogged your minds, at which juncture two of your Children would wake the rest of the human race.

These two Children would force you to see our souls, and who we truly are. And then we were to teach you.

Our Mother instructed us not to hate you, no matter what your species did.

She provided us with the details of the Scent of the two Children, so that we would be able to know and find them. She told us that the first of the Children would be a boy. The boy would be awake, and coming into his power, from the moment of his conception, and would, immediately, be known to us.

The other, a girl, would come later. Her life would be difficult, and the power within her would remain in hiding, to keep her safe. She, and her power, would not awaken until she turned nine years old.

We cannot hide and raise the Children in the heart of the Motherland, because it would be difficult for them to leave. Moreover, they

222

must be enculturated by humans. Their mission requires that they go willingly out into the world of the human race.

We love our Mother. We obeyed her. We made the transformation and put on these shapes. That act was a steep price. It was paid, not just for your stupidity, but also for the pride of the scant few of us who had enjoyed your adoration and who had believed it to be merited.

Then, our Mother disappeared. She no longer spoke to us. We could not find her, nor could we *feel* her. She is not under, above, or around us, anymore. There is an awful silence in her place.

We have debated the issues of what she meant by your becoming awake, and how—and what—we are supposed to teach you. We have not discussed the absence, or even the possible death, of our Mother. We try to think about it, and we recoil. The thought cycles, similar to the way a human touches a bad tooth with a tongue, flinches back, returns to the inflammation, withdraws, and then touches the hot spot again.

A small percentage of you are still able to sense us. Those of you who do not sense us at all—and even some who do—put us in cages, eat us, rip off our skins to make coats, shoes, and bags. Grind up our hooves to make cheese and gelatin. Melt down our flesh for shampoos and cosmetics. Scrape the insides of our stomachs for our enzymes, to be used in your breads and cheeses and gelatins. Pull collagen from our connective tissue, joints, skin, and bones, so that you can smear it on your faces

223

and bodies and pretend that you are not getting older. Burn our discarded, plundered remains into char, to be used in processing your sugar. We suffer.

The world was full of joy, before you came. Now it is full of your narcissistic cruelty and ignorance. We wish that we could hate you, but our Mother forbade it, and we honor her. We live, we are tormented, we die, and we are reborn, to be tormented anew. We suffer.

Even in our flesh and blood animal bodies, we are graceful and exquisite and full of spirit. The most beautiful of you are caricatures of what we were, and what we still are, in our camouflages of flesh. We suffer.

Do not ever forget that *we* are the prototypes of your gods, your angels, and your demons, and that out of us sprang your religions and heavens, and your hells.

Eli finished reciting the text on the laptop. He sighed. "This is a *lot* to process."

"I think you're doing amazingly well, so far," Beau responded.

"It's like we thought we knew so much about the world, and we really know nothing at all," Maya said.

"Some person, over a century and a half ago, learned about the Deor and the Creed and the Children. She wrote a story about it," Annie said. "The author called it *The World Tilters*. She must have been close to one or more of the Deor. I keep meaning to ask Falke about it. And I wonder how many people read it and dismissed it as fantasy?

"Anyway, we've been talking all day. I need a volunteer to help make dinner."

"I make a pretty good vegan stew," Maya said. "I'm assuming you guys are also vegans."

Beau smiled. "Goes without saying."

"Why don't you show me around the kitchen, then, and I'll take over? You've done enough for us already. I need to feel useful. Cooking helps calm me down, and allows me to think."

"She makes a pretty good vegan everything," Eli noted.

"Works for me," Annie said. "Just go ahead and root around in there. See where things are for yourself. That'll be easier than me showing you. And there's a big full pantry in the hallway beyond the kitchen. If you need some other stuff, let me know. I'm sure we'll have whatever it is, in the basement supplies."

"Speaking of the basement and supplies, we'll take you on a tour of the place tomorrow," Beau said. "I think you're going to be pleasantly surprised."

"That'll be interesting," Annie whispered to him.

"Yeah," he whispered back. "Wait 'til they get a load of the "forest.""

∞

The group had Maya's vegan stew with a side of bread for dinner, once again, on the all-season porch. Kate and Ben cleared the dishes and did the washing up, and then went back to the porch and settled onto a sofa. They stretched their legs.

"So... animals are Deor. And because we're at the edge of the Motherland, they're in their actual

225

forms. Rather than their flesh-and-blood bodies, which you say are their Camaflur shapes," Ben said. "If that's the case, where are they? Why can't we see them?"

"Give it a little time," Annie replied. "They don't want to overwhelm you. How about this? We'll introduce you to them tomorrow."

Maya looked at her father, and then at Kate, and then at Ben. "This is going to be something."

Annie and Beau got up to bring out a bottle of cabernet and four glasses. Kate, of course, could not partake, and Ben decided to join her in her abstinence. He smirked. "You're too young to drink legally, anyway." Kate looked at the bottle and made a face. "Yuck."

They sat in silence for the next hour. No one was tired. They were energized and, at the same time, relaxed. They were becoming attuned to one another. The baby Kate was carrying appeared to be the tuning fork.

The last of the light faded from the sky. It was a warm summer evening. Eli broke the silence. "This is kind of like your classic battle between good and evil, isn't it."

"You *might* think that," Annie said. "But I'm not ready to say the Killapaka are bad. I think they're just... off-track. If and when they meet the Children, maybe they'll get back on-track."

Beau snorted. "You've got to be kidding. They're after the Children. What do you think they want them for? They want to twist them in some sick way. Use them."

Kate rubbed her stomach and looked at Ben. Ben jerked his head at Beau. "I don't think we should talk about this in front of Kate."

This time, Kate snorted. "Really? Please. Give me a break. What do I look like, a woman who has the... what did they call it in the old days? The *vapors*. Do I look like a woman who has the vapors?"

"Sorry," Ben put his hand on her knee. "No, you don't look like you have the vapors, whatever those are."

"You kind of did, when I first met you," Maya said.

"I probably did come off that way. It seems like ages ago, doesn't it? But it's really been no time at all." She leaned against Ben, considering. "I want to know–I need to know–everything about the Killapaka, so that I can help us figure out how best to protect Sam."

Maya winked at Kate. "Yeah. Me too. Don't hold back. Lay it on us. I promise that we women won't freak out."

"Something else I've been thinking about." Eli took a small sip of wine. He looked at his daughter. "Your mother. I've been thinking about my Jennie every day since the day she died, and the pain has been... Well, anyway, I think I'm starting to heal. I'm able to think about her without the memories hurting my heart. This has never happened before."

Maya looked back at her father. "You know, Dad, you're right. I'm feeling warmth and happiness now, instead of sadness, when I think of Mom."

"Same here," Ben said, "with my parents, I mean. I know I don't talk about them much. I couldn't. It was like an open wound. That doesn't mean that I don't think about them. They'll

227

always be a big part of me and in my heart, but now, I feel like I'm not hanging onto the grief so much."

"I know what you mean," Kate said. Her voice was soft. "I was always sad and angry that I didn't have parents of my own. I always wondered what they had been like. I had a vivid dream last night. I haven't had a chance to tell you about it, with everything else going on. My parents were in the dream."

"I hope it wasn't another nightmare." Ben took Kate's hand.

"No. Not at all. In fact, I haven't had any bad dreams since we got here. Anyway, I dreamed that I was a toddler again. I was riding on a train. It was full of people. A man and a woman were sitting on either side of me and holding my hands. I don't remember what they looked like, but I know that I loved them and they loved me." Kate's eyes started to tear, but she didn't look sad.

"The train pulled into a station. They both stood and walked into the aisle. The man said "Stay in your seat, Kate." And the woman said, "This isn't your station." They walked down the aisle. They turned, when they reached the door to the vestibule at the end of the car. They smiled at me. Both of them threw me a kiss. Then, they went through the door to the vestibule and got off the train. No one else got off with them, and no one got on. A moment later, the train started moving.

"I looked out of the window at the man and woman. They were standing in front of the station and waving at me. I watched them become smaller, and smaller, and smaller, as the train pulled away. They waved the entire time. And I could just make out other people emerging from of the station house. Those people joined my parents and also started waving at me.

"I felt better about losing my parents, when I woke up, after I thought about the dream. I felt like I understood how life and death works, and it didn't feel so terrible. We ride together for part of the journey, and we each disembark at different stations."

Everyone's eyes filled. Each one of them had experienced loss. Ben squeezed Kate's hand. The others remained silent. There was nothing to say.

Eli waited a few minutes, before broaching another subject. He looked at Ben. "Speaking of those who have gotten off the train before us, your mother left something to you. I've been holding it for you. Maybe I should have given it to you when you were younger. I don't know. But now feels like the right time." He nodded at Beau and Annie. "Remember I said I had another reason to believe your story? Well, this is it."

He retrieved a wallet from his pocket, flipped open the velcroed flap, and pulled something out of it.

"Your mother, Ben, was the firstborn child of my parents. That's why *my* mother left this to *your* mother. And, because she died, it goes to you, her first and only child. That's how this gets passed on. It's our family heirloom."

Eli opened his hand. A miniscule, shining object was in the center of his large palm. Ben stood, walked over, and picked up the object between his right thumb and forefinger, and then laid it out on his own left palm.

229

"It's a tiger," Ben said.

"Yes. A necklace and a locket came with it, but I imagine you wouldn't mind if I gave that to Maya. She can put a picture of me in it." He smiled at her. "Anyway, I guessed that this was the same thing you guys were describing. A *Masque*."

"It sure looks like one," Beau said. "I wonder what his or her name is. Maybe the tiger will join us later, and we'll find out."

Eli looked at Ben nervously, and then toward Beau. "How do they... manifest? Do they just jump from being a tiny gold object to a huge... angel-thingy?" He smiled, embarrassed.

"Pretty much."

"I guess we'll have to bite the bullet soon and meet these Deor of yours," Eli said. He watched Ben, who was examining the little tiger figurine.

"What about the ones you mentioned, your hawk and your dog. May we see them?" Maya asked.

"I wouldn't call them *ours*," Annie said. "Usually, Apalacheela only stay with a person and his or her progeny who have part of the Scent. They do that to protect the line. They want to make sure that the Deor will be there, on the scene, if and when a descendant of that line turns out to be one of the Children.

"Neither Beau nor I, however, have even one molecule of the Scent. And, anyway, no one has a possessory interest in the Deor, or anyone else, for that matter."

"Then why do these Masque Deor stay with you?" Kate asked.

She had repositioned herself so that she was lying straight out on the couch, with a couple pillows under her head. Ben also stretched out, with his head on the opposite end of the sofa. He wiggled his bare toes under Kate's nose. She pushed them away. Ben held the little tiger close to his face and peered at it. Was it, at any moment, going to turn into a real tiger, or even a giant light creature?

"The Cheela wanted to protect us, as well," Beau said, "because we were given our own, very specific mission when we moved here, a long time ago. They told us to prepare this place for the eventual coming of the Children, and to make sure they were cared for and had everything they needed to thrive and to succeed."

"Wow," Maya said. "What did they do, just show up and say, "Hey! Let us introduce ourselves. We're the Apalacheela, a subset of a race called the Deor, who were created by the Mother and the Father, who, in turn, were created by the Living World. Do you think you could help us out with some kids who are going to be born someday?" She grinned. "And did you both need to change your pants?"

"It wasn't like that," Annie said. "They recognized, when each of us were kids, that we were especially open to interacting with them. They'd been getting us ready since we were toddlers. Appearing to us in dreams. Showing us tiny glimpses of themselves. Deconditioning us from our fear and awe of them. They–surreptitiously–caused us to meet each other. We married soon afterward. They also planted the idea of our moving here. And we did. Then, it happened gradually.

"It wasn't such a scary thing, when the big reveal finally came. We were both ready for it. It's a long story for another day. There are more important things to discuss now."

"Wait. You mentioned you had two guest cottages, up in the woods behind this house," Eli said. "And I can see your solar array in the field, and the one on your roof. I'm sure there's a bunch of other stuff you haven't shown us yet. How did you afford all this? You both must have done extremely well, in whatever you did formerly."

Beau grinned. "We did fine, but not fine enough for all this. The Cheela took care of the expenses."

Eli lifted an eyebrow.

"A little history," Beau said. "Owego was founded at the end of the eighteenth century. Trade in the region was mostly done by boats on the Susquehanna and Chenango Rivers. A number of them sank, or were purposely sunk by enemies. Some of the boats carried small amounts of French or English gold coins. The Deor have been able to locate a lot of these coins in the deep silt at the bottom of the rivers.

"The Deor are composed of the element of light. It's not natural for them to carry physical things, and they don't like it. They did bring us a lot of those coins, despite their aversion to handling matter."

"Could they lift one of us?" Eli asked.

"Oh, yes. Again, they wouldn't enjoy it," Beau replied.

"*You* wouldn't like it, either," Annie said. "It feels like you're getting an electric shock when— in Deor form—they touch your bare skin."

232

"Man," Ben said. "You have old gold coins?"

"We did, but now we don't," Annie replied. "We sold them. We had to be careful not to draw attention to ourselves. We have a good friend, an attorney who lives in Florida. He served as our middleman and sold them to coin dealers for us."

"We made a small fortune," Beau said. "Now we don't have to worry about finances."

"So, can we see the Masque charms you carry with you?" Eli asked.

Annie pulled a thin gold chain out from under her shirt and flicked open a small, heart-shaped locket dangling from it.

"It's empty, as you can see. Falke is around, but she's up in the forest right now. We're past the point of needing to carry them with us at all times. It's not like we'll be leaving this property, anytime soon."

She looked hard in the direction of Ben and the tiger he was currently scrutinizing. "I'd hazard a guess that the tiger is staying here in the house because he or she is a designated protector of the Child. Eli, you thought the tiger was supposed to be passed on to Ben. I doubt that's the case, any longer. I believe the tiger is actually here for Ben's child, who happens to be a Child with a capital C."

Eli nodded. "There's a letter that goes with the... the Masque. Ben, I don't know if you remember the day my mother passed away. You were only three. Her heart had been failing for months. She picked a Sunday to die. She straightened up her house, went into her room, and laid down in her bed. My sister, Frances—your mother, Ben—always visited her in the morning on the way to work, and I always stopped by on my way home from work. When I got there that evening, Mom was so weak she could barely speak. I called Frances and told her everyone had to get over there right away, including you, Ben, and your father. And then I called my Jennie and asked her to come over with Maya, so that we could all say our goodbyes."

Ben nodded.

"I remember," Maya said.

"Everyone came and crowded into the bedroom. Mom whispered that she wanted to talk with me and Frances by ourselves, so I asked everyone to leave the room.

"Mom always wore a thin gold necklace, with a locket hanging from it. Right before she passed, Mom gave your mother the necklace, Ben. She told your mom to take it and to open the locket. Frances was fooling with the locket, trying to figure out how to unlatch it, when Mom gasped, and then died. Frances stopped what she was doing, of course, and stuck the necklace in her pocket.

"She put it in her jewelry box when she finally got back to your own home the next day. She forgot about it until a few weeks after the funeral. When she finally opened the locket, she found the tiger inside.

"In our mother's effects, we found a letter in an envelope. The letter was very old. Mom had written "Frances" on the outside of the envelope."

Eli stopped speaking. He had put his wallet on the coffee table. He reached for the wallet, opened it, and drew out a letter.

"This is it." He handed the letter to Ben.

Ben read aloud:

Descendant:

You are the newest holder of the object. It has been handed down through our family for generations. My father was a freed slave. He passed it on to me before he died, along with the legend surrounding it. The legend has been imparted by word of mouth, until now. I am afraid that the chain may be broken, that one of us may die before having the chance to relay the story to the next generation. The lore would be lost, which is why I am writing it down.

The little object is called a "Masque." We do not know what a Masque is. We've come to understand, over many years, that the term is significant. The Masque is in the figure of a tiger and is made of gold. It was brought to the United States from Africa, by one of our ancestors.

The tiger is magical. Those of us who are familiar with African magic know that this is not that. It has a completely different feel to us. It is older, and more powerful.

You are the new custodian. You will not be able to lose the Masque, even if you try. He—the tiger—will not allow it. We have tested this. You may drop him on the street, or throw

235

him down a well, or toss him into a river, or fling him from a cliff. He will always find his way back to you; that is, until you pass him on to your own descendant. This is a part of his magic.

The tiger may enter your dreams and talk to you. This has happened to many of us who have borne it. This is how we know that the object is called a Masque. He has told some of us, in dreams, that his name is "Ingwe."

Our forebears believed that Ingwe contains considerable magic, that he has a significant purpose, and that one of us will finally learn what that purpose is. This will happen in Ingwe's own time. You may be the one he picks.

The Masque must not leave our family. It is clear that Ingwe and we are bound together. You must give him to your oldest child before you die. If you do not have a child, you must find a young relative who is close to you on the family tree, and pass the tiger on to that person, along with this letter.

Ingwe is alive, as you have gathered from the words I have used in this letter, when referring to the Masque. That is my belief, and it was the belief of our ancestors. Ingwe has taken two different forms, when he

has spoken with us in our dreams.
One is a living tiger. The other, well,
I hope that you will witness this for
yourself in real life, and not just in a
dream.

-Your Ancestor, in Life and in Death

There was no other signature on the letter. Ben wondered if it had been written by his grandmother, or one of his grandmother's parents. He'd have to ask his uncle whose father had been a freed slave. That was a discussion for another time.

He held up the little tiger, stared at it for a moment, and said, "Well, hello there, Ingwe. You're with me, now. Or with my son Samuel, I mean."

He pulled out his own wallet and placed the figurine in a compartment.

What about *me*?" Kate asked. "I'm the mother of one of the Children, and I never had a Masque." She felt left out. "I must have qualified. It took both Ben *and* me to create a son with the full Scent, as I obviously have the part that Ben doesn't."

"I guess the Deor weren't able to find you," Beau said. "That does seem strange, however."

The feeling of being a foster child, whom most of her foster parents had considered too odd to love, returned to Kate for a fleeting moment.

She touched the little locket that hung from her necklace, and shook off the feeling.

"What do you have there?" Beau asked. He nodded at Kate's hand on the necklace. "May I see?"

Kate looked up. She hadn't realized she had been rubbing the heart-shaped locket.

"Oh, sure. Ben, can you get the catch for me?"

She twisted so that her back was to Ben, and swept her hair from her neck. Ben unlatched the necklace. Kate let it drop into her hand. She got up, walked across the porch, and carefully placed the necklace onto the small table in front of Beau.

"I believe it was my mother's." She stood, waiting, and wondering why Beau wanted to look at her necklace.

Beau's reading glasses were perched in their usual resting place, *i.e.*, the top of his head. He grabbed them, put them on, picked up the heart on its chain, and held it up to his face.

"Have you ever opened this?" he asked.

"Opened it? What do you mean? How can I open it? It's solid."

"It's not solid. There's a thin line around the sides, where you can see it will open, and it has a tiny catch."

"What are you talking about? I've had it all my life. There's never been a thin line around it, or any catch. Believe me, I would have seen that."

Kate thought of how, on the countless occasions as a child when she'd felt lost, unloved, and alone, she would hold the locket in front of her face, rub it between her fingers, and feel less lost, unloved, and alone. She certainly would have noticed that the thing could be opened.

"Check it out again," Beau said.

He leaned over and handed it to her. She looked down at the heart. There *was* a catch.

"How is that possible?" Kate asked herself, aloud. She gently turned it on its side with a forefinger. There was a little line running around it. She flicked the catch. The heart popped open. There was a tiny golden octopus inside.

Everyone else in the room stood and crowded around her.

"There's you answer, then," Ben said. "A Masque has been with you all your life." He rubbed her shoulder.

"WTF," Kate breathed. "I have an *octopus!* This is *brilliant!*" She beamed, and turned the charm over so that the miniscule octopus fell into her hand. "I wonder what the octopus is called?"

"And when will the Cheela show themselves to all of us in their Deor forms?" Ben asked.

Beau shrugged. "I think we can make that happen tomorrow. Anyway, the local news is on. We need to pay attention to what's happening around us and in the rest of the world, in case there's some news item that relates in any way to the Children, or to you."

Kate nodded, and put the little octopus back into the heart-shaped locket. She closed the locket, kissed it, and put the necklace back around her neck. "An octopus," she whispered to herself, "with me all my life. Awesome!"

A television was mounted on the interior wall of the porch. Beau picked up the remote control from the coffee table and turned on the television. Ben plopped back into his spot next to Kate. She leaned against him and closed her eyes. The others relaxed as much as they could, watching the news.

Chapter 2

The Heart of the Motherland

The group in Owego watched the local news out of Binghamton, New York, and then the national news. No stories rang any alarm bells. Annie changed to a channel that carried programs about home renovations. They enjoyed the respite and the boring, soothing normalcy.

Maya and Eli put in their two cents about the manner in which the renovations were being done. Everyone was sound asleep within the hour, sprawled on the sofas and the big, comfy chairs.

Beau woke himself up with a loud snore at 11:00 p.m. He shut off the television and stood. "Hey, everybody, I think we should all head to our beds."

"I'll sleep out here on a sofa tonight, if you don't mind," Eli said. "I'll get my pillows and stuff from the family room. It's nice out here."

The porch's air conditioning was not turned on. The large, screened windows were open, and the lights were off. It was a warm night with a slight breeze.

Eli brought his bedding onto the porch. He snuggled into the sofa and laid, with his eyes open, feeling the breeze and watching the trees limbs move back and forth in the moonlight. His eyelids became heavy, and he fell asleep.

He did not see or hear the light-filled beings who visited him much later that night, to see the man who had raised the father of the first Child. They also, of course, paid a visit to Kate and Ben.

Maya, Ben, and Kate made their way through the house and up to the second floor. The two upstairs bedrooms were in a loft space that opened onto a short hallway and overlooked the big family room. The walkway was protected by heavy oak railings. The ceilings of the upstairs rooms sloped sharply on one side. The rooms were connected by a small, cozy, windowless bathroom.

The back bedroom, which Maya was currently occupying, faced the deep woods behind the house. The gardens alongside the edge of the woods were full of bushes and perennial flowers.

Beeches, maples, aspens, oaks, and poplars would throw out their young leaves and deepen the green of the forest, already lush with pines, in the spring, which the newcomers had yet to experience. Rhododendrons would burst into color: light pink, white, dark pink, red, and lavender. The rhododendron petals would carpet the floor of the forest two weeks later, and flowering azaleas would take over. White flowers would next appear on dogwood trees, followed by bright yellow Stella d'oro lilies, purple alpine dog violets, and mountain laurel bushes full of pink blossoms. Summer would bring lavenders, oranges, whites, reds, and bright yellows to replace the pastels of spring, accented by small, white Quaker ladies.

The purple asters, lavender Joe Pye weed, lavender-blue campanula, blue mist Russian sage, and yellow goldenrod of autumn would soon supplant the riotous summer colors. Snow, in the coming winter, would cover the grass, the bushes, and the branches of the trees, making the green of the pine needles appear darker. Snow would stick around on the property for two or three weeks longer than on neighboring lands, when winter turned to spring, as if the property were in its own micro-climate.

Ben and Kate wished Maya a good night's sleep and retreated to their bedroom. The curtains were drawn over the windows in Maya's room. She opened the curtains on one of the windows, sat down in a chair next to the window, and tried to peer into the forest as the night deepened.

She felt very alone for a moment, and called to Ben and Kate. "See you later, alligator." She barely heard their muffled reply. "In a while, crocodile."

The spaces between the trees darkened to a deeper black, in direct proportion to the distance from the edge of the woods. Her loft bedroom was lit by lamps that cast a soft, inviting glow, and it seemed to her that she was in the top of a tree house, floating above the rest of the house. The forest behind the house felt fantastical, unfamiliar, and full of power, but she felt safe and secure in her snug room.

There were solar lights on the vine-covered arbors, in the gardens, and hanging from trees. The lights made the outdoors seem eerier. It was as though elves and fairies, who had no business with the people in the house or even with the Deor, had taken over the outdoors. Maya savored the contrast between her sheltered nest and the perilous woods.

She finally had enough of the sensation. She closed the curtains to shut out the looming night and the hazardous forest, turned on the bedroom fan, turned off the lamps, and went to bed. A slight, warm breeze ruffled the curtains.

Kate and Ben were already falling asleep. As she drifted, Kate opened her eyes for a moment. She looked toward the open windows in her bedroom. She thought, "Do I smell salt spray?" They were hundreds of miles from the Atlantic Ocean. She dismissed the thought, and went back to sleep.

The Scent floated throughout the house. Everyone slept well.

∞

Eli was the first to get up the next morning. He took the Walds at their word and decided to act as if he were in his own home. He started a pot of coffee and went outside. He sat on the front deck, waiting for the coffee to finish perking, and looked at the huge pink lotuses blooming in the pond out front. The door opened and Annie joined him.

"How did you sleep?"

"Great. I woke up thinking about those Kills though. I really don't understand why they could track us across the country, but not here."

"The Deor's Mother left some of her essence, her magic, behind," Annie said. "The Cheela add to that, by actively providing protection to this property and to the surrounding area, every second of every day. Beau thinks it's like a bubble, but I think it's more like a hard shell. Anyway, the only way the Scent can get out is on a person leaving here. That's why Beau and I are trying to minimize any excursions. We need to stay put, to the extent that we're able."

"But didn't they follow us here?"

"I have no idea. It doesn't matter. The Susquehanna River is the border of the Motherland. The Kills *do* know Kate and the unborn Child are here, though."

"So why haven't they tried to come and get her?"

"It would be difficult, if not impossible, for them to abduct her from this place. We're at the edge of the Motherland, as I've been trying to explain. This area is full to the brim of the Mother's magic and it's protected by the strongest of the Apalacheela."

"Ok, I'm convinced. We're safe here."

"Coffee's ready," Beau said, coming out onto the porch. "Thanks for getting it going, Eli. Ben is making oatmeal. We'll eat, and then we'll start the tour."

∞

"None of you asked about the online order I placed yesterday." Everyone had gathered on the all-season porch to have breakfast. Annie noted that none of them, including Maya or Kate, had made specific requests. "Just so you'll know, I ordered all of you the basic clothing you would need for four seasons. We do still have four distinct seasons up here, by the way, however long climate change will allow that to last.

"I also ordered Kate maternity clothes, including maternity jeans. It's supposed to be a one-day delivery but, because we live out in the boonies, it'll probably be more like three or four."

"Thank you so much," Kate said. "What about Sam? I should have thought about it yesterday, when you were placing the order. The baby'll need—"

Beau cut her off. "Pretty sure we've got that covered. You'll see for yourselves, later today."

Annie stayed behind to clean up the kitchen while Beau led everyone else outside. The group followed him into the large, detached two-car garage that was off to the side of the driveway. An old van and a much newer Dodge Grand Caravan were inside. Gardening tools were hung on three walls. Behind the parking area were two small rooms, in which bags of organic fertilizer were stored.

Eli eyed, with approval, a lawn tractor, a wood chipper, a pressure washer, and a snow blower lined up against one wall of the structure. "I see you've got a little OCD, man, the way you've got everything organized. I've got a touch of that myself."

"I wish everyone did. Annie sure doesn't."

"Men," Maya huffed to Kate. "They think they're better at organization than women."

"Uh... I think it depends on the person. I, myself, have never been particularly good at organization," Kate answered.

"No one's got you beat in that department, Maya," Ben said.

They walked back outside and around the building. Beau showed them the protected overhang on the side of the garage that faced away from the house. Most of the area was filled to the roof with bags of hardwood pellets, which sat on skids and were covered by tarps.

"For the pellet stoves," Beau explained. "One in the house and one on the all-season porch."

There were also two garden carts, a metal wheelbarrow, and a large ATV cart.

They passed the overhang and walked down to the big pond. A stream ran to the east, across the property, from the base of the pond. They walked along the side of the pond. A covered pedal boat was moored by bungee cords to a dock.

"The boat goes under the garage overhang in the fall," Beau said, "after we scrub her down."

Maya looked out over the pond. Lotuses covered half of it. The plants had huge floating leaves and, also, wide aerial leaves that shot up several feet into the air. The aerial leaves flapped in the breeze. The lotus flowers were enormous pink blooms that smelled like bubblegum.

Maya squeezed her eyelids together to blur her vision a bit, which made the flowers on the pond looked like a painting by Claude Monet. "Awesome," she said.

Beau smiled and waved his arm.

"The field is through that strip of woods on the side of the house. We've got solar panels there and a vegetable garden. There's a root cellar at the top of the field, and the shed that contains the battery bank. The main house and the two guest cottages are connected to the solar service and to our septic field. That was a job, I'll tell you."

"Nice," Ben said.

"I'll show you what we've got stored in the basement. Annie has all of our inventory listed on her laptop, by the way. And pretty much everything down there is labelled and dated."

They walked toward the house, passing by a flower garden that was between the house and the pond. Maya looked over her shoulder at the wildflowers that were blooming under the trees in the strip of woods. They'd had to leave their own garden behind in L.A., and she appreciated that there were blooms all over the place here. There was also a huge vegetable garden.

They walked back to the driveway. It dead-ended at the house, in front of double garage doors that were separated by a windowed access door, leading into the basement. The shape of a lotus was at the center of the window pattern in the door. It matched the two entry doors on the upper deck.

Beau opened the door and led the others into the basement-garage area. The staircase to the first floor, inside the garage, was separated by an interior door. A small enclosed office was on the left at the bottom of the steps, through the interior door.

An ATV and accessories took up the smaller space on the left. Ladders hung from the walls. The space on the right was larger. A covered generator sat near the garage door. An upright freezer and five chest freezers were lined up against the far wall. Maya walked over and opened the upright one.

"Lots of seeds and nuts," she said, and grinned.

"Lots of everything we need, hopefully," Beau said.

A wall and another door separated the front of the basement from the back section. A long workbench and shelving ran along the front of that wall. The workstation and shelves were neatly stocked with assorted screws, nails, drill bits, manual hand tools, caulk guns, a circular saw, a table saw, power tools, respirator, face masks, hearing protection, safety goggles, stepladders, utility knives, squares, levels, tape measures, adhesives, tapes, outlets, switches, electrical boxes, wall plates, cords, receptacles, fuses, conduit tubing, connectors, and other items Beau had accumulated over the years.

Eli looked at the work station. "Not bad," he said.

"Come on through here," Beau said. They walked through the next door, to the back half of the basement. The water system, furnace, solar charge controller, and water heater were to the left. Water treatment supplies were stacked next to the water system. Beau pointed out the filled shelves and the labelled rubber storage bins that were stacked to the ceiling.

A shelving system on the right held bottles, tins, and boxes. The rest of the space was filled with rubber storage bins. Everything was labelled.

"A couple of trays filled with compost are tucked away in a corner somewhere down here. Annie is growing mushrooms in them. I'd like you to come back down here by yourselves, so that you get a better idea of what we have in storage, and really get familiar with the stock. It's all part of making this place your home. We have six extra laptops, brand new, in the box. You can use some of those. We'll download the inventory list on them. You can get online, by the way, to do research or whatever. But do *not* go to any of your own online accounts, or send any emails. We'll give you our login information. And don't have any contact with any of your friends or family—"

"None of us have any family, other than each other," Ben interrupted.

"I'm sorry to hear that," Beau said. "Anyway, no contact with friends, and no social media. Ben, I think it's a good idea for you to transfer whatever documents you have on your laptop to one of the new ones, and then we'll destroy your old one. Please don't go online when you're on your old laptop. I don't think it can be tracked, otherwise."

"Will do. I'll take care of today. I'll get whatever I need off it and then take a sledgehammer to it. And, of course, I won't go online. "

"Oh. You'll notice that there are instruments over there on that shelf." Beau pointed to a stack of musical instruments. "The previous owner of the house used to be a music teacher at the local high school. He left them here when he moved to a retirement community in Maine. Annie and I have looked at the instruments inside the cases. They seem like they're in pretty good shape. There's a flute, a violin, a piccolo, an oboe, and a clarinet. Do any of you play an instrument?"

They each shook their heads.

"Well," Beau said, "if you get bored during the winter, maybe you can teach yourselves by watching videos online. Over there is a section of workout equipment." He drew their attention to a tucked-away corner in the back, which contained a yoga mat, weights, a boxing bag, and an elliptical exercise machine.

They heard footsteps coming down the steps. The group walked to the front of the basement. The door at the bottom of the stairs opened, and Annie joined them.

"Are we ready to take a walk up to the cottages?" she asked. "And, afterward, maybe take a little walk farther into the forest?" She winked at Beau.

"Sure," Maya said, speaking for the group. "Let's go. I'm dying to see these cottages."

"Before we do that, I want to move our old van out of the garage and over to the parking pad next to the garage overhang, on the side. Then Eli can put his truck in the garage. We don't want anyone to spot it," Beau said.

"I didn't even think about that," Eli said. "I hope no one noticed it."

"I wouldn't worry about it," Annie said. "The foliage blocks the view of the driveway from the road during the summer, and the people who live around here are sound and trustworthy. People who *aren't* sound and trustworthy find they can't stand it here. The phenomenon has something to do with the Mother's essence. It attracts people who are drawn to the animal kingdom and drives off people who aren't."

"The Killapaka know, though, that you guys are in Owego and didn't just disappear from the face of the Earth," Beau said.

"Can the... the Killapaka, as you say, can they come here and find us?" Kate asked.

"They can't even send a tiny Killapaka mosquito in here without our Cheela knowing about it," Beau said. "But they might send human spies. We don't know whether they have any people working for them. If they do, those people could slip in unnoticed, and even use low-flying planes or drones to scout around."

"Which means it's best if you stay inside as much as possible," Annie added. "Unless you move up into the cottages. No one is going to be able to spy on you up there. The forest is too dense. You can get all the outdoor exercise you like, in the woods."

Maya grumbled. "I really wanted to work in the vegetable garden."

"How about this? I have an assortment of large gardening hats and Beau has about twenty baseball hats. You can do stuff outside, but make sure your heads aren't exposed, and wear sunglasses, unless you're up in the forest. That means you guys as well," Annie said, looking at the men. "And keep your hoods up in the winter. That should work, right, Beau?"

"That should do it," he replied.

"I didn't bring any sunglasses," Kate murmured.

"Me neither," Ben and Maya said. Eli always kept a pair in his truck, so he was covered.

"Don't worry about that. We have—" Beau started to say.

"Let me guess." Ben cut him off. "You have two dozen pairs in your basement inventory."

"Not in the basement," Beau grinned. "In one of the upstairs bedroom closets, I think, right, Annie?"

"You are correct," she replied. "Check the closet in your room, Maya. There should be a box labelled 'sunglasses.' Right next to the box labelled 'flashlights.' I think there's only about ten pairs, though, not two dozen." Annie looked concerned. "Should I have gotten more?"

Ben laughed. "I think ten should be enough."

"Do you really think it's likely that the Killapaka are working with *people*?" Eli asked.

"Yes, unfortunately," Beau replied. "We know of at least one. There was a man watching your house in Los Angeles. At least, the Cheela *think* he was a man. They're not sure. He looks like a man to them, but they say he smells like he has a touch of the Killapaka substance in him. Either he's been hanging around with them and it's rubbed off on him, or they did something to him."

"A man watching my house?!" Eli asked. He was stunned. How close had they been to coming face-to-face with the Killapaka?

"They don't need to hear any more about that yet," Annie chided. "They need to settle in first and feel safe."

"I'd like to know," Eli said.

Annie sighed. "You got out just in time. That's the important thing. Thanks to Samuel and his alert mother," she nodded at Kate, "and his cooperative father. And, also, thanks to the Cheela who were there. Who still are, in fact."

"Cheela were *there*?" Eli asked. "At my home? Wait... You were saying something about that yesterday... "

"The animals who visited me when I was a kid," Ben said, "when I spent nights at Uncle Eli's and slept on the gazebo, were they Deor? The Apalacheela?" He stopped, and recalled Beau's comment, the previous day, something about the Jackson home having been protected by a "knot of toads."

"*All* animals are Deor," Beau clarified. "Some of them are Apalacheela, some are Killapaka, and the rest of the Deor—which is the vast majority— have completely forgotten who they are. They've been in their Camaflur, flesh-and-blood bodies for too many generations. I'd say that ninety-nine percent of them no longer remember that they're Deor. It's like they're asleep. The Cheela call them "Somnambuli." Sleepwalkers. I guess the Children will wake them up. That's the hope, anyway.

"The Deor don't usually pay much attention to humans. The ones you saw at your uncle's house, Ben, *were* Cheela, very much awake, and they were paying attention to you and your family. Serious attention, because of your smell. Ingwe the tiger, in his Masque shape–that is, your little gold trinket–apparently had already been incorporated into your family for generations. But then, between your Uncle Eli, Maya, and finally you, there was enough of the Scent that the Cheela sent toads to live in Eli's garden. The toads have been protecting you guys.

"It was just a matter of time before the Kills noticed one of you. And, of course, it was *you* they noticed, Ben, as you have more parts of the

Scent than anyone else in your family. The Cheela think the Kills dispatched that man to find out whatever he could about you. Or, maybe, he was just randomly in the vicinity and picked up on it. He would have been able to contact the Kills while you were all sleeping if things hadn't happened as fast as they had. And that would have been that."

"That's freakin' lovely," Maya mumbled.

"Water under the bridge," Beau said. "Water under the bridge."

"Shall we get the vehicles moved?" Annie asked.

Beau rubbed his hands together. "Yes. And then they can *really* meet some animals."

∞

"On to the cottages." Beau was in the lead. He gestured with his arm and waved everyone in the direction of the dense forest.

They walked out of the basement to the driveway, up the slate steps that curved around the left side of the house, on up a grassy slope behind the house, and into the forest.

"The air is so refreshing up here," Kate said.

"It's the *forest*," Beau said, as if no further explanation was required.

They walked for about ten minutes, and arrived at a stand of pine trees growing so closely together that their trunks almost touched.

"I've never seen anything like this," Ben said.

The branches of each tree overlapped and bent over the branches of the trees next to it. He thought back to the dendrology–that is, the study

254

of trees—section of an advanced botany class he'd taken. Kate looked at him. She hadn't gotten as far in her studies as he had but, based on her knowledge, this growth formation did not seem possible.

"We're in the forest," Annie said. "I'd advise all of you to suspend disbelief while we're up here."

Beau walked around the wall of pines and arrived at a narrow opening between two of them.

"Here we go." He pushed his body through. The others followed.

"Cottage number one," Beau said. "Kate and Ben will probably want to take this one over at some point. It's got all the baby stuff in it."

"How did you build this?" Eli asked.

He walked to the picturesque, one-story stone cottage, and put his hand against the oak door. "How did you get the building materials through that?" He waved at the surrounding tree fortification.

"The trees weren't there when we had it built. The Deor did most of the heavy lifting—in Camaflur form, so handling the materials wasn't an issue for them—with respect to the construction. We hired a local contractor, who is quite discreet, to do the finishing work, the electrical, plumbing, septic hook-up, etc. He was well paid, as were his employees."

"What do mean, the trees weren't there? How long ago did you have this cottage built? These trees must be two hundred feet tall, if they're an inch!"

"A few years back. They're white pines. White pines grow fast." Beau smiled.

"White pines grow fast," Annie repeated, and snorted. "I think it's more like, they grow fast when a Deor *tells* them to grow fast."

"May we go inside?" Maya asked. Her father was still staring at the unlikely trees.

"Sure." Beau unlocked the front door. He pointed at a window next to the door. "In case I forget to mention it, those oak shutters latch from the inside, if you ever need them. You obviously have to open the window first, to do it."

"Why would you have them latch on the inside?" Eli asked.

"Extra protection, just in case. You can never be too careful. You guys go on in and look around. Explore. Open things up. We'll wait out here."

Annie had already gone to the side of the house. She sat down on a bench, which was surrounded by wild flowers. Beau joined her.

Eli, Maya, Ben, and Kate came out twenty minutes later.

"This place is *awesome*," Kate said. "I'm ready to move in today." She looked at Annie and Beau. "That is, if it's all right."

"Of course," Annie said. "That's what it's here for. Let's go on up and see the other cottage."

"Wait a minute," Beau said. "They need to see the basement first."

"There's a basement?" Eli looked at the foundation of the house. "It appears to be built on a slab. I don't see any basement windows."

256

"That was done on purpose," Beau replied. "Come on. I'll show you."

He led all of them, except Annie, back into the house, through the kitchen, and into the hallway. He pointed at the rug in front of the bathroom.

"This is the way into the basement," Beau said.

He leaned over, ran his hand under the rug, pulled on the latch, opened the hinged trapdoor, and leaned it against the wall. A light automatically came on in the depths below them.

"Cool," Ben said. "Look at this, Kate! It's pretty wild."

"There's a motion detector light," Beau said. "The steps are pretty steep. A little better than a ladder, but not by much. Be careful."

Ben lowered himself into the opening. Kate went next, and then Maya. Eli gave them a few moments to get out of his way, and stepped down. He stopped when only his head was visible above the floor.

"You coming, Beau?"

"Naw. I know what's down there. I'll wait here."

Eli noticed two heavy, galvanized steel housings set into the ceiling on each side of the stairs. He glanced back at the trapdoor leaning against the wall of the hallway, and saw a double set of six-inch side locks. The trapdoor would be virtually impenetrable when those locks were fastened from the basement.

"Not screwing around with security down here," he said to himself, and continued down the stairs.

Voices drifted upward. "Look at this!" he heard Maya say.

Eli reached the bottom, and turned around. Soft lighting fixtures were set into the ceiling, which was only about a foot and a half above Eli's head. The basement was very small. Despite its size, it was finished, which was interesting. An alcove to the right contained two sheet-covered, queen-sized mattresses—one on top of the other—and a thick stack of blankets and pillows. Maya was already sprawled out on top of the mattresses. Cases and containers of supplies were stacked against the wall on the left.

"Taking a nap?" Eli asked her. She ignored her father and stretched.

Eli turned and saw Ben examining solar batteries in the farthest corner. An electrical panel above was connected to the solar batteries. Two water treatment tanks, a reverse osmosis system, and a heater were next to the side of the panel. Eli looked up. A ventilation system was inset into the top of the wall that was at a right angle to the solar control panel wall. Under it was a refrigerator, a sink, and a stand that held a few dishes, glasses, and flatware. He turned back to the steps and noticed a small door behind them. He stepped forward, opened the door, and saw what appeared to be a brand-new toilet.

"Is this a tornado shelter? Do they even *get* tornadoes around here?" Eli asked aloud. No one answered.

Ben walked to the steps, finished with his brief battery exam. He knew nothing about solar batteries. He'd better learn.

"This is a safe room, Uncle Eli. I guess this is where we're supposed to hide if we're ever attacked by those Killapaka things."

"I hope we never need to use it," Kate said. She glanced from Ben to the bedding in the cozy alcove. "Well, we could use it as a kind of basement getaway," she said with a little smile.

"Hey," Maya said. "Knock it off, kids. None of that. I think you've gotten us into enough trouble already."

"Ok," Eli said. "Is everyone done here? Why don't we go up and rejoin Annie and Beau?"

∞

The next cottage was several hundred yards farther up into the forest. It was similarly situated, in its own stand of white pines.

"There's no baby stuff in this one," Beau said.

The Jacksons and Kate spent less time in the cottage, as the layout was identical. Different supplies, rather than baby needs, were stored in the closet off the second bedroom. A double bed was in that room, rather than a crib and a single bed.

It, too, had a cellar safe room.

"We didn't put sheets on the beds in this cottage, yet," Annie said. "I guess you can handle that if you move up here." She looked at Eli and Maya.

"I don't know," Eli said. "It's kind of nice being around you guys. Would it be all right if I stayed in your house, for a time?"

"Of course. We welcome your company," Beau said. "What about you, Maya?"

Maya was staring at the upper cottage, entranced.

"This looks exactly like an old English cottage. I think I'd like to stay up here."

"What?" Eli asked. "By *yourself*?" He looked at the surrounding trees.

"Maya is as safe here as she is in our house. Safer, probably," Annie said. "She's closer to the heart of the Motherland. Plus, there's a phone system that connects the house and the two cottages. It's an intra-building cable system. You can only call the other houses on it. The point is, Maya can always get in touch with everyone else."

"I take it you did that so no one on the outside can monitor the calls," Eli said.

"Yes. There's a regular landline in the house, and we have a cell phone, but you won't be using either of those," Beau added. "You are officially off the grid, or you've gone underground, or you've ghosted everyone, or whatever the hell it is people do these days." He rubbed his hands together and his face lit up. "That's done. Now, is everyone ready to meet some animals?"

∞

Beau and Annie led everyone farther into the forest. They walked up a steep incline, until they reached the top of a small ridge. The ground in front of them descended for about ten feet and then sloped upward again.

"Ok," Beau said. "Everyone, stand right here. Look in front of us. What do you see?"

"More woods. A bunch of trees," Eli replied.

Annie took Beau's hand. "They can't *see*. I think it's time for a Cheela." She turned to Kate and Ben. "Could you please take out the Masques you're carrying?"

"The little octopus in my locket?" Kate asked, pulling on her necklace. "And the tiger Ben has in his wallet?"

"Yes, please."

Ben pulled the tiger from his wallet. Kate opened her locket and took out the octopus. They held them out toward Annie, on open palms. Annie did not take the objects from them. She stood still.

"Ok, everyone, this is it. Time to *really* suspend disbelief," Beau said.

The two little gold trinkets blurred. Eli rubbed his eyes. He seemed to be having a problem with his vision. The trinkets became misty, and began to shine, spin, and grow, and then two winged beings, an octopus-shaped one and a tiger-shaped one, were floating in the air in front of the group. They seemed to be made of moving motes of light, and were at least twelve feet tall. It was almost impossible to look directly at them.

Maya whispered, "*Deor*."

The beings stayed in their Deor forms, but shrank down to about six feet high. They began to speak to the four newcomers.

"My name is Dedos," the octopus said. His voice sounded like a current rushing through a deep ocean canyon. "I've been watching over you, Katherine Birdsong, your entire life. I'm pleased we can finally meet. This is Ingwe." He waved a tentacle of light toward the tiger.

"I... I... ," Eli sputtered.

"I am happy, at last, to meet the descendants of your noble ancestors." Ingwe the tiger roared the words at Eli and Ben, while gently folding his whirling light form in a bow to Kate and the baby she was carrying.

Two other Deor fell out of the sky and dropped next to the group.

"Seta," one said, introducing himself. His voice called to mind an image of a dog, surrounded by his pack and charging through a forest.

"Falke," the other murmured. The Jackson family and Kate had a mental flash of the hawk hurtling through a river of wind, chasing it to its source.

"You'll get used to it," Annie said.

They looked around, awed. The forest was filled with moving light... wings... animals. The Jacksons and Kate felt like they were in the middle of a soundless and windless hurricane. They could not speak. They could barely breathe.

Dedos floated next to Kate. She found the octopus less intimidating than the other Deor. He was somehow familiar.

"You *know* me, Kate," Dedos said, and Kate felt the current rushing in the ocean depths again. "I've been by your side all your life. Open your eyes."

"My eyes are—" Kate started to say, but then Dedos was touching her face with a brilliant, dizzying tentacle. It felt like an electric shock. Her eyes began to burn and prickle, as though they were being scratched with short thorns. And then

262

she really opened them, and she *saw*. The Jacksons were getting the same treatment from Ingwe, Seta, and Falke.

Annie and Beau stood back and watched.

Eli stood perfectly still. His mouth dropped open. Kate, Ben, and Maya, mouths agape, stood likewise. They looked like statues someone had carved out of stone, with identical expressions.

Beau started to snicker, until Annie stopped him by giving him a small punch on his arm. "You're being inappropriate," she whispered.

"It's the... it's the freaking ocean," Eli said, in a husky voice. He looked down. They were standing at the edge of a cliff that had to be at least twenty-five hundred feet above sea level. And there was the sea itself, a vast blue expanse. Huge breakers crashed against the base of the rock far below them. Countless forms of light whirled above the ocean, dove into it, and shot back out into the clouds. They exuded... joy.

"Welcome to the heart of the Motherland," Beau said.

"Not the heart," Annie corrected. "The *outskirts* of the heart."

Chapter 3

Life at the Edge of the Motherland

"The colors," Maya said. "They were so... saturated. So intense." They were back in the Wald home and having lunch at the dining room table.

"Yep. That is a very blue ocean, isn't it?" Beau asked.

"And the waves, they were so huge!"

Annie watched Maya help herself to a second avocado, bean, tomato, onion, and cilantro taco.

"That's it for the avocados," Annie said. "Enjoy them while you can. Unfortunately, we can't grow avocado trees this far north."

"What about in the... in the Motherland?" Ben asked. "The climate there is so different from this one. Can't we grow stuff there?"

"The Motherland is not for us, Ben," Annie said. "It's not meant for modern people, who bring with them a massive carbon footprint and planetary destruction."

"We wouldn't be burning coal or oil or—"

"More importantly, the place has way too much energy for us to handle," Annie continued, cutting Ben off. "I think it would burn us up and turn us into crispy critters or dried out husks, if we stayed in there too long. We could all just settle in there and not have to worry about anyone finding us, if it weren't for that little problem. It's okay here on the fringes, and it's okay to go in there for short periods of time. But that's it."

"Babies and children, for some reason, are able to move through the flows and fluxes of the Motherland quite easily, according to the Cheela," Beau added. "Maybe because their brains are still forming and they are more adaptable. Who knows? The two Children, however, *cannot* be raised inside it. They'd never want to leave, if they were in there for too long a period of time during their formative years. They would never want to go out into the world of humans, and they would not realize their destinies."

Annie smiled. "But we do often have picnics in there, or just go hiking and exploring. The Cheela always let us know when we've had enough, and when it's time for us to leave."

Eli had an image of parents herding their children off a beach, before the kids got too sunburned.

"There will sometimes be these blasts that shoot across the sky," Beau said. "They look like the biggest lightning bolts you've ever seen. Meska tells us they're power discharges, or magic releases, or something. He says we wouldn't want to be hit by one."

Annie pushed her plate away from her. "Meska suspects that the Living World chose this area because there was already a preternatural phenomenon here, to which the Living World added, and to which the Mother added, after that."

"Who's this Meska?" Kate asked.

"Oh, right," Beau said. "Meska. She's a bear, and the strongest of the Cheela. Kind of their leader."

"Wow," Maya said. "May we meet her?"

"She's definitely around. I'm sure she'll be poking her head in here, sooner or later."

"So, about the Motherland," Eli said. "Is that what it is, a great big ocean?"

"No," Beau replied. "It's much more than that."

"How do you go hiking in there? I don't see how you get down that cliff."

"There are different ways to go in." Beau grinned. "We took you in that way for dramatic effect."

"As if every part of the Motherland doesn't have dramatic effect," Annie snickered.

"I was saying," Beau looked sternly at Annie, "before I was interrupted, that if we had taken you in, say, a hundred feet to the left, you would've entered through a giant redwood forest. And when I say giant, I mean redwoods that grow to at least a thousand feet."

"A hundred feet to the right," Annie added, "and you would have been on a gorgeous, white sand beach in a cove. The water is shallow for half a mile out, and the waves are little ripples. The water is the palest blue."

"We've charted out different entrances. Annie has entered the locations and descriptions of all of them into an Excel worksheet on her laptop. Deserts, glaciers, glades, lakes, savannahs... the list goes on and on."

"How many... regions have you found so far?" Kate asked.

"Sixty-seven," Beau answered promptly. "We're still working on it. And every one of them leads you into a completely different, but equally astonishing, place. The Deor tell us that there are countless localities in there. I've gotten the idea that the place may be infinite."

"Wow," Ben and Maya said, at the same time.

"Are you thinking what I'm thinking?" Maya asked her cousin.

"That it would be fun to take over mapping the Motherland?"

"It's not a piece of cake," Annie said. "The energy of the place makes you exhausted. That's why we've only gotten up to sixty-seven, to date."

"So... what happens to the regular forest, when we're in there?" Ben asked.

"It's still there," Annie replied. "The Motherland is... inside the forest. The Cheela have tried to explain it to us. I wasn't a physics major but, from what I understand, the area of the Motherland is a boundless, expanding universe. It is not part of our universe. It's located in the space between two points.

"So, say a hiker stumbled onto our property and walked up that ridge behind our house. He wouldn't be able to see the Motherland and would keep walking in the forest. He would, in effect, be stepping right over it without noticing. All of us, however—now that you've been initiated—would be able to see it and go into it."

"What about the different entrances?" Maya asked. This was right up her alley. Her education in quantum mechanics might come in handy. "If the Motherland is in a space between two specific points..."

"I should have said that the *entrances* are located in the space between two points," Annie replied. "I don't know if they're specific spaces, or specific points. It's all very confusing to me. Over my head. I'm probably giving it to you incorrectly. You'll have to talk with the Cheela. Good luck with following their explanations, though.

"The one thing I *do* know is that the so-called "regular" forest is affected by it. I've looked at satellite images of it, and the images always vary. The size, shape, and topography of the forest changes, from one shot to the next. There are always lots of blurred-out areas. And the blurred-out areas move around, from picture to picture."

Ben thought about the paper he had been writing, which had turned into a study of a similarly odd place, in Cutter City, Ohio. "You know, I was working on a paper about –"

Maya cut him off. "Paper, schmaper." She pushed her plate away and sighed. "I'll clean up the dishes. How about I stay here tonight, and move to the upper cottage tomorrow, in the a.m.?"

"We'll move tomorrow, also," Kate said. She gave Ben a questioning look. He nodded.

"Looks like you'll have your choice of the upstairs bedrooms here, Eli," Beau said. "You won't have to crash on a sofa anymore."

"I probably should move up with Maya so she won't be alone."

"No, Dad! Please. I want to be in my own place, for the first time in my life. I'm twenty-three, for Pete's sake."

"She won't be alone," Beau reminded Eli. "The Cheela are all over the place up there."

"I do kind of like it out on the sunporch," Eli said.

"You're welcome to keep sleeping out there, but you're not going to get much privacy. We often have coffee there, early in the morning," Annie said.

"Maybe I'll only do it once in a while, then. Or, you can just bring out an extra cup." He grinned.

Annie stood. "Beau and I have some harvesting to do. The purple potatoes and beets are ready to be dug up. We still have cabbage, mustard greens, herbs, carrots, and snap beans coming in. Anyone want to help?"

"Wait a minute," Eli said. "I have another question. Why don't all of the Deor just move into their Motherland? No people are in there. They wouldn't have to be concerned with people worshipping them and starting wars over them."

"We didn't say there are no people in there," Beau said, slowly. "We only said it's not meant for modern people. There are certain people who can not only survive, but who actually *thrive* in the Motherland. We caught a glimpse of them one day. The Cheela wouldn't tell us much about them, nor would they let us go near them. The Cheela will only say that the people there coexist in harmony with the Deor. I think they may be descendants of the original people who lived on this continent. Who knows? Maybe they are the actual, original people."

"Ok. So, the rare indigenous people can survive in the place. You didn't answer my other question. Why don't the Deor pack it all in and just live there? Why not, if it's so damned big? They could forget about us. Why would they want to stay in our land and be tortured?"

He thought about the implications of his words. That would mean no animals would be left anywhere else on Earth. He didn't want to live on a planet with no animals.

"Many of them have considered it," Annie replied. "The problem is that the Killapaka have zero interest in returning to the Motherland. The Cheela would be leaving us at the mercy of the Kills, if they retreated there. The Cheela have opted, thus far, to follow their Mother's instructions. It's a good thing Kate is pregnant with a Child. It has restored their faith. It was getting pretty touch and go for a while there, with some of them."

"Not Meska, Seta, and Falke, and those who have stuck with them, though," Beau added. "They're as steadfast as you can get. They believe that what their Mother predicted will come to pass."

Eli stood. "You're saying that the Deor have stayed here mainly to bail us out. To save us from ourselves. And we've repaid them... how?" He shook his head. "Humans may think of themselves as an intelligent species, but we've got a long way to go before we reach enlightenment. It's too bad more of us don't read the books of the philosopher Peter Singer, or Gary Francione, or Tom Beauchamp, or the works of sociologist David A. Nibert."

He sighed. "Anyway, I'm ready to get to work on your garden. One more thing, though. Can we go back up into the forest later?" He remembered that ocean and how blue it had been. He imagined what the other places must be like. Maya, Ben, and Kate were wondering the same thing.

"We use those little trips as treats, when we feel like we've earned it. That way, we don't go up there too often and get too much exposure to that magic, or whatever it is," Beau said. "We'd be up there every day, if it were up to us. How about we plan on going up there once a week? We can all go together, hike around, and have a picnic."

"Sounds good," Eli said. He was a little relieved. The Motherland was a world made for giants. The landscape there was in sharp focus, the colors vivid. Seeing thousands of Deor dance and swirl across the sky had made him dizzy. The air in the place had been madly delicious, but had been full of something that he could only compare to static electricity, although he knew it wasn't. Eli had felt like a giddy young kid in there. It was probably better to recover over the next week, before he went in again.

"Ok. Let's get at that garden. That'll be fun. I like gardening."

Everyone wanted to help. They knew there would be no more shopping at the grocery store. They'd need to bring in crops, and freeze, can, pickle, or dehydrate them.

Their unique circumstances and their joint passions had caused the group to form an instant bond. The act of tending to the garden, and bringing in and preserving crops, strengthened that bond. They were beginning to grow into one family.

∞

Maya settled into her little cottage.

Her first night in the house was interesting. She made up her bed with sheets, blankets and pillows that were readily accessible in the closet, then locked the front door. She decided to leave all of the windows open in the cottage, and turned off the lamps. She returned to her bedroom, tossed her shorts and t-shirt onto a small wooden chair in the corner of the bedroom, and climbed into bed.

She'd planned to read until she got drowsy, but realized she could barely keep her eyes open. She stretched out and felt a cool northerly breeze, coming from the direction of the Wald home, through the window of the bedroom across the hallway. She inhaled deeply. The breeze carried the smells of lotuses, oranges, peppermint, fir needles, vanilla, cinnamon, and rain.

Maya pulled a sheet up to her chin and settled back into the pillows. She felt the stone of the cottage around her and the fortification of pine trees outside. She listened to the silence and began to drift. A thought intruded. At home, she had been an academic wonder with a bright future. She no longer had that footing. Would she ever get it back? And what was her place here?

Her father had a commanding gravitas. That presence had been amplified by his work history and his life experience. His abilities and common sense were perfect for their new situation and made him a significant asset to their new community.

Beau and Annie had spent several decades of their lives preparing their property for the coming of a Child. The group respected the couple by virtue of that fact alone, in addition to which they were as familiar as a person could be with the world of the Deor.

Ben and Kate were the parents of a Child. What was Maya's role here? Did she even have one? Or was she going to be basically useless, for the first time in her life? The Scent entering the house took over the neurotransmitters in her brain, and soothed her.

The direction of the breeze swung around one hundred and eighty degrees and began to come from the South. The smell of salt spray overpowered and cleared out the Scent which had been filling the bedroom.

It was like a switch had been flipped. Maya's eyes flew open. That astonishing ocean. She had to see it again. She got out of bed and snatched her shorts and t-shirt from the chair.

The breeze shifted a little. The smell of salt vanished. A dry desert wind rushed through the window. The breeze shifted again. A freezing arctic gust swept through the bedroom. Maya stood by the bed, naked except for her underwear. She shivered and wrapped her arms around her chest. What am I doing? I can't go stumbling around the woods, by myself, in the dark.

She closed the bedroom window, latched it firmly, and turned on a fan. She went back to bed and, this time, to sleep.

∞

Maya dreams of a young woman. The woman is as tall as Maya, or even taller. It is evening. The woman is in a forest glade She is sitting by a fire with other people. Maya cannot make out their

273

faces. The woman is leaning forward and using a pestle to grind up acorns in a mortar.

The woman stops what she is doing and straightens her shoulders. She looks directly at Maya. The woman tosses long, straight black hair away from her face.

She smiles.

∞

Maya had breakfast early in the morning, using the supplies in the well-stocked cottage, and then went down to the main house. She joined Annie on the all-season porch.

"Good morning, Maya. Sleep well?"

She did not mention her dream. "I did. How are you this morning?"

"I'm well, thank you. Have you had breakfast?"

"Yes. You and Beau have the kitchen up there fully stocked with everything I can think of, Annie. Thank you."

"Not a problem. You should raid the freezers and fridges in this house and take some of that cold stuff up to your cottage. I'm sorry we didn't get around to doing that. Well, if you're ready to get started, the first thing you can do is grab one of the new laptops and download the inventory list on it. How good are you at organizing things?"

"Pretty good. What would you like for me to do?"

"I thought you could come up with a work schedule. You'll have to talk with me and Beau, and your father, I guess, and come up with a chart of daily chores, so everyone knows who's

274

doing what. Then we'll need a list of seasonal jobs. We'll have to include vehicle maintenance on the list.

"And, maybe you can come up with some ideas for possible larger projects. If the majority agrees, you can add a project to the list and figure out how to approach it. What materials we'd need, the steps involved, who would be responsible for doing what, etc. You're officially in charge of all of that."

"I can also keep track of our supplies." Maya said. She thought for a moment. "You know what? I think I can figure out approximately how long each item will last us with normal usage. Then we can modify our usage, based on the numbers. I'll need to find out how long food items will last, of course, depending on their sell-by date and whether they are frozen or canned or... " Maya's voice trailed off. She was clearly developing a detailed plan in her head.

A sense of peace flowed through the young woman. Her status had been elevated within the group. She was now, more or less, the administrator of their community. It put her on an equal footing with everyone else. She could put her career in quantum mechanics aside, for now.

Annie glanced at Maya. The older woman had conferred with Beau and Falke, earlier that morning. They had all agreed that Maya needed a new purpose to replace her previous goals. Annie smiled to herself, satisfied.

∞

Ben and Kate took over the lower cottage. They spent a good deal of time, the first week,

275

going through baby things. Beau showed the couple and Maya how to maintain the systems in the cottages. The three young people did raid the freezers and refrigerators in the main house, and carried the plunder up to their respective cottages.

Eli decided to take the back upstairs guest room. He actually had the use of both bedrooms in which to spread out his new belongings, as no one else was bunking up there with him. The area of the two rooms, together with the bathroom, was still smaller than his master bedroom suite at home, but he liked the snug, cozy feeling he had up in that high perch.

He started to use the front bedroom as his day room, where he would retire to read, write, think, or do online research, when he wasn't busy with Maya's work assignments. He would retire to the back bedroom at night and sit by a window, gazing up at the dark forest for a few minutes, before going to sleep.

The Cheela came out of the forest, a few at a time and at a distance, so as not to overwhelm or intimidate the newcomers. Eli, Maya, Ben, and Kate began to relax around them. They soon began to feel that it was natural for the Cheela to be there.

Some of the Cheela assumed flesh and blood, Camaflur animal bodies. The property now appeared to teem with wildlife, except that these animals did not go about what humans view as the accepted business of animals, nor did they prey on each other. They instead sat at the edge of the woods behind the house, roosted in trees, or floated on the pond. They returned to their Cheela forms when they required nourishment.

276

Light, of any type, was the only sustenance they required.

The Scent of the unborn child flowed out of every one of Kate's pores. It filled the cottage and leaked outdoors and throughout the property. It caused the group to feel serene, at peace, and unafraid of what was to come. They no longer experienced hunger or fatigue, but they did enjoy eating their meals and they did relish their nights' rests. The six of them moved about their routines in harmony with each other.

The baby had been silent since they had come to the edge of the Motherland. The group assumed that his silence meant Sam felt safe and was content simply to do what a growing fetus was supposed to do. The boy was letting the others lead, until it was his time.

Maya dreamed, almost every night, of the young woman in the Motherland. The dreams were so real that she felt like she could reach out and touch the other woman's face. Maya felt a strong connection to the Motherland, even during the times she was awake.

She kept her dreams, and her sense of connection, to herself.

∞

Morning sunlight caused the leaves of the trees to glow, in the forest behind the house. Beau and Eli were drinking coffee at a round table in the little screened-in porch that was attached to the rear of the home. They heard a noise from the woods and looked up. A large black bear was coming toward them on all fours. Eli was startled for a moment, then quickly composed himself. The bear stopped outside the back porch and sat on the grass.

"Good morning, Meska," Beau said. "It's good to see you. We've missed you."

The bear muttered a low growl. She couldn't speak in her Camaflur, animal shape. Bright points of light started to move around her. Her fur sparkled, and then a twenty-foot-high, brilliant, bear-shaped, winged and whirling cloud appeared, floating next to the porch. The motes coalesced, and the cloud reduced to seven feet in height. Eli's lips parted. He took in a deep breath and held it, then let it slowly release.

"I have to be in this form, if we're going to have a conversation," Meska said. Her voice sounded like a freight train rumbling into a station.

"I'm getting used to it... to Cheela, that is," Eli said. "It's just that, well, it's like your Creed says. I can't help but think there's an actual angel standing in front of me. But like I said, I'm getting used to it. It's pretty awesome. *You're* pretty awesome."

He looked away from Meska and down at his hands. He looked up again and gave Meska a tentative smile. "Don't worry. I won't start idolizing you or anything, so it's cool."

"That is not one of my worries," Meska said. "No one in your family would kneel to another, no matter how awesome."

Beau shook his head. "Yes. We all agree you're awesome, Meska. You don't have to advertise it. Anyway, we're starting to figure out our next steps. Eli and I thought we'd come up with an initial plan and then present it to the others, and to you."

"There's a lot to do," Meska agreed.

"First, we're trying to decide what to do with Eli's house in Los Angeles."

Meska's wings moved, and then immediately stilled. "Why do anything with it? Leave it alone."

Eli shook his head. "I can't abandon it. I love that place. It's my home."

"And selling wouldn't be an option," Beau said. "Selling would leave a public records trail, which could lead right here. That's not an issue, anyway. Eli wants to keep it, and I completely understand. So, how do we keep his place up, long distance? Without leaving behind any kind of trail?"

"We still have Cheela there, watching to see if any Killapaka come sniffing around," Meska said. "They will care for your home, Eli, if you would like. They can handle the easier tasks in their natural Deor forms, and the harder work in their Camaflur forms."

"I'll leave you to figure out how to make that happen, Meska," Beau said. "There are also taxes and utilities to pay. We have to get those paid on time, and that will leave a trail."

"I have a suggestion," Eli said. "I have a nice nest egg. I'll have it transferred to you and Annie, and then you can pay my taxes and utility bills."

Beau shook his head. "You can't transfer your bank account to us. We already talked about that. Too risky." He sat in thought. "I have a friend who retired to Florida. Cristian Leone. He's an attorney. He's the guy who acted as the middleman in our gold coin transactions. It wasn't his line of work, but he was very helpful. He wouldn't even let us pay him anything. Can all of your bills and taxes be paid online?"

Eli put his head back and looked at the ceiling fan. He ticked off the bills associated with his property.

"Taxes, yes. Water and sewer, yes. Gas and electric, yes. We can terminate the phone and cable service." He looked up. "Yes. That can be done."

"Ok, Beau said. "I'll get in touch with Cris. I'll make monthly payments to him, and he can pay your bills online. He can also take care of closing out your phone and cable service accounts."

"I'll pay you back, every cent, with interest."

Beau shook his head. "Come on, Eli. I already told you. Gold coins! It wasn't like it was our money. We could carry this place and yours for the next fifty years. Now, as to your mail service. Is there any important mail you normally receive that would cause an issue with your home ownership, if you missed it?

"None that I can think of," Eli said. "We don't have to wait for a tax bill. Your lawyer friend, Cris, can go to the online county website once or twice a year and pay the taxes, if he doesn't mind. He can do the same, monthly, with the utilities. But what about keeping the place clean, cutting the grass, weeding, stuff like that? If we hire someone to do it, wouldn't we be putting that person at risk?"

Meska said, "The Cheela who live in your garden will take care of your home, as I said. Do not concern yourself with that. Your grass will be mowed and your house, furniture, porch, windows, etc. kept free of dust and dirt. Your home will not look abandoned. They will also keep any would-be trespassers away." The bear mused, for a moment. "I think they will actually have fun doing it."

Images of tiny toads pushing equally tiny lawnmowers popped into Eli's head. "Wait... how can the Cheela mow a lawn?"

"I imagine they'll bring in grasshoppers, Canada geese, a few steers, or other animals who can eat grass when in Camaflur form, right Meska?" Beau asked.

"That is how it will be done. In the dark of night, so there are no human observers. We will bring in whomever is needed."

"Thank you," Eli said. "Thank both of you. That's such a load off my mind. I felt like I was deserting her." He laughed. "Deserting my home, I mean. I always thought of my home as a "her.""

Beau smiled. "Just like a boat. Well, let's get to it. I'll make arrangements with Cris. We don't want mail piling up in your mailbox. I'll also have him do an online cancellation of the mail deliveries for Ben, Maya, and you. Kate won't be an issue. Her mail will just continue to go to the home of her former foster parents, until they decide to cancel it."

"Oh. Ask Cris to cancel my subscription to the *L.A. Times*, please," Eli said.

"Done." Beau stood. "Come on. Let's tell the others what we've decided."

"There is something else you should know," the bear said. "We have not told you this before, because you have enough to be concerned with.

281

The Motherland... the *energy* of the Motherland is dwindling."

"Dwindling? How so?" Beau asked.

"We Deor thrive on it, when we are in our homeland. It used to be sustainable for us to absorb it. And then the Mother vanished. It seems she was the battery that powered the place. Without her to replenish it, the energy is dissipating. That is one of the reasons—the *primary* reason, for many Deor—that we cannot just abandon the world outside of the Motherland.

"We think that, with the Mother gone, the energy there is now finite. If too many of us stayed there for long periods of time, we would eventually starve. There, our primary source of sustenance is its energy. We cannot substitute a source of light for it. It overrides our attempts to do so, as it fills us with itself.

"Here, we are able to exist on sunlight, and moonlight, and starlight, and other natural sources of illumination, without the Motherland energy taking priority over those sources."

Beau was stunned. The Motherland energy was finite. There was no safe haven for the Apalacheela. He looked at Eli, who seemed equally stunned.

"Let's not tell Kate and Ben about this, right now," Beau said. "They have enough on their plates."

∞

The two men walked into the house. They found the others sitting around the table in the dining room.

282

"I'm pretty sure you need an obstetrician," Annie was saying to Kate. She looked up from the dining room table to Beau and Eli, who were coming from the porch at the rear of the house. They looked... befuddled. Annie raised an eyebrow, and Beau shook his head.

A piano was crammed into a nook behind the dining room table. Beau pulled out the piano bench and sat on it. Eli sat down on the sofa in front of the cold pellet stove.

"According to what you've told us, if I leave this property, it'll be like putting up a big road sign for the Kills, who might inform their human servants, to the extent they have any" Kate said. "And there will still be medical records, even if you can convince a doctor to come here, and we'd have to worry about the doctor taking the Scent off the property. Then, when Sam's born, there would be a birth certificate. Which I guess he needs, anyway, doesn't he? Especially these days. But he can be traced, if he has one. It's a Catch-22."

Kate knew that she should be getting upset. She was not, however.

"I'll ask Falke," Annie said.

"I'm here," Falke said. The hawk came through the front wall of the house. "I've been listening to your conversation. Kate will not need a doctor."

Everyone stared at the hawk.

"Why not?" Annie asked.

"Her pregnancy will have no problems. The birth will be fast, safe, and painless. Samuel will make sure of that."

"Wow," Eli said. "That's some kid."

"And then no record of Sam's birth," Maya said. "But how will he be able to prove he's a U.S. citizen, when he needs to?"

"He will have more protection from us than the United States, or any country, could provide him," Falke replied. "He will never need to prove he's a citizen of any country."

There was a rush of light and air, and Falke was gone.

"Well," Annie said.

"I guess that takes care of that," Kate added.

Beau looked outside. All of the animals were in Camaflur. Those in their Deor shapes had vanished. He heard the sound of a truck coming up the driveway. "Your delivery is here, Annie. The rest of you stay here. Annie and I will go out and get the stuff."

"It's going to be a lot of clothing," Annie remarked. "After the delivery person leaves, we'll use the ATV to haul everything but Eli's stuff up to the cottages."

∞

Charlie Waddell, their short, red-haired delivery man, had been on this route for a couple years. He'd moved to Owego from Ohio to get away from an ex-girlfriend and from city life. He was currently staying with his cousin.

He had thought he hated city life, but found that he *really* hated the country. It sucked. He had to get back to where things were happening. He was going to quit this stupid job and move back to Cutter City. Maybe his ex would take him back.

He was thinking about this while unloading the deliveries onto the driveway by the house. The house, the forest behind the house, the two old people who were carrying the deliveries inside, and Owego's ambience, in general, freaked him out.

~

Beau reached out to Cris Leone, his attorney friend. The man, however, was in the process of retiring. Cris asked his son, Luca, who lived in Venice Beach, California, to handle the matter for him, as a favor to an old friend.

Luca was a patent attorney. Luca talked with Beau by phone, and then with Eli. He didn't quite get why they thought the Jacksons had to be untraceable, but he found Eli to be compelling. He graciously agreed to act as the Jacksons' intermediary with respect to their finances, even though handling finances was outside of his field.

Two little rescue dogs lived with Luca. He turned to the smallest one, a brindle-coated chihuahua-terrier mix. "I don't think the Jacksons are criminals on the run, eh, Georgie?"

Georgie snuggled into his lap but did not answer. She was a Cheela in Camaflur form, and very much awake. She had been posted to the West Coast, along with Reggie, the other rescue dog in Luca's home. In her last incarnation, she had been a black chihuahua-terrier mix by the name of Lucie, who had lived with Luca for twelve years. She had died a natural death in Camaflur form and had, when reborn, immediately been reassigned to him.

Cheela had been with the Leone family ever since Cris Leone had taken on the projet of handling the Walds' gold coins, decades earlier. They had latched on to Luca as a precaution. This had paid off, now that Luca was involved with the Jacksons and the Walds.

The Cheela were making sure that everyone connected with Samuel Jackson, in any way, had protection.

"What do you think, Reg, huh buddy? You agree with me? You think these are good people who, for some unknown reason, are in fear for their lives?"

Reggie jumped up next to Georgie and stretched to lick Luca's nose.

~

Summer had passed, and autumn was nearing its end. The group had fallen into a comfortable rhythm. Eli and Beau had become as attached at the hip as twin brothers. Their personalities complemented each other's. Annie was glad Beau had the male companionship he'd been missing. The two men even watched sports together.

The entire group was sitting on the all-season porch. The fire in the pellet stove was keeping the room warm and cozy. Kate sat in an armchair. She was covered with a blanket, and blowing on a mug of hot chocolate almond milk. Her feet were propped up on an ottoman. Maya was in another chair at the small table, sipping an identical drink.

Ben was lounging on a sofa across from Kate. His uncle was on the other end of the sofa. Each of them was gulping down a cup of herbal tea. The group got together frequently, but had a standing engagement every Friday evening. It was their formal weekly meeting, with dinner afterward.

"What's on the agenda, Maya?" Beau asked. He and Annie were curled up on the other couch.

There was an open laptop on the table in front of Maya. She leaned forward and peered at it.

"I think we should go over what we've accomplished and then decide what's next," she said. She looked out of the large windows. Snow was beginning to fall.

"Sounds like a great idea," Ben agreed.

"Ok, let's go through our master list: Harvest the vegetables, as each type is ready. Check. Make sure we always had our heads covered when we're outside, to prevent detection by spies."

Maya smirked. Life had been so pleasant and easy in this place that it was difficult to keep in mind that they were still hunted. "Check."

"Process vegetables, in accordance with Annie's instructions. That includes canning tomatoes, beets, green beans, carrots, peas, Swiss chard, spinach, pickled cabbage (aka sauerkraut), and pickles, corn, sweet potatoes, pumpkins, and squashes. Check. By the way, Annie and Beau, you guys were excellent canning and pickling teachers."

"And all of you were excellent students," Beau smiled. He thought about that controlled canning chaos in their small kitchen. It had been fun.

"Put the root vegetables in boxes, according to Beau's specific directions for each particular type of vegetable, and store them away in the root cellar. Check. Again, great lessons, Beau."

"Any time."

"Cook, boil, bake, or sauté whatever vegetables we like, in our own discretion. Then vacuum seal and cram same into the–already too full–freezers. Check."

"That was the most fun, of all of it," Kate said. "It will be nice to pull out a bag of frozen sautéed peppers, when we want to add them to something."

"Just as long as we know what we have in there, and we rotate the stock," Maya said.

"Yes, chief," Kate replied.

"Set up a schedule to feed the mushrooms that are in the compost trays in the basement, which mushrooms are to be routinely harvested." Check.

"Set up a maintenance program for the solar panels and batteries. Check." Everyone rotated through that job.

"Make sure there is sufficient firewood for the two cottages. Check." She looked at Beau and Annie. "You did that before we came here. That definitely will be something we have to do ourselves, next summer, assuming we're still living here."

Eli nodded.

"Get all our winter gear ready and accessible."

Maya looked toward the far end of the sunroom. Winter coats were hanging from a rack.

Winter hats, scarves, face masks, ice cleats, and gloves had replaced the gardening hats and baseballs caps that had been stored above the coat rack, on a long shelf. Winter boots were lined up on the floor below the coats.

"We keep all our winter stuff next to the kitchen door," Kate said. Ben nodded.

"That's where I keep mine, too," Maya said. "Ok, winter gear, check."

"Learn to maintain the well water systems in this house and in the cottages. Check." She turned to Beau. "We were on public water all our lives. I had no idea how much was involved with treating well water."

"Be glad we have the reverse osmosis systems for drinking water," Beau said. "That water is actually much cleaner and safer than public water or so-called spring water."

"Have Beau show us how to operate and maintain the wood-burning stoves in the cottages. Check."

"We'll show you how to clean the chimneys, in the spring," Beau added.

"Keep an eye on Kate and make sure she and the baby are okay. Check."

"You guys are driving me *crazy*," Kate responded.

"Take weekly picnics in the Motherland. Check." Maya smiled, thinking of the Motherland. "And that wraps up my summary of our accomplishments. I'm sure there are some I've overlooked, but these are the important ones. Now, does anyone have any thoughts about projects for the winter?"

"We're caught up on all of our work projects," Beau said. "I think we should each concentrate on individual activities we'd like to do. He glanced through the French doors, toward the dining room table. "I wouldn't mind doing a jigsaw puzzle or two."

"Wow. And we needed to have a meeting to establish that," Annie said.

"I'd like to learn to play the guitar," Eli said.

Ben stretched his back. "Kate and I have been working on our Spanish. And reading up on caring for an infant."

Annie looked at Beau. "I've always wanted to learn Spanish. That's a great idea. Want to do it with me?"

"Sure. Sounds good. And how about you, Maya? What are your immediate plans?"

"I'm constantly verifying and modifying my projections for our supplies. So, there's that. I should be a little bummed that I haven't been able to pursue my career in quantum mechanics, but, what is happening here is so much more important, that it hasn't bothered me at all. I'd like to order some books in my field, though, if that's ok, Annie? So that I can keep my hand in. I could download books, but it's not the same."

"Not a problem," Annie replied. "A book is normally delivered to our mailbox which, as you know, is across the road from the bottom of the driveway and not on our property. Mail delivery is, therefore, safe. Give me a list of what you want. We'll order one book at a time, so the delivery will fit in the mailbox. Otherwise, the mailperson might have to drive the delivery up to the house."

"Thanks. I appreciate it."

Annie stood and walked to a window. "It's really coming down out there."

Maya also stood. "Wow. I've never seen snow like that."

"I've never seen snow in person, ever," Kate said. She got up to get a better view. The snow was amazing.

Beau also looked up. "That's what happens here. We never get used to it, and we absolutely love it."

"You guys aren't going back to the cottages tonight," Eli said. "You're staying here."

"Dinner is in the oven," Annie said. "I'll set the table." It was her turn to cook for this Friday night meeting, per Maya's exacting schedule. Ben was up at bat next Friday.

Maya walked to the French doors. "I'll help."

∞

Eli and Beau did the cleanup while the others, now sitting in the family room, decided who was sleeping where.

"I'll sleep on the porch," Eli called.

Beau, working next to Eli in the kitchen, nudged him. "Not a good idea. The stove is out of pellets and I forgot to bring another bag from the garage overhang. I don't think it's safe to go out there to get a bag, right now."

"Never mind, then. I'll sleep in my own room," Eli called, so the others in the family room could hear him.

"You and Ben can take the front upstairs bedroom," Maya said. "I'll sleep down here, on a sofa."

There was a large chest, which was used for storage and as a coffee table, in front of the L-shaped sofas. Annie leaned over and opened the lid. She nodded at the sheets, blankets and pillows inside. "There you go. Everything you need."

Eli and Beau finished up in the kitchen and joined the others. The lights were off, with the exception of a single lamp in the family room. Everyone curled up on the sofas. Ben grabbed some blankets from the chest and distributed them. They relaxed in silence, and did nothing but listen to the howling wind and the snow whipping against the uncovered windows.

Beau opened his eyes. The house was chilly. Annie always kept the heat low at night. He sat up and looked around, in the glow of the single lamp. He and Annie were bunched up together at one end of a sofa, their legs propped up on the coffee table in front of it. Maya was curled up in a ball at the other end. Eli was snoring quietly on the one to the right. Beau assumed that Ben and Kate were under the mass of blankets on the sofa to the left.

Beau gently shook Annie awake. She stretched, yawned, and stood. Beau got up and closed the shades and curtains. He was so tired that he stumbled as he made his way around the room, and forgot about the back window that faced the forest.

Annie turned off the lamp. The couple made their way through the house and into the main bedroom. "Nice to have a houseful of people again," Annie whispered. They climbed into bed and pulled the covers over their heads.

∞

Kate awoke, her bladder yelling at her to get up. She carefully stood, trying not to disturb Ben, and made her way upstairs to the bathroom. She heard low voices coming from the family room as she came back downstairs.

"What *is* that?" Ben was asking Eli. The two men were standing next to the rear window and peering outside.

"What's going on?" Kate whispered.

"Look," Ben replied, and moved aside to make room for her.

Kate stared into the darkness. Wait, she thought. It wasn't completely dark. There were tiny, individual glowing spots, high up and spaced feet apart. The snow coming down around the lights sparkled. The lights were located where the tops of the tree branches would be, if the branches could have been visible in the dark.

"What are those? Cheela, do you think?" she asked.

"They're so small. I don't know. Maybe they're Cheela insects? Or some large Cheela who, for some reason, made themselves that little?"

Eli cupped his hands above his eyes, as if that would help him see, and leaned against the glass. "It's not the same kind of light the Deor are made of. It's different, in some way. More sparkly. Less intense." He squinted, involuntarily, trying to focus his eyes more.

He spoke more loudly. "They almost look like tiny windows, with glittering lights behind them."

Instantly, the tiny lights went out.

"That was freaky." Kate pulled down the shade and drew the curtains closed. She looked at the sofa. It no longer seemed inviting. She wanted to sleep in a safe, secure bed. "Let's go upstairs," she said to Ben.

Eli, too, withdrew to his own bedroom. Maya, still asleep, had the entire family room to herself. Her father tucked her in before he went upstairs.

∞

Eli was normally the first one up in the morning, rising at 5:00 a.m., but had overslept today. He glanced at the clock. It was 7:30. He heard Annie and Beau moving around downstairs, and smelled coffee.

He opened his shades and looked out of the bedroom window. The snow had stopped, and the sun was starting its climb up the eastern horizon, It blasted the snow with an orange blaze. There appeared to be about a foot of snow on the ground. His gaze traveled up the trees, where snow covered the branches. He examined the tops of the trees. Nothing there, other than tree limbs and snow.

He quickly showered, brushed his teeth, dressed, and joined the Walds on the sunporch.

"You missed it last night," he said.

"What's that?" Beau asked.

Eli told them about the strange, tiny lights at the tops of the trees.

"Huh," Annie said. "Why don't we ask one of the Cheela about it?" She pulled out the chain around her neck, and drew the locket from under her sweater.

She was about to open the locket, when Eli asked, "May I do it?"

Annie looked quizzically at the man. He turned toward the French doors into the house and waved his hand in the direction of the kitchen.

"Oh. You mean the bell."

"Right. The bell Meska brought you from the Motherland."

Meska had, a decade ago, gifted the Walds with the bell. "It was made in the Motherland for you," she had explained. "It has been charged by an energy strike there. A Cheela will always answer when the bell sounds."

Everyone was very careful, when working in the kitchen, not to accidentally knock the bell. The bell was made out of some unknown metal. It had strong harmonics, and produced a perfect, pure, and bright sound, when rung.

"Sure," she smiled.

Eli jumped up and rushed into the kitchen. He stood in front of the bell for a moment, then lightly tapped it with his forefinger. The bell made an ethereal, silver sound. There was a rush of movement and there was Meska, floating in the dining room. She took up almost the entire space.

Annie and Beau got up and came inside.

Beau looked at Eli. "Go ahead," he prompted.

Eli was a bit tongue-tied. Meska was the most intimidating of the Apalacheela the man had met. "We have a question, Meska," he managed. "Can you tell us what the little lights are, that appeared at the tops of the trees last night?"

"Oh, those," Meska rumbled. "They have nothing to do with us, or with you. Leave them alone. Don't even look at them."

"Sorry?" Annie asked.

"Things sometimes get... confused, at the edges of the Motherland, where you live," the bear replied.

"Confused?" Beau scrunched up his face in thought.

"There are an infinite number of other... other... I am not sure what you call them. Cosmoses? Spaces? Ethers?"

"Do you mean universes?" Maya stifled a yawn with her hand as she walked into the kitchen.

"Yes, Maya, universes. There are an infinite number of universes. The edge of the Motherland is pliable, not completely in the Motherland and not completely in your world. It is *soft*."

"Wow," Maya said. "What did I miss?"

"We'll fill you in later," her father muttered.

"Sometimes, the boundaries of other universes overlap with the borders of the Motherland."

"So those lights are from another *universe?!*" Eli exclaimed. He didn't know why he was so surprised, considering the very fact of the existence of the Deor and the Motherland.

"I was not present to observe them, last night, but I assume so. I have seen them, in the past, and talked with them. I think their universe is on an orbit that periodically–quite often, actually–crosses here."

"You *talked* with them?" Eli asked. "Are they dangerous?"

"I would not say they're *dangerous*, but they are not benign. They clearly do not want to interface with humans. Leave them alone, if you see them again, and you will be fine."

Annie moved closer to Meska's hovering, bear-shaped, maelstrom of light. "Are they another species, altogether?"

"I suppose that is how humans would categorize them. There are numerous "species," in their universe, including faeries, elves, griffins, selkies, brownies, kelpies, dragons, water horses, mermaids and mermen, sea serpents, unicorns, sprites, pixies, sphinxes, krakens, sirens, hippogriffs, fauns, wyverns, phoenixes, leprechauns, werewolves, sasquatches, centaurs, moon rabbits, basilisks, and gnomes, to name a few. Some of your classic tales about those entities are likely based on past, perilous interactions between them and humans. Again– the next time your universe intersects with theirs–do not try to approach or speak with any of them."

"Good to know," Maya said. She was more at ease with Meska, and with all of the Apalacheela, than was her father. She started to ponder the implications of the intersection of two universes– actually three, counting the Motherland–and wondered whether she should start writing a paper about it. But how would she get it published? She could still work on it, though, and push off publication to some future date (maybe, even, as an ostensible work of fiction), when her group was no longer being hunted.

"Is there anything else?" the bear asked.

"No. Thank you for coming, Meska," Beau replied. There was a whoosh, like air being sucked into a vacuum, and the bear vanished.

"So, Dad, can you tell me now what I missed last night, please?" Maya asked.

~

Ben, Kate, and Maya spent the three weeks before Christmas at the Wald home. The constant snow made it difficult for the three to travel back and forth to their respective cottages. They wanted to spend the holidays with the others and, therefore, decided to move in together for a time.

Maya was especially happy about staying at the Walds. She desperately wanted to see the faerie lights. The faeries, however, did not make an appearance during her visit. The group did manage to make their way up to the Motherland, several days before Christmas. They went to the sandy cove and swam in its calm blue waters.

Beau and Eli had anticipated the Christmas holiday for months. They had dug up a five-foot tall, live balsam fir tree in September, and planted it in a large container. They, with the help of Ben, brought it into the family room, to be hung with lights and decorated. Maya brought up boxes of decorations from a corner of the basement. Kate and Ben were in charge of decorating the tree. The others worked on the rest of the house, doing as they pleased with the various Christmas whatnots Annie and Beau had accumulated over the years. Annie had a large collection of Santa Clauses, about which she was unapologetic.

They each made their favorite dishes for Christmas Eve: Kate, a lentil Bolognese; Annie, a butternut squash risotto with onions, mushrooms, and spinach; Beau, a vegan shepherd's pie; Eli, a miso tofu wrap; and Ben, tortilla chips and a dip made of cooked cashew cream, nutritional yeast, a bit of salt, and tapioca starch. They sat in the family room, after dinner, drinking mulled wine. (Kate had hot apple cider.) The only illumination came from the lights on the Christmas tree, which reflected on the ornaments and beaded garlands.

None of them were particularly religious. They toasted the friends and family members who had gone on before them.

"To you, Mom," Maya whispered, and drank a sip of wine.

"To you, Jennie," Eli agreed.

Maya occasionally, throughout the evening, looked out of the back window to see if there were any sparkling lights at the tops of the trees. No such luck.

Falke appeared in the Walds' bedroom at midnight. Annie rolled over and sat up. She shook Beau awake.

"What is it, Falke?" she asked. "Is everything okay?" It was odd for the hawk to appear in their bedroom, especially at this late hour.

"Bring everyone up to the Motherland, tomorrow afternoon. We have a little surprise for you," the bird whistled.

∞

Beau looked at Annie. They and the others were dressed warmly. "The snow is fairly deep, but I think you and I can handle it, Annie. Will you be all right, Kate?"

"Sure." Kate was now five months pregnant. She had had no morning sickness or fatigue. She felt great, in fact, like she could run a mile without breaking a sweat.

"Let's go, then," Beau said.

They left the house at 1 p.m. and trekked up through the snow to the woods. Falke appeared in a tree above them, about fifty yards in.

"This way," she said, her voice like golden shards. She veered to the right. The group followed.

Annie was starting to tire, just as Falke stopped, fifteen minutes later, in a small clearing.

"Here," Falke said. The group joined the hawk in the clearing. Falke shimmered and said, "Focus!" and then vanished. They heard Falke add, in the distance, "Take whatever you like. They made it for you."

"Who are *they?*" Eli asked. There was no answer.

They all stood in a line and, without thinking about it, took each other's hands. No one spoke. They focused, as instructed. The trees around them suddenly disappeared. The trees were replaced by stalls covered in twinkling strands of Christmas lights.

Ben looked around. They were in the middle of a European-type Christmas market. There were no other people there, no one manning the stalls.

"This is *fantastic,"* Annie said.

Kate was beaming. "I can't believe this."

Ben and Maya had already started to inspect the closest stands. "There are all kinds of handmade things," Ben said, delighted.

Kate joined him, and they began to walk down the row of little buildings, looking at mugs, ornaments, candles, figurines, pottery, jewelry, and star-shaped lanterns.

"This really feels like Christmas, now," Eli said. "This is great!" He had found a brightly lit booth that had, in addition to a display of mugs, a pot of simmering hot, chocolate almond milk. He leaned over and smelled it. Eli ladled the hot liquid into six mugs and handed them around.

Ben was searching through a display of jewelry. He was drawn to a simple silver and turquoise bracelet. He picked it up and held it out to Kate. "Here, Kate. Do you like it?"

"It's awesome. I love it."

"Merry Christmas, love," Ben said, and fastened the bracelet on her wrist.

Eli was examining the strings of lights that adorned the hot chocolate stand. They weren't plugged into anything, they weren't battery operated, and they didn't have solar panels. He called, "Beau! Come here. Look at these lights. What's powering them?"

Beau walked over to the stand. He glanced at the lights and shrugged. "The energy of this place is powering them. Come on. Look for something you like."

The two men wandered off together. "Check out these rings!" Maya called. She was scrutinizing a display of silver men's rings, some inset with oval-shaped turquoise, others with onyx, and others with malachite.

Eli and Beau were drawn to the rings. Beau slipped one with an onyx setting on his right ring finger. Eli liked the malachite, and did the same. "See? I told you," Maya grinned. Eli picked out one with turquoise for Ben. "Hey, Ben," he called. "I have your Christmas present!"

Annie, meanwhile, had found a glazed bowl with geometric patterns that she thought was perfect, and a silver necklace with an onyx pendant she thought Maya would like. She walked over to the ring stand, where everyone else was now standing, and held out the necklace to the young woman.

"Do you like it?" she asked.

"I love it." Maya bent her neck so that Annie could reach up and slip the chain over her head. "Thank you."

Kate had moved to the booth that was farthest from the entrance. "Hey, everyone, look at this."

Eli went to grab the pot of hot chocolate. He noticed, on his way to the back of the market, that darkness had fallen. His senses told him that it should be about 10 a.m. but, clearly, it was nighttime.

He joined the others, now standing next to Kate. They were peering at the scene in front of them. Eli refilled everyone's mugs before he allowed himself to look at what was laid out on the booth's countertop.

"What the... " Eli muttered.

It was a miniature village. There were small shops and townhouses and a square in the center. It was surrounded by tiny, snow-covered trees and, on one side, a long hill. The village was decorated with Christmas displays and lights.

Tiny, brown-skinned people, with long, flowing black hair tied into elaborate knots and braids that were twined with bright fabric, were dancing together in the small, snowy square. The people wore colorful, flowing clothing. A few stood at the edges of the square and played fiddles and drums. The sounds coming from the instruments were barely audible to the larger humans.

The group, mesmerized, stood and watched. Some of the little people stopped dancing and skipped over to booths—similar to the ones in the Christmas market—to grab miniature fried bread pockets stuffed with some type of filling, and teensy mugs of beer.

Maya held out her mug to her father for a refill, without turning her head away from the small-scale village.

"Look," she whispered, and pointed. There was a large hill next to the village. Wee children were piling onto toboggans and racing down the incline. They spilled off the toboggans at the bottom of the hill and rolled into the snow. Maya could just make out that the children were laughing and shouting.

The fiddlers and drummers suddenly stopped playing. The dancers bowed to each other. Some of them hugged. They walked over to the children, who were now having a snowball fight. The children stood up, shook off the snow, and raced over to their parents.

All of the villagers slowly walked to their homes, went inside, and shut the doors behind them. Curtains were pulled closed. The Christmas lights went out, leaving the miniature village dark, except for the small lights which came on inside the homes and caused the curtained windows to glow. The only movements in the village, now, were the falling snow and the trickles of smoke coming from the miniscule townhouse chimneys.

∞

There was a flash of light at the entrance to the Christmas market. Falke hovered over the snow. "It's time to leave," she said.

"It seems like we just got here," Maya complained. She looked down at her empty mug, and realized that she had had two refills. They must have been here longer than she had thought.

Eli had begun to feel a bit odd. It was like he was being filled with electricity and being drained of energy at the same time. Maybe it was hitting him so hard, after what seemed like a short period of time, because this was the second time within the week they had visited the Motherland. Or, perhaps, they'd been there much longer than it had seemed.

"Yes. It is time to leave," Annie agreed. "Thank you for bringing us here, Falke. This was wonderful."

She glanced at Eli. He looked befuddled. "Time sometimes gets wonky up here," she said.

"It would seem so," Maya agreed.

"It will be waiting for you again, next Christmas," Falke replied. "A tribe of the residents did this for you. They know about the Children, they know about what humankind is doing to animals, and they know you are the support system for the Children. It makes them happy to bring you some joy."

"How did they know about Christmas markets?" Kate asked.

"Seta and I gave them all the information they needed to make this. They enjoyed it very much, themselves, and will continue the tradition."

Everyone had walked toward Falke while they talked. Maya stopped, before she exited the market. "A tribe of residents? Is that them?" She gestured back toward the booth at the far end, with its tiny village.

"No," Falke replied. "They *are* residents, but not the ones who put this market together."

Maya thought of the young woman about whom she had been dreaming. "May we meet the people who created this?"

"You may not." The hawk led them back down through the forest, her brilliance lighting the way. Maya looked back at the Christmas market. It was slowly fading into the trees. She thought she caught a glimpse of a tall woman, with long, black hair, standing next to a tree, and then the market and the woman were gone.

∞

Kate was stirring a big pot of vegetable soup. She glanced down at her new bracelet. "Today was the best Christmas I've ever had."

Ben was slicing a loaf of bread, fresh from the oven. "Mine, too." He stopped what he was doing, grabbed her hand, and squeezed it.

~

Samuel Eli Jackson was born at 11:53 p.m., on April 20th. (Kate and Ben had previously decided to give their son Ben's surname.) No physician was in attendance and no record of his birth was made. As promised, Kate experienced no pain or discomfort.

The birth took place in Kate and Ben's cottage. The Scent vanished the moment Sam was born. No part of it emanated any longer from Sam or the adults. Sam, himself, had only the normal but wonderful, intoxicating baby smell.

Ingwe the tiger's Masque form seemed to explode from Ben's wallet and, suddenly, there was a gigantic tiger light display in the hallway outside the bedroom. Dedos the octopus erupted from Kate's necklace. His tentacles moved as quickly as the motes of light of which he was composed. He stayed close to the wall and near to the bed.

"Dedos," Kate smiled, "and Ingwe. Thank you for showing yourselves. I know the two of you will be the best protectors our son could ever have."

"I shall guard him with my life," Ingwe said, in a quiet roar.

Meska the bear, Falke the hawk, and Seta the dog also entered the room. They shrank, so as not to overwhelm the room's human occupants, and floated, looking down at the baby.

Hundreds of Cheela hung outside the house. Thousands waited in the forest. Their Mother's words had not been empty. The prophecy was coming true. The world, and the fate of animals, was going to change.

"Hello, little one. Welcome to the world," Meska said.

Ben was sitting on a chair next to the bed. His fingers were wrapped around his son's tiny ones. "The *Scent* is gone," he observed. It had become an integral part of the background. It felt odd that it was no longer there. "Why is that?"

"It is still here. Your son is stronger now, and he is able to hide it."

Eli, Beau, and Annie had left the bedroom and were sitting in the small den, to give the new parents some space. Good luck with that, Annie thought.

The night was cold and a dusting of snow was still on the ground. The three of them relaxed into their chairs. They were content. Maya remained in the bedroom to help with the baby.

Maya bent over Kate. She looked at her new family member with pride. "Now that the Scent has vanished, does that mean we can leave the property?"

"No," Meska replied. "You and your family are not safe anyplace else. For now."

"Hmmm. Well, that's ok, because we actually *do* get to leave. That is, we get to visit *your* home, Meska. That's so much better than going anywhere else."

Maya thought about the places they'd visited over the past months. She'd grown to love this place. The Walds' house, her cottage, the garden, their daily activities. Most of all, she loved spending time in the Motherland.

The Walds and the Cheela had enforced the directive that their group could not go up there more than once a week, and then only for a maximum of four to six hours at a time. Currents of magical power continually coursed through the Motherland. The amount of time their group was allowed to stay was dependent on where and how the currents were flowing on that particular day. Maya wasn't convinced it was as big a deal as the Cheela claimed.

Falke floated toward the bed. "All of us would like... that is—we *need*–to see the Child. Would that be all right, if it is only a few at a time?"

"It's getting late. I think it would be better in the morning. Do you think it'll be too hard for them to hold off for a bit?" Ben asked. He looked down at Kate. She was already sound asleep. Sam was nestled against her chest. Kate had a little smile on her lips.

Falke nodded. She and Seta disappeared through the ceiling. Ingwe, Dedos, and Meska remained behind.

The door to the bedroom was open. Ben and the Cheela overheard the others talking in the den.

"Well, the Scent is gone," Beau was saying. "I wonder what *that* means."

Meska left the bedroom in a flash of light. Her big form manifested in the family room. Annie flinched.

"Yikes. A little warning next time, please."

Meska looked as apologetic as a gigantic light display could, and shrank down to a more appropriate size for the small, crammed room. "Sorry. I came to answer Beau's question. The Scent is not gone, as I explained to Maya. The Child is pulling it in, and hiding it."

"What about Ben and Katie? They each had parts of it. It's *all* gone now," Eli said.

"You must not have noticed," Meska replied. The Scent left them the moment Samuel was conceived. Every part of it from their lineages went into the Child."

"But... Katie projected it everywhere during her entire pregnancy," Eli protested.

"It was coming from the Child she was carrying, not from Kate, herself."

"Oh," Annie said. She sighed, and pursed her lips. "

"What is it?" Beau asked.

"Well... I'd been thinking that, if Ben and Kate had one of the Children, maybe they could have the other one. But if they don't have the Scent anymore... "

"They may have other children," Meska said, "but they will not have another *Child*."

"On the upside," Beau said, "if the Scent is no longer detectable, would it be ok for Annie and me to leave the property?" He looked at Eli. "I understand that the rest of our group had better stay put. No one knows who Annie and I are, with respect to the Child, but you... well, that's another matter."

"All of you must "stay put," as you call it, Beau," Meska said. "We do not know whether the

Killapaka have discovered where the baby and his parents are. They may well have humans in their employ, in which case you and Annie could be taken as hostages, if you left your home."

Eli looked toward Meska's floating form. "There's plenty to do here to keep me busy." I think I'll start keeping a journal, for posterity. Someday, it might be important for people to know what happened here. But I'm sorry we've put you in this position, Beau and Annie."

Annie snorted. "*Thank you* for putting us in this position. Everything we need is here."

Beau patted Eli on the back.

The Cheela came in pairs to see the baby throughout the following days. Humans see Deor as shapes of moving light. Sam, like other newborns, could detect light and motion. He stared toward the Cheela with his dark brown eyes, which held the knowledge of an adult, and he reached his fingers to them.

Part IV
Chapter 1
The Rise of a Racist
Edward L. Doheny High School, Los Angeles

A short, plump boy, by the name of Rex Boner, ran his fingers through his dark hair. He sat at his desk in his tenth-grade history class and stared at the sweaty, balding teacher at the front of the class. The man was giving a lecture about American Indians. American Indians. Unbelievable. Next thing you knew, the teacher would be making them study the history of slavery in this country. What a jerk.

Rex knew everything he needed to know about Indians, as in, they were *not* white, and they drank too much. Rex tuned the teacher out.

Rex acquired the skill of cheating by the second grade. He considered this to be his first great accomplishment. He was now in the tenth grade, but hadn't learned much that the school system was trying to shove down his throat. He had, instead, added to those abilities he did consider to be important. He had become an expert liar, manipulator, schemer, misleader, and con artist. Those skills had provided him the means to achieve a series of report cards consisting of straight C's, without the need for study.

History, in particular, had no relevance to Rex Boner's life, with certain exceptions. For example, the Civil War and the prominent figures on the side of the South were enthralling: Robert E. Lee, Stonewall Jackson, Jefferson Davis. They were men out of their time. The world needed people like that, right now.

Rex discovered that there were entire sections of history not taught in school. He had felt compelled, beginning at the age of ten, to investigate these matters for himself.

One of the non-curricula, historical matters Rex discovered, for instance, was that slaves had been used as specimen subjects in medical experiments in the United States during the 1800s. He spent hours poring over obscure treatises about James Marion Sims, the father of modern gynecology. (Dr. Sims had reached the height of his chosen medical field as a direct result of his experimental surgeries on enslaved women.)

It made Rex's skin crawl—while, at the same time, a sharp thrill shot up and down his body— to read that Dr. Sims (being of the opinion that Black people had inferior physiology, which made them incapable of feeling pain the way *white* people did) had not provided anesthesia or painkillers to the screaming women on his operating tables, while he sliced them open like heads of cheese and dug around with a scalpel in their uteri.

Rex was amazed and impressed that a statue honoring Dr. Sims had been erected in Central Park in New York City, of all places, and another in Columbia, South Carolina.[7] He was astonished

---

[7] The mayor of New York City ordered the statue of J. Marion Sims to be removed in 2018. It was moved to Green-Wood Cemetery in Brooklyn, which is the resting place of many rich and powerful men. The statue now sits in a place of honor in the cemetery, as does another disturbing statute, the misogynistic Civic Virtue, which depicts a man standing over

that none of these events were mentioned in the history texts that were part of the public-school curriculum.

He thought about it, and concluded that was for the best. He would take a lesson from that. Plausible deniability, as in, "This country has *never* been racist," even though it has been *saturated* in it since its inception.

Rex intended to visit those monuments when he reached adulthood. He would take a long educational tour throughout the United States to see, first-hand, the numerous monuments honoring those historical men who had promoted and venerated slavery.

Young Rex also spent much of his free time reading about Hitler, Nazis, and concentration camps. He read about the unbelievable daily tortures, deprivations, and starvations to which the interned Jews had been subjected. Who knew that people like Dr. Josef Mengele had conducted such brutal, horrendous, disfiguring–and usually fatal–experiments on the Jews?

Rex read everything he could about the details of those experiments. He read about the twin children who were sewn together to become conjoined, and the things that were injected into children's eyes, and the babies who were ripped from their mothers and thrown into furnaces. It must have been a pretty wild time.

Rex believed he had been born into the wrong time and place. He should either have landed on this earth as the son of a plantation owner in the Deep South, or as a decent,

---

two writhing female figures, who are dubbed "Vice" and "Corruption."

upstanding Nazi. His own generation was pathetic.

He started to realize that, possibly, he hadn't missed the boat, after all. There might be a way to resurrect a right way of thinking, even in this day and age. He knew there had to be many other people, in this country and around the world, who also despised non-white people. He, himself, would find a way to bring them together in a great cause.

More and more of Rex's kind of people had been coming out of the woodwork like roaches, in modern times, thanks to encouragement from certain white supremacist politicians. The things those politicians had been able to accomplish were a start, but were trifling, compared to what Rex had in mind.

Sixteen-year-old Rex sat at his desk and stared at the teacher in front of the class. The man walked back and forth in front of the blackboard while he lectured. The tenth grade was a waste. Rex hated it almost as much as he hated the Black and Latino and Asian kids in the class. He seethed. Why was he stuck in here with these lowlifes?

The problem, as he saw it, began with desegregation. He hated desegregation, he hated non-white immigrants, he hated Lyndon B. Johnson and Martin Luther King Jr., and all those S.O.B. marchers in the 1960s. They should have gone back to their own country, wherever that was.

Rex felt anger boiling up in him. He was beginning to feel like he was going to explode. He had to do something to release it, or he'd have a stroke.

314

The teacher turned and began writing on the blackboard. Rex rose from his chair and looked around the classroom. A lone, blue, hard-plastic chair was at the back of the room. Rex left his desk, walked over to the hard little chair, picked it up, spun around, and threw it straight at the back of Mr. Watson's head. Rex was already jumping back into his own desk chair, the second he released the chair.

The chair missed its intended victim. It whizzed by the man's left ear and crashed into the blackboard. Mr. Watson spun around.

"What?" Mr. Watson shouted.

He felt his ear to make sure it was still attached to his head, and looked around the room. The class was silent.

The man took in a few short gasps of air, then asked, "Who threw that?"

The students looked down at their laps. Rex's desk was at the back of the class. The only witnesses had been the members of Rex's gang, who all sat in the back rows. They looked at each other and smirked.

"Threw *what?*" one of the boys–by the name of Edwin Perdet–sneered. Edwin leaned back in his chair.

Rex stood, stretched, and walked to the front of the classroom. He picked up the blue chair, carried it to the back of the room, placed it in its former spot, and then went back to his desk and plopped down in his chair.

"No one threw anything, Mr. Watson," Rex said.

The other students stared at Rex. There was something about him. He was feral. Scary. They did not want his attention to be directed at them. Who knew what he was capable of, what he would throw at them when their own backs were turned. Or worse? The other students looked down at their desks and stayed out of it. Not their business.

Everyone except Benjamin Jackson, that is. Ben looked up, alert. He glanced from Rex to Mr. Watson, and back to Rex.

"It's the *government*," Rex said. "They've been pumping chemicals into all of the classrooms in every school building."

"I... what are you talking about?" Mr. Watson asked. The man sat down, leaned his elbows on the desk, covered his eyes with his hands, and began rubbing his temples with his fingers. He was tired.

"It's simple," Rex replied. "These chemicals are making all of us weak. They're making us lose our hair, they're making us sweat a lot." Rex stared at Mr. Watson's sweaty, bald head. "No one threw any chair. It's all in your mind. Those chemicals are making everyone hallucinate."

Mr. Watson didn't know whether to let Rex go on with his usual asinine babbling, or just to send him to the principal's office. He wanted to call the police and have Rex arrested. The boy was crazy, violent, and a troublemaker. The thing was, he had no proof Rex Boner had thrown the chair. The teacher stopped rubbing his forehead, took out a white hanky, and patted at the beads of sweat.

"They're doing it to control us," Rex said. He was looking down at a notebook hidden in his lap and flipping through pages of doodles and drawings. He glanced down at the current page. There it was. He'd been so bored in chemistry the day before that he'd actually written down basic chemical formulas.

Rex ripped the page out of his notebook and whipped it over his head. "I found this outside the HVAC closet," he said. "This is what they've been putting in our air. These are the chemicals they've been running through our HVAC system."

Mr. Watson felt a perverse interest in the measures that Rex would take to support his deranged conspiracy theories.

"Let me see that." He gestured at the paper. The teacher hoped that going along with the kid for a few minutes would tamp down the boy's capricious anger.

Rex strode to the front of the classroom. He slammed his hand, and the page it was holding, onto the desk in front of the teacher. Mr. Watson stared down at the handwritten formulas. It was all Greek to Mr. Watson. He knew history and many other subjects, but had long forgotten chemistry. He had no idea what he was looking at. He was sure, however, that the paper had been torn from a notebook owned by Rex, and that it had not been accidentally dropped in front of the HVAC room by the "government."

Benjamin Jackson had been taking notes on the lecture and looking down at his own notebook, when Rex had heaved the chair at the teacher. He had not witnessed anything other than the aftermath of the event. There was no doubt Rex had done it, though. Rex was bat-shit crazy. Ben decided that Mr. Watson needed help defusing the situation, before Rex's acolytes at the back of the room decided to join in.

Ben interrupted the other boy's performance. He said, as if speaking to child or to a patient in a manic phase, "Rex, please. No killer chemicals are being pumped into the school. None of us are hallucinating. Someone threw a chair at Mr. Watson." Ben looked around the room. "It doesn't look like anyone's going to say who did it. So, let's get on with the class. Why don't you just go back to your seat and relax, Rex."

Rex stood in front of the teacher's desk. His mouth opened a little. A fellow student–a Black kid, no less–had had the balls to challenge him. He pressed his lips together into a thin, hard, compressed line. He wanted to tear off Ben's head with his bare hands.

Mr. Watson looked at Ben. Just as there was something about Rex Boner that the other students found to be off-balance and menacing, there was something about Benjamin Jackson that captivated the teacher. Plus, whenever Mr. Watson stood over Ben's desk to collect a paper or a test from the boy, he smelled something unidentifiable and elusive. The scent did not come from an applied product. It floated from Ben's skin. Mr. Watson was married, straight, and not a pedophile. Ben's attraction, for him, was not sexual. The man was drawn to Ben the way a hummingbird was drawn to sugar water.[8]

---

[8] Mr. Watson was one of the few hundred living people who had a very small percentage of the relevant genetic coding that allowed him to detect–just barely–Ben's Scent.

Ben started to stand, saying to Mr. Watson, "Let me see that."

Rex snatched the paper off the desk, shoved it in his pocket, and snapped, "No way." Squinting, he walked toward Ben. "You're part of it, anyway. You just want to destroy the evidence."

He let his eyes travel from Ben's face down to his feet, and back up again. "I know all about you, Jackson. They[9] say you weren't even born here. You're from someplace like Nigeria. And... and I saw you standing outside the HVAC closet yesterday. You're working with the government."

His voice got low. "I know the plan," he whispered. He turned his head to make sure everyone in the class stayed quiet, so that they could all hear him. "Kill off as many white people as you can, then keep all the resources for yourselves."

Rex's assertions were unquestionable to his devotees in the back rows of the room. Their faces went slack. Their mouths hung slightly open. They hunched their bodies forward, as though they were ready to leap out of their desks and beat the crap out of their new enemy on Rex's order.

The other students in the classroom, by contrast, sat back in their seats. They looked alarmed and were muttering to each other. Mr. Watson was able to overhear a student near the front of the class whisper to his neighbor, "That Rex is one crazy bastard."

---

[9] "They," meaning either or both of: (i) Rex Boner's inner-circle sycophant associates, or (ii) an amorphous, indeterminate and, essentially, non-existent group of people.

"Wow," Ben said. His voice was quiet and his face composed. "Calm down, Rexie. First, my parents were born in Georgia and I was born in Los Angeles. Second, I think that if you get the key from the janitor and look in the HVAC closet, the only chemicals you'll find in there are cleaning products. Third, I'm not interested in taking resources from you or anyone else."

Rex stared at Ben. His mind was racing and he was furious. So, Ben's parents were born in Georgia. Most likely, somewhere down the line, his ancestors had been brought to the south as slaves.

Slaves. Rex's brain flipped from the arrogant Black boy, who'd had the audacity to stand up to him, to the connotations associated with slavery. The torments, the agony, the mastery of an inferior race by his superior one. Those horrific associations caused a flood of endorphins to be released in Rex's brain.

Rex managed, "I'm watching you. I'm going to call Immigration and tell them to check your birth certificate, you maggot." He glowered at Ben, turned, walked to his desk, and sat down.

Benjamin Jackson. Rex wanted, more than anything, to kick him in the nuts, over and over again until the other boy screamed. Girls *liked* Benjamin Jackson. Girls did not like Rex and Rex didn't like them, right back.

He wondered if Ben liked girls. Rex had never seen Ben flirting with anyone. They were in a lot of classes together. Rex would know about it if Ben was going out with someone, because Rex kept an eye on Ben.

Rex thought about Ben, and how maybe Ben didn't like girls, and how Ben had probably descended from slave stock, and how Ben's skin was so smooth. On the one hand, Rex wanted Ben to be dead. On the other hand, Rex wanted Ben to be in chains and for Rex to be standing over him with a whip. The thought made his stomach tingle, an echo of the old thrill Rex could not allow to shoot through his body, at this particular moment.

"I think I'm going to dismiss the class for the day," Mr. Watson said. He did not bother to reprimand Rex about anything that had just happened. What was the point? "Go to Study Hall until next period. I'll let the teacher in charge there know."

He picked up a phone on his desk. He also had to see the principal. He needed guidance figuring out what to do about Rex Boner. The boy was, on a daily basis, becoming more and more of a problem. Worse, the size of his gang was increasing at a disturbing rate.

Rex's followers—including Ethan Miller, Arnold Mudak, Maynard Arshloch, and Edwin Perdet—were, for whatever reason, angry teens. Some were messed up and traumatized by their horrific home lives. Others, who came from apparently stable homes and seemingly rational parents, were still angry and seething.

It was as if the condition resulted from a recessive gene, or from spending too much time listening to outraged radio or television hosts spitting fabricated and simpleminded conspiracy theories to increase their ratings and, thereby, their political power and the size of their financial portfolios. He'd overheard Rex's boys referring to each other as "inspector," "captain," or "lieutenant," and–most frighteningly–to Rex Boner as "general."

He wished the principal would expel the teen. Mr. Watson didn't have any proof that Rex had thrown the chair. The man wished he'd been more forceful and had handled the situation better.

Instead, Benjamin Jackson had felt compelled to intervene and, as a result, Rex had turned his psycho gaze toward Ben. It was clear that Rex was crazy and was likely capable of anything.

Mr. Watson did not want something bad to happen to Benjamin Jackson.

~

Ben's uncle was–shortly after the confrontation between the two boys–able to get Ben a placement in a charter school which provided an advanced academic program, so Rex was not able to keep his eye on Ben, after all.

Rex Boner decided, in the twelfth grade, that he required a girlfriend, for the sake of appearances. He talked a pretty girl with long blond braids into dating him. Her name was Rebecca.

He wasn't crazy about the whole thing, especially as Rebecca expected that he would routinely kiss her and do other things. He went along with her, but his heart just wasn't in it. He did appreciate the fact that his girlfriend had pale skin and long, styled blonde hair, and wore high heels and expensive clothes and lots of nail polish and makeup and perfume.

Rex often found himself wondering what Ben was doing, during the times he and Rebecca were getting physical. His thoughts would inevitably move on to what Ben looked like in shackles. The images made the whole sex thing with Rebecca more tolerable. Ben Jackson was not only Black, he was also probably gay. Rex *hated* gays. He hated them more than he hated Blacks and Arabs and Jews and Indians and Latinos and Asians and most girls, and anyone else who wasn't a white male.

~

Boner's America First, Last, and In-Between Militia, or BAFLIBM, was doing quite well, within three years of Boner's graduation from high school. It was legally organized and validly existing in the state of California as The Unidentified and Incognito P Company, LLC.

The Pee Company, as they called it for short, had been renting space in an office building in Los Angeles. There wasn't enough space for all of the eager, rabid white men who had joined the ranks of the Pee Company.

Moreover, Rex was becoming increasingly itchy with all of the minorities and illegals and leftie movie stars who lived and worked in L.A. He wanted to move to another state, a *whiter* state, where he would be surrounded by like-minded people.

~

The Stone Face stood at the top of one of the mountains ringing the burial ground. The being's gigantic face was turned to the West. It had tried, countless times, to leave the Park. It was impossible for it to do so alone. It lived on the Park's dark energy, left behind by the Father, and also by Saklas, when the goat had brought the Stone Face to life. The creature found that it became more and more *stone*, and less and less animated, the closer it got to the Park walls.

The treatment given it by Saklas had made the Stone Face's composition much denser and heavier than normal granite. It was so heavy that, wherever it moved, its weight carved a path in the ground, be it earth or rock. It left in its wake a smooth ravine, the way a snail leaves behind a trail of slime.

None of its attempts to leave the Park had succeeded. Its freedom was curtailed. The Stone Face could not travel beyond the wall-enclosed boundary.

There was a person out there, though, who could free it. The Stone Face had stood motionless on the mountaintop facing West, for days, appearing just like the original stone monument the men had carved in 1918 (except that it was now ten feet tall and its eyes were open).

The Stone Face did not human thought processes. It could not conceptualize clear ideas. It, instead, had three competing energies that coursed through its mineral crystals.

The strongest energy came from Saklas, the Killapaka Deor who had originally animated it.

The second energy, a very small amount, came from Tembo, the elephant Apalacheela who had almost given all of herself away, as she'd poured much of her essence into the deceased ex-slaves in the burial ground.

The third energy came from the Father deity who had, millennia ago, hidden himself for a time in the City Park. He was long gone from the place but every molecule of the Park remembered him.

The Father was the reason no one was able to map the City Park. *He* was the reason for the disappearances in the Park. *The Father* was the reason planes flying over the Park vanished, and satellite images of the Park were always blank. *The Father* was the reason the size of the Park could not be determined. *The Father* was the reason the Park returned no telemetry. *The Father* was the reason Cutter City residents avoided the Park, or even thinking about it.

The Father was the progenitor of both Tembo the elephant, who had followed the freed slaves into the Park while they had buried their deceased brothers and sisters, and of Saklas the goat, who had animated the Stone Face.

The sources of the three energies were adversarial. Two of the energies—that of the animating force of Saklas and that of the father—flowed together smoothly, for the time-being, through the minerals of the Stone Face, and suppressed what was an insignificant amount of the third energy from Tembo.

Those two energies caused the Stone Face to stand on the mountain and search. It had no idea what it was searching *for*, until it sensed a man in the West whose immense rage, fury, obsession, and hatred matched the primary energies fueling the Stone Face. Facing in that direction, the creature cast a chaotic miasma of what passed for its thoughts to the faraway person it had found and singled out, a certain Rex Boner.

First contact had been made. The Stone Face could feel it. The interaction had drained the creature. It turned to go back to its place at the head of the burial ground, as it always did when it required rest.

~

Rex had recently been feeling a strong, unexplainable pull to the Midwest. He could attribute it to the notion that he'd find a lot of people who thought like he did, in that part of the country. Yes, he liked its anti-minority, anti-immigrant, anti-woman vibe, and its pro-gun policies. It was more than that, though. He felt like something was dragging him there.

He couldn't put his finger on it. He had gotten where he was because of his instincts. He never ignored his instincts.

He had no idea that the Stone Face had been focusing on him and pulling him toward the City Park, much less that such an entity even existed. It had, seemingly out of the blue, become crystal clear to him that he and BAFLIBM had to leave the West Coast and head into the middle of the country.

"Find real estate agents in each of the midwestern states," he instructed Inspector Mudak and Colonel Miller. "Tell them to find a suitable command center for a large operation."

"Yes, sir," the other two men said, in unison.

~

"We're all set. The Pee Company has been re-established with a paper-only address in Cyprus," Edwin Perdet said. He was sitting with General Boner in Perdet's apartment living room, in Los Angeles. "No one will be able to track our finances any longer. The icing on the cake is that we can stop paying taxes to the government."

The Unidentified and Incognito P Company had kept Oliver Schlau on retainer. The lawyer had advised Rex that it was best to move the company, on paper, to a country where officials would turn a blind eye to the illegal sources of funds and the value of the assets held by the company. They would be able to conduct whatever business they felt like, anywhere in the United States, simply by registering as a foreign entity in each such state.

"But it's still called The Unidentified and Incognito P Company?" Rex asked.

"Of course. No reason to change the name, just because our "principal office" has been moved, on paper, to another country."

"All right," Rex said. "One more item, checked off our list. Now on to another. I've instructed Mudak and Miller to get in touch with real estate agents in the Midwest."

"What? Why?"

"We're going to move there. Be among our own kind."

Boner's phone rang. He pulled it out of his pocket and looked at it. It was Colonel Miller.

"General," Miller began. "A realtor in Ohio just called. She says the federal government is auctioning off a building. It's called Primp Tower, someplace in Cutter City. It's being sold "as-is.""

327

No warranties. Interested parties aren't even allowed to conduct a pre-auction walk-through. What do you want to do?"

"How many floors is it?"

"Fifty-eight."

"Hmm. I would have preferred something higher than that. At least sixty-eight floors. I think any building that's worthy of headquartering BAFLIBM should make a statement."

"We want to be inconspicuous, General."

"Yes, you're right. Check it out. Send Mudak. Tell him to perform a walk-through, authorized or not. I don't want to spend money on some jacked-up piece of garbage."

He thought for a moment. "Will we be able to afford it?"

Miller snorted. "General, the Pee Company could buy ten skyscrapers in Cutter City, without feeling the pinch. It's not just that our company is prosperous. The economy out there is terrible. Prices have bottomed out."

Cutter City, Ohio. A familiar, warm, and tingling feeling ran through Rex's gut. Cutter City felt *right*. And he liked the building's name, Primp Tower. That, too, gave him the tingly feeling in his tummy.

"Also, tell Mudak to see if he can find out the history of the building."

~

The federal government, in the 1960s, had caused a fifty-eight-story building to be constructed in Cutter City. The project was

328

undertaken during, and as a result of, the Cold War with the Soviet Union. There was an ongoing threat of an actual nuclear war, during that period.

The building was named after Damien Primp. Mr. Primp was the congressman who had sponsored the vaguely worded enabling legislation for the project. He represented the good people of the district in which Cutter City was located. His expressed concern about a nuclear war was a pretense. He was more interested in the federal dollars that would be allocated to his home district.

A contractor by the name of Ambrosi Russo submitted the winning bid for the construction of the new building. Two men, in dark suits and sunglasses, paid Mr. Russo a visit, the week before work was to start. They handed him additional blueprints and stood in silence, as he reviewed the blueprints at a drafting desk.

Ambrosi flipped through the prints, scanned them, and looked up. "You're kidding, right?"

The men shook their heads. "You are to follow the prints exactly. Keep them in a safe place. Don't let anyone see them, except on a need-to-know basis. And don't show them to any other person from the government."

"This is a massive undertaking. It increases the scope of the project immensely. My bid price doesn't begin to cover it... " Mr. Russo began.

One of the suits lifted a black leather briefcase. He flicked open the latch. The briefcase was filled with hundred-dollar bills. Mr. Russo stared at the bills. The wheels of a calculator turned in his head.

"How much is in there?" he asked.

"One million," the suit answered, smugly. "There are nine more briefcases like it in the car outside. I think this will more than cover your costs and the price for your cooperation, and for your silence."

"You'll need to use some of it to pay your workers for their discretion, as well," the other added. "The performance reports you submit to the federal agency overseeing this project will not mention this... extra project. You'll have to fudge the reports, as necessary."

Ambrosi was uncomfortable with the proposal. It smelled bad. He glanced at the briefcase and the two men, and then at the blueprints that he had already examined. He realized they were not making a proposal. It had gone beyond that. He was *in*, whether he liked it or not. Ambrosi was quite intimidated by the quiet men. He did not dwell on the thought of what might happen to him if he didn't agree to the proposal.

The men left Mr. Russo's office and returned a few minutes later. They carried two stacks of suitcases, which they deposited neatly on the floor.

"I take it you have a secure safe?" one of the sunglassed men asked.

"In the back. I'll keep the...briefcases in there," Mr. Russo said, "until I need funds for this project. And I'll put the prints in there when I'm not using them."

"You'll notice there are eleven suitcases in total. The eleventh contains a four-digit combination locking mechanism. We want you to install it on the entrance hatch to the below-ground levels. Right now, the combination is 1-2-3-4. Our people will reset the combination after your work is done and you've cleared out. You'll see, on the plans, that the hatch is to be hidden under the linoleum flooring."

The two men turned to leave. One of them stopped. "Oh. One last thing. Have privacy fencing installed around the site during the excavation process. We don't want passersby to be able to see what you're doing, until you start work on the aboveground levels of the building itself. At that point, we won't care."

Mr. Russo followed his instructions to the letter. He had the privacy fencing installed over the next few days. It could not, however, hide from the public the thunderous sounds of blasting that came from the site.

The blasting was finished within several weeks, and the excavators took over. The site became a vast hole that was two hundred feet deep. Then, Mr. Russo's crews went to work building a massive bomb shelter. The work went on twenty-four hours a day, seven days a week, three shifts a day.

The building itself was only there as camouflage for the shelter. The shelter was the real purpose of the entire project. The bunker was earmarked, in the event of a nuclear attack, for the use of high-ranking federal officials, other powerful men, and their families and friends.

The two men in dark suits and sunglasses never paid a return visit to Ambrosi Russo. Mr. Russo paid his crewmembers well for their silence, and kept the secret blueprints in his safe.

Mr. Primp lost his bid for re-election, several months after the building was completed. It had been his baby. No one else in Congress had paid much attention to it. They were concerned only with how much money was going into their own home districts.

The threat of nuclear war abated, over the years. The Soviet Union eventually disbanded. Those officials, who had caused the shelter to be constructed, retired or died off. No one who still worked in the U.S. government remembered why the administration owned a building in the middle of nowhere. The building had never been used, and no one occupied it.

~

A manager in the civil service, and employed by the General Services Administration of the federal government, was in charge of reviewing— and, in his sole discretion, disposing of—the government's inventory of outmoded buildings. One of his clerks brought the building in Cutter City to his attention.

"This building has been sitting empty for *decades*," the clerk said. "It should go on the chopping block, yes?"

"Hmm," the manager said. He scanned the paperwork. "Why did we even build this, in the middle of nowhere, in the first place? It doesn't look like we ever used it. Has it been sitting empty all these years?"

"I think so," the underling replied. "There were supposed to be offices and apartments set up in there, of all things. Weird. No one from the federal government ever moved in, and none of the spaces were leased. We've been paying to heat and air condition an empty building for decades. Maintenance, not so much. I don't think we've had anyone go inside it since it was built. The water was never turned on. At least we don't have to be concerned with leaking or ruptured water pipes."

"Ok. Process the paperwork to put it up for sale," the manager said. "Fast-track it."

Ambrosi Russo never knew that no one from the government had ever inspected the bunker, or that no one had come to change the combination code to the bunker hatch.

~

Inspector Mudak called the general with his report from Cutter City.

"I took the initiative and brought Ensign Wilson with me to help inspect Primp Tower. The ensign is a structural engineer. He says the building is sound. The interior also seems to be in good shape. You might want to replace the floors, though. That stuff is bad. And I don't mean bad, as in good. Some kind of crap linoleum."

"What do you think? Would Primp Tower be suitable headquarters for the Pee Company?"

"Ooohhh, yes," Mudak replied. "You would not *believe* what Wilson found."

Ensign Wilson was a structural engineer of the first order. He had located the hatch to the underground bomb shelter during his inspection.

"There's this metal hatch, right under the cheap stuff they put down as flooring," Mudak continued. It's really a blast door. Made out of steel and concrete. It has a combination locking mechanism. I played around with it, and guess what? The combination is 1-2-3-4!"

"What's under the hatch? Is it a panic room? A safe?"

"No, sir. It's a bit better than that. Twelve *beautiful* stories of an underground bomb shelter. Never used. It's pristine."

"You're freaking kidding me." General Boner was practically drooling.

"Nope. And it has its own ventilation system, which has never been turned on. The controls for that, and for the lighting, are right inside the entrance to the shelter. Wilson switched them on before we went down. The system works like a charm. It's spotless, because there's never been any airflow going into the bunker. It's completely sealed off and encased in metal. And the bunker is totally furnished. Desks, cabinets, tables, chairs. There's a common kitchen on each floor, common bathrooms, and a number of small, furnished apartments. I haven't had the time to count them yet. It's crazy! Everything is brand new. Well, brand new from the 1960s. That's when Wilson says the thing was built."

"Where are you now?"

"Back at our hotel."

"Did you hide that hatch when you left?"

"Absolutely, General Boner. Ensign Wilson and I made sure no one would find it. We didn't rely on that crummy linoleum to disguise it. We moved a desk over the top of it, and scuffed the dust around on the floor to hide our footprints and the place where the desk used to be." The above-ground floors were covered with decades of dust, unlike the bunker.

"It's weird. Half of the upstairs floors were set up as offices, the other half as apartments. Everything is completely furnished. None of it has ever been used. It's untouched."

"I'm going to relay this information to Captain Perdet and have him put in a bid," Boner said. The thought of the building and its remarkable bunker was energizing. "Don't come back to L.A. Hang tight. The bids are due in tomorrow, and will be opened next week. I want you on-site, so you can get the place ready for our move there as soon as we close on the building. The ensign will be useful as well. Perdet's IT people will find out who's submitting bids. He'll send you the info. You'll clear the field. Visit each of these would-be bidders. Convince them to back off. You know the routine."

"No problem, sir."

Rex Boner hung up. He was smiling, a rare event.

Primp Tower was the tallest skyscraper in Cutter City. This wasn't saying much. Cutter City was one of the smallest cities in Ohio. Most Ohioans viewed Cutter City with distaste, for reasons they did not understand. It certainly wasn't representative of what they thought of as their proud and beautiful state. They tried to ignore its existence.

It was not a destination place. Virtually every citizen was armed with a handgun and an assault rifle and, in addition, high-capacity magazines. Ohio was an open carry state and had minimal, if nonexistent, gun laws.

Cutter City took the gun culture to the next level. Few investors were interested in purchasing Primp Tower. That would require dealing with the locals and with the odd city bureaucracy: that is, the Cutter City Planning Commission. Rex was not at all concerned about the gun-obsessed civilians—who, after all, were probably *his* people—or the old City Planners who ran the city.

The Unidentified and Incognito P Company, LLC, aka Boner's America First, Last, and In-Between Militia, aka BAFLIBM, aka the Pee Company—through the diligent intervention of Inspector Mudak—was, of course, the highest bidder on the building.

The Pee Company went to closing on Primp Tower two months later. Colonel Miller joined Inspector Mudak and Ensign Wilson. The three men researched the history of the building, during the two-month interim before the settlement.

Miller ordered Ensign Wilson to spend his time at the library and go through old newspaper clippings. Mudak hit the Cutter City Land Records. Miller spent his first few days in Cutter City chatting up street people, with the goal of starting a local network of informants. Some of the guys he approached were desperate-looking and tough. They did not frighten him. He was armed to the teeth and well-trained in judo, karate, taekwondo, Krav Maga, and the use of weapons.

The ensign hit pay dirt on his third day in the library. He was reading the *Cutter City Gazette*, a newspaper dated September 25, 1964. A small paragraph, in a section entitled "Announcements," read: "The Russo

336

Construction Company has been awarded the contract to construct Primp Tower."

"Russo Construction Company," Colonel Miller said. He looked down at the piece of newspaper, which Wilson had ripped out and brought back to the colonel's hotel room.

"They're still around," the ensign said eagerly. "Here's their phone number." He started to hand a slip of paper to the colonel.

"Do you have the address?" Mudak asked. He was sitting in a chair at a table in the corner, with a stack of copies of documents from Land Records in front of him.

Inspector Arnold Mudak had grown into a tall, hefty man. His head was shaved and he had a long scraggly beard, which looked like it was composed of an old man's gray pubic hair.

"It's on the paper."

Mudak stood. "You stay here. Hold down the fort. Colonel Miller and I will see if we can find out anything from the contractor. The guy who was in charge is probably dead. The company may have changed hands by now, but it's worth a shot."

∞

Ambrosi Russo *was* still alive. He and his wife had retired to Hollywood, Florida, several decades ago. They had built themselves a palatial mansion by the ocean, funded largely by the windfall given him by the two federal agents. His son, Matteo, was now running the business.

"Can you contact your father? Tell him we want to talk to him about Primp Tower." Colonel Miller said.

He and Inspector Mudak were sitting in two leather chairs that faced Matteo Russo's desk. Matteo was in a huge leather chair on the other side.

"Why do you want to talk to him about Primp Tower?" Matteo asked.

"Our company is buying the building. We want to find out everything we can about it." Mudak said. He looked closely at Matteo, then added, "We were also thinking he could handle the building renovations."

Matteo held Mudak's gaze. "You can deal with me. I know everything my father knows about Primp Tower. He told me the story before he retired. Not only that, he kept the blueprints, which *I* now have."

Mudak and Miller looked at each other. They nodded. This Matteo guy had the freaking blueprints, on top of which he could keep his mouth shut. He had known about Primp Tower's secrets for years and obviously hadn't told anyone. Otherwise, there would have been many more bidders, and it would have been extremely difficult to get all of them to withdraw.

"So, you're in?" Mudak asked.

"What do you want done?"

"Well, new flooring, and...," Mudak started.

"We want to turn the first three levels of the building into parking," Miller said. "The above-ground levels, that is."

Matteo smiled. "And what do you want to do with the bomb shelter?"

∞

And thus, the first three floors of the building were converted to parking areas. The lowest parking floor was restricted to Pee Company personnel. A garage door closed off that parking level, which was protected by a fingerprint locking mechanism. Three elevators (one of them for General Boner's use only) ran down from that level to the underground floors and up to the top six levels of the building, with no stops in between. The other two parking levels, with their associated elevators, were for the use of the civilian tenants who would be renting space in the rest of the building.

The construction and renovations were completed within six months. BAFLIBM made the move from Los Angeles immediately afterward. Boner's men took over five of the top floors and, of course, the bunker below the building. The penthouse on the 58th floor served as Boner's living quarters.

Rex liked his new digs. His private elevator required a code to activate it. Rex had given the code to Miller, Mudak and Perdet. The elevator had doors on both sides of the car. One of the doors opened onto his private living quarters. These took up half of the top floor. The door on the other side of the elevator opened onto the common area of his apartment, the kitchen, dining room, living room, and a large bathroom.

The interior had been completely renovated. It looked like the end product, shown as the big reveal, of an HGTV episode. No cozy little rooms for Rex. The common area was one big open space (except for the bathroom). It looked like someone had blown out the interior and turned it into a gymnasium, one that happened to have the most expensive and trendy appointments. Lots of marble, glass, leather, white cabinets, and dark flooring.

An art-encrusted entryway, directly in front of the elevator door, opened onto the huge living and dining room area that was full of white leather furniture and accompanying end tables and a coffee table. Shelving along the walls held tastily-placed pieces of expensive artwork from around the world.

A sparkling white kitchen, to the left of the entryway, contained a huge island with a white marble, waterfall countertop. A massive metal and glass-topped dining table was next to the kitchen.

There were no extra bedrooms. No one would ever be spending the night there, other than Rex Boner.

An obligatory, high impact feature in the living room drew the eye. A designer would say the feature had good feng shui. The entire wall was composed of a large glass window. The window provided an incredible view of the city below and the City Park, with its anomalous ring of mountains, in the distance,.

General Boner ordered Inspector Mudak to hire locals to keep Primp Tower clean and in good repair. The majority of those hires were given jobs on the non-Pee Company floors of the building. Mudak vetted a dozen whom he deemed discreet enough to work in The Unidentified and Incognito P Company sections. These men were paid twice as much as the other local employees.

The inspector assigned two young, muscular, blonde-haired men, Private Connor and Private

Cody, to the care of the penthouse, and to the care of Rex himself. These two men were also given his elevator code.

Both men sported "high-and-tight" hairdos (lacquered with a large quantity of hair product), which coiffure was now *de rigueur* in the Pee Company militia. All militiamen, with the exception of those at the top, had been required to drop the bald-headed, bearded caveman look. The new style put other people off-guard and at ease, and caused them to view the young militia men as harmless hipsters.

Chapter 2

Two Beasts, Mano a Mano

It was Boner's first week in Primp Tower. Connor and Cody were in the process of stocking the kitchen with groceries. Connor was putting things away. Cody was carrying groceries from the elevator. Rex was standing by the window and staring at the Park.

"Do you know anything about the City Park?" Rex asked suddenly. Cody put his bags on a side table and walked over to the window.

"Not much, sir. It's a weird place. Not a good place to take a girl on a picnic."

"What about those mountains? Everything else is flat around here. Has anybody, like a scientist... (Rex stumbled on the word, which he found offensive) offered an explanation about them?"

"You mean, like how they were formed?"

"Yes."

"I haven't heard any scientific stuff about it, but people say those mountains just popped up out of nowhere, sometime in the early 1900s."

"Right..."

"That's what they say." Cody looked at the Park. "I went inside the gate once, when I was a kid, on a bet. Nothin' happened, except I won the bet and made five dollars."

Rex ignored the young man and turned back to the window. The germ of yet another conspiracy theory tickled the back of his mind. The mountains cropped up out of nowhere in the early 1900s? Maybe they really *had*. Maybe the government had done something that had caused the phenomenon. Another matter to have his people check out. Or, he could do it, himself.

The mountains seemed taller, on some days, than they had been the day before. This was one such day.

Cody moved to retrieve the grocery bags, and stopped. "You know about the slave burial ground, don't you, sir?"

Rex turned from the window. It was sunset and the light behind him was fading. Cody looked at his boss, all five feet eleven of him. Rex had a dirty mop of graying hair that fell forward over one side of his brow and covered an eyebrow, leaving a streak of grease on his forehead.

His face was bloated, with puffy lips and pock-marked skin. There were several sores along his fat-filled, blown-out jawline, which was covered by gray scruff. Rex wore two button-down shirts over a black t-shirt. He was overweight, had poor circulation, and was cold all the time.

"What is this about a slave burial ground?" Rex's voice was as soft as a young teenager's. It had freaked Cody out, at first, such a childlike voice coming out of such a heavy man's body, but he was getting used to it.

"Well, they say there was a big flu epidemic here in the early 1900s," Cody replied. "Almost everyone who got the flu died. A lot of freed slaves were working in Cutter City at the time... "

Cody related the rest of the story, as he knew it.

"So, it's supposed to be in a meadow full of poppies," Rex said.

343

"Yes, sir."

"It's already August. Do poppies bloom in August?"

"I don't know, sir."

"If they're not in bloom, how would someone find the place?"

"Supposedly, they went in a northwest direction. Those ex-slaves were told to go in at least five miles, but who knows how far in they actually went." He snorted. "It's probably more like half a mile. I mean, they were *Blacks*. They said they left some kind of stone monument, some African thing, in the middle of the field. It would probably stand out."

"Hmm." Rex sat down on a sofa facing the large window, and watched the light over the Park fade. He began to think about what it would be like to walk on top of those buried slaves and to tread on the very earth covering their bones. To experience that old thrill, which was harder and harder to get. He was like a junkie, whose tolerance to narcotics had maxed out.

∞

Boner's America First, Last, and In-Between Militia had two missions at that time: the recruitment of suitable new members, and the procurement of new financial sources. Operations were running smoothly. Rex thought he could leave BAFLIBM in the hands of Mudak and Miller for a little while.

"I don't know how long I'll be gone. Maybe a couple days, maybe a week," he told Colonel Miller. "I understand there won't be any cell service in the Park. Don't worry about me. I'll be armed." He thought for a moment, then said,

"We're only using the top six floors of the building, in addition to the underground complex. Why don't you work on leasing out the rest of the space that we're not using, while I'm away? It should provide some nice additional income and more than offset the building expenses."

"I've already started, General," Miller said. "There won't be any problem finding good tenants. I just leased the 33rd floor to the Cutter City Planning Commission. They're an odd bunch, twelve old men and a youngish-looking woman. And they run the whole show in this town."

"For now, that is," Rex said. "But not bad, Miller. Not bad. A lot easier for us to keep an eye on the most relevant assholes in Cutter City, having them in our own building. Tell Perdet to have his IT people bug that floor."

"Already done, sir."

∞

Rex had been obsessing over the Park. He was, once again, following his gut. He looked forward to the hike. Maybe it was the mysterious Park itself that had called to him, all the way from Cutter City to Los Angeles. Maybe there was something about the Park that he was supposed to experience. Maybe it was the graveyard. He expected that the little camping trip would inspire and refresh him, so that he could continue with the daily grind of taking over the world.

He brought top-of-the-line camping gear and supplies with him, packed away neatly in his backpack. He wore a Glock 20 on his hip and carried plenty of extra ammunition in his pack.

The single gate to the Park was located on Harbinger Street.

The gate was never locked. Rex left his car in front of the building across the street from the Park, took the backpack from the trunk, slipped it on, and walked over to the gate. He pushed it open and went through. It swung shut behind him with a loud clank. It was 6:00 a.m.

The next fourteen hours tested Rex's endurance. He walked in a northwesterly direction, through forests of massive trees and long fields of high grass. He waded through streams and forded a torrential river. He marched through the Park until nightfall, without encountering a single animal. He set up camp at the base of the odd ring of mountains he'd spotted from the Primp Tower penthouse. Rex was exhausted and dirty and every muscle in his body ached. Cody's snide remark about the Blacks probably only having gone in half a mile, Rex thought, was clearly incorrect, unless Rex had missed the burial plot or gone in the wrong direction.

He slept well, however, and awoke refreshed. He drank a bottle of juice and ate an MRE. He wanted to get moving and didn't want to waste time building a fire to brew coffee. He rolled up his sleeping bag, packed it away, and started his trek up the mountain. The angle of the slope, on this side of the mountain, was gradual.

Rex reached the summit within a few hours. He released his backpack, stood on the edge of a cliff, and took in the view in front of him. He would have been dumbfounded, if he had been anyone other than Rex Boner. A solid wall of high mountains surrounded a vast field, far below, that was blanketed in bright red flowers. He tried to understand how this geologic formation could have occurred. He came up with nothing, other than maybe a meteor strike.

Rex did not know that the flowers were, in fact, red corn poppies, or that in Ohio, those poppies should have finished blooming no later than the end of May. (It was now August.) He retrieved his backpack and walked about the summit, careful not to trip on the rocky outcroppings.

He was looking for the best way to descend the mountain. He picked a spot, and started down toward the poppy field. The drop, on this side of the mountain, was steep and treacherous.

He clambered down about a hundred yards, and came to an abrupt halt. A five-foot-wide ravine, with curved sides, was carved into the ground in front of him. It was smooth, and looked like a narrow luge track. There was a bend in the course.

The upper end of the ravine proceeded in a westerly direction, and the other side traveled straight down the mountain, toward the valley of flowers. Several hundred yards below, dense forest engulfed both sides of the channel, so it was difficult to see how far the channel went.

It would be easier to continue his descent in the smooth channel than it would on the rough, uneven ground, Rex decided. He sat on the edge of the ravine and started to place his feet in the middle of it. His feet slipped off the surface and flew straight up into the air.

Rex fell backward onto his pack, away from the ravine. He struggled to his feet, leaned over, and peered at the odd gully. The interior of the channel was carved out of solid rock. It looked like it had been polished until it was as smooth and slippery as a well-tended ice-skating rink. This was not a natural phenomenon.

"What the hell?" Rex slipped off his backpack and dropped it next to the ravine. "Who could have made this?"

He looked around. He saw fir, hemlock, spruce, and pine trees. No people and no other structures, not even any animal sounds. He did hear a distant roaring noise. It wasn't a river. It was the wind picking up. And then he heard thunder. A storm was approaching. This mountainside was no place to be in a storm. Rex looked at the smooth ravine, and then at his backpack.

He sat down next to the pack, opened it, pulled out his sleeping bag, and unrolled and unzipped it. He closed the backpack, shoved it inside the sleeping bag, and then sealed up the bag. He looked at it. The backpack was a big lump at one end of the bag.

"I think this will work," he said. He picked up the sleeping bag, held it in front of him so that the lump stayed at the top, leaned over the ravine, and threw the bag and himself forward.

The sleeping bag immediately shot off down the mountain in the polished ravine, taking Rex with it.

Rex had no experience sledding, having grown up in Los Angeles, but he quickly got the feel of how to tilt his weight from side to side so that he didn't flip out of the ravine, and how to hold onto the edges of the bag, keeping his head on the backpack lump so that he could see what was below him. The ravine went all the way down the side of the steep mountain.

Rex reached the bottom in five minutes. The strange channel continued on the flat ground. Rex's speed slowed, and he finally stopped. He sat up on the sleeping bag and turned his head. He was in the middle of the flower-filled field.

He carefully pulled himself out of the channel, and then reached for the sleeping bag. He stood. His eyes traveled along the gully. It ended a few yards away. He looked up. The ravine butted up against a ten-foot-tall, carved granite face. Other channels, like the one he'd traversed, radiated out from the place where the stone sculpture stood.

Rex had found his burial ground.

He dropped the sleeping bag. He would start his experience of the graveyard by checking out the apparent slave-made monument. The thing was huge. Rex was, grudgingly, impressed that the freed slaves had managed to create such a thing.

The wind picked up. The poppy blooms waved. Rex walked alongside the ravine toward the Stone Face, smashing his heavily booted feet on the carpet of flowers. He tripped on a patch of rough ground and lost his balance. He threw his hand against the effigy to catch himself.

The Stone Face touched him back.

∞

Rex Boner returned from the Park *changed*. He, himself, wouldn't say that he was a changed "man." It wasn't clear to him that he was still a man, at all.

349

Whatever he was, he could no longer interact directly with anyone outside of his circle. Normal people, who got even the slightest glimpse of him, cowered in fear.

He did not know that he was no longer *just* Rex Boner. The Stone Face had left some of its murk behind when it had invaded him. That murk caused Boner to undergo shifting, physical alterations and augmentations.

Boner's continual physical transformations were of no significance to the Stone Face. Of significance to it was that the murk also gave the creature an eye to the world from its Park prison. Two of the three energies coursing through it— those of the Father and of Saklas—were in agreement that the Stone Face should not reveal to Rex that they were now connected. (The third energy, which had come from Tembo the elephant, was dormant.)

Rex did not tell his men exactly what had happened to him when the Stone Face had sprouted arms, and *another* appendage, and had reached for him.

It was fortunate that Ethan Miller, Edwin Perdet, Arnold Mudak, and the other associates who had been traveling this path with him since elementary school, asked no questions when he came back to the building, a few days later, seemingly a different person. Different *people,* depending on the light. Well, not different people. Different *monsters.*

His men recognized that Rex was still somewhere within the hideous demon that had replaced the slovenly slob he'd been before. No one, other than Rex, was able to intimidate and cow them with a single look. Plus, the building security systems recognized his voice patterns, as changed as those patterns now were to men's ears.

Rex ordered, on the day of his return from the City Park, that all of the mirrors in the penthouse be removed. Cody and Connor were sent to fulfill the request.

They were quietly moving through the common area side of the apartment, carrying the mirror they'd torn off the bathroom wall, when the elevator door opened and a stranger emerged. He appeared to be in his mid-fifties. He was of short stature. He had washed-out blue eyes and fat, steroid-pumped arms that stretched the fabric of his black, military-style shirt.

The odd thought sprang into Cody's mind that those muscles would pop like balloons if he stuck them with a pin. That thought was replaced by a mental image of the man walking puppet-like, with arms dangling at his sides, and smashing right through a concrete wall, like a shorter version of the Frankenstein monster.

The man had a childlike pout that made him appear sullen and angry. He had an ovoid face, heavy jowls, a rounded smudge of a nose, and a double chin. His forehead was huge. Its massive size was accentuated by his receding hairline. His hair—what was left of it—was dyed a weird reddish-blonde color, and he had a meager, new-growth beard framing his face, as if to compensate for the lack of hair on his head.

They did not know this person or whether he had authorization to be in the general's quarters. The man moved toward them, into the sunlight streaming through the large window. They watched, in horror, as the man's face and body twisted and changed.

For a moment, Rex's form was amorphous and difficult to describe. His arm muscles shrank to a normal size. His ovoid face thinned, his large forehead crawled backward into a flattened slope, his ears became long and pointy, his lips became thin lines, and the top of his head elongated and narrowed. His formerly blobby nose lengthened into a pointed spike that almost touched his weak upper lip. His jowls and double chin disappeared.

The odd red hair morphed into pure white hair that crested into a pompadour, seemingly the result of years of hair-plug inserts and hair transplants. His eyes shifted and moved closer to each other. A piece of the darkness behind the man swirled around the too close-set eyes, and converted into a pair of small, round, black-rimmed glasses that perched themselves on the man's long nose.

The man had previously been wearing a tight, dark shirt. The clothing blurred. It came back into focus as an outmoded, chalk-striped, dark blue suit with padded shoulders, an expensive silk tie, and brown suede shoes. In the light, the man no longer looked maddened. He looked, instead, haughty and scornful.

Connor's heart was beating so hard that he was sure the other two men could hear it. He was petrified. He couldn't breathe. He could only pull fear into his lungs, instead of air.

"Well? What are you staring at? Keep working!" Rex growled. His mouth formed a large oval as he spoke, and he disgorged spittle into the air with each word.

"Good god," Connor whispered to Cody. "It's the *general.*" The thing in front of him was unrecognizable as an actual human being, but Connor knew in his bones that it was Rex Boner.

It struck Connor that the general's voice had a bit more gravel to it, but was still not deep. It was weak, and it was irritating. It made Connor's brain itch. The image of a yapping bulldog popped into his head. It was immediately replaced by the vision of the horrifying transformation he had just witnessed.

"Yes, sir," Connor answered for the two young men. He bowed his head, and looked away. Cody, bewildered and terrified, followed his cue.

Chapter 3
The Goat and the Lawyer

Saklas the goat decided, around the time of the Civil War, that he needed a lawyer. It took him a long time to find one who seemed suitable. He finally found, in the late nineteenth century, a potential prospect. This was a struggling young attorney living in New York City. Saklas followed the man for a time, to determine whether he was, in fact, a good fit for the Killapaka.

The man, an odd-looking person by the name of Arthur Anthill, was tall and skinny. He had a long, thin neck, and a small round head, which was covered in thick, black hair. His eyes were brown and shifty. He had a meager law practice.

The goat decided that the man would do. The man was made of different stuff than most humans. He seemed introverted, intense, and cold. He would have been diagnosed as a sociopath had he lived in the twenty-first century. No feelings for others, and zero empathy. He did not seem to be the type who would fall down on his face if Saklas revealed his true form.

Saklas had learned, over time, to alter his Deor shape so that it resembled a hybrid human/Deor goat. He used his hybrid shape to *play* with humans. It was more terrifying to them than his actual Deor form. He'd even used that appearance on occasion, when the mood struck, to rape one or another of their women, just for fun. (For him, the "fun" part wasn't the actual sex, it was that he caused the women horrible pain and terror.)

He thought it would be amusing to make first contact with the weird man in this hybrid form.

He chose the middle of the night to make his appearance. Why not? Humans seemed smaller at night. They were certainly more easily frightened, when it was dark.

Mr. Anthill was sitting at his desk in his small, cold office and drafting a court pleading. He dipped his steel-point pen into the inkwell.

The room was suddenly full of whirling light.

A huge, muscular man with white hair, high cheekbones, yellow eyes, and skin the color of burning orange lava stood in front of Mr. Anthill. The lower half of the man's body was that of a goat. He seemed to be made of fire.

Mr. Anthill sat back in his chair and regarded the figure.

"Yes?" Mr. Anthill asked. "Can I do something for you? Do you need legal assistance?"

The thing floating in front of him appeared to be the devil. Supposedly, one could make a Faustian bargain with the devil. Mr. Anthill was certain that he, himself, was extremely intelligent, and was equally certain that he'd come out on top in any deal.

The monstrosity boomed at him. "Yeshhh! I wand youff to establish a... a... what be it called? A craperashun? A cooperation?"

Saklas stopped, confused. He had spent the past hundred years learning how to speak human and, specifically, English. This was his first attempt. It was harder than he had thought it would be.

"Corporation?" Mr. Anthill asked, helpfully. "Go on. What type of corporation? What would

355

you like the name to be? How many shareholders? What kind of stock?"

"Chairholder. What is that?"

"Like an *owner*."

"Me. Only."

Mr. Anthill began to take notes. "And your name is... " He waited, expecting the thing to answer, "Satan."

"Saklas."

"Last name?"

Saklas was silent.

"What *are* you, exactly?" Mr. Anthill asked, looking up.

"A Killapaka!" Saklas roared.

"All... right." Mr. Anthill looked down at his notes. "One shareholder named Saklas Killapaka. Why don't we call it the Killapaka Corporation, then?"

The creature nodded.

"And how will you be paying? There's not only my fee, but also the costs of setting up the corporation." Mr. Anthill looked into the distance. "For now, I can use my office address as the principal office," he muttered to himself.

"Cannot pay. Yet."

Mr. Anthill looked back at Saklas. "I'm not sure how I can proceed if you... "

"Find an old human. Wit money. Lots of it. No fambly."

"And that will accomplish... ?"

"Make a thing humans use to pass on money. Put me in it."

"You mean a *will*," Mr. Anthill said. "But the person would have to sign it."

"Yes," Saklas said. Fire flared from his nostrils.

Mr. Anthill looked at the fire flare. "Hmmm. All right. The good news is you've basically described my client base. A bunch of nasty old skinflints who always short me on their bills. I think that's how they got so wealthy. I'll get the corporation filed this week. There is an additional matter, though. We need two people to witness the execution of the will."

"Find some people. *Disposable* people. Tell me where they live. They will witness." Saklas's verbal skills were quickly improving as he interacted with the human.

"Disposable. Hmm. Well, don't dispose of them until the will is probated and the estate closed."

"What means that? That means what?"

"Never mind. I'll tell you what you should do, and when." Mr. Anthill paused. "I guess this entails you disposing of the testator. Otherwise, what's the point of all of this? You could wait for years to collect."

"Testator?"

"The old rich guy. The one who's signing the will."

"Yes. The testator."

~

The plan went forward. Mr. Anthill set up the corporation, drew up an unauthorized will for one of his rich, old clients, found two witnesses, and gave Saklas the addresses of each of the prospective witnesses.

Saklas went to their houses late that night, to "meet" with them. The petrified men, after cleaning themselves up and changing their clothes, did as Saklas ordered. They showed up at the mansion of one Mr. Alexander Clark at midnight.

Inside, Saklas was showing himself to Mr. Clark.

The old man signed the will, with a shaking hand, and immediately proceeded to have a heart attack. Saklas let the two men into the house. They witnessed Mr. Clark's signature, and left. They ran to their carriages and rushed to their homes, glad they had, so far, survived the night.

Servants discovered Mr. Clark the next morning. He was in a coma. He stayed in a coma for a month, and then died. Mr. Anthill processed the will. The Killapaka Corporation was funded.

They did this procedure five more times, using different witnesses on each occasion. The witnesses to a will disappeared, courtesy of Saklas, after the will was finally probated. Saklas also paid a visit to anyone who objected to the wills.

Rex Boner and his crew, unknowingly, duplicated this foul tactic more than a century and a half later, when they were starting their campaign as young men in Los Angeles.

"Who's next?" Saklas asked, popping up in Mr. Anthill's office. He had quickly become fluent in human speech, as a result of his discussions with Mr. Anthill.

358

Saklas had done well by the man. Mr. Anthill could now afford to have a suite of offices. The man, instead, chose to live frugally and to stay where he was. He had begun to amass his *own* stashed-away fortune.

"We're going to go a different route, from here on out," Mr. Anthill said. "There's this thing that just opened up. It's called the New York Stock Exchange. The Bank of New York is listed there. We can buy stock in the bank."

"If you think this is a better way to create wealth, do it," Saklas said, and disappeared.

∞

And, so it continued, until the Killapaka Corporation was one of the wealthiest, privately-held corporations in the country.

Saklas felt it was safest for the Killapaka to be near the Cutter City Park. The City Park still contained part of their Father's essence, which would make the Kills stronger.

He had Mr. Anthill buy them a large apartment building on Harbinger Street, across the street from the City Park, in 1952. He then had his Kills—assisted by his own dragon-type fire—make a deep tunnel that terminated in a massive cavern, right under the building. This was now the headquarters of the Killapaka.

~

Saklas looked at Mr. Anthill one day and realized that Mr. Anthill had, somehow, become *old*. He was actually *dying*. Saklas did not want to lose his human assistant, who had almost become like a pet to the goat-man.

Saklas came to Mr. Anthill's bedroom, that very night. He stared at the weak, frail, dying man. He wondered when Mr. Anthill's hair had become so thin and white.

The goat said, "I cannot make you immortal, as *we* are, but I can extend your life."

Mr. Anthill reached his hand weakly toward Saklas, then let it drop back to the bed. "Do whatever you can," he said. "I don't want to die."

Saklas said, "You won't be the same."

"I don't care," Mr. Anthill replied.

Saklas wrapped wings of light and energy around Mr. Anthill, lifted him up, and *infiltrated* him, twisting and converting the molecules that made up Mr. Anthill, so as to coax more life out of them. It was torture.

When it was finished, the man's white hair fell around them like snow, as Saklas dropped him gently back to the bed.

Saklas looked again at the man lying in front of him. Anthill's tiny round head was now as shiny and smooth as a billiard ball. Mr. Anthill opened his eyes. His eyes were white, and blind.

"There," Saklas said, satisfied. "You'll be with us for quite a while now. Maybe long enough to see this through to the end."

The man on the bed began to scream. He screamed for twelve hours, until he passed out from exhaustion.

~

He still screamed inside, silently, even today. The tortured cells in his body had a longer life span, but he felt every one of them, and each one of them was in agony. Not even hospital-grade narcotics could put a dent in his anguish. He knew, because he had tried.

Mr. Anthill *hated* Saklas for what the creature had done to him. Saklas should have let him die. He hated all Deor; Killapaka and Apalacheela alike. He continued to work for Saklas and let the creature believe that Anthill was a devoted and loyal employee. The entire purpose of Mr. Anthill's life now, however, was to pay all of them back, for what one of them had done to him.

Mr. Anthill knew he had once had a first name, but he could no longer remember what it was.